# Where the Road Goes

*Also by Joanne Greenberg*
*in Large Print:*

Simple Gifts
Of Such Small Differences

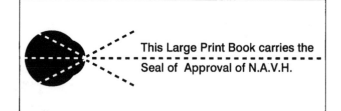

# Where the Road Goes

## Joanne Greenberg

**Thorndike Press • Thorndike, Maine**

Published in 1998 by arrangement with
Henry Holt and Company, Inc.

Thorndike Large Print® Americana Series.

The tree indicium is a trademark of Thorndike Press.

The text of this Large Print edition is unabridged.
Other aspects of the book may vary from the original edition.

Set in 16 pt. Plantin.

Printed in the United States on permanent paper.

**Library of Congress Cataloging in Publication Data**

Greenberg, Joanne.
    Where the road goes : a novel / Joanne Greenberg.
        p. (large print) cm.
    ISBN 0-7862-1356-6 (lg. print : hc : alk. paper)
    1. Large type books.  I. Title.
    [PS3557.R3784W48    1998b]
    813'.54—dc21                                    97-47231

*To David and Maureen*
*The glow from the east*

# Acknowledgments

I would like to thank Marta Palos for her help, and Franklin Folsom for his book *The Great Peace March* that validated the possibility of a sea-to-sea walk.

Thanks also to Diane Doe.

I've done it — the first day of The Walk: air soft, sky lowering. The wind gave the slaps and kisses of children in a game.

We began late, frustrated over endless forgotten details. The water truck that should have gone ahead had to be signaled to catch up, the portable toilets were out of sight at rendezvous, but by three, we had gone far enough to know we had begun.

Sore tomorrow? Yes! Blisters? Shin-splints? Yes. But now I want to yell and cheer. I'm sight-drenched. Have I never looked at anything, earth or sky or other people? We started from Fresno. We will walk to Washington, D.C., and thence to Woods Hole, Massachusetts. It will take us a year and a day. And we've begun.

# *April*

*Dear Marz:*          *April 1, Fresno, California*

We're on the road and beginning to move toward you. My thanks and love go ahead of me to Boulder.

We've finished dinner and cleaned up, the biggest of all big deals on an environmentally pure Environmental Walk. It's worse than the kosher demands of my great grandmother.

When we stopped for the day we did introductions: name, job, reason for being on The Walk. "Tig Warriner," I said, "part-time librarian." I couldn't give my reason(s) for being here; they're too complex, so I told them about you, that you had tried to talk me out of going, and when you realized how much I wanted to go, helped me choose a tent. There were sounds of amazement and now I have a reputation as a liberated woman. I told them we had two daughters, but I didn't give their names. One eccentricity is enough.

This tent is excellent, and I found the envelope with your note and the money when I unpacked my toilet things. Write to me. I know it's hard, but with a hundred of us on The Walk, wherever we stop, phoning will be

9

a hassle; I'll always be calling from some campsite's public phone or at least in a wrangle of impatient callers lined up for miles, urgent as the ladies' room lines at the intermission of a play. I've asked Justice to write; I doubt she will. Maybe Solidarity will want to put in a word. Even the younger generation might. I'll keep their letters, and together with mine, they might form a document of this year for all of us. Someone's calling. More when we get organized and there's time.

*Love, Tig*

P.S. Poppy says hi — she has put her tent on the extras truck and come in with me. There's plenty of room and it's nice to swap foot massages and talk over the day.

*Dear Marz,*                                        *April 2*

We started collecting answers to our questionnaire today. We're to use our eyes, too, and keep a record of what we see on the land we pass.

Poppy imagines hundreds of houses and apartments all over the country where our itinerary is being spread out on desks or flutters from magnets on the sides of refrigerators. Yet, here we sit at our second campsite: we're arguing about the rightness of having an evening fire. A young man, Kevin (?), makes a plea for the fire as being necessary to the soul of The Walk even though it may affect the natural environment. He says we'll need to gather, for announcements and rubbing our bunions.

The purists murmur. A fire would be one of our few luxuries. The food won't be. It comes hot(ish) from the cook-wagon, and it is tasty only because we are exhausted and ravenous.

The group is diverse — singles, families, a few children, but Poppy and I seem to be the oldest here. There's some prejudice, or daintily expressed <u>fastidiousness</u>. "What is the policy toward Walkers unable to keep up?" a young man said, looking directly at us. This Walk isn't supposed to be a marathon. We have five trucks and five cars following us, and if people tire, they can catch rides. Grumbles. Someone behind us said, "With time off for trips to the beauty parlor." That was a shot at Poppy.

Poppy at sixty-five isn't gray; her work in Hollywood incorporates that place's fear of age, and when I asked her if she would let her hair go for the duration she looked as though I had asked her to do the walk barefoot. Her hair is even redder than when you met her, and she wears the same hard, red lipstick with eyeliner and mascara right out of a Queen of the Nile remake. Fear of surgery has kept her from having a face-lift, so, as she describes it, she is a redhead with a face that can hold a five-day rain.

Do you remember that there was, in 1969, a wanted poster on me? That's the face I remember, not the one I see in the mirror. I'm always surprised at what's actually there.

The Walk thinks of us as potential drawbacks. Poppy is a <u>bizarre</u> and I am a relic, a tall, stocky old lady, with a recent fling of moles and a habit of picking at them when she thinks no one is looking. Antigone. No one knows <u>that</u>. I whispered to Poppy that we should find out who made that beauty parlor crack and fix his sleeping bag.

The meeting goes on, mired in detail. I'm fading fast. I want to make this Walk. I hope I can . . .


DIARY ENTRY     *April 4, Sequoia, California*

More arguing. We have a council and five committees. During the evening's Bunion Rub, they report. Some people want all the rules in detail, <u>carved</u>, <u>etched</u>. I dozed. Kevin: suggestion about a social meeting on Sundays. We have been walking in good mountain country, refreshed. Soon we will be going down into Death Valley, all the challenge and glory anyone could want. Thank God we don't carry our own loads; we're followed by the equipment trucks; we walk unencumbered. NO PURSES!!

I keep measuring. I'm sore, slow. I'm worried about not making it. We've been lucky so far, but our strains and sprains take longer to heal. <u>Our</u> bodies forget and forgive nothing. The young people <u>dance</u> when the day is over.

Weather: warm. Something I can't identify is in bloom, filling the air with a perfume that mixes with the smell of the cedar that grows here. We seem more sensitive to smell, flavor, touch, sound — not since childhood —

We meet with tourists in the campgrounds, and the residents of the towns we pass. Questionnaires: we're surprised at the eagerness everyone shows to register an opinion, to tell the story of the changes that have come. The yes-no stuff takes three minutes; it's the verbatim statement that takes the time. People's hands form a shape for their thoughts. Their faces are perplexed. They have not been able to say what they suddenly wanted to express.


*Moms,*                          *Detox, May something*


Hello? Are you there? I have a creepy feeling of not being able to get to you, and it reminds me of stuff I thought I had forgotten, like that time when you were camped out at nuclear sites in California, and during the Vietnam War when you were protesting, or in jail.

Are you okay? Sixty-two isn't old. In some

13

places, it's not even old enough for senior citizen discounts, but marching across the country and camping out in the wind and rain for a year? I called Justice and she said, "It's Mother doing her thing again." I called Dad and he said he had learned years ago that if he wanted to stay married he had to take you as you came. He said this would be a hard one, though.

Remember when you dragged me to the camp-in at Rocky Flats? I was married then and had Sam. When Cary was born and Lewis and I split, you wanted me ready for life five minutes after he left. We said things and I flipped. It took a year before I felt like it was me in here, living. This morning I was thinking about that and how it has worked out. I wouldn't have gone into social work originally if not for you, and Detox is part of that.

Childhood memories: some painful, but some heroic. Remember New York — the big anti-war demonstration in 1969? We were in a park — Central Park, I guess — and you were teaching the Vietnam protesters what to wear and how to go limp and what to do to protect themselves from blows — things you'd learned in the civil rights protests. It was the first time I thought of you as more than my mother. I was thirteen, self-conscious as hell. People were arguing tactics, you were telling them about keeping clean, wearing clothes that didn't show the dirt, simple blouses, no

14

frills, hair short and neat, etc. You said they should try for a middle-class look, and never yell. The arguers were loud, repulsive. They were dirty and they wanted the dirt to show — they were middle-class kids trying for low-class identity. They thought their rags and stink would unite them to the poor; you said it would only make people laugh at them, the poor along with everyone else. "We want our mess in the faces of the captors!" a protester yelled — and he stuck his face into yours, messing his long greasy hair. I saw your nose wrinkle. I was furious. If I had had a gun I would have blown him away without breaking the rhythm of my Juicy Fruit. Isn't it funny what's dug up, walking through the old castle? Keep dry, Moms, keep clean. Wash your socks and underwear every night. Try to get good food and stay away from greasy snacks.

*Sol*


*Dear Solidarity,   April 8, Paniment Springs, Cal.*

I never told you the details of how I came to be on this Walk. I guess you and your sister do think "put a cause in front of her and an invisible orchestra tunes up, banners start flying, and a scarlet cape ripples out behind her." At Thanksgiving I told how I was planning to do this Walk and how long it would take. I saw Justice's eyes shoot up — you know her

15

ceiling-inspector-God-help-us look. You shrugged. Hope and Ben cheered. Sam and Cary cheered. My big support came from our grandchildren. Hope and Ben knew their mother thought I was being ridiculous, but they wished me well. Who else's grandmother does such exciting things? I think Ben actually said that.

I had thought to stay tucked up in my retirement. Being sixty hit me in a way that being fifty had not. One day, at a protest, I had a vision of myself as one of those gritty old parties screaming through her dentures and waving her cane in protest against everything. I decided to hang up the old cape and banner and take up what Justice calls Sensible Good Works, or grow something, or knit something.

Then, last June, I was at the mall, idling, and I stopped to watch a woman put up a notice on the outdoor board. She was my age, but one of those "protean" dames — twenty from the rear, and seventy from the front. She had flaming red hair, but when her hands went up to hold the poster, I saw the rolling veins, the arthritic thumb, the liver spots. Then, she turned to go and saw me, smiled, but instead of moving on, stood staring, and I stared back at her. This went on as we peered through the tops of our bifocals. I saw Poppy. She saw Tig.

Our senior citizen disguises blew off and we

16

were revealed to one another as our true selves: Poppy Irwin and Antigone Klein, now Tig Warriner, from the civil rights days of the 1950s <u>before</u> the Civil Rights Days of the 60s. We shrieked, we chirped, we hugged — all the things I hate seeing old ladies do. Where did she get that <u>hair</u>?

Where did I get those boobs?

We finished doing the notices, and she came back home with me. I asked her about the posters. They showed an astronaut walking on the moon, then the earth seen from the moon. EARTHWALK, JOIN US. There was a date and a place to write for info.

What was it? It was a Walk of Inquiry. The Walk would start in Fresno, California, and end at the big environmental meeting at Woods Hole. We would look, gather impressions, and give out a questionnaire about the respondents' own environment.

The Walk would not be random. We'd be doing something like a core sample, one long probe through the middle of the country. We'd be talking to people in small- and medium-sized towns, on farms, in suburbs, but not in big cities, which other surveys cover. We'd be getting our own impressions, too. The main thing is that we'd be informing ourselves, learning how to see the environment, how to hear people talk about it.

Poppy told about meeting Patricia at an ecology seminar, where they had the idea. She

17

reminded me about the 50s and 60s protests when we had jumped in without knowing much about life or how other people saw it. This Walk would be about learning, not teaching; about listening. We would present our paper, based on the questionnaires and what we had seen. Poppy thinks it's a chance to do one last wonderful thing, one last crazy thing without its being politicized or parodied. They were having final planning meetings in Los Angeles. Would I go and be part of it?

I didn't go, but I stayed in touch. The group was collecting money from hundreds of donors and many businesses big and small. In August I went out and met the Californians. In October I went again, and then I helped raise some money. I talked long and hard with your father. He wasn't ecstatic about it, but he did see how eager I was to go. The Walk will be coming through Colorado, and he'll travel out to meet it here and there through the year.

*Love, Moms*


*Dear Marz,*                    *April 9, Lone Pine*

It rained the day before yesterday and we got to test ourselves against hard weather. The rain made us all feel self-reliant, baptized. We sang, we took out our rain gear, and went our full day, and it was only waking damp and

18

crabby yesterday morning that we learned the full story. It took us all day to dry out.

Food: We break into age and levels of elitism here. The higher the educational level, the rougher the food we demand. "I can't walk on garbage!" Herb Kvarner declares, shouting for whole grains, bean dishes, and the coarse bread the younger people have a disgusting name for. The younger ones — the teenagers — want burgers, fries, doughnuts, and corndogs. Iron-gutted youth. Coke and Pepsi. Each assumed his reasonable standard fare would be provided. Each faced a ghastly awakening. It was our first true crisis and the conflict was resolved by compromise.

There are eighty-nine of us, now. Eleven of the hundred left on the second day, realizing suddenly what a year-long Walk would mean.

This evening at Bunion Rub Kevin suggested we sing a goodnight song to end the day. "Oldest first!" Poppy yelled, and before we knew it, she was teaching everyone Brahms' Lullabye, and by the time we were done, some people were crying.

You'll understand why, if you imagine us. In almost darkness, fire dying, eighty-nine people were singing that very simple song. Our mellow sound rose backed by some heretofore undiscovered deep bass voices, resonant, powerful, but soft as water. We didn't want it to end.

I was moved, too. Rituals like this will bring

The Walk together and we need that, because there's so much to argue about. Kevin understands the need. He reaches instinctively for what will heal the animosities that build up — he laughed about the food crisis that might have ruined The Walk and after the compromise, made us see the joke. He's a powerful force on The Walk, a good angel.

Poppy has become less impressed with him than she was, and has pointed out the number of pairs of female eyes, their scleras white as milk in the now brown faces, all turning toward Kevin as if they were watching tennis.

It's April, I remind her: Moon of the Throbbing Gland. We passed a big ranch on the way here and the new-born colts were out with their mothers. Even as we have left the farms and vineyards of Fresno for the drier, barer, land here, there's something about the air, the wind, and the smell that tells us it's spring.

We're making a list, checking it twice. We don't want to break down in the desert. The trucks were donated and are fragile; a food and a water truck — that golden oldie kept running by Murray Siger, mechanical genius of The Walk. The bus is another invalid.

Ecological comments? Only that this country is bigger than I thought, and thank heaven we don't have to do the desert in July.

*Love, Tig*

I miss you already and I am saying so in spite of not wanting to. You explained the trip; I know what it means to you, but I have had a week of returns to this empty house, a sad nudge at the end of each day.

I do understand your reasons for making the trip — that we get our ideas of America from the bad-news dispensers with a cataclysm every day. You wanted a fresh picture. I think you really believe The Walk is your last hurrah; no jail this time, no civil disobedience, no admonitions from platforms. Most urgently, you wanted to know if you could still make such a walk.

As much as Poppy's showing up kindled all that in you, I can't help but think my sickness and long convalescence last year did its part. We're getting on. How long will the knees hold out, the eyes, the wind? You wanted one more try at something big and you saw this year stretching clear ahead of you, with a door closing slowly and inexorably, and you squeezing through one more time.

Why not? You haven't been arrested since the Rocky Flats sit-ins of 1983 — thirteen long years without a single appearance before a judge. The year lay open — the girls are grown and mostly settled; our grandchildren strong and healthy; our friends beginning to fade and some of them to die; our parents

21

gone, with no more need for sudden calls to New York or Grosse Point.

I am reconciled, but I won't always be, I know. I will be lonely and angry sometimes. I will try to build ways of overcoming the empty feelings. I will learn to use my advantage as father and grandfather and see the girls more often. I might, for example, get roaring drunk and wind up at the detox so Solidarity can take care of me; or babysit her boys; or get Justice to send me some of those savory senior-shut-in-meals-on-wheels she administrates. Then there are Justice's children: Hope might need a chaperone and Ben a mentor. I think I'll get him to go skiing with me before the season ends. Jason skis too fast for me.

Here's something else: some of the library people and the women at my job think you have done me wrong. I can get signed up for at least a dozen pity dinners a month.

*Love, Marz*


*Dear Gram,*          *April 8, Grant Street*


I know Mom and Aunt Sol will be writing to you about me, about what they think is my big mistake, but it isn't a mistake, it's the most wonderful thing of all. I'm in love, yes, really in love, and he's shy and proud and because of that he didn't want to admit he loved me back, but last night we went to a school basketball game together. He's not on the team so we sat together and later he told me he liked being with me, close to me. I felt my insides melt with joy and love for him. We've known each other for two years, and I've been in love with <u>him</u> for one whole year before he started arranging to be where I was, or sit next to me, and then it was a while after that that we started to talk. That's been for six months, but last night was the first time we kissed.

If I can't keep seeing him, I'll die.

There's a bad part, though, and that's American racism. Larry is Native American and people are against him because of that. I can't exactly explain, so I'll give you an example: Larry likes to wear the Feather. It doesn't stick up on top of his head like they show it in books, which is just racist, too, because they make it look funny, and a feather is really a symbol of manhood. Larry had to buy his feather because the government won't let people kill the special birds you need, and forbids the tests of bravery Indians are supposed to do. He wears two and they're on his neck near his hair and here's more of the racist part because the boys laugh at him and call him Tonto and Chief.

He's so wonderful. He's very spiritual and when he's sure you aren't laughing at him, he shares his thoughts which few boys do, and which are <u>not</u> about how good he is in sports or how he's going to compete for some award.

Remember how I said if I can't keep seeing Larry, I'll die? That's because he's thinking of dropping out of school and because Mom and Dad are down on him. Mom and Dad are good people, but they are part of a racist society and they can't help themselves. Ben and Jason are against Larry, too, saying they're afraid of him. Jason saw him fighting on a school visit once. Ben heard it from Jason. They don't even know how he is at school, because both of them are still in junior high.

I love Larry and I want to show him that love is stronger than bad things, stronger than everything. Please be on my side. No one else is.

*Love, Hope*

*Dear Hope,*         *April 12, On the Road*

I remember the lunch out we had before I left for The Walk. You told me I should write to you when the going got tough. It's been tough for reasons I didn't expect.

I wondered if I could walk the distance, if heat, cold, rain, or weakness would stop me. I'm older than all but one of the other Walkers who's a lifetime hiker.

But this isn't a hike over bad terrain, carrying forty pounds of gear; it's a Walk along secondary but reasonably good roads, two breaks for water, breaks for lunch and the johns, and the possibility of hitching a ride with the scouting car or gear vans, if necessary.

We write short reports, give out questionnaires, and every now and then pick up the trash we find. There isn't time to do it all and we have to fight a drift into species-self-hate when we see spontaneous garbage dumps and evidence of stupidity, greed, and neglect. It's difficult then not to become angry and bitter at the thoughtlessness of it all. Pessimism can settle like a second hat. Yet, looking up, there are horizon-shattering spaces in this country.

The spaces shimmer, and at dawn and twilight go iridescent as though they owned the light of the sun. Light is the preeminent feature here, and every hour its changes pick out or retire the shapes it chooses, this heave or stone, that line of cliffs; now the soil is dun-colored, now honey-golden, now silver-black. The rocks come forward and retreat like dancers against a sky someone on The Walk described as "drop-dead blue."

In these light-intoxicated spaces, the wrecked car rusting, the laceless leather boot, the festoon of beer cans intrude in a way they never would in a lusher place. This isn't land where the garbage gets vine-grown in a day and disappears in a forgiving, green tangle.

You probably don't remember, but I met

your young man, Larry. It was last spring at your school picnic. We only said hello, but he made enough of an impression on me that I remember him. Please tell me how things go between you. You and I go back quite a while as friends, and friends really talk to one another and aren't defensive or afraid of being harshly judged.

I wasn't always wrinkled and gray. Remember that.

*Love, Gram*

DIARY ENTRY
*April 12, looking down on Death Valley*

After Bunion Rub this evening, we were sitting around. Kevin started talking. America's government and administration are too big, he said. All the systems that heal, police, educate, and feed us need to be scaled down to tribal size; we should be preaching that. Poppy reminded him that the purpose of The Walk was to learn. I said we needed to encounter life directly, the land and the people. He stared at me, his face shadowed as he stood in front of the fire, and said he was looking ahead of The Walk. The moment passed. The night song was "Bridge over Troubled Water" and I had a hard pang of nostalgia because Justice and Solidarity used to sing that song around the house years ago.

26

The group broke up, Poppy and I went to our tent. We have an illegal cooker — a Sterno set — just enough for evening cocoa. She's troubled that Kevin wants to change The Walk, to make it political, that we're going to have to fight him before long. She thinks people like him too much.

I think he is idealistic and that the by-laws will rule.

"Kevin wants power," she says.

There are fewer sounds here than anywhere I have ever been — the whrrs, ticks, hums of domestic machinery, the background wall of noise is gone. There is no scratch of dry leaves underfoot, either, no sound of wind in leaves. What sound there is, is a wind-up insect chuttering its mechanical love call To Whom It May Concern. Here and there, the call is answered.

Then, from far away, seas readied themselves and a wave began. I could have sworn it was water, in some vast form, all along the line of the distant mountains. It was wind. It was on us suddenly in a roar, fingering its way into the tents. I thought: what isn't well-staked will blow away. We heard shouts. "The campfire!" I crawled out. Our tent was flapping and yawning dangerously, a fearful billow. I was thinking of the embers of the fire I had insisted on, how they would wake in the wind and swarm to light on the treated and coated synthetics of our tents. The wind had taken the side panels of tents and made sails of them, pulling the tent pegs up and setting all the loose items inside to flight. I caught clothing and bedding in midair and had to let them go again. I fought the wind, pushing in slow motion to the circle where the fire had been. The earth there was warm but not hot; embers and ashes had been borne away in the mix of clothing, toys, pebbles, shoes, sand, and loose weeds.

The wind increased. I couldn't walk in it so I crawled, and then lay flat on the ground, wishing I could interpret the sounds around me. A flying tent-stay hit me. There was no escape from what was breaking and coming apart around us. I was in the open, prone and trying to guard my head, deafened, and blinded, and at last losing my sense of direction when I got up again and tried to move toward our tent.

Then, like a fast curtain down at the end of a play, it all stopped. Most of the camp was gone — tents and their contents, blankets, sleeping bags. The trucks and cars had been banked with blown sand. People called to one another, flashlights bloomed. When we were sure no one had been hurt, we decided to save the picking up for daylight. I found a blanket — tripping over it, shook the sand out of it, made a bed. I never expected to sleep.

We took today out to recover ourselves and find our camp. First time luck: the water and food trucks had been pulled over to the side of the road, one on each side; the cars had pulled over at an angle to the camp. Clothing, blankets, bottles, boxes, toothbrushes, hairbrushes, laxative bottles, and sunglasses had all been swept into piles at the lea sides of both trucks. The cars had been sandblasted and pitted with wind-flung pebbles. I found this notebook with its rubber band and pen in the pile by the food truck. Other possessions, which we spent the day recovering and returning to their owners, were not so easily restored. Clothing had to be shaken and the three Porta Pottis had been overturned and were a hideous mess. We thought we would have to take precious water to hose them out, until John Duda, our "Dr. D.," thought to use recovered wash water. We had tents to sew and patch.

Some items were not recovered and people kept digging in the blown sand all day for this or that lost thing. Sometimes they opened sand-hills only to find the blown bones of small animals, sand-cleaned.

It's tonight that we won't sleep. We'll lie wide awake in our repaired, dust-smelling tents, alert as foxes for the horn sound of the wind.

*Dear Tig,*      *April 10, The Hill, Boulder*

It's been five days, and I've written five mental letters to you. This morning I realized that I'll have to schedule regular times to write. If I wait to gather interesting things, the daily this and that will have faded like old newspapers in an attic.

We had a big, wet April snow. Instead of handling it manfully, I burrowed up with some books and canned beans, called in with an eye complaint ("I can't see working"), and took two days off. I have material at home and have been able to put some necessary work on the computer. Wave of the future? With the snow banking the walk, it seems like a retreat into the past.

I'll meet The Walk at Pueblo, where I will see you blooming in situ and hear your war stories from your own cracked and desert-parched lips.

The office has become an encounter group. "How can you let her go?" Bayler demands. I remind him that you are a person as well as a wife — a person first; I tell him that had I been the woman and you the man, your year away would have seemed much more normal. Wars, jobs, sabbaticals at the Sorbonne are all perfectly acceptable reasons for men to spend a year away. Had I believed in the cause with the enthusiasm you have for it, I would have gone with you. Mitzi, the secretary,

30

weighs in. She forgets that if I took a year's leave of absence I would lose my seniority. She's worried about the sexual possibilities now available to both of us; Carson says things about love between husband and wife. I hold to my point, and reduce him to muttering, "Well, I wouldn't let my wife do that."

And it's all true, and yet I spend (waste) some time each day missing you and resenting our separation, going over your reasons and punishing you by eating tuna fish out of the can.

(I'll tell the woman I don't miss her. I'll tell the woman I'm doing splendidly without her.)

I don't miss you. I am doing splendidly without you. A year is a long time, but I held you back once before on work you felt you were called to do, and lived to regret it, deeply, deeply to regret it. Things are fine here at home. The damage from the fire hardly shows. I buried the two intruders I shot, in the backyard. The smell has gotten pretty bad, but if the police come, I'll just act confused.

*Love, Marz*


DIARY ENTRY         *April 16, Death Valley*

Descended, graceful as night falling? No. The dull ground has salt on its lips.

Eyes are on us. Burrowing animals live here

31

and the nakedness of the ground allows us to see an underlife of mice, skinks, and tiny lizards. Evidence of sidewinders. The snakes eat the mice. What do the mice eat?

The Walk starts out singing, but the immensity of this place stifles cheeriness. We put up the snake guards on our tents and the next day see sand-signs of struggles we cannot read.

Even Poppy has to admit that Kevin is vital to The Walk. He goes up and down the line like a friend, capable but not obtrusive. The children get whiny in the heat. With them he is miraculous. They live on his smile and pattern themselves on his walk, his way of stretching to ease a stiff shoulder. They do impersonations: "O — Kay" the way he says it. The four adolescents try not to be unworthy of his magic smile.

He has made a family out of us, or a tribe, reconciling the stubbornness of the Dudas ("Let's push on") with the dreaminess of the Dorns ("Let's wait and see . . ."), the pleasure-loving singles with the peace-and-quiet marrieds.

I started badly, after a bad night. Poppy, too, and we gritted our teeth when the starting signal was given. It was Kevin who came to the back of the line where we were wading through glue. "You are the only ones on this Walk who haven't spent time in the follow-up car."

We don't need his permission. The rule is that no one asks and no one apologizes, but the way he said it took the worry from us, worry we haven't vanquished about our being equal to this Walk. We looked at one another and then, Poppy and I, without another word, stopped and let the first of the follow-up vehicles pick us up.

*Dear Marz,*                    *April 16,*
*    on the road, to be mailed in Las Vegas*

It was wonderful to hear your voice in the treasured five minutes while the line stamped and sighed behind me. Even though we can't say much, it's the voice, the very "hello," that works the miracle. The weather has been "good" — 90° and upwards, and the road is good.

Sometimes we talk. Someone starts a song, and clumps of Walkers answer with another, or with punning and joking up and down the line. People walk in small, habitual groups. These are:

1. Young, single men and women up front, usually, with lots of place-changing. There's an inner flow, like the liquid in an amoeba, a moving and jockeying for place beside this girl or that young man, and, of course, near Kevin, who's often in the lead. He's the

only one who, after starting out in front, will fade back and spend time walking the long snake-line of us.

2. The Middle-aged, using The Walk as a combination ecology statement and proof of undiminished vigor.

3. Marrieds and families with kids, and they are in the middle to make sure that the kids — the youngest are seven or eight — don't get left behind.

4. The Aged and the Misfits (Poppy and my group), the out-of-condition, the social failures from group 1, the bad day people from group 2, the loners, and the boring ideologues. Attempts to "distribute us" more homogeneously start well and an hour later we are back to our natural groupings.

Yesterday I learned that Poppy has been sharing the choicer parts of my bio, the facts of which have been percolating through The Walk, and I've been met by people at the water truck or the johns with questions: Did I really go down south before the civil rights protests and Freedom Summer? Was it true that I had been in the original Vietnam protest group and knew the SDS people and the Chicago Seven? Did I know all of them?

I've achieved a dippy fame. I am quaint. Now, as moss-grown as the Civil Rights Movement itself, as venerable and non-threatening as the old wars, I bring a brittle-bone presence, like a relic skeleton, to this enterprise. How long ago were those ancient days? they ask me. I'm sixty-two, not one hundred sixty-two.

Poppy says it does the kids good to know that the back of The Walk has its distinctions. Maybe we'll need our reputation for feistiness later.

I didn't follow up on that part. I was too busy wondering why I felt so dislocated by what she had revealed about me.

My life is being handed back to me in cartoon form by youngsters who see those days as "simpler." And those people as "simpler," too.

She has also blabbed that my name is really Antigone, and then I am obliged to tell them that my parents were idealists, also. She's holding out about Justice and Solidarity. She says that's to use later.

Funny? I don't know. We don't share a lot about our non-Walk lives. Lesson: Never lend money to friends. Don't travel with them, either.

*Love, T.*

*Moms,*                              *April 12, Niwot*

Thanks for your letter about the why of The Walk, Poppy, etc. Dad read his to me over the phone. I was antsy about you and Dad breaking up again. Surprise — it brought out a lot of old feelings. You were heroic back then. You were selfish, too. I was proud of your going this time, but I started going funny and depressed. Dad must have sensed that, because he called and then he came over and we talked. I know you hate to be explained and excused, but there it is.

I'm okay. Ever since the divorce, I've been worried about Sam and Cary, who are still small and vulnerable. Lewis never calls or visits. His new wife and family take up his time. Child support has leaked to a stop. The boys can't understand why he isn't here anymore. I worried about having to move to a smaller place away from friends, theirs and mine, but with the new job, and living like mice, we may squeak by (joke).

But ten months ago, a gay couple moved in next door. Blake and Anton and Blake's two little boys have become our friends. At first it was good enough that the two of them enjoyed Sam and Cary and we all pulled up in a bigger, happier family. Now I see that when Lewis took off, something about trust in men went with him for the boys and for me.

Blake and Anton needed reassurance, too. One evening we were sitting in Blake's kitchen, talking, and I asked Blake if he thought either of his boys was gay. He said they didn't think so. I wanted to ask how he knew, what word, look, gesture, preference would tell him. I asked what it was like to raise a child who was in some ways a stranger.

Blake said it had happened in his own raising, but at least the secret-keeping wouldn't be there.

My niece is in love, glowing like a two-dollar sparkler. Justice rants and raves. She's frightened of the precocious sex, and she can't accept the "love" Hope talks about for what it is, a mile wide and an inch deep, and an issue that may have disappeared in two months. Hope comes over to tell me all about Larry. Jussy probably won't write much because she's not a letter writer. Today she was up at the junior high where Jason and Ben go, protesting the use to which the school is putting its bond money. She won't win this one.

*Sol*

DIARY ENTRY                    *April 21, Pahrump*

No sense of forward movement. Valley has yielded to up and down. The land lies watering away in false mirages. The Walk defends itself. Knock Knock jokes. Knock Knock. Who's there? Effervescent. Effervescent who? Effervescent for this Walk, I'd be in Hawaii. Next day — Tom Swifties, the next, What Did The jokes. These idiotic word plays are funnier than they were when we were six. We laugh uproariously and from the substrates of her memory, Poppy draws up amazing numbers of them. She pulled a tendon and limps. She cut my hair — a feather cut — all the charm of wet feathers.

Next big stop — Las Vegas. Kevin's lip curls when he says the name. Such places are excrescences that should be wiped off the face of the earth. The Puritan in him shines forth in its blunderbuss fustiness. "Get him," Poppy smiles at me in the shimmering twilight. Have I noticed the night arrangements around here? If we stayed in one place, there'd be a path worn eight inches deep leading to Kevin's tent.

I was ashamed to admit I hadn't noticed. I looked. At first, I thought it was the girls preening before him. Poppy said I should watch him move through The Walk, combing it, grooming it.

So what? He makes us feel merry, courageous, necessary. The Walk, his moves say, is important. You and you and you are vital parts. Had we heard what the Park Ranger said about us and our questionnaire? The best group he'd had all season; an excellent focus on environmental issues. I found myself smiling up at him. I looked over at Poppy, whose face was gleeful and smug.

Yes, I saw him, combing and grooming, as she said. He put his gaze on two of the girls, just for a second. It's normal enough. The Walk must have elements of a year-long lark, if you're young. Kevin is attractive — I, too, feel the warmth of his approving smile and am cheered on by his approving word.

*Moms,*                    *April 14, Niwot*

I got a raise! A grateful community has decided that what I do is valuable. On it, I met Jussy for lunch. She's still frantic over Hope's relationship with Larry Walks Away. I asked her if it was because he's Native American.

Native American is an idea, not a people, she says. She's against the relationship. She told me how he summons Hope and she goes like a wind-up doll. When he comes to the house it's to lie around on Sunday afternoons, delivering Holy Writ and being waited on hand and foot, ordering Hope here and there. Twice, she thinks, he was a little drunk. You know how Jussy idealizes work. She told Hope to find something to do. "I have something to do," Hope told her, "it's Larry."

Then Jussy said, "Hope wants to marry him." She went on to describe Hope looking up at her with that inherited <u>Here</u> <u>I</u> <u>Stand</u> look and saying, with the inherited <u>Here</u> <u>I</u> <u>Stand</u> tone, "The age of consent in this state is fifteen. The state wouldn't have set it so young if it didn't think fifteen-year-old women are mature enough." Jussy flipped and called Hope an idiot and reminded her that that law was the state's torn umbrella over the swollen bellies of pregnant fifteen-year-olds with strap-wielding fathers. Hope stared at her, Jussy said, her gentle stare, her little smile. "I love him." When Jussy told me that, she pounded the table. "She <u>loves</u> him, and disapproval is racism. Case closed."

Has Jussy forgotten what <u>we</u> loved first time around? I remember, among others, a drugged-out jazz musician, a forty-five-year-old history prof, a feckless flunk-out with bedroom eyes and no visible means. She shouldn't yell at Hope, no matter what.

Or will I yell when Sam brings Bobbie Bimbo home and says, "I love her," with stars in his eyes? Hope says her only ally at home is Ben, "and he's still a kid so nobody takes him seriously."

*Sol*


*Dear Grandma,*                    *April 16, Grant Street*

Mom said to write but it's okay because she said I could tell you anything I wanted to. I want to tell you this because I don't want to talk to Mom and Dad about it yet.

I've been skiing a lot with the guys in class this season and I'm pretty good. Everybody,

Jason included, wants me to go out for ski team next winter, but I don't know if I want to. Last night I made a list, and here it is:

| REASONS FOR | REASONS AGAINST |
|---|---|
| 1. Makes you ski better | 1. Makes skiing into work |
| 2. Friends will think you're neat | 2. Makes you secretly mad at friends |
| 3. Seems neat | 3. It's dangerous if you don't really want to do it, and you're scared all the time |
| 4. I don't want the kids in school to think I'm a loner or a nut | |

I know this makes me look like a wimp-out, especially number 3, but I've talked to guys on the team and they're always pushing about competition. It's not only in skiing, either. If they find out you like dogs, they think you should join some group that races or shows them, or if you like to run they want you to be on some team. Mom and Dad don't push or anything, but I get a feeling they would be proud of me if I was on a team. Can't a kid have a hobby — just something he likes to do without other people making a big deal out of it?

I thought I could say it was the money, that

I couldn't afford it, but then I found out Chad Backstrand's dad works for a company that gives ski team scholarships to kids who can't afford to go. How can I tell kids I don't want to do what <u>they</u> say I <u>should</u> want to do? In the summer the ski kids have a hiking club and it's the same thing, there.

*Love, Ben*

P.S. Life around here is not so peaceful. Hope is in love with a scary Indian.

Even the kids in high school are afraid of him. She says he's deep, he's sweet, blah, blah, and Mom tries to argue her out of it. Jason stands around and laughs and soon Dad gets pulled into the scene. The thing is, he — Larry — has been around here a couple of times and none of us can figure out why Hope likes him.


*Dear Ben,*                           *April 22,*
*a dusty road 1 day out of Las Vegas*

In regard to your skiing, I must tell you that I think it would be irresponsible for you to join the ski team that would take up all your spare time when your grandfather needs so much help around the house, especially with me away. In winter, there's all that snow to be shoveled and window screens to be taken care of and many other home chores. In summer there will be yard work and painting to do. This is not to say that you will have <u>no</u> opportunity for skiing in the time you have left, or hiking now and then during the summer with your friends, but I do think family responsibilities have a call on some of your leisure time. I think you should tell your friends this. Right now, I'm sorry to say that a commitment to a team would be letting me and your grandfather down and I know he will feel the same when you tell him.

I'm glad you're thinking, feeling, and learning what you want to do. That learning will give you confidence and that confidence will make you respected in a way no phony enthusiasm ever would. The phony thing gives itself away. I was twenty-four or twenty-five before I learned that and you have an extra ten years to discover, investigate, and enjoy what you really want to do. I hope it's not something too difficult for you to explain to me.

*Love, Grandma*

P.S. Have you tried to talk to Hope's boyfriend, alone?

*Dear Gram,     April 17, Grant Street, Boulder*

I want to tell you about Larry. Nobody around here likes him or cares about why he is the way he is, why he wants to drop out of school, and why he doesn't have a job. I used to watch him when I was in class with him. They wanted him to be like everyone else. They picked on him because of the feathers and his long hair. In the end they let him keep it long, but you could see the teachers looking down on him and some of them made comments.

His father was half Navajo and half white. His mother is half Sioux and half white, but she never lived on the reservation and she doesn't speak Sioux. She used to live in Denver but Larry doesn't know where she is now. His father was never around. The way Larry describes him, I think he was an alcoholic. Mom's down on Larry because he's not a real Indian, but whose fault is that? He was raised in Denver, mostly among Chicanos, and even there he didn't fit in.

He is hanging out with a bad crowd. I never admitted that to Mom and Dad because they'd go ballistic if they knew. All the kids in that crowd are putting themselves outside ordinary life and they think that anything is okay to do or say. Even they use Larry in a way, and I think he knows it, but he also knows that at least he could get some strokes from them.

Larry's at a group home here, and they sent him to Boulder to get him away from the crowd he was with when he was at the Lookout Mountain School for Boys. It was a pretty dumb move because Boulder schools are full of kids like me whose families are professionals and who are book-smart and know all about intellectual things. In downtown Denver Larry might be just another kid. At our school he sticks out like Dad would at a rock concert.

The two of us started hanging out and you should have heard everyone scream. My own friends — even Denise, my best friend, is down on me for being with Larry.

He wants to be an Indian, but he doesn't know how. He can't really study it because all the books are written by white people. Once he did go to a ceremonial, but he said it made him feel imprisoned because although there were Indians there, he couldn't get over the fact that they were captives. He said they were like lions and tigers in cages. He hates white culture but he can't live on the Navajo reservation or be Sioux either. It's not his culture anymore.

I want to marry him. He sometimes goes to an Indian group in Denver, and he's going to find out if we can have an Indian wedding.

Larry feels free with me. When we're alone together, he laughs and talks about what he wants to do. In the Indian world, everyone respects everyone else and they respect nature and the earth. I feel all those things and I know I could be Sioux and if we lived as Sioux he would feel that respect. His real problem isn't his drinking because he only drinks when he's low. When we're together he doesn't drink at all. When we get married, we'll be together and he won't have to drink.

White people will never make it up to Native Americans for taking their land, but one white person can come together with one Indian and help rebuild what was here before and what was taken away.

*Love, Hope*

*Dear Gram,*        *Sunday night, Grant Street*

I'm writing to you before everyone else gets their two cents in about what happened today. It's late and no one is talking to anyone else.

There was a big snow on Friday. Grandpa invited everyone over today to go sliding on that hill near your house.

We came with sleds, inner tubes, and even cardboard packing boxes. Aunt Sol's kids and their friends had those plastic slides. It's a great hill for sliding, fast enough for fun, but the snow was really soft so no matter how fast anyone went, if a sled tipped over he couldn't get hurt. Aunt Sol came in that weird coat of hers that makes her look like a show poodle. (Don't tell her I said this.) She brought a guy she works with at the detox center.

Mom and Dad came and Jason and Ben with one of Jason's friends and Grandpa asked me to come specially and bring Larry, so there were sixteen people.

I knew it would be a bummer from the start, for Larry and me, anyway. Larry hates crowds and useless activity, parties and stuff, and I had to beg him to come. I knew when we got there that it was a mistake.

Jason and Ben knew Larry from when he was a junior at school and was hanging out at the 7-Eleven parking lot. They were afraid of him then, and when he comes to the house they are uncomfortable with him. It makes him defensive and angry even though they're only kids.

We had all decided to treat the littlest kids, just for fun. We'd haul them up the hill instead of making them walk, and give them pushes and cheer when they did <u>anything</u>. Everybody went down the hill a couple of times, even my stodgy old Dad and Grandpa, but one or two runs were enough for them and they went into the house. That left Ben and Jason, Aunt Sol, and Larry and me with the little kids. Aunt Sol was asking Larry questions and telling him about life in the county detox unit and I guess it was all meant to get him to know her, but I could see he was pulling back from her.

By that time the snow on the run had packed down and the ride was faster. The kids started to goof around, bumping into one another, and we were all getting cold and tired, but we thought we would tell them, okay, three more runs.

Larry said he was going in. I was kind of nervous because if I was out on the hill, what would happen if he got angry in the house when I wasn't there? But if I went in with him, maybe he would think I was following him, crowding in on him, which he sometimes says I do. I said I would go down at least one more time. Larry said he would go down with one kid.

They got on the plastic slide and Larry pushed off. There was an icy patch about halfway down and they hit that and went over. Larry was wearing one of those slippery shell-jackets so he just kept sliding and couldn't get up.

Everyone had dumped at least once during the day. The kids were doing it on purpose, so when Larry did it, Sam and Cary and their friends began to laugh and that made Larry so mad the day was ruined for him. He wanted to go right then. We should have, but I knew that Grandpa wanted him to meet the family, so I talked him into going in the house.

He was cold and wet. When people saw he had only that light shell over a T-shirt, they gawked at him and Jason asked why he didn't have more on. Larry said that not everyone has fancy down jackets and expensive winter clothes. That shut them up. The secret is that Larry does have a heavy jacket but he didn't wear it. I don't know why.

Things got worse after that. He started fighting with Grandpa about old people — you know how sensitive Grandpa is about

48

being old. Larry said a lot of the things about politics that Aunt Sol would say, but no one liked hearing them from him. By the time we left, he had argued with everybody and no one felt like answering him when he said things. It made him mad because he said people were treating him like he wasn't there.

So we left early and then he was so sweet. We walked almost to the highway and he said he wanted to be himself but he didn't know who that was, and that he had never had a family to fit into, a family with aunts and uncles and cousins like I did. We went to a place we know and made love. He says that the body doesn't lie the way words do. Too many teachers and cops and social workers have told him things that were lies, he said, but body to body, giving everything, people can't lie.

Don't tell Mom and Dad. They wouldn't understand. I love Larry and I want to make up to him for all the heartache he has had. If I did tell them about making love they would ask me about the pill or about Larry's using a condom and he can't stand insincerity like those things. I have to be there totally for him and Mom and Dad wouldn't understand that, either. I feel all right letting you know this because you promised not to tell. Indians value loyalty above everything and they need to find it in an angry world.

*Love, Hope*

*Dear Tig,*　　　*April 18, The Hill, Boulder*

The oddest thing happened the other day. Ben came over and said you had sent him to help me around the house. I hadn't been planning to do anything and it's not quite warm enough to work outside, so I gave him my special peanut butter, banana, and coconut sandwiches and got him talking. I'm not sure I got it right but it went something like this:

1. He's not going out for any formal team or for sports this summer.
2. You told him he didn't have to.
3. In an excess of gratitude he lay himself down on the rack of filial assistance.

A couple of numbers must have slipped by me because this still isn't clear to me.

He's a nice kid, though. He's bright, well, not too bright — because he promised to come back and help me with the lawn this summer.

*Marz*


*Oh, Marz! —*　　　*April 23, before Vegas*

How daily this is. When I remember our time down south together, I remember the declarations, the strength, the high spirits. I remember you and I and all the tutors

50

crowded into those pine-slab churches to hear black pastors urge us to give the best we had, and to raise ourselves along with our students. How it all gleams, now, without vanity or silliness. Where did all this dailiness come from, arguments over bathwater and mail and having to decide organizational questions about seven times a day, <u>every</u> day?

Kevin has been organizing small groups to do demonstrations in addition to our questionnaire. I'm against the idea. When we do the questionnaires, people relax with us and talk freely. We are going to lose this comfort if The Walk goes political. Our scouts travel five days ahead of us and do a little P.R. People greet The Walk with enthusiasm. We meet at churches and little stores in towns, and at campgrounds, where we go in groups of three or four. There's a personal feeling, and an ease with questionnaires.

Yesterday, I suggested to the committee that we consider neatening ourselves up a little. Since Vietnam, most marches have lost any easy, friendly quality they may have had. It was one reason we called this enterprise a Walk instead of a March. People are afraid of violence parading as civil disobedience, and when a rag-tag bunch carrying signs and flags converges on a roadside, you can see eyes narrow and postures stiffen. The young people take pride in grungy clothes and trailing shirttails. Can I convince them?

Hope has written about Larry and it's serious, she tells me. I met him once, you know, last year. He looked aggrieved and sullen. Justice insists that Hope is too young. Of course she is, but nagging will only drive Hope to do something foolish. Justice is still the more conventional of our girls, and has always been very protective of the kids. It must have been difficult for her to grow up in a family where Mom was marching, organizing, and now and then in jail. When she was with me, the environment was overheated, too intense; then she would go to you and be de-pressurized into ordinary life. I've tried to talk to her about those days, but we always end in defensiveness on my part and anger on hers. She did grow up well, even with uncertainty and some instability. Infiltrate and let me know how things are between Hope and Justice, who needs to be careful where Larry is concerned.

*Love, Tig*

P.S. Take full advantage of Ben's gratitude and tell him you'll expect him to help with a paint job this fall. Don't look a gift grandson in the mouth.


*Dear Hope,*                    *April 24, Las Vegas*

We are in Las Vegas, and before you begin to wave your hand around, let me tell you that there is more than one Las Vegas. One is the casino town, where we were not successful with our questionnaires on the streets, and not allowed into the hotels or casinos. The leisure of the people there has the intensity of work, of oil-well capping.

But there's a city, too, and churches and schools, very clean and somewhat defensive about being supported by the wealth coming in from those hard-working vacationers. The people of that city greeted us with marvelous hospitality, invited us in, and gave us cake and tea and the time for thoughtful responses. There are lawns here, and lawn-sprinkler suburbs pulled out of a desert that given ten years would own the city again.

For Poppy and me, Las Vegas will always evoke the memory of a couple we met at a church. They invited us to dinner, and over the questionnaire, they talked about what life is like in a tourist town.

The house was adobe, and they have let the desert come close. We sat under a brush arbor, in shade, and they talked about their lives before coming here and how they had to make a conscious decision to find the kind of life they both needed. The sun went down and we sat in the dark, our sounds only minimally louder than the insect noises.

It was an evening I want to remember. There was a quiet awareness in that couple's life that my own life seldom has. Dear girl, I know that you have gone away from a conventional path and I know that's difficult. I'm glad you and Larry talk together about things that matter. It sounds as though he's sorry he can't take advantage of the good things life has to offer, but maybe he will, some day. What does Larry like to do? What gives him pleasure? You haven't said. Your little brother is beginning to examine what he likes to do and how he likes to do it. The four-year difference between your ages still seems cavernous, but it will shrink as you both get older. I know he loves you and I think you can confide in him. Maybe Jason is a little too tied up in sports and his own friends to be the best confidant, but your little brother is a sympathetic listener.

Keep writing and tell Ben to write, too. Your letters are especially valuable because there's a sense in which The Walk touches people and places but doesn't linger and after a while the Walkers feel cut adrift even from one another. We need the lifelines of old friends and close family to remind us of deeper relations than The Walk can give.

*Love, Gram*


*Dear Marz,*     *April 26, Kingman, Arizona*

I just got Hope's letters, one of which described Larry being a pain in the neck at your

Sunday sledding party. It was a wonderful idea, that day, and that makes its upsets even more irritating.

What were your impressions of the day?

A couple has left The Walk and two couples have joined it. They are young students who seized the chance to interrupt the grind of school for what one described as A Long Walk In The Country. In one, we have a jewel, another mechanical talent. As usual, Kevin was the catalyst and recruiter. He draws young people to him seemingly without lifting a hand. It has occurred to us with a surprise that says something about our naivete that people will be leaving as well as joining The Walk, and that by the time we come to the East Coast, we may have had considerable turnover. Patricia mentioned it at yesterday's Bunion Rub and said, ". . . that wouldn't affect the Fresnos." So we charter members now have a name — we're Fresnos.

Keep writing. Tell me about what is happening to you, to Solidarity and the kids, to Justice and Frank, including Hope, Jason, and Ben, to Whom It May Concern.

*Love, Tig*


DIARY ENTRY    *April 26, Kingman, Arizona*

Walking in the city remembering the Berkeley protests of 1970. I never wanted this

Walk to be a reprise of those days. I pick at the sore — the aggressively messy look of some Walkers. It makes the questionnaires seem political. Kevin leads the defense: "Our message goes far beyond how we look." His eyes are intense. The five or six people who have gathered around, who are always where Kevin is, nod. "How do people relate to clowns?" I ask, "How to bag ladies?"

Their faces freeze. I try to make it better. We shouldn't be preaching or teaching, anyway. We should be asking and listening. They will want to see us as worth talking to. "We want to be ourselves," sweet, blond Shari says.

They want to be they. I want to throw rocks. We are losing chances to reach people who might have much to tell us.

The same damn communal arguments draw me back to Mississippi in 1952, to Chicago, New York, on and on. The problem of who works, who loafs, who gives extra, and who not enough. It's all familiar as sweat. Yet, those times, those other times now seem bathed in light and when Solidarity evoked that Central Park protest in her letter, even the angry argument she remembered had a glow to it.


*Dear Tig,*                      *April 23, The Hill*

I gather Hope wrote to you about the sledding party I had for the kids. The snow up on the hill was so perfect — it was probably the last big snow of the year, and I couldn't resist. I was remembering how the kids and I used to go sledding up there. I called around: "Come quick, the snow is perfect." To my delight, they all said yes. I went out to buy chestnuts (good God, do you know what's happened to the price of those things?), cider, cocoa, popcorn. I found your recipe for those cookies the kids used to call dog tongues, and baked them. They came out a little doughy, but still edible. I made a batch of your pepper-nuts.

Everyone came; big success, I thought. Solidarity and the kids and their friends had brought those new plastic "sleds" to try. They are lighter than sleds and seem to work as well. You sit up. We all took three or four runs on the big hill, even <u>Frank</u>, yes. Justice was amazed. I am imagining your surprise. Hope brought her heart-throb, Larry; Jason, one of his friends. Ben used the old sled I gave him years ago.

After a few runs I got a bit tired and one by one, the second generation followed me to the house. The women went into the kitchen and Frank and I set up the table. It wasn't really cold, but we had a fire going — I thought how good it felt, how much fun it was to have everyone here, all talking and laughing and enjoying one another. You know, as soon as anyone starts thinking <u>that</u> — pow!

Hope's young man — he'd be good-looking if his expression weren't a sneer or a pout — came in later, pointedly Not Enjoying Himself, and when Larry Walks Away is unhappy, EVERYONE is. I was amazed at how good he was at his misery. It was as though he had X-rayed everyone in the room, found his or her nerve of discord, and played it like Paganini. Themes were Justice's looks, Frank's politics, my age, Jason's machismo, Ben's size, Solidarity's single motherhood.

After a few more parting salvos, Hope got him to go. All of us were sad for her and that, as much as Larry's rudeness itself and the hurts he had so liberally dispensed, soured the day.

Before she left, Solidarity, whose work at detox has sensitized her to the problem, said she thought Larry might have been on something, booze or drugs that he might have been using during the afternoon from hidden stashes, though he wasn't visibly impaired. I thought it was his real dislike of us, singly and together, and of our lives. We are not Indians. We are not hunter-gatherers. He had played that motif as a theme all afternoon.

Now here's the odd part: I encountered him yesterday, by accident, on the mall. I'd come out of the hardware store and he was walking — sauntering toward me, hands in pockets. I wondered if he would greet me — our afternoon at the house had not been pleasant, but he nodded my way and so, pursuant to what I knew was Hope's deep wish, I spoke — something witty and trenchant, like, "Hello, Larry, howzit going?"

He answered, to my surprise, "Not too good. I'm looking for work and it's not easy." We began to go up the block together; he talking freely with a natural ease, and I found I was following his talk with interest. He apologized indirectly for the circumstances that had brought on the bad mood at the house. We talked about job hunting. He's still living at the group home but at eighteen, in another two months, he will be on his own. Minimum wage jobs don't pay enough to support him here, and the hours of those jobs are so long that school or training classes are almost impossible. "I'm trying to put something together," he said. I made a few suggestions, which I thought he would brush off, but he asked intelligent questions and seemed to give my ideas serious consideration. We've had people in the office who come up with elaborate reasons for why none of the ordinary answers fit their special cases, and I've become alert to that kind of brush-off. Larry offered none of those excuses.

I found we had walked all the way home together, talking. The boy has been in lots of heavy situations: children's shelter four or five times before he was in elementary school, foster homes, then the reformatory, and from there to the group home he's in now. About that, too, I expected a diatribe, or at least a bitterness, but he only said, "They tried. They talked to me. I want to start to be a Native American but living in the Anglo world and having strengths in both cultures." I asked him about the time he was laughed at for wearing feathers in his hair. He looked at me hard. "Hope told us about it," I said. He said, "I wore them to cheer myself on, a kind of pat on the head I felt I needed. It wasn't a religious thing, although the kids thought it was." Just that.

I asked him in for coffee; he declined, with thanks. He said he had a job prospect to check out, and he turned and then turned back and gave me a wave. I felt it was sincere, good-hearted.

We wondered what Hope sees in him. I think I know, now. My only problem is how to compare that Larry Walks Away with the petulant, injustice-farming boy I met at our party. It only matters if Hope stays with him. In spite of his good meeting with me, I hope she won't. She's too young for the bronco ride that relationship would be.

Another snow nipped our lilacs in the bud and froze them all to the ground, so there may not be any blossoms this year.

Love, Marz

While you sample the delights of Vegas, we're shoveling snow. Blake, Anton, our four kids, and I made an evening of it, snowmen, snowfights. I hate a winter that goes on into May.

After Dad's party — a good event, soured by Hope's pain-in-the-ass boyfriend — we all met to get the shoveling done.

The guys are freer with me, now. They're interested in how I look. They're into looks. Blake said to Anton, "Did you know Don has AIDS?" Anton said, "How does he look?" This was not the first question I would have asked, looks.

They talked about friends who had died, about changed notions of friendship. Blake was never into the bar and bathhouse scene. Anton was — "When I came out it seemed <u>so</u> <u>sophisticated</u>!" I laughed at them — "You should have seen me at sixteen." I told them how my girlfriends and I mimicked the street prostitutes we thought were so with it, getting that open-mouth gum-pop. I popped the look for them. They both broke up.

Then we tried to think of all the things we had done as teenagers that we thought were sophisticated. Blue nail polish. Tattoos. Anton had an anchor, and a banner with the name of his ship. "I didn't know the tattoo would last longer than the ship," he said.

After the kids were in bed we talked about Anton's hitch in the Navy, his learning how to hide his gayness better than he had in high school. He and Blake met at the University, where he was majoring in architecture and Blake was a law student. They argued all the details, like you and Pops do. Anton saw Blake on campus. They talked. "Is he gay? Is he straight?" Anton said he was terrified of approaching Blake. Hints were dropped like Victorian ladies dropping handkerchiefs. Anton was local, Blake wasn't. Anton's hints about gay bars and meeting spots went past Blake. One day Anton bit the bullet. "Listen, I need to tell you something." Blake laughed about this. "I hope it's that you're gay, not that you've got AIDS."

It was dark by then. I hadn't put any lights on in the living room; there was only the light coming from the kitchen where the cleanup mess was.

Talking in the dark is easier. I opened up about Lewis, about how he thought experience was obvious, so why talk about it. Hell, two people in the same house would come up with the same numbers, wouldn't they; what was real and what wasn't? Disagreement was someone choosing to be a drag. I was surprised when the clock began to chime. We got up and did the dishes, and they left their kids, who were already asleep, with me.

After that I walked around grinning. Why?

Good feeling. I stayed up for another hour just sitting in the dark, feeling good.

What's all this about? That I'm okay — better than <u>just</u> okay, and getting more out of my life than pride at being independent, which I thought was all I could hope for.

Walk well.

*Sol*

# May

❧

*Dear Marz,*                    *May 3, Peach Springs*

We are 40 miles behind schedule and may have to catch up by riding to make the Grand Canyon on time.

I've written to Hope, trying to keep an even tone about Larry and first love, and I wish Solidarity would get back into the full flow of life again. Where will she meet the husband she should have if she stays in a social backwater with two gay men? Careful with Hope, careful with Solidarity. These thoughts are secret between us. I won't <u>touch</u>; I'll just <u>feel</u>.

The Walk imposes formality on us. We're too close for yelling or crying to go unheard. Tempers flare and must be put down ruthlessly. I think some couples who have left The Walk did so to go where they could have a decent fight. Clean anger goes to sulking like fire to smoke.

There's a quest for privacy, too. When Poppy pointed out that all the flirting is physical, in body language, not speech, I was amazed. No one mentions it but everyone knows where Kevin is walking, where Kevin is eating, where Kevin has set his tent.

We're getting used to answering questions

about The Walk. What is never asked about is the tribal quality we have developed. Consider the tenting: The young singles pitch their tents in the middle of any area where the camp sets down. Their tents are so close together they form the heart of the camp, loud and busy, with lots of visiting back and forth, and lots of jockeying for position. There's a little trail or walkway around that center to the water trucks, the Porta Pottis, and the food wagon. On the other side of the trail and more widely spaced are the tents of families, their extra space to give kids room to play and to provide some privacy. This group tends to keep the same neighbors. Because the families need more time to do everything, their schedules dominate the camp's understanding of time. The families are quieter, in spite of the kids, than the singles. I like the presence of the kids — most of them.

At the edges of camp are the loners, some of whom face their tents away. Some give the feeling they are traveling at the same time as The Walk, but not with it. Scattered among these loners, but all facing inward unless the view is spectacular, are the tents of friends, older friends like Poppy and me, and older singles. These tents sometimes move closer to the family tents when we form special friendships. When kid noises get too loud, or friendships cool, we pull away a little. Just now Poppy and I have families on both sides.

We could be said to be grandparents, neighboring with families we have adopted.

The weather has been good, a bit too hot and getting hotter, and we go past rockfields, up escarpments that look like the mud castles of a race of giants. There are huge open spaces here, impossible for Kevin to doom-preach about population explosions. Water could be brought in and they would bloom.

I got a cheering letter from Solidarity, who says she is doing fine, my doubts notwithstanding, and I'm happy about your meeting with Larry, although his personality difference is puzzling. Maybe the family-ness of us was daunting for him on the snow day. Have you talked to Hope?

*Love, Tig*


*Dear Marz,*          *May 6, The Grand Canyon*

The Grand Canyon: Poppy and I couldn't let the occasion go without giving Kevin and party a well-deserved critique. We arranged it when everyone was at the canyon rim. I showed up in a borrowed cut-off tank top the size of a postage stamp and low-riding cut-off shorts. My belly button hasn't seen so much light since I was six. Poppy was similarly attired. We whistled for attention.

Poppy: Look at the devastation industrial

society has accomplished in a few short years!

<u>Me</u>: What erosion! What unconcern for the environment! Why, it will take generations to bring back this area to agricultural productivity.

<u>Poppy</u>: And but for <u>your</u> indifference (pointing at me) this would be productive organic farmland today.

<u>Me</u>: No doubt about it, THIS WILL ALL HAVE TO BE FILLED IN!

As we were doing this, a prairie dog poked its head up from behind a rock as though it were part of the show. Poppy pointed a trembling finger at it and shrieked, "A Special Interest, there, hiding behind that rock!" The prairie dog disappeared.

Kevin came by our tent in the early evening and praised us. Maybe he had been taking things too seriously, and needed more of a sense of humor. We agreed.

Poppy, who was illegally washing underwear in a small basin, said, a little too pointedly, that we were not supposed to disagree about the <u>purpose</u> of The Walk; the by-laws were there to tell us what The Walk's purpose was. I thought I saw Kevin's face tighten. Poppy should have been decently quiet; our washing is to be done in the wash-house with the water specially disposed of. We were in the red-gloom of the tent's inside in long shadows cast by the tents around us. Subtle

68

facial expressions drowned in the gloom.

Kevin spoke slowly, saying that we were going to cross mountains, and the long plains. We were to be in rain, cold, heat, storms. Days of all of it. To be <u>interviewing</u>, <u>observing</u>? That wasn't enough to keep us going.

The point, Poppy said, was to <u>be</u> where the questionnaires were being done, to understand what the respondents were saying by being there.

Kevin said we needed to bring a message, too. He went on about the need for building a "tribal" feeling in The Walk. Tribal sounded too aboriginal to Poppy and too self-conscious to me, but we do need to discuss where we've been and to reach agreement on our purposes. When he left, Poppy only grunted. Later, she wondered why we rated all this care from him, and said that he only did what furthered his own plans. Why had he come to us?

Because we're Fresnos, even though Fresnos are now only three-fourths of The Walk. Poppy and I are, if one gets tribal about it, The Walk's Elders. Kevin knows we disagree with his ideas. He knows he'll have to convince us or fight us, and he doesn't want to fight a burned-out radical and a sweet little old two-tone-haired lady. Poppy laughed.

I don't like Kevin's idea, but at least he's not coyly pretending he's not the leader. He's trying hard for agreement. Because we aren't in agreement. The Left on this Walk thinks that environmental Armageddon is at hand.

In five years we'll be standing on leached-out soil, pressing our overpopulating footprints into other footprints at every step. The leftists want to go pre-tech, use manual power for everything, and scale the cities back to the size of Jericho.

The Right believes that technology has the answer to clean air and water. These philosophical questions are not academic on The Walk.

I'm beginning to wonder what the members of each faction see and experience, what that "data" will look like. Will our realities be so different that there won't be any agreement even on what we see? Above all, I don't want this Walk to become political. When the protests of the seventies went political, they lost credibility. Good Lord, I'm talking like the people I used to hate!

*Love, Tig*


*Dear Ben,*            *May 6, The Grand Canyon*

I'm sending you and Jason T-shirts from the Grand Canyon. I suppose officially I should deplore all kinds of tourist garbage at popular national sites, but my grandmother status wins out over my political correctness every time. Best wishes from the canyon.

*Love, Grandma*

*Dear Hope,*      *May 7, The Grand Canyon*

I wanted to write a big, inspirational letter about the Grand Canyon — vastness, beauty, importance as natural wonder, etc., but at first sight I was <u>embarrassed</u>. I had seen so many pictures and heard so much about it that my first sight made me think, "Yes, that's it, all right." I saw the blown plastic and the soda cans and someone's used Huggies. All around me, people were expressing what I should have been feeling. It wasn't until late afternoon that I felt the wonder.

The canyon is <u>alive,</u> which no one told us. Heat lifts from it as the sun sets, and birds lift on the rising shaft of warm air like so many blasé commuters on a moving staircase, going up, no need to work at it, just a spread of wings. Butterflies pour up through the golden tunnels of late light and that made my mouth drop open and brought the "Ah!" I hadn't felt before. Later, bats streamed out of innumerable caves and crevices to cry themselves aloft. Crickets wound their watches and something else that wore a carapace came out to love-dance with castanets.

And there are lots of people, too. Some of our people hate them. Back at the campground, RV, radio, and TV noises are loud enough to drown out all else. There's an anti-human prejudice on this Walk. Some of the featherless bipeds camping with us are graceful and lovely, and some are funny-looking. I'm sick of the noise, but it's human and that's my species — love it or leave it.

*Gram*

*Dear Marz,*          *May 15, before Tuba City*

We are becalmed. We saw the maps but didn't face the fact of more desert after the high of the Grand Canyon, where we stayed for two days and did 300 questionnaires. The Walk seems endless. There are long, desolate stretches where in three hours we may encounter only one Navajo staring at us out of the glassless windows of a truck whose engine would pass no state's emissions test. We crossed the reservation we have romanticized into acceptable poverty because it's so bare.

There's a feeling of being in a foreign country, into which we have intruded. We see people moving outlined against the sky as though they had slipped through a slit, in and out of visibility. There are no jokes now up and down The Walk, no knock-knocks or Tom Swifties. The weather is fine, but the day seems endless and the land unchanged from the day before.

Even Kevin's ebullience is blunted here. He can't reconcile his idea of the world as a warm, green Eden with this barren place, overgrazed in its hunger, leaching water in its thirst. Except, he thinks, white people must have been responsible — he told me so last night. We were camped off the road about an eighth of a mile. Only the rare passage of a car or truck kept us from losing all sense of other people, of a world of people beyond these scarped and rocky cliffs, this landscape of rocky floors.

I couldn't sleep, and rather than bothering Poppy, I went out into the shadows of a three-quarter moon and picked my way past hazardous guy-ropes and vindictive tent stakes.

There was someone sitting fifteen yards away, smoking. I caught that evocative smell before I made out a shape. Someone was perched on a large, flat rock, legs up, arms enclosing them. I went close.

Kevin's voice, and he unfolded himself and made room. I said something about this country having its special beauty. "Who knows what this was like before the Spanish and the prospectors raped it for gold and silver?" he said. Kevin isn't from the Southwest, but I remember no heavy mining operations around here, no population ever powerful enough to produce the smallest effect on its unyielding inhospitable realities. He went on to say that he didn't like the cross as a religious symbol. What would he use?

"A bunch of wheat sheaves tied together," he said.

Who teaches history to kids these days? I

73

told him it had been done before. He seemed surprised.

He began talking about his idea of the ideal society.

It's small; its model, though he wouldn't have known it, biblical, Book of Judges, maybe, and even the trade implicit in that book, nonexistent. The Nature he described, even as we sat <u>here,</u> was as mellow as might be spoken of by a suburban kindergarten teacher.

I listened to dreams, visions, nonsense pour out of Kevin. He is some years past twenty, but part of his development stopped at fifteen, stunned by the confusion of wish with reality. The nonsense from <u>him</u> began to scare me. My silences grew longer and he didn't notice my change from interested conversant to appalled listener.

At last, and it was the cold that forced it, he stopped, rubbed his arms, and said he was ready for bed. He got up, stretched, wished me good night, and walked toward his tent, at the very center of the camp. I watched him glide, even though he must have been weary at this late hour, with a dancer's grace, missing all the stakes and ropes and the piles of gear people left outside for a little extra tent-room now that the night was fine. He made a beautiful shadow in the night and left restless shapes in my mind.

So, the need is urgent. Please send a list of

74

sane men and women with lives that are lived in ordinary ways, people who pay their bills, hold responsible jobs, and raise families, and who, at the same time, hold outrageous, bizarre, and dangerous points of view, who will die in their beds surrounded by grieving family even as they continue to hold such views. This is not a joke. I am trying to recover from half an hour of Kevin's philosophy.

*Love, Tig*

*Dear Gram,*            *May 10, Grant Street*

Larry asked me to marry him! Anyway, to be his woman. I'm so happy! Here's how it happened.

Larry is really proud of his heritage and being Indian, but he doesn't know a lot about it because he was separated from his people and lived in Denver where there didn't seem to be Sioux, and very few Navajos, his father's people. We have been going to a group where they talk about Indian ways and racism. Someone got up and defended how the Indians have babies. White people say that Indians just squat down in the road and have their baby, and then get up and go on their way. No. The whole group is very reverent and careful of the new life and there are all kinds of religious and spiritual things they do. The same is true of Indian marriage. They brought someone in to talk about courting customs of Plains people, and it is really a big thing. Later we were coming back to Boulder with one of Larry's friends who has a car and Larry whispered in my ear that he wished he had a whole string of horses he could give me. I forgot to tell you that this part of the courtship ceremony is that the groom-to-be brings the bride's father lots of good horses. We started to giggle about how it would be if Dad woke up and there were thirty horses grazing on our lawn. Someone would call the police and the health department and the ASPCA. We were laughing and then Larry said, very softly so no one else heard, "I love you, you know." I wanted to cry with joy, but I said back to him, "Will you ride up to me on one of those horses and tell my father?" He said, "I'll put on my ceremonial clothes," and we laughed, but then he said, "I mean it. I want us to get a place together."

I don't want you to think that was all, or that I'm naive. I know boys say things they don't mean when they want sex. Then, when they've had sex or are away from the girl, they think differently. Yes, I have my joy and happiness and my whole heart jumping, but I am not naive.

So I called him before he had left for school so he wouldn't be seeing me or near me and the sex thing wouldn't be there. He's at the group home, and they don't like girls calling the boys there. They put a five minute limit on the calls, and you're not supposed to call until after school. Luckily, one of the kids Larry likes answered the phone and said it was Larry's teacher.

I was very formal when he got on. I said, "Do you remember what you told me last night, about wanting to have a place together and be married?"

He said, "Yes."

I said, "Do you still feel that way?"

He said, "Yes."

I said, "That's all I wanted to know," and I hung up.

I don't see him a lot in school. His classes are all different than mine and even his lunch period is different, so we can only see each other in three passing periods and homeroom.

Here's what he did: Two days after the phone call, some kids were talking in second period about horses. Someone said there was a long line of horses strung up one staircase to the senior three homeroom. In the passing period I saw Larry and he was dressed up and he had four feathers, not big ones, but all fanned out in back of his head and he was holding a cut-out of a horse he had drawn and painted on construction paper. Did I tell you, he's really good at drawing — the horse was attached to a string and the string led to another horse at the door. The horses were about seven inches long; the first was brown with white spots and the other horse was white with brown, and that led to another and another, all different colors, and some were running and some were grazing and some were tossing their heads, all down the hall and up the stairs, 6, 7, 8, 9, 10 up one flight; 13, 14, 15 — thirty in all, and they led right up to my desk in homeroom and all the kids were standing there with their mouths open. Larry came in with a little leather lasso, braided fine, and he gave it to me, and only I and he knew what it meant, but the kids were all standing there gawking.

I guess I'll have to take a picture of those horses to show you how beautiful they all are. I'm going to put them up in my room and when I move in with Larry to be his wife, I'll bring them with me. I wear the braided lasso around my neck. It's made of very fine suede strands — four of them, and it's so beautiful. Larry made that, too.

That's what I mean by being his woman. He can't afford a ring or anything, but we are tied to each other like those horses and like my little woven lasso. We want to work to bring the Indian spiritual culture and the white culture into harmony and we want to do it with our bodies, our minds, and our spirits.

*Love, Hope*

The Walk is allowed here by the Navajo tribal authority. There's overgrazing here and the tribe is multiplying too rapidly for its resources. They let us go through and give our presentation at schools and at chapter houses. Here we came, allowed but not received. People are polite but something in us or our message falls through a net. In the schools, no wonder or surprise kindles the children. Only the young men argue and that's about jobs and the implicit criticism we made about their wrecked trucks abandoned where they died, graveyards of whiskey bottles, cans, torn plastic sheeting at roadsides. Old people agree with us, but don't speak. At one of the chapter houses, young people postured around, shouting at us. We had a moment of real fear because suddenly our strangeness was on us like our clothes and we couldn't put our arms past it because we were sleeved in foreignness.

Young men were angry for the sake of anger. They yelled at us, blaming us for what neither of us controlled or had made, so the anger went around and around, circling wasps of it, the vagueness a menace. A relief to get out of there. Others said they had heard our message. One woman admitted that the young men needed to hear it because it was really a Navajo message.

The Walk is making us aware of weather,

water, dryness, roads, falling and standing water, cut-over places, torrents and dry creek beds, rain. In the future we might have to measure water by the drop. I remember camping by water when I was a child; we never feared disease if we swam in that water and swallowed some of it. We are making ourselves strangers, extra-terrestrials — divorcing ourselves from our bases.

Hope wants to end racism; it's a good cause.

What could we do to further that? I see the anger on the faces of the young Navajo men at the meeting. It was a group anger. I wonder if any one of those young men spoken to, befriended, seen separately as <u>himself</u>, might speak out of a different framework and say other things.

*Dear Tig,*                    *May 20, The Hill*

Pursuant to your request of May 16, inst., herewith the list as requested: salt of the earth types personally known to me, the baggage of whose minds should be impounded at the borders of sanity.

1. Charlie Elster, 59, Lawyer. He believes in astral projection. Bodies must not be buried until the fourth day after death to give slow souls the chance to disengage.

Near-death experiences are due to speeding souls leaving the body before it is dead.

2. Cassie Jurnigan. What's she got, an MA at least, in lib. sci.? She once told me she believes that extraterrestrials are among us and are the psychics in our society.

3. Who was that boyfriend of Solidarity's? You know, the one with the eye condition. He believed so much in the control of individual lives by planetary forces that he based all his relationships on it. I think he told me he stayed home and in bed on days of negative planetary conjunction. I thought he was an escapee from the Clair-de-lune commune until Sol told me he was the star physicist at the university's Institute for Advanced Studies.

Are these enough? I think that when Santa and the Tooth Fairy are unmasked as Dad and Mom respectively, lots of us keep on dreaming, winding up the dream on some spool of the mind that turns separately from all the others.

I've known Charlie Elster for forty years. He's a smart attorney and a solid volunteer on the water board. Astral projection, for Pete's sake!

*(Signed) Mandrake the Mandala*

*Moms,*

Screwy letter; screwy day.

I told you about Blake and Anton, my friends next door. For Blake's birthday I had a special invitation to a cello evening at one of the Stately Homes upscale and uphill. Anton hates chamber music, so I would be Blake's date for the affair, black tie, black dress — the lady and the gent. I was jumping-eager to deliver the tickets to Anton, who had arranged it all as a surprise.

I got the invitation and ran next door, which was open. His "come in" sounded strange.

I went past the dining alcove. There was food set out, cups and plates for ten people, maybe. It was a classy setting. I started to say, "Big doings —" as I crossed the kitchen to the sun room they had built on.

A woman was putting flowers on the side tables. She had her back to me but even from behind I thought of misshapenness in her. She turned; I saw a big chin in profile. What an ugly woman, I thought, and she makes it worse with all that makeup, and her dyed hair piled up like cotton candy. She was in a tight, red dress, low cut, and stiletto heels, whorish, and — not a woman. It was Anton. I was scared; I stood there scared and wishing I could run.

When he saw me, he went white under his foundation. We stood there, staring. Then I thought: It's a parody, burlesque.

Anton's voice was caught in the crack between his male and his female mood.

Then he came forward and I saw he must have shaved, then shaved again. I took in the heavy eye shadow; lipstick, too red; blond wig, teased, sprayed, curled; it gave his face a hard look. Who advised him that a heavy chin needed the balance of heavy earrings? His were huge. His bust was a shelf you could rest a dictionary on and he was carrying pounds of costume glass. I asked what his perfume was.

"Night of Love." Night? More like a full month.

It was the parody that got me. Beyond the shock of his gender change, hell, what did he see us as being? I tried for that look when I was thirteen. I think I said something like, "Your makeup's too heavy," and he touched at the lacquered ringlets, and said it was about freedom.

In that girdle?

He stared at me for a minute and then smiled, and said he was still Anton.

There were other voices from the door, male, but high; he called out that they should go downstairs. He would be with them in a minute.

I reached out gingerly. All that work — I didn't want to disarrange anything — and handed him the tickets.

He smiled, and thanked me. We were almost mute with embarrassment. Then he turned and with a simple gesture, one more graceful and feminine than I'd ever managed, waved good-bye and went to join his group.

I didn't get the nap I was supposed to get. I lay on the bed and thought about Anton and what he had said; that it was about freedom.

Whatever we have as women, it's not freedom. I've always been mediating something, fixing something, tied in — soothing, smoothing, the kids, Lewis's mother, worrying about how Lewis and she got along, how Lewis and the kids got along. I see the mother gig playing way beyond Sam and Cary's eighteenth birthdays. What do the teased-up wig, the greasy makeup, the heavy brassiere and girdle have to do with <u>freedom</u>?

*Sol*


*Dear Grandma,*          *May 15, Grant Street*

Thanks for the tee shirt. It's neat. Everybody here is in a hissy fit about Hope and Larry Walks Away, her Indian boyfriend. She says she's engaged. He made her a rope that's supposed to stand for something in Indian life.

It's true that his friends were all the worst kids. A guy who wears braids and a feather in his hair, if he's a guy he better be tough. Ma goes on like he's radioactive.

So it isn't so good to be in the house these days. Jason stays out with his friends and I asked Mom if it's because Larry is Indian that she's so upset. She says they are too young to think about getting married. Larry isn't really an Indian, either. When he used to bully us and take our lunch money, it wasn't because of what Columbus did. It's a month until school is out. Jason says he likes high school. I'll never get there. I'll die in junior high.

*Love, Ben*

P.S. I'm going to help Grandpa this summer. Don't think it's a chore for me. We talk about stuff I'm interested in.

*Dear Solidarity,*

My first experience with a cross-dresser was seeing a classmate in a stage production in which he played a man disguised as a woman, then seeing him on the street a week later in the same clothes. We've now got unisex clothing worn differently by men and women, but cross-dressing must be something different. Sort it out for me, if you can. It's a world I have no knowledge of.

I think about you and Justice a great deal. The Walk gives me time to do that. We sing and talk, but there are long stretches of silence, our bodies taken up with the work, the rhythm of pace and pace. In <u>this</u> landscape there is no relief in green vistas, trees, landmarks, but we are light-struck. Light dominates the earth, changing its colors throughout the day and moving the shadows here-and-gone, hide-and-seek.

I remember you as babies, as children, as girls. I think of you as you grew into what you are. The biggest surprise has been the different paths you took, the different outlooks you have. We watched you face the increasing problems in your marriage and your strength in the divorce from Lewis. Did I see you as a counselor in a detox center? Who would have dreamed of such a response arising out of a spirited, willful little girl? Justice resented my leaving to protest the Vietnam War, and then war itself. Who would have imagined her reaction would be her own group of causes — the water system, the school system, less idealistic but much more practical. Mankind is not at peace, but there is less waste in the Boulder County schools. If I put that on my tombstone, Justice would think I was mocking her. She would be mistaken.

I have changed as well, but I don't know exactly how. The Walk's maps get wrinkled and torn and we keep replacing them. Symbolic, huh?

*Love, Moms*

*Dear Moms,*                    *May 19, Niwot*

Anton has stayed away since I found him in that getup. When I go over, he's shy.

Jussy and Frank have not calmed down about Hope's seeing Larry. I've had Hope over twice to babysit and I think Larry has met her here, but I can't prove it. I can't ask her. I mention his name and she lights up like July 4th, but she's cautious about bringing him over when I am home. And we're all too serious. They're kids. This is a malt-shop moment, not West Side Story. She'll go away to college next year and he'll find someone else and we'll all remember this like a case of hiccups, and she'll remember it as sweeter than it was.

I keep imagining Anton in all that makeup. Maybe he's only carrying the male preening instinct one more step.

*Sol*


*Dear Marz,*                    *May 25, Tec Nos Pos*

I got your letter about local solid citizens who harbor deep weirdness. Thanks. It put Kevin's ideas into perspective. When Jesus said, "Be as little children," he didn't know what he started. I'm years further away from childhood and I don't remember it as an innocent time. Why does Kevin, I wonder?

87

He wants to amend the by-laws. I wanted a dress code and didn't get one; he wants a mental code. Walkers should <u>demonstrate</u> simple living, he says. Many of us feel we do that already. Kevin means preaching. He wants us to lead a back-to-the-soil movement — spiritual, he calls it. "Religious," Poppy says, "full of unexamined dogma." I don't understand why Kevin needs this unnecessary unanimity. I am trying to give him psychic support without supporting his ideas. Poppy says that this is too subtle for him to see. At one of the Bunion Rubs he called for a rule on simple living. Poppy, in an undertone, asked if simple living shouldn't include monogamous sex. His attitude toward Poppy has chilled visibly, while to me he is gentle and gallant.

Magically, as out of the desert, three people have joined The Walk. Many people walk along with us for a day or two, but don't become permanent members. We've learned to ask them for a food-and-water donation and for certain work around camp. Some walk along for an hour or two, or an afternoon. I think this is one source of Kevin's wish to define us more clearly. The "tourists" bring a rag-tag-pied-piper kind of behavior to us. Occasionally, for example, motorcycles and bike riders join us. Kevin wants us to be as much of an entity as possible. In this, even Poppy agrees.

We'll be in Colorado by tomorrow, and the

effect on our Coloradoans is amusing. We feel hostlike. We have begun to worry about the weather, the altitude, the welcome. Populations will increase from here on. We got a good response from the people in Tuba City proper. Will Colorado be as hospitable?

Our mountains — still all white — will soon fill our view, rim to rim. Colorado means closer and closer to Pueblo and that means seeing you. I'll call you from Cortez.

*Love, Tig*

DIARY ENTRY                    *May 27, Colorado Line*

The weather is holding — occasional rain. It's cold at night. We feel the pilgrimage quality of what we are doing. We don't want a parade of Winnebagos, bikers in black leather, and cyclists in Italian helmets and designer sport outfits following us. Some people argue that everyone should have a part in The Walk, and be welcomed. Kevin addressed the problem of people joining for a day or two, eating, drinking, using equipment, then melting away, often with said equipment, into the night. Such guests could bankrupt The Walk. Our advance people find us free camping places and scout for gifts of food and money.

I want to support Kevin. An overnighter left us last week, taking a tent and blankets. Kevin also goes out of his way to cheer the advance people who have to work two or three days ahead of us and often feel separated from The Walk. The advance people's sense of connection with us is vital and but for Kevin's concern would be forgotten. These are the things I want to concentrate on, not Kevin's nutty visions of the future.

Poppy wants more control of Kevin's leadership. We talked so long last night we almost didn't make the wake-up call.

*Dear Hope,*                    *May 28, Cortez, Colorado*

We're in Cortez, and we'll be moving east and north, slowly, up and up to where Grandpa plans to meet The Walk and where, if you can come, you can sit me down and tell me about you and Larry. How about it? We'll be in Pueblo on June 4, and plan to leave early on the 5th. You could come down on either of those days and we can all have talk alone and talk together.

I'm going to take a grandmother's privilege to give you some advice. You and Larry are making love regularly, so please, <u>please</u> protect yourself in every way. Take the pill, insist that he use a condom, and don't promise each other things you can't fulfill. You love Larry, and because you do, you won't want to burden him with responsibilities he isn't ready to face.

Can you come? I'd be happy to share your joy, even though I think it's too soon for some of the commitment you are making. It's good that you are learning about his heritage. It's good to be in love. Don't think both of your parents haven't been in love as deeply as you have. Don't think I haven't, or your grandfather. I didn't have sex at your age, and that's a big difference, but the feelings — oh, yes, all of them. That's why our advice may be of some value to you. I'd love to see you so we could talk about it.

Let me know if you can come, as soon as you can —

*Gram*


*Dear Gram,*                    *May 24, Boulder*

Enclosed is a picture of all the horses Larry made for me, put up around my room. It was my idea to shorten the strings between them and now they run and prance around the top of the wall in invisible fields of flowers, my herd. In Indian life, my father would be the owner of this herd, but everyone in the tribe would know that all these horses were a gift for my hand in marriage, so in a way they would be mine.

I hate how jealous people are. The girls were buzzing about the horses in school. Even Mrs. Chandler, our homeroom teacher, was smiling in a soft, sort of long-gone look, and she only came over very quietly and said, "Take them up quickly, Hope, before I have to say something." But the boys, who were as interested as the girls, later began to make fun of what Larry had done and mimic the girls who were really impressed: "Ooh, isn't that row-man-tic!" Then the girls caved in to their insults and stopped telling me they envied me and stopped saying things to their boyfriends about how they couldn't think of something as nice as that. It's all just jealousy.

Now they laugh at Larry even more. When people are so jealous and ugly it's hard to be around them. Larry is going to get a job and when he's eighteen, he'll be eligible to get a GED and then go to community college and take classes there. In the meantime, he's going to save up and get a small room, and when I get out of school, we'll be married. I'll be happy to wait until I graduate if I know he's working and saving like the tribal Indians did, to be worthy to be a husband. I love him so much I hate to see him sad, even for a minute.

*Love, Hope*

*Moms,*

I'm hearing big plans for us to come down when you hit Pueblo. It's working up to a family reunion. It would be good to include

Sam and Cary but they'd get antsy on a three-hour trip. Blake and Anton said they'd keep them. Jussy and Frank said they would bring Jason and Ben; Hope is making eager noises. I'm trying to convince Dad that he should ride with us.

I think I told you about how stiff Anton has been since I caught him as a walking wedding cake. The <u>man</u> is my friend, a confidant, a buddy, a Navy man (demolitions), an architect, with humor, rather than wit. Yesterday I went over to see him.

I stayed for a couple of hours, listening, mostly. Anton says he is one of the few openly <u>gay</u> cross-dressers he knows. Most men who cross-dress say they're not gay. Many are married. What's there for them in all those padded bras, those depilatories and high-heeled shoes that we kicked off as torture and suppression of our natural figures <u>years</u> ago? Freedom, he says, again, color, texture, flutter of a dress against the leg, caress of clinging silk and sensuous velvet. He talked about what he called The Feminine Side of his nature, easy tears and easy laughter, he says, an openness to life that women have and men don't. In the getup he was wearing it would be difficult to be open to anything. I asked him when women seemed most womanly to him. Was it as they baked, sewed, made love?

"Not <u>women</u>," he said. "My <u>idea</u> of women."

So it's still a man thing after all. I asked him when he started. He said it was too far back to remember, but when he was a kid. It was fun to pull back from the serious stuff, boy stuff, fights and competition and sports and guarding his gayness. I said it must have been tough in the Navy.

He said that then, cross-dressing was a thing he needed to do. It was the only way to cut the tension of the lies he was telling about being macho male. He was terrified of being outed as gay, of being beaten to death.

I thought about that; I'm still thinking. I said something about the paradox of finding safety in danger and then he laughed and said he wanted to know something — what? what to do to keep panty hose from tearing.

His group meets every week in one of their houses. Some are married to women who don't know about their cross-dressing. Most hide it from their children and all from parents, bosses, and co-workers. The secrecy of gay life isn't a butt-patch to the secrecy of this compulsion. "They don't understand," Anton told me. "You don't understand."

I told him to freeze the panty hose in water before putting them on for the first time.

The act he pulls is no compliment to women, but it's not directed at me. Late yesterday we went out to the park and gave Sam, and Blake's son Erik, bike riding lessons. The three of us had more fun than the kids.

I can't believe that in two weeks you'll have walked close enough to give us a look at you. You — a Fresno. It's almost half the country!

*Sol*

*Dear Solidarity,*                    *May 30, Durango*

I want to tell you without gushing how grateful I am for your letters. Contact with home is more than news, a cheery wave, a kiss of affection. We need it. Two months of hammering out stupid compromises about shower water and potty stops, food preferences and leadership styles are supposed to have forged us into a strong group. It hasn't. I have been tiring; I'm frightened of falling, doing the careless or stupid things tired people do. All around us the peaks pull the eye up to where they lift into an earlier, rarer light, but my day is spent watching for rocks and holes on the shoulders of the road. At Bunion Rubs I doze through the arguing. Kevin wants us to make street theater. I dozed through the vote and was horrified the next morning to hear his motion had passed. Poppy has been too tired to go at all.

Three days ago it rained and we went into the supply truck for warm clothes and rain gear, only to find that tiny white spiders had seized the opportunity to go into an orgy of reproduction, and their children — born in

95

the thousands — had begun the work of spinning guy wires to hang from as they attempted to find their way into the daylight. They had all died in the fold-on-fold of damp wool and the airlessness of rubber and plastic. We tried to brush off the wools, blankets, sweaters, pants, but there was a greasy odor we couldn't get out and all day we felt invaded, our clothes busy with imaginary armies of crawling things moving up and down our legs inside those webby, smelly clothes.

Some places I recognize from trips I made with you and Justice the summer I came home again. There are surreal sights here that make The Walkers gasp — juxtapositions of incompatible things: cupped flowers cradling snow, green moss and cress on the lace-edged doilies of ice that line the creeks. There are rocks finger-combing the run of melting snow on which ice rests thick and black as obsidian.

But I am cold and cranky.

Yesterday we had enough sun to dry out the spider-invaded blankets and woolens. Some of the things were ruined, more had holes and weakened places. At any other time this would have been joke material. In our present state, it was enough to bring tears. Then I got your letter, and the words transmuted my annoyance into optimism and energy that made me able to breathe deeply again.

I've had news from Hope on this stop, letters crossing in the mail. She loves Larry. They want to <u>marry</u>. This isn't going to happen, is it? Hope is too young. Larry seems too immature. Hope has always been reasonable in her demands of life. Can't someone talk seriously to her? I know she won't listen to Justice or Frank. Could you?

*Love, Moms*

*Dear Marz,*                    *May 30, Durango*

I'm waiting, impatient as a three year old, to get to Pueblo, to see you and as many of the family as can come. The rain and snow have stopped at last. It's still cold at altitudes now, colder as we climb. With no choice, we put on spider-haunted woolens and walk in a permanent odor.

A family has left — a couple and three singles have come. Kevin goes around the campgrounds where we stop. He brings people to see us. They stand curiously before us, like viewers at a monument. "These people are walking across the country," Kevin says. We want them to join. We become artificial to ourselves, too pleasant, too visibly enjoying our closeness. Kevin calls on one or another of us to explain. We put an exaggerated emphasis on community and the interrelatedness of people. We pass out the questionnaires with slight theatricality. You could be learning

97

about the soul of the country, our gestures seem to say. Join us and you will come to speak with authority about what Americans believe.

And it works. It works because Kevin is utterly convincing in his expansive, male enthusiasm. I saw him doing it at the campground last night. It was late and I was hurrying up from a creek bank. I heard them before I saw them, men and women laughing. I came up over the ridge and saw Kevin with a group of attentive campers. He seemed larger than I knew him to be, and suddenly doing a dance step. He paced, then stood, then squatted at the center of their sitting circle, his hands moving as he described, made a point, joked, debated. I was too far away to hear the words, but their sound and laughter made me ache.

I had few moments of belonging in girlhood, which you know. My parents preached brotherhood but their friends were prickly intellectuals who talked about the masses and never enjoyed or sought one another's company. Their children inherited their fastidiousness. The summer I met you was the first time I knew the joy of a group of happy, cooperating friends who liked one another, who had lives and work and jokes beyond the Cause and who were . . . gladsome, I think is the word, gladsome together.

I realize now that this was a great part of

what led me to join The Walk. I thought that when we had stripped down to the basics, pared away comfort, houses, cars, TVs, VCRs, we would befriend one another on the deeper levels of soul to soul in a group enterprise that would make us a body, a <u>we</u>.

It hasn't happened, or not yet. We are a <u>we</u> but we never hit the deeper chords of friendship. I have Poppy, whose friendship of years ago is deeper now. We camp near the families, who are Fresnos. Abner Dorn and John Duda are becoming friends. I like many of the young people, but the magical group, the <u>we</u>, hasn't emerged. Most people look to Kevin, and we pursue a fragile constitutional democracy and live what are essentially private lives on The Walk. Kevin knows about the <u>we</u> — he reaches toward it with all that street theater, mistaken, I think, and the attempt to make us political. I know what he yearns for. I walked past the group he is convincing and heard their laughter. No one saw me, with my kerchief full of mint and my eyes blinking away tears.

*Love, Tig*


*Moms,*                                    *May 26, Detox*


It's 2:00 A.M.; the place is quiet. I did my bit with Hope and Larry. I think he's a loser, but try telling that to Hope. Jussy called a couple of days ago; could I talk to Hope? Larry is a bad influence. Hope thinks she's in love and why did such a sweet, well-brought-up girl wind up with someone like him? I didn't laugh in her face — the kid is my niece; I thought I would see for myself.

So I had them over. I have Indian friends from my trip to the rez in New Mexico. Two of them live up here, now, and I've been wanting to see them. Good idea? Wrong. Hard-learned wisdom: don't combine motives. Killing two birds with one stone wounds one bird and the second flies over your head and drops the stone on it.

Along with Hope and Larry at my little get-together were three friends who work with me in Detox, Bobby and Luis (the Indians), Blake and Anton, and a couple from social work school. Twelve people. By 8:00, H. and L. hadn't shown up, but everyone else had come and was mixing well. People found mutual friends, mutual interests. You know how it is when a group clicks and people let down and start enjoying an evening — it was going to be one of those.

Then Hope and Larry showed up. It had started to rain, a fine drizzle, and they had come on a motorcycle so there were little pinhead-sized drops on their hair. (Why no helmets?)

As soon as he got into the room, Larry started to crab at Hope, and damn if she didn't fall down like a dog at his feet and accept the blame for the rain, the time, and the appearance of Columbus on the continent.

Everything stopped. People began to move away, to leave them in their own space in the crowded room.

Working in Detox you get to know the subtle drunks. He wasn't obviously drunk, but half the group are recovering alcoholics and the tension level shot up like the strength-tester ball at a county fair.

Was there anything to drink? I said there was juice and soda. Some of our friends don't drink, but I had beer and wine for those who did. "<u>Beer</u>?" He did that macho thing I hate.

Leonardo, my Detox buddy, tried to help, introducing himself, and trying to introduce the other people, all standing by, silent, watching. ("Where's the damn beer?" That was Larry to Hope.)

While he ranted on I found myself hearing him and watching her. After getting through three beers, he began what must have been a set piece with him. Whites don't understand Native Americans' souls. Luis, whose boiling point on this issue is only a few degrees higher than Larry's, went over and said, "Hey, man, this isn't a thing we discuss here. Wait till you're in the right place with the right people." He told me later that it was a violation of his people's rules to intervene like that, but

101

the effort turned out to be wasted. Larry had no intention of calming down. Four beers, five. Everyone was watching him, dreading and fascinated.

I kept my eyes on Hope. She was standing by her man, literally, moving closer as he went on in his tirade. And she wasn't annoyed or irritated but sympathetic, with a tinge of shame, the way a mother would feel for a sulky kid kept up past his bedtime.

We were all in the lock-step — and we all began to think that Larry would soon start swinging, and if he did, someone would have to take him down. If he left, he was too drunk to operate the motorcycle. I didn't have the equipment I depend on at the Detox center to restrain him until he sobered up. Luis has had lots of experience and I think he realized that Larry needed the male, not the female, presence, as skilled as it might be. He began to talk to Larry, almost in a whisper, and soon Larry was nodding and then he folded away into sleep.

Hope was blowing apologies all over the place. They'd had trouble with the cycle. There was that awful rain. Larry had terrible social fears. He had had a little too much to drink in too short a time. When Larry was happy, these upsets wouldn't happen. He was really warm and kind. Really, we hadn't seen the Larry she knew, really the loving, the spiritual . . . blah, blah, blah.

102

We took the Loving-and-Spiritual into the other room to sleep it off. Hope looked helplessly at me and went to sit with him. I surveyed the wreckage of my evening, a group that looked as though each of them had just buried his mother. Bobby (one of the Indian men) was crying. He leaned over and took me in his arms and said, "Jesus, Sol, does every lush take the women he loves into that hell? I looked at your niece and there was my girlfriend, Pauline. I listened to her and there was my sister, Pat. One's dead and one's gone out of my life so completely I don't even know where she is. Cry? I want to scream the place down."

It was on this merry note that the evening ended. Great stuff, huh? They drifted away around ten, although Blake and Anton stayed to help in case Larry woke up with an attitude. Even they were depressed and we barely talked. Larry's "Ode to Joy" had hit everyone at the party. He was like one of those tests the psychologists give you. Everyone had some ugly or guilty or defensive association with what he had said.

He came to about one (A.M.), and they went home, Hope still perfecting her drill. "I know he's so sorry for what happened." I had had enough. I told her it was not a <u>what</u> that had happened, but a <u>who</u>. Larry would have to admit he has a problem and so would she. I told them to go to A.A. I told <u>her</u> she needed to set limits and be prepared to live by them. She looked at me with her beautiful, large, dark hazel eyes, and that lovely, rapturous look and said, "You don't understand." Larry went to the bathroom.

I'm infuriated by that daffy-duck innocence of hers. "You don't understand," she says, armored in her smooth innocence and proof against any reality there is.

What I said had no more effect on her than a breath of wind has on the petal of a daisy. "Love," she said. Had I loved enough, had I trusted in my love, I could have healed my suffering man, restored him, blah, blah. With a smile like the smile on the Patron Saint of Maple Syrup, she gathered up her sodden pancake and left.

I'm irritated, I'm impatient, I'm scared. Where did she learn that shit?

*Sol*

# *June*

⤳

I was tired, exhausted. On the map the upward gain is 300 ft. but it ⌇⌇⌇ goes like that. For the young people, it was a challenge; for Poppy and me a nightmare revelation of age and weakness. How could we have thought we would walk the country? Twice, we were overtaken by the follow-up cars.

We went up into snow at the pass. At the head of the line someone saw a short-cut trail that would take us to our campground. The way down looked easy and there was a path made by years of hikers.

"Let's go!" from the front part of The Walk, and we started down. The way was slick from the lead walkers and those behind had to make new trails or use sticks to secure their footing. There was a series of large boulders and passing around one of them, I slipped, then skidded, half falling; trying to recover on the slick ice I went forward and saw — nothing. I had gone over. I began to fall, not outward, but down the hill, sliding and dislodging stones and rocks that overtook me as

105

I struggled to find something to catch on to without breaking an arm. I thought once it was a shame to die so in the middle of things, Marz alone and the family not knowing why . . .

Then, suddenly, I stopped falling. I was on a tiny ledge no larger than my butt and pocketed with a slippery wad of snow. I was half sitting, half lying, head and one arm off into space. As soon as I received the messages — arms, legs, feet, hands, and fingers — that nothing was broken, I began to try moving. I had to dig into the hill to widen my perch, carefully scraping the snow from under me. There was a sound above me, but I couldn't make out any words. I shouted back. Rocks had hit me on the head and blood was beginning to run through my hair.

The voice came again, louder, this time. "Can you stand up?" I shouted back that there wasn't room, and I was afraid to change my position for fear of dislodging anything that might be supporting this tiny ledge. "Can you climb down?" I looked. It was an almost sheer drop to the next stage, rocks. "No," I hollered up.

Then a rope whipped past my face, but I was too frightened to grab for it, and a voice above me, but closer, said, "Don't move. Don't reach for the rope," and suddenly he was beside me, Kevin, leaning out from the rope that was around his waist, and walking

106

like a fly on a wall, smiling down to me. He said, "You rang?"

He took a long look at my situation, whistled through his teeth, and called up the hill, "Send down the other rope." The rope came down and he moved close to me, leaning against his foot, weight into the rock side so that his hands were free to help me knot the rope around my waist. "This won't slip," he said matter-of-factly. He called up to the people above to take up the slack.

His idea was to have me "walk" up the cliff as he was doing, but I found I couldn't stand. When I tried, my legs gave way. Somehow, using him to lean on, and with the rope slowly pulling us up, we made it back to the top. Just before we made it to "floor level," Kevin, supporting me against his body, whispered in my ear, "This was my mistake, Tig. Anyone could have fallen."

"I was waving good-bye to a friend," I said. "I was hailing a cab."

He grinned into my face as we hung there. We were pulled up onto a flat rock, and suddenly everyone was gathered around us, cheering, feeling elated, even jubilant. Someone had a thermos of coffee and Poppy came and gave me a cup. When I looked around for Kevin, he was gone.

But I was shaky all the way down to camp. When I stripped, I found I had been scraped all the way down one side of my body, had sore places even where nothing showed, and three significant bumps on my head. Doc Duda crawled in to see me and declared that by tomorrow I would be too sore to travel. He said he thought I could get by without stitches in my scalp and put a butterfly dressing there, after he had shaved an area of bloody hair the size of a silver dollar.

Poppy offered to bring dinner, but there was a withdrawal in her manner and I wondered if she was someone for whom sickness or injury is so ugly and fearful that she can't face it, even in a friend. Later, I asked her if she wanted to take her bedroll to one of the spare places allowed for the odd guest. She said she was sorry and ashamed. When the accident happened, she was well behind me, cursing that the front of The Walk had decided to take the shortcut. She hadn't seen me go over, but when the cry went up, knew it was I, somehow, and the first thing she thought was, "She can't leave me here like this — the oldest one on The Walk." And then, shame. "To face the fear of you being hurt or — worse — selfishly . . ."

Kevin said it was his fault. Poppy accused herself. I said I wished everyone would get off my accident and stop trying to horn in on my act! Then we laughed and everything was all right again, although Poppy did say before we fell asleep, "It was Kevin's fault. The whole thing was Kevin's fault."

That's Poppy's prejudice against Kevin, who saved my life. He did it quickly and gallantly and daringly.

We won't be taking shortcuts again soon.

DIARY ENTRY                    *June 5, South Fork*

We took the day off in the Wolf Creek Pass campground for my benefit. Kevin used the time to get up a street-theater production. I was sleeping when I should have been fighting.

His preparations became real to me when I got up to go to the Bunion Rub. The evening was damp and equivocating with a hint of rain or snow, so light we wondered which, but it would soon be cold and we huddled and shivered around Bunion Rub's small fire. Kevin was speaking his standard line, good enough, but not what we had decided for this trip: a production with costumes, miming, Mr. Clear Cutter, Mrs. Polluter, Helpless Child. The people who don't agree about People's Theater won't have to participate, Kevin says. He has it sold under the rubric of Having Fun.

So we will go into Pueblo, where I will be meeting Marz and the girls and the grandchildren, sleep in a bed with Marz beside me, bathe in a bathtub and lie there soaking and dreaming while he sits on the edge of the tub and talks to me. I promised Poppy a room as well. We have informed the council we will be leaving for a day and a night of the two days The Walk is scheduled to be in Pueblo and environs, but will rejoin before it gathers to leave the city.

I ache all over. I have been beaten up by skilled professionals.


*Moms,*                              *June 2, Niwot*

We're coming to meet you in Pueblo, all at the Holiday Inn — seven of us: Dad, Jussy and Frank, with Hope and Ben. Jason is staying home with a friend. Hope says she wants Larry to come on his motorcycle but he won't stay over — he's due back at the halfway house. I'm coming with Sam. Cary will stay with Blake and Anton.

In spite of Dad's plan — he says we should also do some tourist thing — I'm getting into this. Can I tease Frank? Sam needs a family outing. Can I tease Jussy?

Your itinerary tells the day you're supposed to come, but not the time. Let us know when you'll be coming and we'll wait for you. I'd like to meet Poppy, too. Are you allowed to sleep out, away from The Walk, for a night or two? We can catch up to you wherever you'll be, if you stay over. Can I tease you?

*Sol*

*Dear Marz,*                    *June 14, Pueblo,*
                                *right after my call*

First things first: it was a pure joy to see you all and be with you; it was good of you to include Poppy in the doings for part of the day. Let me give you my version of what happened. By now you will have seen or read or heard about the confrontation. Hope's version might be melodramatic and my call could give no details.

As I told you, Kevin has gone in for street theater. Pueblo was our first big city after Las Vegas, and the first where he could try it. Our advance people had us booked for presentations at libraries and schools and a public meeting in the city park. By the time we hit town, there was a script of a sort, costumes, even music.

Poppy and I, citizens of Wrinkle City, who couldn't run half a mile if our lives depended on it, are, as it turns out, the only ones on The Walk who have known violent protests first-hand, club-swinging police, rock-throwing mobs, strangers whose faces were twisted in hate. Those who have not known such violence may have a secret hankering for it.

Warnings had come to the advance people even before we reached Pueblo. We found out later that Kevin had sent announcements ahead, demanding the end of all polluting industry in the state. Lots of Pueblo's industry

111

has been sent off to other places and jobless locals are less prissily particular about what they breathe and drink.

Ignorant of all this, Poppy and I left The Walk to be with you, enjoying every moment. While we were away, people from The Walk gave ten presentations in groups of three or four and street theater by Kevin and eight performers. They were all psyched up to do the big one in the park.

You left in the morning, and we did some questionnaires. I was missing you and off my concentration. Except for the belief that what we are doing is valuable, I would have quit The Walk and gone home with you for a week or two. The bright spot was that Hope had decided to stay over with us in camp. Poppy moved into one of the guest spaces and my darling granddaughter and I talked into the night.

The news is reasonably good. Larry, she says, is going into an alcohol treatment program. The evening they ruined Solidarity's party made them realize the seriousness of the problem. All the radiance and energy of Hope's fervor is to be given to Larry's need. She says they will do the program together. I told her some but not all of my reservations. Caution and worry are old people's crosses; why hang her on them?

Larry came down that morning. After an initial period of caution and measuring, we began to relax. We spent part of the afternoon talking. He admitted acting stupidly at Solidarity's evening and also during the famous sledding afternoon. He said he would be beginning the treatment program as soon as he got back to Boulder; the group home people have approved it and made arrangements with his caseworker. He has always worked the system, he said, because he grew up doing that, but he wants Hope, a normal life, and a chance to forget the foster homes, group homes, and phony homes of his growing-up years.

Poppy came and it was time to work. They decided to stay and watch. Kevin's street presentation interested them and the whole city was out for the wonderful Sunday weather. The street theater had set up posters in the park and put one up for the performance. A little crowd had formed, parents and children mostly, drawn by the color and the promise of a show. We saw Kevin and took Hope and Larry over to meet him. He turned his blue gaze on them, smiled that smile that could charm stone, and invited them to join The Walk. He said it would be a famous day. (Fame and famous are words he often uses.) Reports from yesterday's presentation had been positive. The show had been applauded, even cheered. He smiled and went off to get in costume. We were sitting off to the side so as not to block the view of the passersby.

The skit began — mimed with placards to describe the characters.

The four of us were sitting in a half-circle, talking quietly, when I looked up at Hope and saw a movement of people behind her. A phalanx of thirty, perhaps, was moving toward us. My eyes must have gone wide or my face pale as I recognized them not as visitors to the performance but as a group, then as a gang, a mob, a mob holding things — stones, rocks, sticks, bats. The odd thing is that I don't remember any sound they made. Surely there must have been sound — a mutter, a flurry of epithets sent ahead of them like the first throw of pebbles before the rocks they were carrying.

We stopped talking and I told Poppy to get up and move smoothly, walk slowly past the performers, then go and get a cop. Tell him a mob thing was happening. She left. Larry turned and saw them from the side. He said, "They think we're part of the audience. Get up and dust yourselves off like we're leaving. Follow Poppy. Slow. This could get bad. Don't run. I'll be covering you." We sat, indecisive, wavering. I didn't want to leave the Walkers to the mob. Hope said she thought she could talk to the mob — reason with them. It was just a play, a performance —

The performers were fully involved in their capers; the black leotard figures of Pollution and Toxic Waste jumped and cavorted, throttling The Child and menacing The Mother and The Elder.

The group stopped just in throwing range. Some of the performers noticed them and stopped. Larry said in a whisper that they were giving the audience a chance to leave.

By then the onlookers had become aware of the mob and realized that they were between it and the performers. Fathers picked up their kids and the families moved away quickly.

Larry looked miserable, his patience with us straining against his knowledge. I could see then how little he liked being balked.

Then the group sent up a yell and began shouting slogans. I caught Kevin's eye, mouthed, and mimed — run for it. I looked around for the cops.

Instead of getting the group away, Kevin yelled a slogan to them and they all began to cry it in unison: "Don't rape your mothers."

Stupid? Sure. Except that it had gone over so well with the college students camping at a dozen campgrounds and with the young people at the college library. It was such lovely rhetorical overkill. College students love rhetorical overkill. It's common as motes on their eyeglasses.

These weren't college kids and Kevin realized his mistake in the moment of their shocked silence, tried to shout something, but all words were drowned in the yelling that followed it. The mob began to run toward us. Larry pulled Hope and me to him, and pushed us down behind him. He peeled his leather jacket off, and threw it over Hope. Under the jacket he had a T-shirt and a belt made of flat chain. He took off the belt and as the mob came toward us, chose someone and leaned out toward this boy. I had my head down, covering it with my arms, but the urge to look was irresistible and now and then I took quick sight before ducking again. The boy, who had only the general idea of throwing his rock and then moving in to use his bat, was unprepared for an attack and went down. Larry got the bat and moved the two steps back to us, and for the rest of the time fended off all attackers, hitting with the bat and swinging with the chain while we squatted behind him, covering our heads.

Eventually, the police arrived and at the sound of their sirens the mob regathered itself and melted away, leaving five of its number stunned at Larry's feet. "Let's disappear before the cops show." We disappeared.

His courage amazed me. We had disregarded his completely practical advice, making the strong defense necessary. He could have been beaten senseless, but after we made our escape and were acting like innocent strollers, in another part of the park, he grinned at us and told us to get street smart. "I won't always be here for your gang rumbles." I apologized for disregarding his warning. I had seen violence in the South and during the Vietnam years, but that had been a long time ago. I had obviously lost my edge for sensing mood and danger. He was quiet for a while and then he said he wouldn't have been a protester in those days. He said, "I like things that are clear, friends, enemies — that's clear. Us and them — that's clear. Loyalty is what I think about. Loyalty is what I believe in."

I was moved by his honesty; it unlocked the paradox of all the Indian talk from someone who knew so little and practiced even less of an Indian heritage. Hope began to talk about their plans. So much of Larry's trouble had been caused by drinking, she said, that once they were on the program, a new life would begin for them. At that moment, it was she who sounded immature and he who struck something deeper. I felt in the small, slow shake of the head he gave then that he was disagreeing with her easy answers. He was comfortable with a bat and a chain and a clear set of enemies. Fighting in a fog of ambiguity, fighting himself, was another matter. We allowed ourselves to drift back to the scene.

There was still the wreckage of signs and torn clothes here and there but the people were gone. We went back to where The Walk was camped and helped clean up bloody noses and black eyes. No one had been badly hurt

117

but several people needed stitches. Dr. Duda was hard at it; his wife, Kim, is a nurse. By the way, as a result of that day, our first-aid kit is now much more complete. Hope and Larry said good-bye. I had a sudden urge to take Larry with us — to give him some of our strength in The Walk — its cooperation, its sense of purpose. When I hugged them I said something maudlin, wishing them strength for the challenge they faced. I meant it.

They are both immature. Neither is ready for marriage. If only they could be friends it would do them both so much good . . .

Left on that exalted plane, I tripped over the reality of Kevin.

I watched him walk the camp. I saw him talking to the people who had been in the attack, and I realized that he had loved every minute of it, every taunt, every rock. He was going tent to tent full of flowing cheer, his face cut, his eye blackened, telling everyone that The Walk was now blooded. We had confronted evil and faced it down. The polluters and the Special Interests couldn't stand before their unmasking.

In those hours I came very close to leaving. It was Poppy who convinced me we needed to stay, to vote for moderation, or The Walk would end in violence and discord. Outside Kevin's tent, excited young people came and went. The fear at this remove was now being remembered as excitement, the mistake as courageous integrity, the escape as winning. He came to our tent and I told him I thought that mob was no more made up of polluters and special interests than The Walk was.

He said he realized they had gone overboard on the street theater. Families with kids were fearful and needed reassurance. He didn't like getting clubbed, either, and if the authorities thought we drew violence, they would deny us camping space. He was saying that, but I had seen him, full of the joy of shoving ambiguity away, of pushing it down, clearing a swath through paradox and argument, pure will. He looked at us in the fading light. He told us to have faith in him — he knew how to lead. When he left, Poppy, who had made us some tea on her illegal burner, looked after him and shook her head. "Tig, my girl, that man sleeps in a corkscrew."

I don't want this to sound as though I'm not taking precautions. I was scared, and the fear came in waves during the night along with memories of other violence. Poppy and I aren't the only ones re-thinking The Walk's activist trend. Many of the family people are troubled about how The Walk is changing. I'll call you the next chance I get. Please fix the answering machine so you don't miss the call.

*Love, T.*

Long Bunion Rub yesterday about what happened. Most of the Walkers hadn't been at the street theater, but doing questionnaires, and news of the violence came to them as they returned to camp. After a long discussion, we voted to discontinue the street theater. The more polarized we are, Poppy said, the less likely to be listened to when we make our statements at Woods Hole. This Walk is not an end in itself.

The competing argument was about waking people up. Some people thought the need was for more élan on The Walk itself. I told them The Walk is as important as it needs to be. People are drawn to us because we're doing something exceptional, something many of them have a hankering to do — it's true travel. They come to me asking if someone my age can do such a thing, if my feet don't get too sore. They don't come asking my advice about changing an industrial society back into an agricultural one. Some of the other Walkers said that the act of filling out the questionnaires was enough to make people think about the issue.

So Kevin's dream was voted down and The Walk's political thrust is blunted. We will see if he droops or sulks. Poppy says Kevin will leave The Walk. I say he will find fulfillment as unifier and spiritual energizer. Poppy looks at the young girls blinking at him like emergency vehicles around a wreck and says, "Maybe he'll father a race of people all named Walker."

*Dear Tig,*                    *June 15, The Hill*

When have I ever convinced you away from something you wanted to do? Don't tell me not to worry; it's a useless request. Living with your dedication and enthusiasms has never been boring but it has been full of anxiety. Sometimes the level of anxiety is low, sometimes high. Someone might have shot you. Someone might have brained you with a club. I remember what mob scenes are like. I remember the one we were in together, unreported and unnoticed, before the Freedom Rides. It makes me shiver when I remember it. No, I don't dwell on your danger, but I can't help seeing nightmare pictures. They were a good part of the reason for our separation — not the first, the second. The first happened, I now think, because of my feeling that the kids and I didn't come next to your causes, but last. The second separation was about the worry I couldn't take any more. Your letter brought some of that back.

O.K., I believe in your causes, most of the time. I hate that a better cause is sacrificed, me, the kids, the grandchildren, our lives, our

121

ordinary lives. You're not idle or self-indul-
gent with the problems of our aging, and
you're not bored or pitiful as some of our
neighbors are. But I'm angry, annoyed,
scared, and yes, it's true that if my job took
me abroad for a year, I'd go and expect you
to do all right with it, but that wouldn't exactly be by choice, would it?

I'm alone here and will be, basically, until
next April 3rd or 4th. Last night I dreamed
of myself sitting by a window in a castle,
dreaming out and down the road by which
you have gone. I was a woman in the dream
— long skirts and a veil. Men are supposed
to go, women to wait for them. Maybe some
of my angst is sexism. But . . .

I saw the mess on TV: standard fight scene;
it took up less than thirty seconds. Someone
taking home movies of his kids got the foot-
age. We saw fists, bats, the usual. The an-
nouncer mentioned you were walking from
Fresno to Woods Hole, Mass., but failed to
explain anything. Facts: 5, Truth: 0. I didn't
see you in the melee. Next time, wave.

*Marz*

P.S. The visit was nice, wasn't it? And now
I'm mad as hell. I agreed. Yes; I'll stand by
the agreement. But.

*Dear Grandma,*        *June 16, Grant Street*

I saw you on TV!! Not you, the fight. It was exciting, but they didn't tell about why it happened. They thought showing the pictures gave us what we needed to know. The reporter said no one was seriously hurt. That was a fact I wanted to know because if someone was hurt it might have been you.

It was Hope who really told us about it and how Larry was a hero. She told us that Larry wouldn't let anyone get to the three of you and how the place in front of him was full of guys who had tried to attack you and how he knocked them all down. Hope was proud, but it scared me. How will I act when it comes my time to stand up and defend some people, women or someone? Will I be able to do it or will I just be the wimp Jason says I am? Jason drives me crazy. I hate him. You're supposed to look up to your big brother, but he stands there waiting for it like an emperor. I think: Get stuffed. I hope you stay safe. Run if you see them coming.

*Love, Ben*


*Dear Gram,*        *June 16, Grant Street*

I'm back home again and Larry is back at his group home. He says living there is more trouble than facing the mob. His counselor says he can still get back to H.S. and graduate if he goes to summer school. Because he's eighteen, the group home wants him out. He just got a summer job, so when is he supposed to go to school?

"Nothing new," he says. "This system is a seven-legged horse and all the legs get tangled up in each other; the horse keeps falling over but nobody's supposed to notice." The summer job is working for a carpenter. I think he was lucky to get it. He likes working outside and no one will care how long his hair is.

My best news is that we have started A.D.E.P.T. — a drug and alcohol treatment program. It's at night so people can work during the day. Part of it is like AA meetings and part of it is information, and for Larry, part of it is a culture program the Indians have that Larry will join. Part of the program he can do in Boulder, but he'll be going into Denver once a week for the Indian part. I go to AlAnon meetings.

I need a summer job now because I'll be saving for when we get married. Mom wants me to spend the summer "like a normal girl," she says. What is that? Playing, swimming with the swim team, going to parties, or helping her with her volunteer work.

That's busy-work to me. I want to help remake a human life. I want to help save Larry! A man I love is in danger and Mom wants me to turn away from him and play! "Go hiking," she says. I do. I hike over to Larry's building site and spend his lunch hour with him (<u>hour</u> comes to about twenty minutes). There's no kissing but we hold hands. We escape behind the building. We have made a little clear place there to sit. We have to be very careful because Larry doesn't want to be fired.

He's starting over. He is not drinking, I mean <u>not</u> <u>anything</u>, not even a beer, and he goes to his meetings, every night. He is cleaner about himself, too. He's trying to eat better — they told him in the orientation that he has to watch his nutrition, vitamins, and eat good food. Isn't it better to help that fight than to go hiking or swimming or go to meaningless teen-age things with friends who are only interested in clothes and gossip? Everything I do has meaning, now. It's for Larry and me and for our lives together. Tomorrow I'm going to apply for a job at Wild Duds. I'll tell you if I get it.

*Love, Hope*


*Dear Ben,*          *June 17, Rocky Ford, Colo.*

The Walk is going faster and life is going slower. We're on the Plains, now, and we do about twenty miles a day. We stop at farmhouses and do our interviews and questionnaires; we stay overnight at campsites near small towns, and talk to people, and the pace

125

of everything is easier and slower.

People are treating us very well. Population here is shrinking. Use of machines increases the capacity of each farmer, so farms combine. Then a big shopping center goes in just outside of a town, and the small stores in all the towns around dry up and people start leaving. They move to Denver or Boulder.

I think Denver and Boulder are getting too big. The population crowding up against the mountains is the loss of small farm towns here on the Plains.

Thanks for your letters and yes, I will take care of myself. T-shirts will be sent from Bent's Fort, when we get there, if they have them.

*Love, Grandma*


*Dear Gram,      June 13, Grant Street, Boulder*

I got it! I got the job at Wild Duds. Living at home it means I'll be able to save <u>lots and lots</u> of money! for when Larry and I get married.

I'm so glad you're on my side. Daddy won't talk to me about Larry. He says I'm too young and immature to think about a steady boyfriend. Mom yells and cries. Jason asks me how often we make out. Ben looks confused. None of them understand.

*Love, Hope*

Five more Walkers have joined us. They are college students ready to walk the summer with us and then go back to school. Two families left after Pueblo, the braid I told you about.

The core of the braid, we said, would be the Fresnos; they would provide the stability. The reality is that each of these new people must be taught the lessons of The Walk: cooperation, shared work, mingling, not forming cliques, although cliques do exist here, and a sometimes forced cheer. The new people join us in a burst of eagerness. After four or five days of learning the rules, they begin to chafe at them: Why doesn't The Walk have a complete democracy? We argue and teach and it drains energy and slows everything down. In spite of all the chin-music about democracy, new Walkers have a tendency to let the leaders lead while using the system for special perks, or to argue with everything and obey nothing. Suddenly we are running an eighty member civics class.

The new mood of The Walk is even more anti-civilization. As we move out onto the Plains, Kevin goes up and down the line, declaiming. His hate word is <u>plastic</u>. The Walkers who have come on lately are too young to remember what drudgery rural life used to be without it.

Are Justice and Frank working carefully around the minefields of Hope's fantasies? I liked what I saw of Larry in Pueblo, but they're children! He's courageous but he's all immediacy and no forethought. I suggested to her that they not marry until she is out of college and has worked for a year or two. She looked at me with the stare of a whipped child.

We're on to the Plains and no city until Wichita. When will I see you again? The drama in Pueblo temporarily obscured the joy, deeply felt, of your visit. Come again to Carthage.

Poppy sends her love. She bought a bottle of hair dye in Pueblo and says if she hadn't, she would have used Rit out of the box and done it in one of their bright reds. This is a political statement on her part although it makes her look like one of Toulouse-Lautrec's soiled doves, wizened, hennaed, and hard as flint. Battle flag, she says. The Walk is too organic, too ecologically correct. Kevin wants street theater — this is Poppy's role. I reminded her that it would be half grown out by Wichita. "In Wichita perhaps I'll be a blonde," she said.

Can you come to Wichita and see Poppy blonde?

*Love, Tig*

What does my sweet nephew Jason say? The feces has fanned.

I told you about Anton in women's clothes, and a group of cross-dressing friends. Here's the pitch: Blake was once married to Louise. She knew he was gay and that was okay with her, but she used his gayness at the divorce.

Six months ago, Louise remarried. She had had no problem giving Blake sole custody, but the minute the paint was dry on her new name, she began to push for the kids. This is from dead silence except for gifts at Christmas and cards on birthdays.

She called. "I need the kids." <u>Need.</u> She said she had married into a socially prominent Atlanta family, and her husband had told people that her divorce had been from a gay man. That Blake had custody put her in a bad position and now she felt trapped. She needed kids.

Partial custody? That wouldn't have done any good. She has a big, empty house in Atlanta, a ready-made social life, and, she says, advantages. She called. Blake started recording the calls. He said he never heard a word from her about loving the boys.

When we got back from our trip to Pueblo Blake told me someone had photographed Anton with his group and had sent the pictures to Atlanta. Louise is going to court with a charge that he is an unfit parent. He is scared shitless. I started to tell him I hadn't done it — he gave a cough-laugh and said I didn't have the smarts required for a job like that. These weren't some amateur candid shots, but clear enough to give Louise's voice a confident lilt. Blake says she hired professionals. Cameras could have been planted, friends bribed or threatened. "I hate to think it was a friend," I said. Anton shrugged. He said that every sea has its sharks. The world of cross-dressers is small and secret, and the sharks in those waters never rest.

Some of the cross-dressers disapprove of Anton because he's gay. Some are homophobic; almost all of them hate cross-dressing's fear and creeping around. Few are <u>friends,</u> not really.

Anton looked at Blake. Blake went to him and held him, and Anton said, "I'm sorry, so damn sorry." I think he was crying.

They're going to fight for custody. Blake knows the best lawyers in town and I've been in social work long enough to know the special problems of this fight, because it will be a fight, and it may be a dirty one.

So here I sit, divorced, trying for a low profile. I don't know what Lewis will hear of, up in Idaho with his new family, but there's bound to be trouble here. Sonic boom.

*Sol*

130

P.S. You've heard more than enough about the minute or two The Walk was on TV. I missed it. By the time I heard, I knew you and Poppy were okay. She's a hoot. I'm glad you two got together. It was great to see you, and we got in some good talk. I even liked the sightseeing. Be careful.

S.

DIARY ENTRY                 *June 29, Hasty, Colo.*

Stealing in camp. We are on guard in ways we haven't been before. I talked to some of the children. An older child was bitter, saying that now that it's happening to <u>us</u>, we're looking at it. She said petty thievery had been going on among the kids for some time but hushed up by parents so as not to make trouble.

Why? People don't have many valuables, but there are watches missing, cameras, a ring, a necklace. There are camp luxuries missing: a specially designed cup, a buck knife, etc., set down as lost. The thief couldn't show his takings; we live too close; we recognize one another's camp items. I have been LOPER (last out person) of the week and checked the camp each morning when the group had gone. Twice I found forgotten items, and by recognition and deduction, returned them.

The stealing problem came out at Bunion

131

Rub three days ago and reports have begun to mount. People need to watch their things more carefully, Kevin says. We have begun to look at the teenagers on The Walk. They sense this and are angered. We look at the new people, but the camera and a watch had been missing before they came.

I went to Kevin and said we should turn out the camp. We're between towns now. If we reach a town the thief will get to a post office and send the stuff away.

Kevin says the thief will stop. We've put him on notice. This stealing isn't a matter of need. In a fair society there would be no reason to steal.

Poppy is also for turning out the camp. People need a look at all their possessions laid out on the grass. Things put a strain on us, she says. I asked her where she learned that.

"Hollywood, Cal."

We were in a swelter of our own exhalations — two days of warm rain. I told her that if we turned out the camp as soon as the rain stops, some of her illegal knickknacks would be uncovered, to wit, the stove that is illegally drying us out and that illegally provides our evening tea.

We need the stove, she says. I counter: The thief needs three watches, a buck knife, rings, money.

People know, anyway, she says.

They do know but they choose not to see

132

our little flicker. They choose not to know it's from a camp stove. They choose not to see Kevin's choices for the evening and the gentle waft of pot over the center tents in camp. We make these little hypocritical sidesteps because we need to live with one another. Why did you think The Walk could cure problems a million years of group experience couldn't fix?

# *July*

꙳

*Dear Hope,*        *July 1, Granada, Colorado*

We are out of the rain at last, moving toward Kansas and the middle of America, a
third of our journey. It's sugar-beet country,
and a once huge industry was here with big
factory buildings, many now closed, and I
think of a sick man wearing clothes that once
fit him. We have learned a great deal since I
saw you and Larry in Pueblo. Because of the
riot, The Walk seems to have lost some of its
arrogance. We listen more sympathetically to
people whose jobs have been shortened, their
lives narrowed. There was a lesson in the
mob's anger.

We are feeling our otherness as we did in
the Navajo country and the contact is cool.
We no longer describe ourselves as Environ-
mentalist, which here means a tourist moan-
ing over the tiny impurities in air and water
while the people she passes are stuck jobless
in houses they can't sell. I hope it's making
us quieter, more ready to try new ways of
approach.

We have begun to exploit the interest people take in what we're doing — "You started

135

in Fresno? <u>Really</u>?" That, not our talk about the environment, usually starts things, now. The down side is that too many of the young people tune in only to the names of the places we have been: Las Vegas, especially. They look around at where they are and yearn to be gone to the lights and excitement they think Las Vegas has waiting for them. Some still say that if work came back they would stay. Their families are here, their friends. They murmur it as a secret. When they're in a group, they're loud to be gone. "Get me out of <u>here</u>."

Yet the mornings "here" shimmer from the sky and the vastness is always alive and in motion, sun, clouds, storms, a pouring of shadow as there is a pouring of light. Flocks of birds stitch pockets in the blue, slip through the seam they have made and disappear. On the farms green crops go on for miles and we are shy because except for corn and wheat, we are too ignorant to identify what the crop is. How can we talk about environmental matters when we don't even know the simplest facts of these people's lives?

How are you getting along? Tell me about your job. My first jobs were all political, really. Mother and I took jobs to organize the workers or expose substandard conditions. Sometimes I liked a job and wanted to stay. I had to dream up excuses because personal happiness wasn't considered a valid reason. When

I talked about wanting nice clothes, my parents talked about decadence. My father used the word <u>style</u> as though it were a curse word.

My trip south was the first time I picked a project for myself. My parents were stumped. They couldn't criticize its idealism. I met your grandfather down there, a great reward for my independence.

So you come by your independence and idealism by long family tradition. That's fine, but don't sacrifice your own needs and wishes, your own personality, your own safety to the cause of Larry's redemption.

Please, my beloved Hope, protect yourself. Honor yourself. Hear your <u>own</u> voice and the voice of your wishes and needs as you go along with Larry. I've fought in many causes all my life. You've heard about them all, I know. In each of these movements and protests there were people willing to sacrifice their personal truths for someone else's. This sounds melodramatic, but great causes can destroy a person's sense of what is real and what is not. Pacifists end by beating up their antagonists and justifying what they do. Lovers surrender the very thing that makes them loved. Men and women preaching respect and individuality end by screaming obscenities in the faces of people they see as enemies. Please, dear Hope, don't surrender yourself.

Love, Gram

School is out and I'm riding my bike a lot. I've been all over town, and something interesting is happening: I'm learning stuff I never thought of before. I call it Body Voting.

If you go into a poor people's neighborhood, you see the houses are small and run-down. Anybody can see that, but I started to wonder when and how the poor people got there. They didn't build those houses. The houses were there before and richer people lived in them. Why did the rich people go? Where did they go to?

It's cars. When cars are your enemy, like they are for me, you study them. Poor people don't have cars so they have to live near where they shop and work, or near the bus line. Old people can't drive so they live where the poor people do. That means downtown. It starts with a decision one person makes, but all those make a group decision that ends up as a slum or poor neighborhood.

And here's something else I thought of. People can get rich by figuring out what's going to happen when these decisions get made or something new gets built, like a road or shopping mall. I like studying about why people make the choices about where they live. Is there a job like that?

One of the places I've been riding over to is Larry's construction job. We go out for a drink after his work (it's a 7-Eleven for Cokes, not a bar) and Larry tells me about quitting drinking. It's more than just switching to Cokes. There's a lot of other stuff to it. I used to be scared of Larry, but I'm getting to like him. Sort of. He's still scary because he can change in a minute if someone gets on his wrong side, and there's no list you can read beforehand.

Jason has joined a hiking club. Let's get to the top of all the 14-ers quicker than anybody else. Big deal. Ma and Dad say Hi.

*Love, Ben*


*Dear Marz,*                     *July 3, Syracuse, Kansas*

Over the line into Kansas. After a blistering criticism of the randomness of all state lines, arbitrary lines drawn for political expediency, blah, blah, John Sievert, a Fresno and self-proclaimed rationalist (a bit of a stuffed shirt) showed up at the line crossing and danced a hula across it. Kevin did an Irish reel back and forth. I did the Lindy Hop. Do you know there are adults who have never heard of that dance? (!) Poppy did the one-step, another revelation.

So we danced our way into Kansas and hit a horrific, blinding storm. We tried to put up the tents as soon as it began, trying for a place against the wind on high ground. There were

139

no such places. We ended camping on the shoulder of the road, strung out double-file in the lea of trucks and cars through the hardest part. The fields on either side of us turned into rivers. We hung out flashlights to warn passing cars, which luckily weren't too many. Wise drivers had waited out the worst of it. Those two hours were fearful. Poppy and I were glued to a stalled truck. When the wind eased we crawled up into its bed and lay under a tarp. There were twenty of us.

Did I tell you, we've had some theft on The Walk? We warned everyone to be more watchful, but in the end it paid off. We were swimming in the Arkansas, a group of women laughing and enjoying the skinnydip, when someone screamed from the shore. "She stole! She stole!" Maya, our six-year-old, had come on Parie Baker, who is eleven, going through the pockets of our clothing. Parie had run away.

Two people reported losses — one a little gold necklace that would have been recognized immediately had it been worn.

The Bakers are very reserved. Because Parie is only eleven, we thought they should be told first. They stood in front of our group together and Dick Baker said, "The Walk needs to assert itself. Let The Walk do what it needs to do. We will abide by its decision."

Someone found Parie hiding and told her how terrible theft was. Throughout the day

140

and into the evening, one by one, kids included, we went to her and spoke about how the theft had hurt us.

I thought it might be too heavy for an eleven-year-old to stand, but The Walk has a process, a law with which we can all live. I'm proud.

*Love, Tig*

*Dear Hope,*        *July 4, Syracuse, Kansas*

Best Wishes on the Fourth of July! We stopped in Syracuse, had a lovely time, old-fashioned July 4th with a parade, picnics, and an ice-cream social, windy speeches, music, and bunting. When I was a girl our group used July 4th to march on the Capitol with a list of grievances. I'm getting old enough to like community celebrations even when I know that the small towns we pass harbor all the nit-wit-ery one gets anywhere else. Still. They had fireworks. I <u>love</u> fireworks.

*Happy 4th to you and Larry,*
*Gram*

DIARY ENTRY      *July 5, Garden City, Kansas*

The storm that hit us on the Kansas line brought killing hail to this area only a few miles away. The fields look as though a six

141

year old had planted them. In town there's a tension in many faces.

Kevin preaches to us, though, at Bunion Rub and as we walk. "If the soil could be invigorated with organic material . . . and left fallow part of the time or planted with trees . . ." He sees it so clearly. This is all to the good, I tell him, as long as I don't have to face some gnarled old party who has been farming all his life and tell him something I didn't find out until last Thursday.

At Bunion Rub, the idea came up, and was decided, that Kevin should have the largest spare tent. The rationale for this was that so many people were needing to meet with him that more room was necessary. "It's Munich," Poppy said. She was rubbing oil on her arms and legs, an activity that evokes spirited speech and strong opinions.

I said it wasn't as bad as that. It's just a <u>tent</u>. I don't want to argue about Kevin any more. Who else besides Poppy and me sees him as something more than a catalyst — the Necessary Rebel on this Walk?

*Dear Tig,*                                *July 2, The Hill*

Have I told you that it gets lonely here? I bring work home and I've developed the single man's schedule which has all the spontaneous joy of an afternoon with the IRS.

142

Sulking loses its charm, so I've been calling our daughters and grandchildren in to help. If I have an evening or two a week with friends and corral a kid or grandkid for supper, the weekends begin to serve as R and R.

Seen in a group, as we have been seeing them for years at Thanksgiving and birthday celebrations, etc., the personalities of our Near and Dear tend to flatten. We ask banal questions, they return in kind. Taken one by one, the N. and D. have bloomed for me like roses. I have been inviting them kid by kid and grandkid, singly, and have several revelations to note.

I started with Ben, the most open and easy of our grandchildren. He's been riding around town and looking, studying old maps, talking to people, learning. His subject is why people live where they do. How are communities formed? he asks. I told him we'd take some trips to mining towns, company towns, and farm communities, maybe to Colorado Springs and Pueblo, too. I can tell him about civil engineering problems in those communities, but what really interests him seems to be a combination of demographics, sociology, and urbanology. Whatever it is, it lights up his eyes and makes him intent and voluble, and I sit and watch it, and am moved.

I invited Solidarity out for dinner last week, to a Place of Her Choice. I thought it would be some upscale restaurant but we went ethnic, and had a Near Eastern grain dish, wonderful breads, and salads in which at least a few of the ingredients were familiar.

She is still building siege ramparts in undisputed country, our daughter. "Of course, you want me to stop working at the detox center . . ." Later it came out that she thought I had wanted her to have been a boy.

I answered her halfway honestly, that I couldn't remember what I wanted. What was born became <u>her</u>, a person I came to love, very much.

She wouldn't have understood had I told her she was born on the scree-covered 40° slope of a marriage tipping into avalanche, and that her gender had nothing to do with what I wanted. She was the one for whom I felt the most misgivings, with you half the time, with me the other half, and brought up by a conservative religious Chicana housekeeper when she was with me and by your atheist activist friends when she was with you.

But now — I don't know if we can ascribe her confusions to this or that decision we made. She lived with both of us; she was surrounded by people who were interested in and devoted to her, people who loved her. We were separated for ten years, but Sol's adolescence, her teen years, were as conventional as anyone could want. Maybe, as time goes by and we talk, she and I can reach some kind of harmony, some stage at which she doesn't have to shock and I don't have to convince.

*Wish us Luck — Love, Marz*


*Dear Gram,*                    *July 3, Grant Street*

Don't flip. I'm pregnant! I haven't told anyone yet but you, not even Larry, because I want to tell him in a special way at a special time. Please, please think it is wonderful! I know everybody will think it's awful — Mom and Dad don't understand that I don't want all the things they keep yelling about and wanting for me: college, fancy clothes, parties, dates, a big career, a big wedding, a house like theirs in the suburbs.

Larry and I have been making love in his boss's cabin and it's two miles off a dirt road that's off the road to Nederland. Do you understand what that means? It means Larry really loves me. He isn't seeing me just to make love, because then we would go out in the park or in someone's car. We could do that every afternoon after work if he wanted to. This cabin is small and doesn't have electricity or water or anything, but when Larry turned eighteen he had to leave the group home and he heard about this cabin from his boss. The boss is letting him live there almost rent free and that's where we go. I brought my sleeping bag there and we bring water

145

when we go and there's a little camp stove. Larry and I go there once or twice a week. Do you understand? <u>It's His Home</u> and he brings me home, like a wife.

When I missed my period, I thought maybe I was pregnant, but what made me know was I had this dream. You remember the horses Larry made for me, and the little lariat rope he wove that I wear around my neck? I dreamed the horses all came alive and were running down the street and people were standing watching all amazed because they knew those horses were my dowry gift. Then the woven rope was tugging, and I saw it was at my waist and I wanted to untie it but it was attached to my stomach and then I felt a pain so I knelt down and a baby came out and it had the woven rope as its umbilical cord. So today I got one of those pregnancy tests at the drugstore and <u>yes</u>, it said, <u>yes</u>, because the color changed right away.

Here's how I'm going to tell Larry. I'll wait until we go to the cabin and I'll make him a special dinner. Then I'll tell him and we'll go to his meeting and tell all of them because they're like family to Larry in a way — he said so. Later, we'll both tell Mom and Dad and I don't look forward to that because they don't understand about Larry or about love, either. Do you think we should get married first? If we get married, they'll know it isn't just for sex or about the ugly things people make out of love — even the words people use for sex. People use ugly words for being pregnant, too: knocked up, in trouble, got the lump. How ugly those words are when what they express is so beautiful. I want to make beauty in Larry's life and mine forever.

*Send us love, Hope*

P.S. I read this letter over and saw I left something out that will confuse you later. It's about Larry's boss. It's a new boss because he wasn't treated well on his old job, the construction job. He left that job and now he is working at a garage. It's steadier work, he says, because in construction times are bad and people are always getting laid off. His new boss is a nice man, or seems like it, letting Larry stay at the cabin for so little until he can get another place.

*Dear Hope,*                                    *July 8,*
    *Between Garden City and Kalvesta, Kansas*

I feel honored that you chose me to be the first to hear your news. I want to share some of my anxieties with you, but I want you to know that what I say represents no change in my feelings of love for you or in my regard for Larry. It's easy for a person to be so in love that she forgets some of the stumbling blocks that are in the way.

147

Please see a doctor and make sure of your condition. Make sure you are healthy. Please don't decide to get married yet. Give yourself and Larry time. Larry's treatment program is hard work. Why load him with this extra weight?

Because, my darling girl, it is a weight for any thoughtful or caring man. Larry will want to support you and how can he when he can hardly support himself? This is <u>not</u> a condemnation of Larry. Young people are at their fittest and strongest but don't have ways of using that strength in work. They have to be trained. Larry will get that training, but if you heap him with the responsibility of you and a baby, it will be like sending a runner into Olympic competition with twenty-pound weights tied to his legs.

Is this the right time for you to be having a baby? If you waited, both of you might be in a better situation to care for it. I'm going to ask you a question, in all love. Please answer it in your heart and let me know. Did you let this baby be conceived in a desire, a fear to try to keep Larry? It's understandable, if you did, but it's making that little baby into an extortioner. Extortioners are hated. Why start this tiny thing you love with such a heavy burden?

I know you just want to be happy, but you won't be happy for long unless you think how others are made happy, too. Write soon.

*Love, Gram*

Some bad things have happened. Right after I wrote to you, I was so excited and happy I went and bought another test and took it and it came out blue again — pregnant. I couldn't wait to tell Larry because I was too happy. Instead I went down to where he works, and after work I took him for a walk and told him.

He was so proud. He smiled and then he laughed and then he let out a big war whoop and began to dance around me. Then we hugged and cried. I was so happy I wanted to explode.

He was supposed to go to his GED class that evening and I was going to go home and tell Mom and Dad, so I went home. But I couldn't find a way to tell them, so I was watching TV, or trying to, and then we went to bed.

Around 12:30 there was a call. I got to the phone before it woke anybody else up. It was from the hospital. They said Larry was there. I got dressed and woke up Jason and we snuck out and rode bikes — I rode Ben's — to the hospital. The people in the emergency room said Larry was in a coma with acute alcohol poisoning, and that he was so sick with so much alcohol in his blood that he might die. He had my name and number on his Social Security card and that was how they knew to call me. It made me start to cry. He feels married to me or he wouldn't have done that.

They let me see him. He was taken over — his whole body was taken over by machines. He had wires and tubes all in him and IVs in both arms and tubes down his throat and even in his nose. They had him tied to the bed where they were working on him because they said he had fought for a while before and then went down below where he could fight. They wished he would come to, a little, even if it meant they had to keep him tied.

A doctor talked to me a little. I told her I was pregnant. She asked me did Larry seem depressed about it and I told her how we had laughed and danced and cried and made plans. I told her Larry was on a program and she said I should call the people later. Jason left, but I couldn't go. I'm glad to be writing to you because it gives me something to do. I told Jason not to say anything and he won't, and Mom and Dad will just think I've gone to work, but I'll call in sick because I have to stay here until Larry is out of danger.

*Later*

It's 10:36 A.M. — I know because there's a huge clock across from where I'm sitting in the waiting room. I thought I could sleep but I got afraid. What if I were sleeping and something happened — good or bad — maybe they

150

wouldn't call me. What if Larry died and I missed it? So I sat and watched the hours go by and played games to stay awake. Each fifteen minutes I would think hard, really concentrate on a scene of my memory of Larry. The time we were up at Gold Hill, camping. The time we first said we loved each other. When I dozed, I caught myself by drinking water or walking. I drank the hours; I walked the hours.

Now it's morning and people are moving around and I realize that I'm smart and I'm mature. I'm mature enough to be with Larry and have his baby no matter what Mom and Dad say. How I can prove it is, I took my purse and address book with me when I left for the hospital. I got the worst news of my whole life but I still had enough mental strength to take what I needed to work with. Isn't that being mature?

I had the number of The Program and Larry's sponsor and at eight this morning I called them and told them, and called Larry's boss and said Larry was in the hospital and very sick. I didn't say what had happened, so the boss thought it was like an infection or something. He was sympathetic and I said I would call again as soon as I knew how things were. The doctor told me if Larry did live, he would be okay relatively soon. Then I called Jason and asked if he would fill in afternoons for Larry for a week and Jason said he would if he could get Larry's pay. I said yes and called the boss back and he said okay, Jason could fill in. Jason said he would tell Mom and Dad Larry was sick and he was filling in part time for a week but not about the alcohol poisoning or our sneaking out.

I think all the things I did, all the calling and the work I did, was mature and proof that I can decide about being Larry's wife and having his baby.


*Later*

It's 12:40 — afternoon — and I've just seen the social worker and Larry's sponsor and someone from The Program. I didn't care too much about their talk about future plans until I realized it meant the doctors had told the social worker more than they had told me. Larry started fighting at about 7:00 and they had him in restraints but they let him fight himself tired and he isn't in a coma anymore but has been sleeping. I asked her why they didn't tell me and she said he was still not out of danger. She wanted to talk about me, then.

I said, "No!" really loud, and got up. There's a lot of time to do that. I hadn't seen Larry in ten hours and I wanted to see him <u>then</u>. She started to talk to me but I stopped her and said I was going back to see him.

They did let me see him. His lip was all caked with blood where they forced the tube in and I cleaned him off and soon he woke up for a few minutes. He was so sorry. He said he had drunk something to celebrate our baby and the liquor hit him hard because he had been dry for almost a month and wasn't used to double shots anymore. Then, he said, he lost control and was so fuzzy he must have been drinking a lot without knowing it. They shouldn't have sold him all that liquor. Why did they sell it?

When he went back to sleep I felt the let-down and went out to the waiting room. Mom was there. It was dumb Jason after all. He was so excited about the job that he forgot to tell Ben that I had his bike. Ben thought I had taken it and called me at work, and of course they said I wasn't there. Mom called the police then because she thought I had run away with Larry. The police told her they had picked him up and brought him to the hospital.

So there was Mom, super angry. She started yelling right away about deception and we started to argue and with one thing and another the truth came out about me being pregnant. Abortion, she said. No, I said, never. I told her I wanted Larry's baby, we want this baby. Larry knows he can't drink, now, ever again. Even to toast his new baby. She said all kinds of things and they all sounded like the social worker.

I was suddenly so tired I couldn't stand up and I just slid down to the couch and was going to sleep, but Mom pulled me up and got me to the car and took me home. I don't remember going upstairs but I must have because I woke up around 4:00 P.M., and now it's 5:00, and I am finishing this letter. After I mail it, I'm going to see Larry.

*Later*

I got your letter. It just came. I am going to answer it as well as I can. I know that you and Grandpa loved each other because you separated but came back together and whenever I see you I feel your love for each other. You only saw Larry and me together that one day. You couldn't know how much we love each other. Larry has to stay away from liquor and that's his test, not lack of love. He is conquering racism and we will make a baby who will carry the spiritual message of our love into the world.

That is meant to be a big challenge. If it was easy, the magic wouldn't work. Larry knows that. We talked about it. His people have strong spiritual magic, stronger than ours. Wait and see.

*Love, Hope*

*Dear Marz,*          *July 10, Kalvesta, Kansas*

By now you'll know about Hope's pregnancy and Larry's reaction to it. It took everything I had to keep quietly reasonable with her. I wanted to yell out of my letter, to scream at her. Yes, I know they're not <u>ours</u>, but their own selves, but must we watch them make hashes of their lives? Can you talk to her? Can you make sense to her? Surely she has some anxiety, some small wake-up call trying to penetrate the dreamy chirp I hear in her letters. Larry mistakes a quart jar for a shot glass and she <u>believes</u> him?

Luckily I got the news as we were walking the undulating sea of ripening wheat. Mail call is first thing at a town stop, and is the big event of any day. I all but hopped up and down as I read; I swore, cried, raged. Poppy took the letter, read it, and said I would have to let this letter season a while before I answered it.

By the time I did, I had had hours to become wise and kind. I am not wise or kind. I am appalled. I want someone to shake Hope until she rattles. I want the God of our virtues to hit her on the head with a brick.

In my anguish over her, I worry about you, too. Are you all right? Are you eating well? I called you from Garden City, but you weren't home and the answering machine with your voice on it made your absence ache all the more. I'll keep on trying.

155

Here we walk in the heat-watering isolation I didn't feel in the mountains. Their monumentality saved us from being crushed by the sky. Someone starts a song in the morning and we sing it resolutely, but here the air grabs it from us. Anyone can see anyone else and anything else for miles away, so intimacy is demolished unless one bellies down and peers into the green corn or the gray-green wheat, and there is such teeming movement, such life, as to astonish and amaze. Ants race, beetles lumber, a million spiders weave and dream, crickets tick, small birds nest in the readying grain, mice scurry, snakes eye and slide, and everything cries its identity, peep and squawk, and a million carapaced insects scratch their names out on their washboard bodies. Stand up, and it's all gone.

I have never been anyplace where the tri-level world is so evident. There's the minute busy-ness of the ground, then the wide, lonely mid-range where humans, horses, houses, fence posts, and fields move slowly against the clouds. The fields seem more alive than the humans because they are in constant play under wind and rain. Over all, there is the vast, everlasting, ruling Blue that seems to organize its own light.

The stars out here are amazing when a city's light doesn't drive them away. It is possible on some nights to walk by starlight alone. We pull our sleeping bags out of the tents and lie under the dome drunk with vastness and stars. God knows what winter must be like, wind and snow with no feature or break in the rolling frozen waves of plain.

I'm writing myself calmer with this description, hoping in the details of what I see to get some distance and objectivity in our personal confusion. Justice won't write to me about Hope's choices and I know it's because she thinks I blame her for them. She fills a picture of me with cartoon bubbles over my head, full of words I would never say.

The defense rests. The defense is going to sleep.

*Love, T.*

*Dear Justice,*          *July 13, Larned, Kansas*

I've learned from Hope's ecstatic declarations that she is pregnant, and I felt her disappointment in us because we don't share her joy. You have my sympathy for the arguments you will present that she won't understand. Were we like that at eighteen? My big rebellion, I seem to remember, was choosing a cause that wasn't Socialist Party–sponsored, and marrying out of a faith we hadn't practiced for two generations. I don't remember what your rebellion was. My parents at first were horrified and then reconciled to my choices. Maybe this choice of Larry is a way-station.

I hope they'll break up. My dream would be that Hope and Larry go back to the treatment program. They realize that he is a boy and they have no chance of making a marriage work. Hope gets an abortion. Larry, alerted by his brush with death, gains in understanding and begins to work and study more single-mindedly. He and Hope graduate into friendship. They stay friends for life even when they go their separate ways, marrying other people.

This dream is brought to you by an accomplished dreamer, a grandmother walking through an awesome land. If Midwesterners have the reputation for being practical, somewhat literal, down-to-earth people, it's because if they weren't, they would be sucked up into the sky on the evening updrafts and forsake the earth which is only a line five degrees from dead flat while the sky fills the rest of the one-eighty. Our dreams float along above our heads as we walk with no mountains or buildings to bump into. Kevin, our leader, dreams about an environmentally perfect lifestyle. Some of the young-girl Walkers dream of Kevin. Poppy says she dreams of having done this Walk.

Keep well darling, and give my love to Frank, Jason, and Ben. Bless Ben, he has been writing, a very delightful surprise in one his age. Love also to Hope. Love and Luck.

*Mother*

*Dear Grandma,*  *July something —*
*I don't have a calendar; Grant Street*

Thanks for the Boot Hill tee shirt. Jason likes his, too. Things are pretty depressing around here. Everybody who isn't weepy is angry. Jason and I stay out of sight as much as we can. He sleeps over at friends' houses and I go over to Aunt Sol's and stay with her.

Two gay guys live next door to her. Jason, who is heavy into machismo, calls them Home Grown Fruits. These guys have two kids who are good friends of Sam and Cary and there's some legal stuff going on with their custody. It hit the papers and there have been letters and phone calls and people driving past yelling and throwing things. The two kids have moved to Aunt Sol's. Aunt Sol asked Jason if he wouldn't be here just to be another set of eyes and ears in case someone came around to hassle the kids. Jason bugged out. He didn't want to stay around, he wanted to be with his friends, blah, blah, blah.

I said I would do it. They all looked at me like I had said something stupid. Didn't I know I was just a kid? I told them that's what I know best. This job doesn't take a genius, just someone who can run fast and knows how to dial 911.

Mom made mom-noises, telling Aunt Sol I'd be in danger. I told Aunt Sol I could be there during the day, and would leave about six when everybody was back. Saturdays and Sundays I'd be home. Weekdays, I'd be staying pretty close to their house.

Guess what — They have <u>computers,</u> <u>and</u> Aunt Sol and the guys chipped in and got me two programs to work on — not games, either. Anton is an architect and he says he will get me programs in city planning and demographics. You need a lot of math for that, but I'm very slowly figuring it out.

*A couple of days later*

It's everything I wanted — it's a blast! I get up at 5:30 A.M., leave at six, and go somewhere on my bike — the streets are almost empty then and I can study things like through-streets, and how bridges and creeks demarcate, and then I go to Aunt Sol's and check on Blake and Anton's house, eat whatever I want <u>in</u> <u>either</u> <u>place,</u> and then sit down and work problems on the computer.

I try to act cool, imitating Jason, who is imitating a movie role. "Yeah," I say, "it's okay." But I can hardly believe it. It's going to be all summer! Every day I get to do what <u>I</u> want to do most. I'm helping someone, I'm eating Blake and Anton's gourmet stuff, studying what I want, and learning so much I can feel my brain cells stretching inside my skull, <u>and</u> everyone (except Jason) says I'm wonderful. Keep my secret, I'm not being wonderful, but <u>HAVING</u> <u>FUN</u>.

Is there big danger? Not really, or not yet. The custody case was in the Boulder paper and there was some stuff in The Denver Post, but they didn't give addresses. Some people found out, and now and then kids ride by and throw things, but that little bank where the houses sit on that block makes it much harder for what people throw to do much damage. Mostly it's just a job of picking up stuff on the lawn. I scared away some other kids who were creeping around and I have various gadgets that will set off alarms and call the police. The neighbor on the other side of Blake and Anton's house isn't too sympathetic to them, but he doesn't want his house worked on so he looks out for theirs, too. It may get worse when the case goes to hearing or trial or whatever happens next.

I am a good brother. If Hope moves in with Larry and leaves home, I'll get her room and be out from under the filthy, greasy thumb of Jason. <u>Still,</u> I hope she doesn't leave and move in with him. Larry still scares me, but he has minutes when he's an ordinary guy.

*Love, Ben*

*Dear Mother,*            *July 18, Grant Street*

First let me say I'm grateful that Hope has

been confiding in you these past months. I know your advice is good and although Hope follows no one's advice in her relationship with Larry, she hasn't cut the lines of communication with you as she has with the rest of us.

And she has no friends anymore. None of the group she went around with were comfortable in Larry's presence, and when she made acceptance of him the only requisite for friendship with her, the kids dropped away. She has no one, now, not even us. Jason is scornful, Ben can't understand what has happened to his sister, Frank is angry all the time, and I'm grieving. There is only Larry, Larry, Larry, Dad and you. Hope is closer to those cut-out horses Larry made for her and which circle her room, than she is to any of us.

I'm writing to beg you to beg her not to marry him. I made her go to the doctor yesterday and she is definitely pregnant. She was in ecstasy. She and Larry are going to end racism with this baby. They are going to demonstrate that class and race and background and all the artificial categories set up by society can be overcome with love. How our family loves The Answer: Socialism, Desegregation; now, Love.

Ben is darling, but my money is on Jason. Jason is normal. He does what his friends do, if it's sensible. Like me, he weighs things. He likes the world as it is and doesn't want to reform it, and he takes after Frank and Frank's family. You used to say they were stodgy. True enough, but they do less damage than the dreamers.

Beg her.

*Justice*

*July 16, The Hill*

*Dear Tig,*

Hope was over yesterday, trying to find someone in the family who'd be happy for her and Larry. I feel sorry for the kid; Ben is the only one who smiles when she talks about it. He loves her and <u>wants</u> to believe in what she believes in. It's all pretty sad.

You have sometimes accused me of indifference, but how much should I do? How much can I do? Hope sat in the rocker you used when you were nursing her mother and tried to talk me into being happy about her pregnancy. She wants to be Larry's wife and a mother right away.

Larry is out of the hospital, and back at that cabin he has. Could we give him the old camp bed and card table we have in the attic? I said yes, we have no use for them. Tomorrow I'll take them over, so I'll see his place.

Later, Jussy came with the excuse of picking up some books I have for Ben. I saw her coming up the walk, shoulder bowed by the huge purse she carries, and it was a shock. I

163

thought suddenly, "There's Tig —" It was the day you came back from the Vietnam War for good. She has your height, your long-boned, slightly clumsy gait, your fly-away auburn hair as it used to be. Jussy can be formidable, but she gets that helpless look sometimes in the middle of a display of strength. She has always posed as the down-to-earth person, dream-free and sensible. She uses that word a lot, sensible. She feels betrayed by Hope who isn't being sensible and who maybe has never been forced to be.

*"Tell Hope . . ." she said,*
*"convince Hope . . . Tell her —"*

Poor woman — you can't tell a deaf girl what "Taps" sounds like and you can't make her feel any of the associations those notes have for you.

We are supposed to be their parents, she says. We are supposed to be responsible.

I asked her if she had told Hope to evaluate things. Certainly. I asked her if she had demonstrated good sense in her own life and thus taught Hope by example. Certainly. I told her there was no more to do. Frank was playing handball. I made her dinner.

After Jussy left I sat down to watch a little TV. I picked up the horse Hope had left on the coffee table. She had brought it to us as a gift — one of the thirty or so horses in the string Larry had made for her. It had been cut out of construction paper — just a silhouette, but it's beautiful, really. Perhaps he had seen his model on a museum trip, the T'ang horses, fat and full of life and spirit. This one is beginning a prance, just a bit back-haunched, and its mane flying. She said each of the thirty horses is different. That certainly beats flowers and candy.

What is it that stops me from Jussy's despair? The boy's too young, he's alcoholic and untrained. He has no visible means. He's also bright, courageous, and gifted. Alcoholism can be overcome, youth will be overcome, training can be given, but courage and intelligence, artistry and wit can't be bought or taught. Now I will confess something: I felt worse when Solidarity brought Lewis home to see us, and when we first met Frank I was depressed. Lewis showed all the intellectual penetration of a grape, and Frank — stodgy and plodding — cast a shadow over Justice that hasn't lifted. Let's help clean up this Wild Horse, help tame and school him. The country is full of unwed mothers and people in treatment programs.

Don't breathe this to a soul, but I'm planning to rendezvous with your madness in Coffeyville, Kansas. Save me a chair and a look at Kevin. Say hi to the gang.

*Love, Marz*

Shimmering heat, a fume of panting respirations from leaves and melon. Our sweat rises like a mist and the green corn sweats, too; you can see the stalks growing.

No traveling between 11 A.M. and 4 P.M. To keep to schedule, we rise earlier and walk later. Sometimes there's water: river, pond, or creek. Some of us have gone dark brown; Poppy and I burn red as we freckle and speckle and spot, but even we have begun to look like the earth. Hair color fades, even hers; clothes bleach; skins darken; shoes weather and wear.

Coming through these small towns, we are treated well. People wave and smile. We give our questionnaires at grange meetings and church choir practices. The people here are farmers and the populations of their towns are shrinking. The land fits well into the technologies of agribusiness. Kevin finds this a violation of basic principles, and so there's a tension between wanting to hate them and the easy friendliness we receive from these people — warm acceptance in the camp of an enemy.

People relish the idea of our walking across the country.

There's an almost religious respect for the land here and that gives The Walk a hint of pilgrimage and makes our dark faces and faded clothing seem worthy. It imputes to The Walk a dignity it didn't have in the mountains where tourists hike for sport.

Kevin preaches to his group of followers. Poppy says he must. We hear him when the wind is right and there's laughter and applause in his big tent in the middle of the night encampment. It's comforting to hear the young people. It must have felt that way to the wandering tribes of Indians who set themselves against the vast openness of the prairie night.

*Dear Gram,*                                    *July 19,*
                           *Wild Horse Dream Ranch*

We had a big fight yesterday, Ma, Dad, and I, and I left them and moved in with Larry. I took my horses down off the wall where I used to live and now they are prancing and pacing around my new home.

Larry didn't tell me, but I found out he had been fixing up the cabin hoping I would come. It's in a sort of pocket down an old side road that used to be a logging road. You go about three miles out of town toward Nederland, turn off on a small side road for two miles, and then on to a path on your left, and the cabin is about half a mile down that little path. There's no water or electricity, but that's okay because we can use camp stoves and kerosene

167

lamps and we have gallon and two-gallon plastic bottles we haul the water in. The roof used to leak. You can see the faded places on the floor where the water ran in and warped the wood. Larry got some roofing somewhere and fixed it. It's fine now and by the time winter comes, he'll have insulation up and a new outside wall. His boss said if we fix it up tight and warm, he won't raise the rent and he'll go half with us on the supplies.

So the money I make at work will be used for wood and nails and lamp fuel and food — real things, not eye shadow and clothes, or doctors who'll tell me to take expensive vitamins and eat fancy food. I'm not drinking or smoking. Larry says he will give up smoking some day, but he doesn't drink now. I'm so proud to be doing this, building something good with Larry.

This is the best thing for me, to be with the man I love and to let him get used to life with me before the baby comes. I haven't begun showing yet, but I can hardly wait. I have to convince Steve, my boss, that I didn't know I was pregnant when I started to work. That's about the insurance money, and the law that says the company has to pay women workers when they have babies. Now, do you see what I mean? It's life happening to me.

I wonder what he will look like, our baby. I want it to be a boy. I'm a little nervous. Grandpa is coming over tomorrow and I want him and Larry to get along. I'll have to be there for them both, really <u>there</u> every minute, in the spiritual way, watching and helping so they don't fight.

Write to me at General Delivery, Post Office; Boulder.

Love, Hope

Moms,                               July 19, Niwot

A social worker from the county children's protective services showed up today, interviewed me, and pumped Sam and Cary for info. Were Blake and Anton good for Blake's boys? I know the drill, but not from the receiving end. The social worker was about my age, but, as Ben would say, with a few hard miles on her odometer. She said the visit was about Blake's kids, about their being subjected to things they shouldn't be. "Confusion about sex is one of those things."

I took a good look at her, asked a few questions, and we found ourselves opening up. I'm always wowed by what Sam and Cary see in people and daily experience. The kids don't cast Blake as father and Anton as mother. Division of labor isn't gendered in that house <u>because</u> there's no mom living there. Sam told her they had a mom, but she was gone and has another family. Then he added, "Anton is Blake's friend and he lives

169

there, but he's not the <u>mom</u>," and he began to laugh as though that would be funny.

The social worker asked if Anton punished the kids.

Cary shook his head and Sam said, "He gives them this <u>look</u>," and did a polite disgust I wish I had on film.

She asked questions about nudity and sexual behavior. Sam was clear: both men patted him on the shoulder and sometimes on the rump, but he said, "You know, like football players."

She asked me if Blake and Anton's parenting was different from the ordinary. I said it probably was but most families have unusual qualities. Men are killed in war, or die, and kids are raised by relatives or grandparents. What if Blake and Anton weren't gay? Her eyebrows went up. Couldn't two widowers move into a house to save money, each with one or two kids? Big deal? Probably not.

She asked about Anton's cross-dressing. I said it wasn't done in front of the boys and if they found any of his stuff he might say it was a kind of game.

When she said they sounded like an ideal couple, my warning-flags went up, so I said that it wasn't a marriage, but a good relationship. Blake is stuffy; Anton opens his windows. Anton is a worrier; Blake chills him out. Blake would be tight with a nickel if Anton let him. Anton would get even, but Blake is very moral and Anton has had that side wakened up in him through Blake.

It got to me that our chin-music was unnatural in many ways. It was gossip, girl-chat, but we weren't girls together. Its <u>context</u> includes her power in the situation. It gave our talk a hard edge. I asked about the hearing.

It will be a hearing in judge's chambers, and Hizzoner will decide the case based on reports like these . . . and she tapped the folder she had with her.

Suddenly the whole idea seemed far out, scary, oppressive — being passed on by strangers who have the power to give or withhold <u>children</u> — your own <u>children</u>. Brrr.

*Sol*


*Dear Tig,*                    *July 20, The Hill*

Yesterday I went up to the place where Larry and Hope are living. It's not as bad as Justice sees, and not as good as Hope burbles about. I brought them the camp bed and table and that old chest of drawers from the yard sale. It's no piece of furniture to feel beholden for.

You can miss the cut-off road easily. I drove at ten mph and back and forward three times before I found the little dip brush and the road shoulder obscured. A path goes down and becomes hidden in brush and foliage, which the car can't pass, so I got out and walked a mile to the cabin.

It tilts on an earth-heave, like something washed up there. The outside is of weathered, warped slabs from which nails protrude like arrows in a target. I think Larry has run fresh cement between the slabs and shored the house on one side. The door was around on the north and there are two nice-sized windows. The entry stone has been re-settled, and more shoring was on that side. I knocked.

The lady of the house opened the door to me and squealed the typical Hope sound of delight. Larry had gone to get water, she said, and would soon be back. She sat me down on one of two reinforced crates and began to Make Tea on a little camp stove. It was the quintessential Guest and Hostess bit and I was moved. It was so womanly. Tell that to any woman today and she'll cut you up for bait, but there it is. Would I like tea or coffee? Could I eat a little bread and cheese? Later, she showed me around the house, pointing to this and that, telling me what they had planned to have here, and how that would be changed.

There are two rooms; the space is bigger than it looks from the outside, but it's still small enough not to overawe a Japanese. On the blind side there's a back bedroom. They've improvised a raised platform on which their sleeping bags are spread. They need that — the floor is so badly warped it's perilous. There are also cubbies made from stacked peach boxes, cardboard with wood frames, and a clothes pole ingeniously making use of a corner and held by wooden chocks.

She's proud of their ingenuity, their ability to have everything a bedroom needs. They needed a wood stove for heat and cooking — did I see where one had been? With that, they could have heat and be able to bake and have hot water. There was wood around for the gathering. An old privy stood upwind of the house. By winter they planned to have it moved to a better location.

The main room is light and with the door open, airy and pleasant. There are plans, too, for the hideously warped floor and the loose chinking on one thickness of wall. With Hope's next month's pay, they'll buy wood — logs cut length-wise — and those will go on the outside and be chinked with cement. "We've got the rest of the summer to work on it, and all fall, too!"

Why not? I sipped my warm tea out of the McDonald's promotional cup; pioneers did it, Okies did it, trappers in high country do it, and the miner who built this cabin did it. Sure, Hope and Larry are too young, but too young is the only way to do a thing like this. They've got just the energy and the madness and the health and strength this dream requires.

Then we went out to the car to begin the

173

long job of moving everything. The chest seemed much bigger in their back room than it was in our attic at home. I asked if I could buy them a wedding present — that wood stove now, so they can vent it safely, and do the work that needs to be done before summer is over. She said she would ask Larry.

When I was starting to turn the car around, I saw a motorcycle tire mark covering the footprints I had made, one that turned in and then circled around the car and went back out again.

Pray with me. Pray to make us clever, you and me and Jussy and Frank, so we can think of ways to help them without offending his prickly honor or compromising her in his eyes. All around the rough walls of the cabin his horses dance and run and rear and toss their heads. They're all high spirit and freedom. Might they make it? Might they just make it?

*Love, Marz*

*Dear Marz,*        *July 23, Wichita, Kansas*

Wichita. We'll work this town like evangelists. I'm yearning to see you in Coffeyville on August 3. Is it all set?

Our reception continues positive, but the interest is in us, as Walkers.

I just got your letter describing your visit to Hope's place. I'm glad you gave them that old dresser; I hope you told them the drawers stick. I want no cause for Larry to be angry at us. Can you tell I'm scared? Is he still sober? Is he still on the program?

Summer bakes here. We lie panting in its oven. I'm cheered to think Hope won't be carrying heavy in summer's heat. A great grandchild, and the thought harrows me. They're too young, too unstable, but I've been getting surges of memory overwhelming logic. I remember the <u>feelings</u>, the milky sleepiness, the labile emotions — tears so plentiful you would think they were food. I remember the long contentment — I was in jail once for a day or two and I was so ripe my cell felt like the Waldorf. I argued with you — I was fearful, terrified some of the time — still protesting, marching, getting violently arrested — No memory remains of my arrest, arraignment. I lie in my sleeping bag drunk with old sensations until I come awake with a start, and it's Hope and it's Larry.

Babies need things. Hope may twitter with joy about pioneering, but <u>babies died</u> in those miners' cabins. Hope and Larry need heat, water, decent sanitation for the baby when it comes, or it may die.

And they're unused to thinking such thoughts because these days a baby's death isn't part of ordinary experience. I think we need to help them quietly because they are sleepwalkers. If we wake them they may be so world-shocked that they turn into wild swans and fly away.

I'm concerned about Solidarity, too, and her boys. Might someone hit upon the idea of bombing the house Blake and Anton live in? What vengeance is being carried out on us for the sins we sinned against our parents! We went south in dangerous days and later, into the riots of Chicago. Back then, I didn't think our parents really worried. I saw them as being fussy and overanxious, and now, in an unfashionable Socialist corner of heaven, they are laughing uproariously at my distress.

Social note: Kevin's late night gatherings have been curtailed by the long enervation of The Walk. His big, central tent is as often empty as full. People go to sleep, these days, even pretty young women.

*Love, Tig*


*Dear Hope,*          *July 23, Wichita, Kansas*


Your grandfather told me about his visit to your cabin. He described it and told me how impressed he was at how much you and Larry had done to make it livable. You are right about the importance of it all, of your life and its building, especially with the baby coming. Are you having morning sickness? The women in our family are good at pregnancy and child-birth. My grandmother had thirteen, all of whom survived infancy, a record in those days. The cousins have all had easy times and healthy children. When your breasts get tender, remember to massage the nipples to toughen them, and then rub them with a good emollient to keep them from cracking. Some people say that using cocoa-butter or a good cream on your stomach (later on) will keep it from having too many stretch marks. Are you beginning to want to sew and knit, or does that come later? It did with me, an urge against all my tendencies and former interests, something primitive, strong as those food urges some women have. When are you due? I plan to be back home on April 4th or 5th when The Walk is finished, and the first thing I will do after I take A BATH!! is to hurry over and see you and the baby.

Write to me often, please. Tell me how things are going. There are sure to be pressures and strains because the challenges are so great. Write about those, too, if you can. Don't keep me away with falsely sweet pictures of your life, and I won't do that with mine. Is it a deal?

*Love, Gram*

*Moms,*                                          *July 22, Niwot*

Bad news. An article about gays' legal problems ran in The Denver Post last Sunday.

There were digs about Denver's neighbor to the north and about Boulder's gay community. Blake and Anton's custody fight was mentioned twice, so more drive-by yelling and rock-throwing. This might have been too much for Ben to have handled on his own, when look who came galloping out of nowhere to help? Leonardo, my Detox buddy. Blake, Anton, and the kids have moved out temporarily; Leonardo has moved in. I think it will take about three weeks for the flurry to blow over, if it gets around the guys have moved. Leonardo! Would you believe it, the dude who seems to walk everywhere with a full orchestra playing "I Did It My Way." His school of diplomacy has always been Rock Through Plate Glass Window. This was done deftly as a bird landing on snow.

We're going to make it, and the kids are growing up with good models for courage and sense. Lewis would never have let us know Blake and Anton and their kids, and even with the wrangle, the drive-by hooting and horn blowing, and the occasional thrown rock, I'm right, it's right. Hope says that, too. Hope is nuts.

*Sol*

*Dear Marz,*          *July 24, Wichita, Kansas*

I'm sorry about the collect call. Poor man

— you hung on the line, barely awake. When I convinced you that everything was all right, you had to try to keep the irritation from your voice.

I'm suffering from a malady common among us, those who have strong ties to home. Instead of things fading <u>with</u> distance, losing definition, they suddenly move ahead of us, they loom, they heave up great shoulders and shove the present away.

Poppy dreams, sloppy, illogical nightmares about her house burning down, her job disappearing. Martin, from California, has come down with earthquake paranoia. Some of us are sent hometown newspapers and go into the sulks if their town weekly gets to them a day or two late.

I saw Hope, and Solidarity. My premonitions were seen by lightning. The kerosene lamps Hope and Larry use will tip over. Hope and Larry aren't familiar with the care kerosene requires. A bomb will be planted in the house next door to where Solidarity and the children are sleeping. Molotov cocktails will be thrown through the window. Nightmare pictures. Mother pictures.

This should tell you that Walkers aren't the strong, resolute, sound, grounded idealists our P.R. says we are. Those with home ties get miserable or frightened at odd hours of the night, yet I think it's worse for the ones with no links to a permanent life away from

The Walk, and there are more of them than there would be in a random sample pulled off the streets of a city. They have other fears, fears about The Walk.

Forgive that call, and forgive the one I'll make next month when the night begins to rain bad dreams.

*Love, Tig*


*Dear Ben,*     *July 26, During Bunion Rub, Winfield, Kansas*

The next few weeks are going to be a rich haul in T-shirts for you. Little House on the Prairie is here, and the Daltons and Jesse James are presences in Coffeyville and environs. It's a day's walk between them and a world of difference.

As we go through these little farm towns, I've been looking at how each one organizes itself, ordering its priorities, setting itself against the plains. You started me on this new habit. People crave order in what bits of their lives they <u>can</u> control. It helps them bear the rest, the parts they can't. This idea is as clear on these plains as it is in the oblong blocks of New York City or downtown Boulder, only expressed in vastly different ways.

*Love, Grandma*

Justice was angry about the wood stove and furniture. You know how that looks. Her face gets tight and her hair seems to fan out like a mane and her lips pull in. I see the little girl she used to be, at six or seven, stubbornly fighting tears of rage. Here it is on her grown-up face, and part of me wants to laugh, so I have to bite back my smile. She accuses us of furthering Hope's lunacy. Without our help (each word was expectorated like a spat pit) Hope and Larry would be having a mere summer's idyll. Around October they would begin to freeze. Without the ability to cook meals they would soon give up the pretense of housekeeping and Hope would come home to have her baby in a warm, serene place. They are camping out. Campers come home in the wintertime.

She has underestimated both modern camping and Hope's stubborn will. They could be warm and well-fed in Klondike conditions, thanks to modern technology. All I am doing, I told Justice, is bowing to the inevitable. Which is more desirable, having them or losing her?

She told me that as Hope's grandparents, we should be setting a higher tone.

Amazing, isn't it, what we cry out in pain? Jussy is suffering, I know, but it was all I could do not to laugh. Authority has taken a header into a snowbank and there's no calling it back to don black robes, even when we need it. I asked Justice to come in and eat with me. Pulling the Lonely Old Man out of my wardrobe of disguises, I hoped to get her to stay, to ease up over dinner, and a little wine. She didn't fall for it. Next week I'm taking Ben to Cripple Creek. I want to show him the bridge we put up there back in the sixties, and I'm interested myself in how it affects the town's development, if at all. I'm happy he's interested in something I can share.

*Love, Marz*

*Dear Gram,*            *July 26,*
*Wild Horse Dream Ranch*

When will this family start loving and trusting me enough to accept Larry as my choice? Mother thinks he is drinking again. LARRY IS NOT DRINKING. He has been sober for twenty-two days and working hard in spite of everything.

I understand so much, now. Look at July 4th — the whole country goes into its joy — American flags, fireworks, and parades. Independence Day. The people at Wild Duds kept talking about picnics and swimming parties. One of the girls was on a float in a parade, representing Silver. How would she feel if she knew she was representing an enslaver? Minorities and Native Americans have to sit on their hands while the rest of the country cheers. What Independence? they say. Larry has explained it all to me and now I see how empty such holidays are because they are celebrated over the dead bodies of Indians and the chained bodies of slaves and the land-cheated Mexicans. It makes the holiday a mockery.

Larry sometimes goes to his Indian ADEPT meetings but it's difficult for him to go because he has to go to Denver on the bus or hitch rides with people. Still, he sometimes goes. You can see by this how strong he is and how spiritual.

And Larry is working hard for me and the baby. We want to name our son a strong name, an Indian name, but one the White culture will not laugh at. Larry hates his name; he says Larry is a cop-out name. Everyone laughed at his last name, Walks Away, when he was in school. I said we should name our son <u>Never</u>. He would be called Never Walks Away — someone who stands and fights for what he knows to be right. It would sound all wrong to Anglo culture but names should represent things. I like your naming Mom Justice and Aunt Sol Solidarity. I like the name Hope, too.

Tonight I came home from work — did I tell you I really like my job and the people I work with. I made a nice dinner — most of what we eat is canned because we have no refrigerator. Then we sat outside. It was so dark. From our cabin you can see the fever glow of Boulder's lights. You don't see the lights themselves, but a kind of heat, as if there was a factory producing steel over there. Its fever is a kind of energy but that glow closes away most of the stars on that half of sky.

But looking west, into the mountains, there's velvet black and we only saw each other as gray shadows against that velvet dark, and heard the tink-tink of Larry's bracelets and tribal ornaments. My braided leather necklace has some beads on it, too, and they make very small sounds striking one another when I turn my head in the quiet. Larry began to say the "huh hun" words of the chant we use, a chant to the mountains and the earth to strengthen us. That way, we'll stay strong.

I have to admit I have a little morning sickness. I don't like Larry to know about it because it doesn't seem right, being sick, when childbirth is such a natural thing. Larry likes to eat sardines and bread in the morning. The smell makes me gag.

My breasts are a little tender, like you said they might be. I'll rub them like you told me.

*Love, Hope*

P.S. ADEPT stands for Alcohol Dependence Education . . . I forgot the rest.

*Moms,*

The ploy is working. Leonardo sunbathes on the porch of the house next door. I go over and we cut the grass, Leonardo in torn undershirt. We look at home and very heterosexual. The teenage drivers cruise in ancient jalopies, straining to check the address they copied off some men's room wall or other. Trying to read and gawk, the cars drift to the oncoming lane, there's a scream of worn brakes and a street full of skid marks. Leonardo, raised in fine, late-sixties style, knows all the tricks of heavy menace and can bring them out at will.

So, we're all right and there's less for Jussy to worry about with Ben. Blake and Anton want to take back their house for the custody visitors. I told you about that social worker. Blake wants the visits done in their natural setting — dig the zoo metaphor. He says they all feel the house is now part of the zoo — mortgage, paint job, lawn. It used to be a laugh. Not now.

They have been back visiting, or we meet them. The lift has gone out of their friendship with our boys. Visits have to be planned, the kids, taken.

Anton looks like hell. He knows he caused this and it hurts. He wants all the parts of his life back.

Is dressing up that important?

185

He told me he hasn't dared to. What if Blake's wife has surveillance stuff?

Everyone is waiting for the social workers and the court-appointed people, and the hearing to be over, so they can have their lives back.

I began to kid him. I said, too bad the mess would die down and he would be back in those revolting earrings.

He tried to smile and fire back a joke, but his eyes went teary, too quickly for him to control. He said, "It's so awful. I'm scared they're going to hurt us and take the kids."

More as it happens.

*Sol*


*Dear Hope and Larry,*          *July 28,*
*Cedar Vale, Kansas*


I want to start writing some letters to you as a couple — some of my letters are for Hope alone, woman talk, but there are some things to share with both of you.

About the dresser: The drawers stick. Don't think you have to keep the piece as it is. If you need to, plane them down. These are no heirlooms; the piece is only <u>old</u>. Make an appointment with your grandfather and go to our attic and get whatever you want out of it. There are curtains and some rolled-up rugs you can use for the draft on your floors.

Go to the garage. In it you will find treasures of half-cans of paint, boxes of nails, screws, and heaven knows what else. You would be doing us a favor by taking what you can use. When I get back, we'll go through some of the fabric remnants I have stored up.

Larry, please don't see Hope's mother's worry about the pregnancy as intrusion. She worries because that's her job. Hope needs to get set up with a doctor for this pregnancy. Even though pregnancy is a normal and natural condition, things sometimes happen that are not normal and it would be a shame to lose this baby because of something that could have been prevented.

Even with your hard work, it seems as though you are enjoying the summer. I envy you where you are. It is blazing hot here during the day and the crops breathe out moisture like a sweat. It's going to be even worse in August, but at least we're not doing the Arizona part of The Walk during these months.

> *Enjoy the cool . . . Love,*
> *Antigone (Gram)*

*Dear Marz,*        *July 28, Cedar Vale*

I wrote to Hope and Larry and gave them permission to rifle our attic and garage. Noblesse Oblige. I need to include Larry in my thinking as a family member and not just a problem that walks.

I like the people here. In stores they bundle things to be easily carried. They point out rest stops and parks with water taps. They stop their cars to tell us: "Don't stop here. If you keep on a mile or so, you'll find trees and a creek." Once or twice we have stayed in their barns to get out of the rain.

It makes us neighbors. Yesterday, we interrupted The Walk to help a man get his hops under wraps before a storm.

I came on Kevin again, sitting up. We were camped in a farmer's field from which a crop had already been taken. The crescent moon was covered so often it looked as though it were being wiped with a cloth. Back from the Porta Potti I saw the light of a joint. Something told me who the smoker was, and I went toward his light. He was sitting in a folding camp chair someone had made for him. He patted the ground beside him companionably and offered me a puff. I declined with thanks. Then he said he was uncomfortable in this country. It was too big, too open, too featureless.

I asked him where he was from. We have only the sketchiest bios of other Walkers. There has been a choice not to know beyond the requirements of The Walk — doctor, mechanic, cook.

It was Oneonta, New York, but they didn't

stay. His father had itchy feet and Kevin has moved often. He spent a year in North Dakota while his mother was divorcing his father. After that he was up and down the California coast.

I told him a little about my parents, mentioning that if all the parks and trees in New York disappeared, they wouldn't have noticed. He said he didn't understand this Plains mentality. I began a defense but he cut me off. The people here were salt of the earth, and all that, but they wouldn't stop using chemical fertilizers and insecticides. They had no creativity.

I had heard these views from Kevin before. Wasn't it a Peanuts character who said, "I love Mankind, it's people I hate"? He's a little sanctimonious. He has taken the spontaneity out of Bunion Rub, but we gave him some permission to do that. He has admirers, fawners, male and female. Whose fault is that? "What bothers you?" I asked him.

He said, The Walk. He had come to think it was a joke. It listens, listens, and says nothing. It's like the little bitches he went to school with — they would priss around saying, "I've got a secret, but I won't tell it." The Walk knows what's needed. It's been listening for four months —

Hasn't that differed from place to place? I was thinking the joint should have made him mellow.

The hand with the cigarette drew an arc. Sure, people want to justify their selfishness and greed, the bigness and sprawl, the fertilizers and chemicals.

I asked how he planned to instruct them. He said, "I was thinking about that when you came."

Marz, my love, why are reformers, like Kevin, so humorless? God bless the energy it takes to laugh. I told him I was sorry for breaking into his thoughts, that it was difficult enough to get time alone on The Walk.

He gave me a compliment. He likes talking to me. I don't fawn or flatter. He needed my help.

"Just don't tell me to start preaching," I said. "I'm not so senile that I don't remember Pueblo and 'Don't rape your mothers.' "

We said goodnight and I went back to our tent. I lay awake with a feeling of having been interviewed for a position of which I had no knowledge, and no job description. I do know that Kevin is reaching for my support. For what?

Arise and come thou, my beloved, to Coffeyville!

*Love, T.*

*Dear Tig,*                          *July 30, The Hill*

This letter might get to you before I do.

I'll be flying in to Coffeyville's airport. Arrange a camp-out for me and I'll join The Walk for at least a part of my summer vacation, Coffeyville to Springfield, Missouri, as I make it.

I've given this a lot of thought. We agreed that I would touch base with you at various points along the way, but I reckoned without my own interest in the problems of The Walk itself. Now, I want to check it out with my own eyes. I want to see you in this environment, <u>ecologically</u>.

We've always had different versions of reality, you and I. The ten years we spent apart were some of the loneliest of my life, even though I had the kids for part of the time. You wanted the freedom to go where you saw a need — the Vietnam protests, the anti-nuclear movement. I realized back in 1978 that if I wanted to keep you with me it would have to be on your terms. I gave in.

But giving in isn't consent. The kids are grown and I'm going to retire soon with no sorrow at all. Bureaucracy is swallowing the department and drowning creativity and initiative. I'll be sixty-five and perhaps there's another career opening beyond the county engineer's office — something we'll talk about on all those starry nights you describe. Then we'll talk about what has happened on the road and I'll be able to get my own view of this cause. Say hello to Poppy. I'm looking

191

forward to seeing her and the other characters of the epic Walk. Will that make me the oldest bloke there? Are there prizes given? Where's that damn wardrobe list you used?

*Love, Marz*

*Dear Gram,*                                    *July 26,*
                              *Wild Horse Dream Ranch*

I know you want to include Larry in the family life, but your letter made him really mad. It was the part about my pregnancy and getting a doctor. Larry is very sensitive and he thought you were criticizing him for not taking care of me. If I get sick, he says, he can take me to the hospital on his motorcycle. We don't have a million dollars to spend. Doctors and medicine are part of the white power structure, anyway. Indians lived for millennia without any of that, and Larry thinks it's a rich people's thing. I did tell you about the motorcycle, didn't I? It's another wonderful thing about Larry. He got a better motorcycle, one that had been wrecked, and he fixed it up and now it runs and we have transportation back and forth to work and even to go food shopping, which I do in my lunch hour or after I'm through at Wild Duds. So you see he can be modern, too, when we need to be and I won't spend my life in a wigwam!

He is really strong. He hasn't had a drink

for twenty-six days, and he wants me to be as strong as he is in my pregnancy. I'm trying hard. I'm not showing yet, but I can tell things. Like:

1. Reds are redder. I can't describe it — the whole world is <u>more</u> <u>itself</u>. It got that way when I fell in love with Larry, but now it's even more. The sky seems brighter, the smell of everything is more intense. Some foods make me sick (how I wish Larry would stop eating those <u>sardines</u>) but that's because smells are — <u>smellier</u>. When I'm sad I cry for the whole world. When I'm happy, I could light it with joy. Last night I fell up into the sky and got stuck to the moon.
2. Here's a secret: the whole world is pregnant, too. All over Boulder you can see them, pregnant women, big and small, all with that little look they have. Do I have that look, that smile, that isn't quite on the lips yet? I wonder.
3. Sore breasts. I told you about that already.
4. I want to start making things for the baby.
5. I <u>don't</u> want to start making things for the baby. What if I make the things and the baby is born dead? What if I make the little booties and the baby is born with only one foot? Don't laugh. I have dreams. I don't

want to make God angry at me by acting like I <u>know</u> what will happen, when I don't. Still . . . I want . . . I stop by the stores, the baby clothes places and the yard goods stores and I want to be <u>starting</u>. All my work money has to go into the house right now. Larry says we don't have as much time as we think to get it done. We have a lot of wood to use and insulation, and Larry says we will get the things you said from your garage.

Write to me. I'll tell the right parts of your letters to Larry, but don't try to come between us again. He is very sensitive about being poor.

*Love, Hope*

# *August*

❧

Marz is here. The arrival of someone eagerly awaited is always sudden. Suddenly, all of him is completely present; nothing here before, all here now. But, when did he get old? It must have taken thirty years or so of inattentiveness on my part.

Poppy moved out of our tent with minimum muttering. There are eighty-six of us on The Walk, now. Couples have come with us, and some of the people we picked up in the mountains have left. When we move across the Plains and into the Ozarks, we expect our full complement of 100.

The mix of us changes. Families make The Walk stable in some ways, unstable in others. Panic at a temporarily missing child clutches us like talons.

More single people give more energy, and also more pain. Love and loss blow through The Walk, moving tent-flaps where some young man has made brief passage on his way through. Here comes adorable Jessica, in her little sleeveless blouses. When her eyes open

195

— morning glories. Three women have left us to be pregnant back home. Did the wandering bands of Sioux change spirit with the demographics of pregnancy, dying, and infant mortality? Has it ever been studied?

Marz is a good observer and his insights are sure to be different from mine. When I asked him to go into his trance and speak, he said, "Not yet, impatient one. Cross my palm with baloney sandwiches."

So it isn't from Marz that I learn The Walk now, but from my presenting it to him. At home, the rake may have been standing at the door for years, the untrimmed tree may beat annoyingly against a window, but it's only when guests come that these things are noticed and cause us embarrassment.

Some of what I see through Marz's new eyes impresses me. The camp is thrillingly efficient. Tents go up and down in a twinkling. With no running or undue noise, morning breakdown and evening setup occur almost magically in sun or rain. Food is readied, eaten, and cleaned up. There's speed but no haste. Having learned what does and doesn't work, we go with no orders given, smooth as a ballet troupe that has rehearsed together for four months.

Marz will work with Poppy and me on our rota this week. Next week he wants to go with The Walk's site-scouts and advance people, who are sent ahead to deal with park officials and others. Towns that two months ago said they would welcome us change their minds. Campgrounds are full, invitations open or close. He will sleep on the road with the scouts and thus will know The Walk in all its parts.

I don't want him to feel I've wasted a year of my life and our lives together.


DIARY ENTRY                              *August 6*

We danced again, this time into Missouri. Marz and I were asked to dance over the line. He whispered to me, "Let's show this bunch." His specialty — the Charleston. "Has Anybody Seen My Gal?"

They actually thought we were that old. We snowed 'em anyway, winding both of us to exhaustion, and impressing the hell out of them.

> *Turned up nose*
> *Turned down hose*
> *Flapper, yessir, one of those . . .*

It ran in my head for the rest of the day.

DIARY ENTRY        *August 7, Joplin, Missouri*

Honeymoon, a few questionnaires, minimal work. We walk, leaving the land behind us to get along by itself.

Suddenly, we are seeing black people. Yesterday I stopped at an AME church. It was choir practice night. I asked the pastor to introduce us and ask his parishioners to help.

He was guarded at first but when he saw the questionnaires were not about race or race relations, he loosened up and smiled, questioning us about The Walk. Later I thanked him for presenting our case so eloquently. "It's the first time," he said, "that we have been presented with evidence that we are simply citizens sharing life in this nation. Poll people and reporters have come down here, but it's always about racial matters." He looked at me through heavy, gleaming bifocals. He and I were separated by two thicknesses of bifocal glass. "Last April," he said, "an apartment complex three blocks from here suffered a fire. Our church families opened their homes to the white people rendered homeless by that fire. No one came. When our men went over to the place to help find and store any salvageable things, they were turned away. I cannot express to you the pain this gave us. We have heard nothing from the white community since. Now you are asking us to help. You offer us nothing, promise us nothing, and your questions are not about race. How could we resist?"

*Dear Solidarity,   August 8, Chetopa, Missouri*

I am on the road with Marz, camping out. We reminisce while we walk, telling each other about our years together and our years apart. Camp business fades.

While I am farther from you all physically, I've learned more about you through these letters than I could have when I was at home, a paradox. It seems that there, our lives got in the way.

Your relationship with your neighbor-friends, Blake and Anton, has made me wonder about the gay people on this Walk. I think two female Walkers may be, but women who share tents and wear each other's clothes, touch each other easily and affectionately, aren't noticed in the same way men are. We have an effeminate man or two, but no overt pairings.

Is there any dropping off of your other friendships because of Blake and Anton? It was a blow to me when I went to work for the Peace movement that people I thought were friends — some quite close — deserted me. I hope you won't be swallowed up in this controversy. I'm proud of you — <u>we're</u> proud of you, and you know that. Just be careful.

*Love, Moms*

*Dear Grandma,*        *August 3, Grant Street*

Thanks for the tee shirts. I like getting the packages and knowing they are something special from the places you go. I was looking hard at the petrified dinosaur shit you sent. I'll take it to show the kids at school.

I went over to visit Hope and Larry yesterday. They are fixing up their place and I helped them even though I'm clumsy and don't know how to do things. Larry is almost a genius. He has a book Hope got him about how to do roofing and put in floors and siding, stuff like that. She said he looked through it once, not reading it, just seeing the pictures and turning the pages. She heard him say, "Yeah, uh-hum," and when he got to the end he said it was a good book. Now he seems to know everything in it.

I didn't believe what she said about him until I went over there. They don't have the money for equipment and supplies, fancy shingles and siding. Larry got a whole lot of scrap wood some place and made flooring out of it. Then he fixed the outside walls. He said he could do that because Grandpa gave him some protective oil stain from your garage. They didn't have enough to do the whole cabin so on the back half, that side that faces the hill, they used regular paint. People can't see that part anyway, unless they go back and look. Hope and Larry keep the garbage stuff and his motorbike back there.

When they moved in, the floors were warped — I think I told you that. They rented a sander and Larry got a machine from the garage where he works and ran the sander off that, don't ask me how, but they sanded the warps down and put water-proofing — it's like a tar-soaked mat — on top of that and then glued the scrap-wood tight together and sanded that and covered it with a finish also from Grandpa's garage and it's really good.

The big surprise is Hope. When she was living with us she never did any stuff like that. She mooned around or read and left her clothes all over the house. As soon as she left she turned into someone else. That's kind of scary, don't you think? It says there's no such thing as a <u>person</u>. I grew up with Hope. There wasn't ever a time when she wasn't <u>there</u>, and now she says she was never happy at home. How come I didn't see it? Was I somewhere else? Will <u>I</u> be someone else at some other place? If I go away to college will I turn into a person I don't even recognize? It makes me scared to leave the house in the morning. Maybe I'll meet someone and be changed into another <u>person</u>.

Because there was Hope hauling rock to shore up the side of the house. She hammers and saws and bucks wood for Larry and when I was watching it I felt ripped off. I was thinking: Why wasn't she ever that enthusiastic at home? Why didn't she jump into <u>home</u> the way she jumps into <u>here</u>, to life with a guy she didn't even know last year, not well, anyway?

Now, she says she never wanted a big, elaborate wedding, but she <u>did</u>. I <u>remember</u>. We used to play it when I was a little kid, talking about the cake three stories high. <u>I</u> was the one who said I would save all that money, go up to the mountains and have the wedding in a big field and have cake and champagne (which I thought tasted like white grape juice). <u>She</u> was the one who wanted to be married in a cathedral in Europe with a long, white wedding train.

How do you know someone? Isn't it by knowing what they think and how they act? I have nothing left of her but stuff only <u>I</u> remember.

Love, Ben

Dear Hope,        August 9, Diamond, Missouri

We are at the George Washington Carver memorial surprised to find more white than black people visiting today. I'm sending pamphlets to Ben.

He tells me you are working hard on the house. I hope that doesn't mean you haul heavy loads. Please be careful and don't strain. These early days of your pregnancy are more risky than the later ones. Your mother has told you the same thing: our opinions are based on solid experience, in this case. You will answer that traditional women worked hard and carried heavy loads. They also lost babies.

I'm suffering from the heat on this Walk. Even the blizzards and snows on the high passes we crossed in May were not so difficult for me. Grandpa has gone to be part of the advance team that sees us into campgrounds and lines us up for appearances at college campuses, churches, libraries, etc. He'll come back for a day or two before he leaves The Walk for home. I'll miss him very much, and may not see him again until Washington, D.C.

Why do I stay away so long? A friend I called last week asked me that, when I told her I missed her. I will be home next year, having walked across the whole country. I will have seen small-town America as I never would have and learned what I can't yet put into words. Maybe then I'll be willing to settle down and be a more traditional great-grand-mother to someone who is also missed and waited for.

*Love, Gram*

P.S. Ben feels a little lost without you because you were his ally at home. I'm glad he's part of your new life.

*Dear Gram,*                                    *August 6,*
                              *Wild Horse Dream Ranch*

Larry has celebrated a complete month of being sober — one month and a day, and he says it has been very hard although he says he is not an alcoholic. Drinking is a habit, though, and it's hard to break habits. One of the things we laugh about is when he says he doesn't have time to be an alcoholic. When he isn't working at the garage he's working on the house. Ben helped us with the new floor and now the drawers in the dresser you gave us don't stick as badly because its weight is evenly distributed.

Floors, walls. They will be finished by September, we hope. The roof is coming along but needs to be redone and we can't afford that, so we'll put something on top of what's there and hope it lasts the winter.

*August 7, lunch break*

I got a raise! My boss, Steve, likes my work and says I have a feeling for design and what looks good on people. He's beginning to train me in the business end, more than just ringing things up and counting receipts at the end of the day. He showed me a little about how to enter things into the computer and how to figure overhead. It's interesting. Larry says it's just capitalism and money and it looks that way from the <u>outside</u>, but when you're in a store you see things and it makes the receipts represent a lot.

For example — it's kind of slow now. Most of our customers are kids — junior high, high school, and some college kids. We sell casual clothes, tops, shorts, skirts, different kinds of pants, things like that. It's what you would use for hanging around but not for a particular sport. Steve says almost all our customers are impulse buyers. When they're doing <u>wardrobe</u>, he says, they go to a big store. They plan there and compare, thinking about how this and that will look together. That's why our clothes have to be more styled than they would be in big stores. Also kids don't have to risk these clothes at school where they might be laughed at. Steve says they fantasize a kind of <u>life</u> the clothes suggest to them.

The designers and fashion houses know that and they send us things they <u>think</u> will appeal to kids. We get in a blouse or a tank top that goes and we put it out — front window, in a big display. For those clothes we don't use mannequins, just the blouse or the top made as though someone was wearing it, using it in action, having fun. Things like that sell very fast or not at all. We order more. Sometimes we guess wrong. Sometimes a trend will build. I've only been here two months and I see it already, the guessing, the betting, the knowing, and it makes the receipts even more interesting.

The raise usually comes after <u>four</u> months. I can work, Steve says, until the end of my pregnancy. He also told me they have a training program for store management. I could be a <u>store</u> <u>manager</u> in a few years, if I'm good enough.

That way we can have money to buy some land, maybe up a canyon that's not so fashionable, somewhere land is cheap, and we can build our house and live the way we want. We could commute to Boulder where the store is or maybe even have a place in a town like Longmont or Fort Collins and live around there and get land.

I guess you've seen by this letter that Mom and Dad and everyone else is wrong about me and Larry. Yes, we're young but we know our love is real and soon we'll prove to you and the world that we're not dippy teenagers having a puppy love romance. Larry has given up drinking and anger because of me and I'm showing him his sacrifice is worthwhile and that life is good even in our society.

With my raise, maybe we'll be able to put a new roof on the cabin.

*Love, Hope*

Marz has left in anger. We both said things. He thinks The Walk is in <u>ethical</u> trouble, that I'm blinded, as I have been so many times before, by the charms of unworthy leaders. It happened in the Vietnam protests, he told me. Two-bit leftists took the stage and overwhelmed the sensible message about our inability to fight such a war. Vietnam was over twenty-five years ago! He said I gave too much trust. I said, not trust, leeway.

He said I could be second-banana for Jim Jones, that I was Alice in Wonderland in Waco. He said Kevin had guns.

It stopped me cold.

One of the advance people dropped a hint, Marz said, and he followed it up. There's money, too, that Kevin has been keeping out.

How could that be?

Marz thinks Kevin has an account he's not telling anyone about, with money he has taken from The Walk. I said he may need a special account — an emergency fund. Marz said The Walk's idealists are not skeptical enough to look any further, that one day I and the other trusting lambs are going to wake up stranded. Kevin is skimming money. Kevin has at least three guns.

If the guns are for protection, why doesn't The Walk know it? If not, what are they meant to be used for?

I said that since Pueblo there have been instances of harassment, kids biking past The Walk trying to force us off the road, pranksters now and then coming to the camp. Now and then there has been an edge to the pranks, letting us know that we are strangers moving through these places, here on sufferance. I told Marz that Kevin is dedicated to The Walk.

We were going down the road to the park campground. Walkers passed us on the way. Marz, in his Humphrey Bogart voice, said, "Sweetheart, I gotta go. I'm an old guy, see, and I can't watch you getting taken without rising to your defense, which seems to be the last thing you want. That gets me sore, kiddo, and it also gets me nowhere."

I was annoyed and defensive.

He shrugged and said I was trusting and naive and he didn't know how I have lived this long.

We started arguing again and I can't stop an argument with anything good left in it. In the end he left, angry, and I stayed, angry.

I told Poppy. She said she liked Marz and was sorry he was going. She doesn't know about money skimming or the guns, she says, but knows about Kevin.

There's no proof. The Walk needs to act without destroying what's good about Kevin's leadership.

She says it's too late. We could have done something conciliatory months ago, but now he's too entrenched. There will have to be a public inquiry.

I thought we should go to the Fresnos, the ones who are most sensible, and let them investigate privately. We can't go to Kevin and get him to admit what he has done.

We were spinning possibilities between lengthening silences, looking out through the open tent flap to bands of purple beginning in the sky. We had talked the night away, worrying the time and reaching no decision. We fell into dozes until the wake-up call and the clatter of pots and the doors of Porta Pottis creaking open and slamming shut.

We have no proof, only Marz's suspicions made on a week's participation and two meetings with Kevin, both brief, and with Marz asking only the simplest questions. I feel raw, annoyed at Marz, here for a week and now leaving a mess of unsubstantiated suspicions behind him.

We need to keep our eyes open, Poppy says. I can barely stay awake.


*Dear Tig,*                    *August 18, The Hill*


Home. Something goes out of homecoming when no one is home. This isn't a plea for sympathy: I want you to know that we are both contributing to your ecological Walk in ways no one could have predicted.

I was angry. I still am. I went out there and you told me to experience The Walk, to look at it, and when I did and told you what I had found, you first denied it and then acted as though I had spoiled something for you. I couldn't stay to watch, but I can't help worrying about you.

Do I think The Walk is another Jonestown? No. I do think Kevin is a con man, even if more Pied Piper than Jim Jones. I think he has been collecting money with both hands. Talk to the advance men. Get Peter Percy to tell you what he told me. I'll worry about you because you're vulnerable and so is The Walk.

You asked me why sober, practical people and couples I met and liked, Fresnos — Siger, the Dudas, the Kvarners — why they haven't seen through Kevin. I now have an answer that's not hasty or angry: The Walk is an amazing venture. You cover up to twenty miles a day, you circulate and collect questionnaires about local environmental matters, you also do the daily jobs of the camp — washing your clothes, making camp and breaking it, and are required to work out internal camp difficulties — the minutiae of group living in somewhat primitive surroundings. There's not much time to inquire into motives, to question advance staff, or keep track of all the money coming in and going out, especially when you're being presented undetailed account sheets at business meetings. Talk to Patricia. She's the group's accountant.

Another reason for your blindness is psychological. Having invested time, love, hope, etc., in the picture we form of someone, we forget how that picture changes. Kevin has changed, unseen and unnoted by you, and The Walk has changed to accommodate that. Reality sometimes buys its supplies from memory. Yes, The Walk is wonderful, but be careful. Why can't you demote Kevin, or get rid of him? Be careful. Get others behind you. Be careful.

*Later — 8:00 P.M.*

I went down to the mall earlier today for a tour through The Hardware Store and when I was done, decided to amble over to Hope's Wild Duds. I watched the girls come and go for a while, enjoying their cuteness, and when I went into the store, a woman nearby eyed me as though for identifying characteristics to report to the police.

Hope introduced me to Steve, the store manager, who looked like a kid with high school freshman problems. There's an ease between them, a lack of front I found refreshing. Hope gave him a little report before she left, her impressions of the day. They had had lots of enthusiasm about <u>this</u> item, <u>this</u> sold less than <u>that</u>, the buyers of <u>that</u> had been younger than expected. He said good-bye to her with real friendliness. We left the store, walking in the summer warmth, hand in hand. "Larry picks me up in half an hour," she said, "so there's time for you to buy me an ice-cream cone."

I said I would buy the cone and take her to Larry's garage afterward.

She likes the store, the work, being in a place where things are going on. I have my misgivings there, too. As I watched her deciding between rocky road and mocha nut, I was aware how much Hope needs people, choice, action. I could tell that from the little report she had given at the store. The manager likes her work; management has an eye on her. What's she going to do up in some isolated cabin in the woods?

The difference I felt at the garage was almost like a casebook study: fig. 1, fig. 2. Larry apparently didn't want us to see him at work. His face fell as hers had brightened. "Be right there," he said, to keep us in the car. We saw him go to his boss, point to work he was leaving, and then to us. The boss looked annoyed. Hope said she would tell him we'd wait.

I said this was Larry's workplace. She can't

be straightening things out here.

She heard my unhappiness as impatience and began that damn woman-like defense, planning, excusing. Do they put it in your baby formula, some chemical that goes to the female brain and makes women rush in, all ready to smooth everything at the fall of a word?

So we waited and I got her to be still and let him walk away from his work, his face pinched with discontent at his boss and us. "What are you doing here?"

She said we had come to pick him up and didn't know he wasn't finished working.

He shrugged, mumbled something, and I offered to take Hope home. They both said no, and Hope skipped out of the car, and turning to me began the smoothing again. "I know Larry is glad to see you, it's just that —"

I said I would see her after work from now on, and sometimes take her to enjoy a mocha nut; Larry would pick her up when he was ready.

She smiled and turned away, then thought of something else and turned back. "You haven't noticed . . ."

"What?"

She put her hand on the well of the open window; a ring, a "gold" band, was on her left hand. They had gone to the courthouse on Friday and gotten married. She gave me her luminous smile and turned away to where

Larry was straddling his bike, gunning his motor, her summons.

*M.*

P.S. Did I remind you to be careful?


*Dear Marz,*       *August 17, Hartville, Missouri*

Hallelujah the hills! It's harder walking and we don't make the time, but my chest opens up and there's a lift of spirit as we crest the mountains. The spaces ease the eye. We were walking parallel to the interstate for a while, before we struck out to the east.

Being a Coloradoan, I used to think that water was all anyone needed to make a paradise of any place on earth. They have plenty of water here, rain, streams, creeks, lakes, rivers, but work is thin.

Have I ducked the Kevin issue long enough? Here it is: <u>We</u> didn't decide what to do; Poppy decided. She came late to Bunion Rub. Kevin was in a spate when she slipped in beside me and proceeded to interrupt the flow several times, visibly annoying our Fearless Leader. I thought she was trying to make him lose his temper and show a darker side. Walkers are proudly, sanctimoniously, against confrontation.

After the good-night song, Poppy guided me — all but pushing me to our tent. She came behind me and pulled me around to face her. She was whispering: "I got the pistols. Kevin's pistols."

For a long time I stood staring. It must have been twenty seconds or so, because I only came to myself when breath demanded breathing. "Where are they? Did anyone see you?" Tents are the ultimate combination of public and private environment; anyone who wants to eavesdrop, can.

Poppy brought out the mosquito repellent; if anyone came, we could talk about — and she mimed spraying.

"Where are they, the guns?"

She pointed in the general direction of the river. She had found three. They were in plain sight in Kevin's tent, which made her think that his nearests and dearests knew all about them.

It was why she had made herself so present later at Bunion Rub.

"When Kevin finished answering me, I slipped away, again. I had the guns in a plastic garbage bag rolled up under my arm."

"My God," I said aloud, "what if you had dropped —"

"Shhh! They didn't and I didn't." The best part was that Kevin wouldn't be able to acknowledge the loss or institute a search. All he could do was sulk.

I began to feel lightheaded and for a while we got silly and began those bilingual puns

215

that get you so annoyed.

So, Marz, there went the guns. <u>Dans le boisson</u>, as Poppy said. We were exultant but I'm not giving this letter to Patricia to mail with the rest. I'll slip it in a box as we pass through Fairview, maybe, so you might get it late. Know that you are vindicated and I apologize for my defensiveness. Now that Poppy is a criminal and I am an <u>accessory</u> (like an alligator bag?) things will change. They will have to change, and we don't know how, but tonight it's the giggle latitudes where successful heist artists exult.

*Love, Tig*

*Moms,*                  *August 13, Niwot*

Hearing is September 10, and Blake's begun to look like a magician whose rabbit has come up skunk. There's fear in his eyes and desperation in his energy. He sees me and begins to argue, presenting his case. I've seen two social workers. I've told them how solid he and Anton are — not flapping fairies but family men. Others will defend . . .

With the boys, they're putting on an act that things are fine. Last Sunday we all went to Water World. It was crowded so we picnicked late. Blake took on the four kids and left Anton and me to clean up the lunch mess. Anton was down on his hands and knees among the Cheetos when he stopped and his head dropped. I saw he was crying. I went and held him.

He said, "Sol, how did Blake's wife get the pictures?"

I had thought there was only one. He told me there was a pile of them, different days, other places. It made it seem as though he cross-dressed all the time. He hadn't seen the group lately and he missed the laughter and the primping. When he went downstairs and locked the doors and dressed up all alone, he felt like a prisoner, a betrayer.

I held him in my arms, and wow, we were a couple, man and woman, lovers, nuzzling on our picnic blanket, while he cried it out. We lay that way until Blake and the kids came back. Later I asked Blake about the pictures.

There were thirty or so — Anton and his gang, dancing, sitting, talking, dressing.

All his friends had denied doing it.

So, it all looks "normal" again — They're back in the house; Cary and Sam still go over there, but when the kids are in bed and we're doing the dishes or watching TV, the fear leaks out. Once or twice I've seen them eye me, a quick look — could I have been the one? Someone had to have dropped the dime on Anton to Blake's wife and given her the weapon she needed. Was I the one?

I want it back the way it was. Those men — that family — did great things for us. They

217

got us through the pain of the divorce, being dumped and forgotten. We make a family — not conventional, but good for one another, and I want us back.

*Sol*


*Dear Grandma,*          *August 15, Grant Street*

Grandpa got me maps, four of them, of Boulder that he found in some antique store. Neat! Now I can see all the changes as they happened and even talk to people who were here in 1932, and then 1946 and '58 and '68, which is when the maps were printed. I'll show the people those maps and get them to remember what the city was like, and we can go over them, seeing how the populations moved and where and maybe why. It's called demographics. I have decided to go to college and study that.

How can I go to college when I feel so lousy about going back to school in only ten days? Answer: because in junior high, you study dumb stuff, and you do it with people who don't care and don't want to be there. Mom says make the best of it, which really means stop bugging her, but it's so boring! I could be finding out about cities and why people move and how neighborhoods grow and get rich or poor and how neighborhoods die — instead I'm studying things I don't want to know about.

I didn't mean to gripe to you. I got up this morning and realized it was August 15. So, I'm going to take my maps and go downtown and start walking, following the first map, the 1932 one. Fifteen days. Cripes!

*Love, Ben*


DIARY ENTRY                    *August 20,*
                               *Bendavis, Missouri*


Our Kevin smiles and leads The Walk slick as raw liver. He hasn't given himself away. He's only waiting us out, Poppy says.

Yesterday we came back from Bunion Rub and found that our tent had been searched. There was, literally, an air. The tent smelled of young, male feet, rank, animal. Pfew! Poppy asked if young men mark territory the way cats do. More like — Bengal tigers.

The search was easy. Packing and unpacking every day has trimmed us down to amazing simplicity.

The johns are the only privacy available in camp. We have the choice of silence — Kevin will replace the guns and be better guarded — or we can announce to The Walk that we found the guns and disposed of them. I'm for silence. Poppy has no proof, now, anyway.

*Dear Solidarity,*                      *August 22,*
*Raymondville, Missouri*

I've just sent another bundle of letters home to Marz so I can't refer to yours of the x, y, or z. It will be fun, I think, to open the bundle in five or ten years and see where we were during this year, spatially and spiritually — though I don't want us to start posing for one another.

Are you seeing Blake and Anton too much, and becoming too enmeshed in their problems? When your marriage with Lewis ended I was sad for you, but relieved, too. You had given it your best and Lewis wasn't a warm or generous man. You scanned the children for evidence of loss and psychological dislocation, and then you told me you would go out again, date, and enjoy male company, give it another try. Your friendship with Blake and Anton has been a harbor for all of you, but how has it fulfilled any deeper needs? They are gay, their friends are gay. Where will you find the male companionship you need, if all your time and energy are spent with a gay couple?

Please don't be angry — it's taken me hours to write this letter, hanging between what I wanted to say and a knowledge that I was interfering. But I'm not interfering, I'm voicing my doubts. Don't think I'm cold or unfeeling, either. Blake and Anton need help in this fight of theirs, and I'm proud of you for that, but I'm worried. The crusader in me cheers you on. The mother worries.

Love, Ma

*Dear Ben,*                              *August 22,*
Raymondville, Missouri

In my high school class there was a boy named Ambrose Hale. We lived in the city and very few of us had pets. Ambrose didn't, either, but he had an overwhelming interest in them, especially in dogs; <u>nothing</u> evoked a response from him like dogs. In art, he drew their pictures, he knew geography through the origins of breeds, history to him was the history of The Dog in America. He knew all the presidents and principal figures by their pets and while some of his teachers went tight in the jaw when he would read his reports (Dogs in the White House; Dogs in Early Philadelphia, etc.), I think his doing that got him through school.

I recommend that you follow Ambrose's example and use school as an excuse to study demography. It certainly has wider application in school than dogs. Some of the courses you'll have to pit bull through, but I think most of what you study can be a mirror of your interest. Let me know if you decide to put this into practice, and tell me how it works.

Love, Grandma

*Dear Marz,*        *August 22, Raymondville, M.*

Something is happening: Kevin has gone quiet. He still moves from one to another up the line in the morning and down the line in the afternoon, giving the news, hearing it, working The Walk like a good politician works a room.

But he used to — exhort all the time. Now he doesn't. He used to share himself with everyone. It was a unifying thing, and a great part of his charm. Now there are those he greets and those he slips past with only a word or a smile. At night his tent is busy but not with women or laughter. People come and go quietly, and there's a purposiveness about their visits. The quiet is so deep that the singles tents where there is sex action stand out like honky-tonks.

The people in the family tents ringing the outside of the camp and the people farther out in the loner tents seem unaware of a change. Or they choose not to notice. The stillness is not the stillness of peace.

Perhaps, I'm projecting guilt pictures on the wall of my cave, seeing things — Poppy says something is going on but she, too, is unable to find out what it is.

I had planned to mail this letter at our next stop, and now I'm glad I didn't get the chance. We were on the lunch break: deviled ham sandwiches for the meat folks, sprout and seed sandwiches for the 'tarians, and we were sprawled adoze against the trees at the edge of a plowed field. Half asleep, I heard a voice and looked up. It was Kevin, asking if he could sit with me and talk. I said sure.

Marz, it's so humid here I keep imagining there are rainbows hung in the trees. Everything vibrates with it, shimmers with undropped rain; the shimmer is the only energy in this place.

Kevin sat in that shimmer and began to talk as I drowsed and dozed, listened and didn't listen. He seemed to want no response from me, as he murmured in his monotone . . .

It was about age. About age and wisdom and how necessary it was to have someone of age and wisdom to be a guide, as to how life should be lived . . . mumble . . . mumble . . . I heard him say that <u>physical</u> energy comes from the lead male, the prince . . . I <u>thought</u> I heard that in my noontime torpor. I thought I heard him say that the <u>spiritual</u> energy, the darker part, comes from the Queen Mother, the woman in purple.

Could I have heard that? It's so . . . <u>purple</u>. Would I have dreamed anything like it? I've

223

dreamed odder things. What makes me think it happened is that I had a queasy feeling about it when I woke up, a sense of my own passivity under that voice. I never agreed or answered but I let myself hear him and doze under the caress of his voice, agreeing to what?

Later in the day, he smiled at me, walked toward me with his wide open look of acceptance and delight which had warmed me in the past. At Bunion Rub, he made a joke at my expense — a kidding that's so warm and inclusive that the person who's the subject of it feels elected to a valued place.

But I slid past the hook this time; I looked down. I'm awake now. The siesta is over. Queen Mother . . . Good Lord, why didn't I laugh?

*Tig*


*Dear Grandma,*               *August 18, Grant Street*

Maps don't work. That's because when they put in the highways and overpasses, the engineers take out the land features that were there before — they level hills, dam rivers and divert them — do all kinds of stuff that changes the landscape so there are only the biggest features of it left — like the Flatirons.

Boulder isn't the city I need to work on — no real city is, maybe. I need to make a model city, begin all over again with mountains and a river, a city <u>like</u> Boulder but one I build myself. Then I can move things around and make my city grow or shrink.

I asked Mom if I could use the storage space in the cellar and she said yes if I didn't take up all of it. The scale has to be really small so I can see everything. I don't think you can buy stuff like that — I think I'll have to make it. Little cubes of wood — balsa, maybe, to make houses.

What's good about it is that I'll be able to work a little on it every day and that will make up for having to go back to school.

Jason is okay, I guess. He's busy with his friends and they don't tell me where they go or what they do and they are definitely not interested in anything <u>I</u> think is important.

Hope isn't showing being pregnant. She just looks regular, but she has done something to her hair that makes her look old. I hate it. She smiles a lot, though. I saw her at work. Sometimes I like to go and have lunch with her.

*Love, Ben*

*Dear Gram,*                              *August 20,*
                          *Wild Horse Dream Ranch*

This is Larry's 44th day sober. I'm really proud of him. We have a calendar on the wall

225

and we mark off each day. In ADEPT everybody knows how many days he or she has. Larry's days are like money in an account. Some people have fewer days than he does, now.

He doesn't like to go to meetings because they are full of middle-class whites, but there's one in downtown Denver where there are Native Americans, and he goes there, sometimes. I have been to some of the open meetings and some for wives and husbands of alcoholics.

I want to argue. The meetings are down on what they call enablers. They say we shouldn't support the drinkers' drinking or make excuses or get in the middle between the drinker and the world. What if you really love the person? What if you know he's really good and sensitive but the world just sees him as a drunk Indian? You should have heard people talk about Larry when he was in the hospital. They acted like they didn't think he was a person. One orderly called him <u>Chief</u>. "I guess Chief has been in the firewater," I heard him say. Later he said to Larry, "Well, Chief, you've had a busy day," when he lifted him up. When they heard his name, one said, "He should have Walked Away from the bottle."

On the job, too, Larry says, they look through him. I don't think everybody treats him that way but when someone does, he feels it a lot.

Still, they say I shouldn't defend him. I

<u>don't</u> support his drinking, but everything depends on so few people. If Larry's boss turns against him, we'll be out of our house and he'll lose his job. If he can't get another job, we'll sink. Of course I'll stand between Larry and that part of the world. All of you are rich and secure and white. You don't depend on only one or two other people for your lives. I really think that's why Larry drank — because he had to deal with people who weren't dependable.

Ben came over here the other day. He's got this bird in his attic about building a toy city. I didn't get it, but Larry said he did. He said that it wasn't about toys at all, but a way of seeing something from above that you couldn't see when you were buried in it. Ben said Larry and Grandpa were the only people who understood him. Jason and his dumb friends just laugh and Mom and Dad are nice but don't understand. I'll tell you a secret. I don't, either.

When Ben came over he stared at me. He asked me when I'd bug out in front. I'm not really showing yet, but my breasts are bigger and my waistbands are all tight. Some clothes I can't get into anymore. Ben acts as though there's something weird about me having a baby. When I told him he'd be an <u>uncle</u> in February, he fell down on the ground and started to laugh and roll around and said he felt funny and old. I said he could think of the baby as his cousin.

We don't have many friends. I work all day and then go home and keep house. Larry is the same. He doesn't like any of the guys at work and the people from my job wouldn't understand the way we live. There might be some people from ADEPT later but now I guess Ben is our only friend. I'm so glad he and Larry get along.

*Love, Hope*

*Moms,*         *August 26, Detox, 2:00 A.M.*

I'm going to duck my head and let your advice fly over me or sidestep and let it pass. It isn't needed and can't be followed. Blake and Anton have made me feel more like a human being than I ever felt married to Lewis. Find someone suitable? The field has gotten rockier. On how many dates has the guy been delighted with me until I mention I have kids? How many weepy or raging soliloquies about ex-wives have I listened to? They say: "Your place or mine?" I pay for my own cocktails or dinner so I don't get any accusations about owing. They say, "Why do you think I asked you out?"

This was the level of savoir faire I was experiencing when my perfectly okay next door neighbors were transubstantiated to Florida and two reserved gay men and two nice-looking kids moved in. Sam went over. He came back grinning and stuffed with cake. Next day he took Cary and they both came back grinning and stuffed with cake. The third day I baked and went over.

You should have seen them: they stood together, close, arms crossed. We shook hands; they gave their names. Their smiles were measured. I told them which neighborhood kids to hire for yard work and which to leave alone. I saw them begin to ease up. They asked me in.

I appreciated what they had done with their house, one just like mine, room for room. At some moment during the house tour I knew they were gay and I knew I had done whatever it took to begin a friendship with them.

They are the brothers I never had, maybe the brothers no one has. Now they're in trouble and I'm happy and proud to be here for the fight. There's more to life than dating and marriage. You, of all people, should appreciate that. I've stopped fighting that war. If someone shows up out of the crowd, stops, sees me, comes toward me, brings me something besides his raw need, I'll be there. If not, that ought to be all right with me, and with you. Please.

*Sol*

I spent the day before yesterday with Ben. He wants to make a model city, the houses for which would be tiny blocks.

I asked him why he couldn't do it all on the computer. He could image anything in three dimensions, build, adapt, destroy and rebuild in seconds.

He gave me a funny look and said he knew there were programs like that, but he needed to be touching, making the thing.

He thought I wouldn't understand, but I do. I said that in another generation, people might not feel that need. Maybe even now, there are people who don't appreciate the feel of <u>putting</u> something here and taking it from there.

We went looking. All the toy houses were too big. I tried calling plastics factories. They have soft, square plastic rods that might be cubed with a razor. We bought some. The lumberyard had our plywood sheet. Frank cleared a space for the arrangement in the basement and even gave us some sawhorses to support the plywood. He may not understand what Ben is after, but he's happy to help. I brought over that ugly floor lamp.

What does Ben want to see that he couldn't image on the computer? I don't know, but I know that at thirteen, Ben has begun to educate himself. He's still a boy in all other ways, but when <u>his</u> subject or any of its elements comes up, he changes before my eyes. We have discussions of surprising depth and range. I don't know whether adolescence will cripple Ben or whether he won't even notice it in the grip of his interest. I'm a little worried that now in his headlong charge at knowledge he may miss some of the things he needs to humanize it. He's already a mile wide and spreading.

His inner teacher is deft, subtle, even sophisticated. And he's still a good kid. At the lumberyard he saw some odd lengths of wood and bought them cheap. We took them over to Hope and Larry's and left them in a pile at their door. I wouldn't have thought of it.

Do me a favor now. You've stopped the "I'm okay" calls. I know they're a pain, that you must wait on line, sometimes in the rain, but I need those calls or I start to worry.

*Marz*


*Marz —*      *August 29, Poplar Bluff, Missouri*

They're gone: Kevin and eighteen Walkers and all our money and a van loaded with food and supplies and a water truck and the cook wagon and two cars, and no sign of where.

I have the time to tell you because we're camped here in shock, regrouping and wondering if we can go on, wondering if we can even afford to go home. We are adrift and without our leadership, not only Kevin, but many of the most active young people, four of our best planners, all but one of the advance people, and four council people. I'd call, but the phone is a mile away and the park service people are here. We're sending letters with the officer who will mail them.

Let me set the scene. We came into these mountains and began to see the bones of old farms, derelict barns, and farmhouses, whose spines and ribs had been hand-hewn oak, and the old mortise-and-tenon work you love.

The holdings are small, far smaller than the smallest farm in Kansas or eastern Colorado, and it's easy to people the land from the imagination because the scale here is so much closer to human size. We re-create the man with mule and a bull-tongue plow, his wife growing flax and spinning. The land here is watered by a hundred creeks and streams and could grow wonderful crops if present undergrowth is anything to go by. What hasn't been set out as farmland in the valleys or on the arms of these hills heaves forests of timber and cover for innumerable animals.

Kevin saw Eden. "This is what we should be doing!" he yelled at Bunion Rub the night I last wrote to you. He said we should be farming land, hewing wood to build, learning wood and stone, earth, animals We looked at him, having walked these days with the same ideas in our own minds, in a kind of bemused agreement.

He sounds incoherent as I write his words, but it was the incoherence of someone responding viscerally to a tidal pull. We were all touched by the dream of sufficiency and independence that overwhelms the most dedicated sophisticate, struggling with a complicated and paradoxical world — come back, renounce, forget.

They have pot, Kevin and his friends, but pot is a bliss-out, not a blow-out, and I don't think any of them have slept from that night on, except during siesta times.

Two nights ago I saw him alone again. We older Walkers have learned that our encampment's most important position is near the Porta Pottis. I was up, wondering what the Sioux arrangements would have been for elders rising on icy nights.

This time he was sitting on a shelf of rock just outside the perimeter of the tents. Solitude is rare on The Walk and an etiquette has emerged to guard it. We nod and pass on, not stopping unless we are asked. I prepared to go by; Kevin asked me to stop on my way back. It seemed more than a casual request.

The dew here falls in a mist, green as frogs and full of their talk. We murmured a word or two. Then he said he was thinking about leaving The Walk. He wanted more than a list of understandings derived from questionnaires. He said his group would need a wise woman. I refused with thanks and said there was a man back home. He began to talk about bringing you to The Group. He didn't see me grinning in the dark. He told me to think about what he had said.

Next morning I told Poppy. We were moving down from Elsinore through the National Forest — you're still following us on the maps, aren't you? We had a two-day stop in Poplar Bluff. There's a VA hospital here, a community college, a reformatory. I didn't see Kevin, so I thought he must be at the new campground with the advance team. As you know, the water and food trucks go ahead, the supply truck and two cars follow, so when the supply truck passed us at about 10:00 A.M. we weren't surprised. Poplar Bluff is large enough and the shopping list had gotten long. Trucks often pull ahead for gas, etc.

We arrived at about five in the afternoon. There were the Porta Pottis on their truck and the supply wagon with what looked like a jumble of tents and equipment, nothing like what we had packed up in the morning. The food truck was gone. The advance team was gone. We stood staring. Who else was gone? How many Walkers were left?

We began to count ourselves. Where was Annie, where was Chas? This couple, that?

We went to the tent and clothing truck to see what had been taken and we were unpacking it when two other trucks drove up and a horde of boy scouts descended from them and began setting up their camp. The advance team hadn't even cleared the site for us. After a lot of talk and frayed tempers, we compromised for space and by ten it was quiet enough for us to meet. Kevin had taken all our cash, too, we learned. Some of us had credit cards and those people would have to go into Poplar Bluff early to get food.

We have no food truck and no water truck. We have no money. We voted unanimously to continue The Walk. We are more than halfway across the country and the thought of disbanding, of going home without a try was too much like defeat. After the vote, we spent three or four minutes fighting tears and then began to cut our problems into bite-size pieces. Poppy asked how long we would stay here.

Tomorrow I will go into Poplar Bluff and ask you to wire some money.

*Tig*


*Dear Marz,*

Early this morning I went to a branch of dear old Uni-Bank and talked to the president. I don't think it was my gift for sudden eloquence. I think I looked old and desperate. Perhaps the man saw headlines about heart-less-business-crushing-a-well-meaning-if-dotty-band of idealists. Perhaps he was a closet idealist himself. He made some calls, then let me talk him into coming back to the campground to check us out. I introduced him around. Others had been working, too, and by noon we had leads on canned and dried food and many of us had also wired home for money. We called our angels, and, of course, I called you.

Back at the campground, Poppy was nowhere in sight. I was annoyed, then worried. I had thought the two of us would work together and I had leads on where we could get money to lease or rent some cooking supplies. As you remember, the food truck had been beautifully adapted to cook and serve.

Three of the men had gone to the police station, hoping they might track Kevin and his group and get our things back. Five vehicles were gone — the water truck, the food truck, two cars, and a van. All of his people could ride. If their group wanted to disappear, the police told us, there were innumerable small back roads and hundreds of trails leading to abandoned farms or logging camps. Kevin had taken enough supplies for his group to disappear for days or even weeks. They could buy food from farmers, or in small towns here and there, taken for campers or fishermen. The area was full of strangers, now. The officers told our men they would ask around. Both trucks were distinctive and might be spotted but the probabilities weren't very good.

In the afternoon, we re-invented our administrative council. We couldn't move without water, which we drink in huge amounts. We need water to wash the dishes, us, clothes. We can eat cold food, but sooner or later we will need to cook. We need more cars — we still have two and those are for our advance team. Where is Poppy? I'm really worried, now.

I'll call again when I can.

*Love, Tig*


*Dear Marz,*          *August 31, Poplar Bluff*

It was a blessing to hear your voice and to do the necessary crying and sniveling in your ear. You didn't say I told you so, to your great credit. I'm raw as someone dragged across a highway. The reality of our situation has barely begun to sink in. We have no money. Kevin has taken thousands from our bank account and cash, which was food and water and rental and service on the Porta Pottis and a cushion against the things that happen, storms, sickness, torn tents, flood, fire, and famine.

We're scared, even as we go out looking for backers. We worry about water and food. In the heat of the day here, we feel chilly, damp with dread. Few of us are wealthy and those few have been tapped so many times they are beginning to be resentful. We can't leave without water and unless we have money we can't leave at all. Poppy has disappeared.

*August 31, Evening*

Poppy. <u>Poppy</u>. She showed up after supper. I was away in town, meeting with men from Rotary and another service club. When I came back, the place was a madhouse. People were running around beating one another on the back, dancing, screaming. Poppy was at the center of it all, her hair a renovated, blazing red, and standing with her was another trompe l'oeil exhibit with raven tresses and a makeup job thick as tub-caulk. I fought through the melee.

She asked where I had been, with that disingenuous raising of eyebrows, and introduced Lucile, with a hand on the stranger's shoulder. Lucile had gotten us a water truck and a food wagon.

Later, after we had wined and dined Lucile (grape juice and lunchmeat sandwiches on hideous white bread), she drove off to cheers and waves. We repaired to our tents and I all but dove at Poppy.

Apparently, even major film studios no

longer keep the props and clothing they need in huge storage areas. A script calls for a 1931 police van, a covered wagon, and a full portrait of Rutherford B. Hayes. It's become cheaper to find these items when they're needed and send them to the location of a shoot than to store them for a possible use that may never come. There are people who hunt down and list such things, then wait for a call. Lucile is one such hunter.

I asked where Poppy hunted <u>her</u>.

They had worked together for years in wardrobe, Poppy said. When Lucile retired she came back home to Arkansas and began scouting. Poppy called her and told her our story. Lucile sat down at her computer and got the closest working water truck, called the man, told <u>him</u> our story, and damned if he didn't give us use of the truck and drive it to Lucile's. She did the same thing with the food wagon. Then she and her son drove them up here.

The food wagon belongs to a defunct circus; the man who has it was glad to put it to use at a very low rate. These things deteriorate in storage.

I leaned over to where she lay on top of her wrinkled sleeping bag. I told her she had saved The Walk.

She didn't hear me; she was fast asleep.

So, we're scraping ourselves off the floor and we'll move tomorrow. There's a feeling of triumph, and an anxiety we haven't had before. I can't put my finger on its cause. The guys who want to track Kevin down and prosecute are furious, but the sheriff told us frankly that if we were going to pursue the case, we would have to stay here. Getting to Kevin and getting our money would mean the end of The Walk and we have voted to continue. The reality of our situation demands we go on. Pray we can —

*Tig*

# September

જ

DIARY ENTRY           *September 2, Road WW*

On Road WW, to Dexton. We move through, passing out and receiving our questionnaires in a dream. We imitate ourselves, smiling, answering questions, telling people that we have put our private lives aside for a year to go and see for ourselves what rural America is like. At evening, we set up camp and the smiles drop off like sheets from a mirror in a house of mourning. We look into our own faces reflected in the faces of other Walkers. We miss Kevin.

What kind of power did we cede to him that we should be so bereft? Was he a brother, lover, son? He helped us along The Walk, cheered us, made us feel competent and graceful, took our fears in his hands and worked them into excitement, and handed them back to us to blow up into party balloons.

Bunion Rub is in chaos. Everyone's needs and ego trips carry us away. Last night it lasted two hours. Bicker-bicker. I want to scream. When Kevin was here, people were ashamed to air their pettiness to the whole

Walk. We've had Better, and Better stole our supplies, our money and morale, and rode off. The Bakers left The Walk this morning before wake up. They've been defensive since the stealing incident with Parie, a problem I thought we had solved so well.

We're still on The Walk and that's what matters, now: to find its rhythm again.

Kevin has left us alone with the heat and the sweating and the road and ourselves.


DIARY ENTRY *September 4, Morehouse*

A rain — I've never experienced such utterness, all water. We woke to it, flooding in our tents. Some of the tents had been staked in easy earth last night, now flowing mud, and the tents moved on a curded wash of muddy water. Water poured down on us, no purchase in the mud to fold up and go. We were near the town, an eighth of a mile from the river, and now the river is here. Some of the hardier men went for help and the rest of us pushed the foundered food truck and then the van and then the water truck up to the road, Highway 60, almost a mile, and there we stayed in the shower that steamed with its own energy. We had to keep counting ourselves. Twice our cars began to wash away and we had to run and heave them out of the push of water and back to the road. Rain let up a little and some people with heavy equipment came and towed us to Morehouse and got us bedded down at the school. People had filled the gym already and overflowed into the auditorium and the halls. It was still raining.

They were all there, singles, families, filthy and marooned, wet to the bone and some with that stare. The trees protect the part of The Walk we had just left, we were told, but east of here floods sometimes took the low-lying farms. There were a hundred creeks, branches, streams to go mad when it rains.

Our questionnaires were back in the trucks, soaked, but we talked to farmers and travelers and stranded tourists and retirees whose mobile homes had foundered outside of town. People wanted to get their minds off the ruin nothing could change, and some we didn't think might be able to respond, pulled themselves together and spoke to us.

The air in the place — close with so many bodies — fumes and reeks with heat and moisture. To sleep is to drown in it. I woke again and again, hanging in the clammy straitjacket of my own clothes.


DIARY ENTRY          *September 6, Morehouse*

Another day of rain, trapped in the school. We entertained kids, we put on a play — Noah's Ark. In the afternoon the downpour slowed and early in the evening, stopped. The worst part <u>then</u> was the sanitation. There was mud in the school toilets, which had begun regurgitating waste. Our Porta Pottis were a godsend. The water systems were fouled, too, so the health department has been bringing in water, inoculating people, and setting up rules for use and saving. Later, they brought more johns. We have decided to stay and help clean up. The radio told us flooding was local.

The sun woke up the next afternoon, too bright, and too hot, over the steaming mud. Trees were down, houses choked. We went out to the trucks. A man who had helped to pull us to the road had pulled the food truck into his own garage. Our food and cooking supplies were saved. The water truck's engine had been soaked but spared the mud because of its high clearance. The cars and the van had been laved with mud, a window broken in the van, and debris washed in.

I saw strength and ego rise among the geniuses of The Walk. Their faces couldn't hide the secret exultation in their powers to resurrect things. Each of the three, Murray, Todd, and Mary Lou, got an assistant and began to take apart the fouled engines. Others of us, including Poppy and me, were assigned to clean the cars, the van, the clothes, and the tents. The rest of The Walk went to help the town pick itself up.

We will be here two days longer drying out upholstery in the cars and getting mud out of the engines. The Geniuses say it may take them a day longer to get everything running again.

The people who have gone to help in town must have done splendid work; each of them brought invitations to eat at houses spared the worst of the flooding. Yesterday women came and pulled us away to a picnic on the swept-off main street. There were tables and chairs brought from everywhere. The gas lines were back in service so food was cooked, and we ate the product of a hundred canning shelves and root cellars saved from the mud. The eating and talking started quietly, but people seemed impelled to describe what they had seen, even though it was common experience. Then an ebullience took us all. No one had died, no one was seriously injured, people told us. The town would rebuild itself. Here and there they joked at the incongruities the flood had produced — two calves, a dozen cats and dogs, and a squall of chickens had been found in the church. Someone said "choir practice" and we found ourselves laughing harder than the joke was worth.

The Walkers had taken places all along the block-long row and after most of the food had been eaten, our hosts began to question us.

Where was I from? Walking the country — really? What kind of work did I do?

I sat next to the principal of the grade school. "Look down this table," he said, "and see where's my Merle and my Laura Anne, who should be sitting here. They wanted to stay but there isn't the work. People laugh, I know; 'Mayberry,' they say, but not everybody needs New York City or Hollywood to make a life in. When your kids move away and marry and your grandkids are raised in Chicago, Raleigh, or Dallas, what good does it do you? Where's the joy?" I didn't answer, but I could have. There are worse things than happy children at a distance. Others talked about better lives than Morehouse allows, and others asked, "What does better mean?" It was night by then and we were under the town's streetlights. Children slid off chairs and benches into their parents' arms asleep and were laid on blankets at the sides of the street. Someone came and sprayed us all with mosquito repellent, as the old people recalled other floods and droughts, hard freezes and hard times. Someone began "Abide with Me," and we all took up the melody. Our exhaustion was part of the evidence of the daily miracle.

*Dear Marz,*              *September 10, Charleston*

We're on the road again and I'm so glad you were home for my call. We're still shaking dried mud out of clothes and shoes, eating grit, pulling lungfuls of the still-sour air of mildew in tents and clothes, but we're away and we have ridden to catch up. That's why we're at Charleston, farther than we could have gotten for leaving Morehouse at noon.

They saw us off, almost the whole town. As we waved to them, they to us, I thought about Kevin again. How much he would have loved the challenge of this flood and its cleanup. The help we gave has bonded us; some of our morale has returned; how much, I can't tell, yet.

This was our departure: We had packed the tents and repacked the stiff clothing. We had tested the trucks, the van, the cars, and we set off, someone singing a pop song from the years after I stopped listening. We walked through the town, seeing no one, and were about a quarter of a mile down the road when we saw a crowd filling the way in front of us and spilling over on either side. As we came closer we recognized townspeople and called out to them. They moved aside to let us pass, and as we did, they reached out to one or another of us, patting arms, shaking hands, saying good-bye, usually with a joke. Someone invited us back for Christmas. Then they all took that up. "Come back for Christmas, we'll be cleaned up by then!" "But then we wouldn't recognize you," one of us yelled, and we heard them laughing as we walked the road carrying Morehouse in our clothes.

But it's good to be on the road again, moving.

T.

*Dear Tig,*                    *September 8, The Hill*

I had begun to worry about not hearing from you. Spoiled people we are; we think any silence is dereliction, not natural circumstances: flood, fire, act of God. The TV news never mentioned your flood — too busy with the local murders and drive-by shootings. I dutifully traced your hypothetical moves on the big map and had put you well into Kentucky.

Let me ventilate a little of my own unease, now that I know you're all right. One of the unspoken reasons we split up all those years ago was that I am used to an organized kind of life. When we met at the training sessions in D.C., I was at the outermost reach of my adolescent rebellion and you were just in the suburbs of yours. When we moved to Boulder and this job, I was happy to settle into it and learn the ropes of its modest bureaucracy. I contented myself with working well inside the net.

But now, I'm tired. The tangle gets thicker, the creative possibilities diminish. We thought computers would simplify things. They don't. I want to leave. I would go except that I'd lose my retirement. I'll soldier on for the four years and try not to strangle in the rules while I serve my time.

It's sad to be saying that. I love the <u>kind</u> of civil engineering I do. Your environmental buddies say the building of roads and bridges separates us from nature. I see it as modifying nature so that we can use the environment without destroying it. I had hoped to retire with a feeling of accomplishment and pride. Rules and paperwork and "channels" grow irrespective of the party in power or its governmental theory. The systems we established to keep us honest and report our work to the world now determine our every move.

What has made it worse for me is the comparison I feel when I watch Ben. As inspiring as it is to see him race to his calling, open it, look at it, turn it this way and that, then to claim it as his, there's a part of me that says, "I was once like that." I feel betrayed by the difference between his joyousness and my lethargy and I want to walk off the job, retirement and all, and try to find some other work, some work I can love before I'm pounded into the floor and become one with the linoleum. 1. We need the money. 2. Might there not be something new I could try for the next twenty years or so? Where should I look? I know I'm competent at least and, in my moments, creative. We're all afraid of growing too old. At work, Hudson dyes his hair like Poppy, and he has gone for cosmetic surgery and starved himself so that he looks like something smooth and salt-dried washed up on a beach.

These are my thoughts and this is my life while you shovel mud and reorganize your psyches after your debacle with Kevin. Perhaps some clever engineering might have eased the effects of the flood on town and Walk. Your people are so enamored of nature left to itself that they don't take advice from either one of us. Alas.

*Marz*

*Moms,*                              *September 9, Detox*

Dad just told me about the con job your leader pulled on you and about the flood. You didn't answer my last letter — almost three weeks — so I thought you were pissed at what I said. Now I find out you were a lion tamer in a cage full of teeth, who hears her phone ringing.

News: Upheaval in Detox. I've told you about Bob Kester — Kester the Pester — well, he has left. I came in yesterday and said to the secretary, "Has someone painted the walls in here? The whole place looks brighter." We laughed.

I've been in my own world for a while, working, getting Sam off to first grade. Yes, it's happened. Blake's boy, Erik, is in his class and that will ease his way. Sam was eager to start, and I don't want one bit of that lost to boredom and the cruelty of other kids. So, I've been a bit of a bitch at the school, checking it all out.

I used to sneer at the women's magazine stories about the big loss moms were supposed to feel when their firstborn went off to school. "That's for the cookie and PTA crowd," I said. Bull. I left Sam, got into the car to go to work, and burst into tears. So much for the tough, modern, professional woman I say I am.

*Sol*

*Dear Gram,*                   *September 10,*
*Wild Horse Dream Ranch*

I went shopping with Mom yesterday for maternity clothes! You should have seen her. She was trying so hard to smile and be proud. The saleswoman was cooing around me and I was cooing back, feeling so excited because I am starting to show — I really am. There were other women there and they were all bigger and some were huge, but I won't be, the saleswoman said, because I'm small boned. I was secretly happy to be there and we took half the day doing it because where I am I don't get much chance to see and talk to other women about women's things — you know, are your breasts growing and how is your morning sickness and things like that. I want to be strong for Larry and not always be talking about how it feels to be sick and feel funny emotionally.

I cry, sometimes, for no reason. I can be bird-happy and then someone will say something, or I'll hear sad music, and off I go. Sometimes I feel miserable and sick and ugly. I looked in the store mirror yesterday and nearly died. There are dark pigment patches on the sides of my face. Mom says it's natural, and will go away. Larry laughed and said I'm turning Indian because I have Indian blood and an Indian baby inside me, but I think it's hideous and it made me cry. I smell funny, too, some of the time.

<u>But</u> yesterday I got to talk about it all and it made me feel so much better. Mom took me out to lunch and told me all about her experiences being pregnant with me and the boys, how she felt and how long her labor was. I've never asked her before, but now it's all stuff I want to know so badly she can't tell me about it fast enough. If Larry had to hear it all, he'd have a fit.

He's been restless at work, lately, and I tell

him it's a good sign. He's now 64 days into sobriety — two months and three days. He told me after he told this in his meeting that he never had been sober, I mean not drinking at all, longer than two weeks since he was 13, and that two weeks was when he was in jail. He has cut down on his meetings, and that means he can be with me more, and do work on the house while the days are still long and the weather good.

He's restless at work because people don't show him any respect. Yesterday a lady came in with a battery to be replaced and yelled at Larry because she said he took the old one out wrong and ruined her alternator. The boss had to give her a new alternator, and while he didn't dock Larry's pay, he yelled at him, too. When I make a mistake at work, it's usually on the computer and Steve says, "Too bad you've got a dumb girlfriend . . ." (meaning the computer); "Tell her again and maybe this time she'll get it right." You can see how my working conditions and Larry's are different. I hate it when he comes home sad and angry. At work people ask my opinion of things and a few customers have begun to come and ask for me specially because they know me and trust my judgment. Larry says people look through him like he wasn't there.

Grandpa was back on the mall today — he <u>said</u> to buy something. I told him there wasn't one thing in the store that would be for him.

He said, "Oh, yeah?" and went away with a purple sunvisor hat with daisies painted on it. I think Grandpa came in to see my stomach.

*Love, Hope*

*Tig,*                      *September 10, The Hill*

I stopped in at Wild Duds to see our granddaughter. She's trying too hard. She's as bouncy and pert as an ambitious clerk at a place called Wild Duds should be, but there's something stretched and strained in her smile. She wanted me to tell her how pregnant she looked, but all I saw was the urgency in her gestures and the strain in her face. She was wearing pants with a pleated top — I seem to remember you in such an outfit, but it didn't make her look any more pregnant than she did a month ago. She showed me the "shadow" that was darkening up near her hairline on both sides of her forehead. It was there, very lightly. I bought something and left and felt heartsick. I didn't know where to go so I sat down on the mall and pretended to watch the people passing.

I remember our first year of marriage as a year lived walking several feet above the streets of Boulder, but if I probe that memory I realize it's almost pure invention, or perhaps the memory of an hour stretched to cover the whole time. We did have ecstatic moments and joyous times. I remember our gratifying discoveries in the area of sex and my happiness with a compatible job, our planning, our hopes.

Then I make myself remember the fights we had, the missteps, the sudden angers, the struggle against our dependence and for our identities inside the mr. and mrs. we were. Yours was so great you had to leave. I'm not dragging that up again, I'm trying to say something about Hope and Larry; I'm trying to convince myself that the strain I saw on Hope's dear face is normal, that she's pregnant too soon and he's untrained and not ready to see how much more training he needs, that both of them are too proud, and that all of that will work itself out in their lives together. It hurts.

*It hurts. Marz*


*Dear Marz,    September 16, Aurora, Kentucky*

I can hear you sighing. I remember how my emotions pitched and veered during pregnancy. If you got Hope on a bad day, her strain might even look like despair. Check on her now and then. Does the mood lift?

We are about to cross Kentucky Lake to a huge recreational area, where there should be lots of tourists to fill out our questionnaires.

Our atrophied steering council has begun

to grind into action; Poppy and I have decided that however harmful it was to the people of Morehouse, the flood was providential for us. Kevin gave us one myth of heroism to live by and when he took it away with him, we had to march without a rippling banner of any kind. Our superman capes were gone, our ruby slippers carried off, The Walk shorn of its glory.

Do I sound like a heroism junkie? I know the Devil with the radiant face: The Walk succeeds, we are understood and appreciated. I meet with the president and speak to Congress. We arrive at Woods Hole to cheers.

Four new people have come on and two might stay the course. The new people show us admiring eyes and in them we see ourselves heroically. Now, we need it. "You've been buried in the snow in the Rockies?" "You've been in a flood?" "How quickly you set out, how deft you are with your questionnaires!"

I'll call you from Hopkinsville. We are still very much "In Country." We have gone many days and will go many more before we come to a population center. Our mission was threefold, which turned out to be one-fold too many; we were to inform ourselves, inform the nation, and collect signatures for our petitions. By choosing to focus on environmental change in rural areas, we have seen our fill of ghost villages, and land going back to scrub, the way it might have been before towns sprang up along the waterways and trails west.

Towns shrink, the ambitious leave. The railroad tracks get torn up for scrap and new industry settles elsewhere.

I had the local's view of this from two old men we encountered at a run-down store still selling fishbait and sundries to sport fishermen and tourists passing through. It had once been a much bigger store, part of the commerce of a town, and we had stopped to ask directions to our night camp. My age does wonders here. A look at this gray hair, these wrinkles, and the locals are off on a ride of reminiscence: The old school was over there, the old mill, there. "We was farmers here, but as much woodmen as farmers because our grand-daddies realized that the old way wasn't going to work forever . . ." If I could only preserve the sounds of those words and the way the men said them. I always thought that "hit warrn't" and "cain't git no hep" were exaggerations, but they are still here, if fading. We sat with the old men for an hour and I would have stayed into the night except that Patricia came and pulled us away. The speech is low and slow but the old men took delight in it and relished its metaphors and colorings. "They have done blowed the lantern out on this place," one of them said, and the other, "Ain't but two songs sung here no more: Too Late and Not Enough."

The humidity slows everything here. In the

weedgrown main street the dogs chased the cats at a walk.

Hope writes that Larry is restless at work. Is he seeing that they will soon have medical bills to pay and winter expenses, even if they burn wood? Won't he take anything from Justice and Frank when the time comes? What about help from us? Can you ask him?

*Love, Tig*

*Moms,*                          *September 16, Niwot*

I went to the Boulder Mall yesterday and took Hope out for lunch. Her boss is sweet on her. She was bouncing along full of plans, and after I left her I found myself in a cat fit, and realized it was envy. She's all lit up with her importance in the world as a mother-to-be. She went on describing their plans to warm their cabin for the baby. Lewis didn't want kids, you'll remember; he acted as though my pregnancies had been achieved without him. He didn't like my pregnant body. Hope says Larry likes her to take her clothes off and that he studies her belly until they both laugh. No wonder her boss is captivated; the whole world is a magic place for her. Everyone cooperates by reflecting the light she casts.

I thought Jussy would like to hear about our visit, so I called. When I told her about their plans for the cabin she hit the ceiling.

Hope and Larry had promised to move when the baby comes, to accept help in getting a place with running water and electricity that wasn't miles out of town. "He's weaseled out of every promise he made. School? No. Moving? No. They spend their time fixing a house they have no legal rights in, no lease. Hope defends his stubborn decisions. Larry won't see us, and when she makes him come, he's frozen-faced and monosyllabic."

I think Hope and Larry promised to move to shut Frank and Jussy up. Jussy makes demands but she also helps. Now, I'm in the middle and will seem to be disloyal to someone, no matter what I do. My phone call did no good and got Jussy steamed.

Sam is in bed at Blake and Anton's with chicken pox, which Blake's kids also have. Cary and I will hole up at our house. Anton stays home on the odd number days and Blake on the even. I hate the downside to this modern independence we've all fought for. Without Blake and Anton, I'd be like other divorced mothers for whom any sickness means risking the job, or leaving sick children in the care of God knows who. I couldn't help thinking of your letter asking why I didn't get out and into a social life that would lead to The Altar. I'm functioning, and thanks to Blake and Anton, safely, and with a masculine presence for the boys. I think I'm coming down with something, too.

We're all trying not to mention the dead elephant in the living room: Blake's custody hearing coming up soon. We pretend everything is the way it was before the mess started. He has been combing cases and calling his lawyer with citations. It looms and we walk around it and listen to our own footsteps tracking us.

*Sol*


*Dear Hope,*          *September 19, Caledonia, Ky.*

Bless you for keeping me company on this Walk. I remember morning sickness and the swings of mood that amazed the men around me. They have their moods, too — fear of being supplanted in our attention, fear of having to support the dependent little being, fear of the absolute difference that having a baby in the house confers on day and night. Modern life is harsh on young parents. It makes them do the job alone too much of the time. You have the advantage of having aunts and grandparents in the area. I'll be back soon after the baby is born and you'll have some of the tribal feelings Larry wants. We can take some of the constancy of baby care off your shoulders.

If it's possible to learn from the mistakes of others, here was mine: During my pregnancy I was so taken up with <u>my</u> feelings and my changes and with my cause (I stayed political through my pregnancy because of a fear of losing my core of individuality, of becoming "the mother"), I forgot that Marz must have been suffering changes subtler and less rewarding than mine. I experienced rapture and despair within moments of one another and thought it strange that he was moving away from me. Give Larry room, take up his cause.

If I have enough of your goodwill for some more advice, it would be that you try to convince Larry that we mean well for you and for him. Haven't your mother and father offered help? Yes, they were against your marriage at such an early age, but they haven't disowned you, have they? Perhaps you can show Larry that he's not in an enemy camp. It's true that your parents don't understand rural living but they are being realistic about the difficulty of having a baby in the poverty real rural living imposes. Think about this.

*Love, Gram*


*Dear Grandma,*      *September 20, Grant Street*

It's working, a little, your idea about how I can exist in school. Any time I get my choice of what to study or write about, I write about demographics. Maybe the teachers don't care what we write about because in our school, most of the interest is on stuff that goes on before or after class. Girlfriends — boy-friends . . .

Which reminds me: Jason has a girlfriend, Kim. They have been having sex since the beginning of summer, but Mom just found out. Then she and Dad took Jason on as a project, telling him about condoms and AIDS and VD. He knows about all that, but none of it matters to him. "Old people count their money and eat vitamins," he tells me. "I'm alive. Kim is alive, too. She's beautiful and free. Nothing is going to turn her into a careful old lady who counts and measures and figures everything."

She doesn't look free to me. She looks like she's twenty-five years old. She has her hair pulled up and then frizzed out like a radish and her clothes are so tight she has no room to breathe. That's not free. Breathlessness must be why she keeps her mouth open all the time. I think she's hoping some air will get to her that way. All I've ever heard her say is "un-huh" or "uh-uh," and once, just once, she said, "Oh, Jayy-<u>sonn</u>."

Mom called Kim's mother and said she thought the two of them were too young to be having sex. Kim's mother told Mom she was old-fashioned and that we should let the "young people" use the guest bedroom the way they do at <u>their</u> house. "If you don't, they'll only do it in some inappropriate or uncomfortable place, like the backseat of a car."

"God forbid!" Mom said.

Kim's mother said that sex repression might mark Jason and Kim for life and make them mentally ill. The funny thing is that if Jason was Aunt Sol's son, his having sex at fifteen wouldn't be so much of a problem. It isn't that she doesn't care as much as Mom does, but she doesn't have Mom's idea of the way things are supposed to be. I'm a lot like Mom, so I understand when she says she wants to shake Hope and hit Jason with a brick (which is what she told Dad she wanted to do).

I think she loves Hope best and is most hurt by what Hope did. Don't ever tell her I said this. She always says we're equally precious to her and Dad, but how is that possible? Hope was meant for big things — to be an artist or a musician. She had all those dancing lessons, remember? Mom and Dad don't see me as having much imagination, and I don't.

Thanks for the Jefferson Davis tee shirt. I'm getting a neat collection. I know Jason likes his, too, and so do Sam and Cary.

*Ben*

*Later*

P.S. I forgot. Hope and Larry had a big fight yesterday at our house. Mom and Dad had invited them over for some barbecue because the weather was so good. I could tell Hope and Larry had started the fight at home. Larry was mad at all the maternity clothes Hope and Mom bought. He was talking about how Hope was shaming him by having a "fancy wardrobe" that made him feel like a beggar. We all tried to be friendly and change the subject, but when they saw it wouldn't work, Mom said that mothers and fathers help. They help on Indian reservations, in Paris, New York, and Borneo. Getting a daughter outfitted isn't a slight to the son-in-law any more than if a tribal family did it.

Jason piped up with something that sounded like, "Like it or lump it," and that got Larry going again. He started cursing and then he and Dad nearly fought. Hope kept trying to quiet both of them down, and Larry started shoving her and Jason said if he did it again, he and Dad would make Larry pay. Larry went home. Dad made Hope stay until it was almost midnight and she was crying and begging him to take her back, and saying that Larry would be over his temper and it was just a time when his frustrations were building up. That's when Mom and Dad started to get angry. Mom was angry that we had let Larry go on his motor-cycle in the mood he was in. What if there was an accident?

Dad: "Is that supposed to scare me? Wouldn't I be devastated if that kid totaled himself?"

Mom got upset. Dad said it was how he really felt.

Hope sat there and cried. I don't think she heard them because whenever they said that stuff, I started talking to cover what they were saying.

Anyway, it's all back to square one. Hope is home with Larry, Jason is over at Kim's house, probably making love, and Dad and Mom are okay when the subject isn't Jason and Kim or Hope and Larry.

*Love, Ben*


*Dear Marz,*          *September 24, On the Road*

Ben wrote about Larry's tantrum during a visit to Justice and Frank. Have you heard about it? Larry doesn't want the family giving her anything. Ben didn't say whether Larry had been drinking. The rage is bad enough, but it scares me more if it comes when he's sober. I want to fly home, go to that cabin of theirs, and beat Larry senseless. Maybe our "niceness" is part of the problem. Maybe he needs a large, screaming family, a father-in-law who threatens his life periodically, aunts who demand, a Gorgon mother-in-law. Perhaps our displeasure is worse for him than overt screaming. Could that be? Can we change? Can he?

Hope needs some iron in her spine.

265

I'm aware that I'm fulminating from a safe distance. "Do this, fix that." Do you think there is anything we can do?

Two more Walkers have joined us. Maybe we'll make up the number Kevin's defection took away. They are an engaged couple and they are so sweet and dear and in love it makes me ache. I see Hope and Larry in them without all the anger and posturing. How I wish . . . How I want such a love for Hope. She's too young to be pulling herself away from us.

*Love, T.*

*Dear Tig,*            *September 25, The Hill*

When I heard about Larry's outburst from Justice, I went out and rented two videos — old movies I had enjoyed years ago. Then, I asked Frank over to see them with me. Ever the respectful son-in-law, he asked me why I'd want to see those old creakers. I said that when you can't fix a situation the best place to go is the video store. I <u>wanted</u> to go over to that shack of my granddaughter's and beat the young man senseless (or let him beat <u>me</u> senseless). Frank passed on the video evening.

I watched "Dial M for Murder" and "Strangers on a Train." Hope won't budge and I can't stand to hear her justifications of his behavior — we're daunting, we make him defensive, he's sensitive to our racism, and on and on. I meet my childhood self in the impotence I feel. For all of Hope's embraces and her cry of joy, "Grandpa!" when I come — and it's a word that sends delight through me in the sound — I'm not free to walk toward her and pull her out of the way of danger and anguish. The delight gives me nothing but itself; no privileges, no special call on her time, her attention, or her obedience. I have no power beyond what she grants to me on condition of my uncomplaining good behavior. TV is better; good wins; evil loses.

Solidarity called and asked me to go with her, Sam, Cary, and their friends, Blake and Anton and their kids, to the state fair. Since Sol's friends don't know how the custody hearing will go, they've decided not to tell the kids anything until a decision has been made. I'm eager to meet the friends, who have come to mean so much in Solidarity's life.

This has its comic side. She briefs me as though for an exam, as though I had never met a gay man before. I've gone on job interviews with less preparation. My own worries are how well I'll hold up with four kids below the age of seven. Seven, I seem to remember, is the age when I started enjoying our own children.

I want to use this outing to get my mind off the questions you asked about Larry's alcoholism. He rages when he's drunk, but alcoholism can be dealt with. If he rages when he's sober, is there a program for that? Does Hope contribute in some subtle way, her very gentleness a spur to his rage? Back to the video store; I can't think these things.

*M.*

DIARY ENTRY     *September 29, Auburn, Ky.*

We have gained a new young couple and lost the Percies, one of our Fresnos. Their kids had developed long-term hacking coughs. They were part of the family notion that keeps The Walk stable.

If we don't see ourselves and The Walk as something larger than life, its details — the sore feet, the colds, the chiggers, the mosquitoes, the damp beds — then The Walk won't be a mission but an exile.

*Dear Tig,*          *September 28, The Hill*

The fair was quite an experience, and saying good-bye to four kids under the age of seven was as big a relief as saying hello had been a joy. We had, in retrospect, a swell old time. There were eight of us — four kids and four adults. Anton has a van he uses in his architecture work and we went down in that, sing-

268

ing. I think I sat through forty verses of "Inky Dinky Spider" before I taught the crew "She Hit Him with a Shingle."

Anton and Blake are good men, and you could see that by the way all the kids acted in their presence, but I did catch them between-times when they didn't have to be cheerful for the boys, and felt something of the awful pressure they were under.

They are both good-looking, and through the weekend I noticed how the pair of them drew the admiring and speculative glances of women young and old. One of them was obviously married to Solidarity, but which? I was obviously a grandfather; the boys, two sets of fraternal twins. Which was the extra man? I was tempted to pass out a cast sheet or players' lineup.

I've decided I don't care if Anton wears lace drawers and a feather boa. I like him. Blake is a little stiffer, a bit more formal, but it was Anton's behavior that brought all the trouble and there's a tentativeness in him I have a feeling wasn't there before. Our grandchildren are learning the give and take of real friendship with Blake's kids. When things get rowdy, a look or word from either Blake or Anton calms the chaos, though they both have more tolerance for noise and argument than I do. Sol says you think this friendship is keeping her from finding someone else to marry. I think you're mistaken. The friendship

269

will help her more than a year or two of desperate husband hunting.

On the trip, Anton and I got into a discussion about my work, job restlessness, and so forth. He thinks I should look into using my engineering background as a consultant, in his area, perhaps studying the feasibility of restoring old houses.

And I ate a wonderful selection of foods at the fair: caramel corn, hot dogs, burgers and fries, ice cream, frozen custard, and cotton candy. I came back bloated, winded, and quite satisfied. Solidarity sends her love.

M.

*Dear Ben,*                    *September 27, Rich Pond*

I'm happy my advice about getting the most out of school is useful. I learned that lesson in harder times.

I've told you how politically active my parents were in the Socialist Party. Some of the heroes of socialism had been guests at our apartment, sharing our meals. I wanted to tell my classmates and teachers about that because, although we were close to being poor ourselves, our prestige in that world was high. I began to write papers about the movement and its heroes.

Disaster followed. My papers came back with terrible comments and bad grades and I found myself at the principal's office explaining why I had written them. Our family was Jewish by birth and culture, but my grandparents had given up religion for politics, in which they were even more Orthodox. The usual anti-Semitic undertone of those years, the thirties and forties, was hardened in our case because of our politics. I had to learn to separate home from school.

Until Miss Riley, my seventh-grade teacher. She encouraged me to write more, and helped with books and information. I began to see that there was challenge in finding the friend who could share my interest.

When I went south I listened to poor and "downtrodden" black people speak of their lives, traditions, and wishes. They were the very same people whose champions my parents and grandparents wanted to be, but the families where I stayed didn't hope for a new world order, or think religion stood in the way of progress. They hated the idea of an abolition of all distinctions between people, and made sharp distinctions themselves, between "fine" and "trashy." The Party had never asked The Poor what they wanted. It was a revelation to me and ended my enthusiasm for my parents' politics.

You can tell I'm getting old. Anything you say evokes my life's story. I hope some of it is interesting, at least. You will learn that your interests will bore or even anger some people, but if you find the right friend or two, you'll be able to speak your mind to a sympathetic listener. It makes all the difference.

*Love, Grandma*

*Dear Tig,* *September 30, The Hill*

It's a few minutes after two A.M. I'm bleary-eyed but I need to let you know what happened, and I won't sleep, anyway. Hope came here at dinnertime, huddled herself in a chair at the kitchen table, and began to shake. She took the tea I gave her and held the cup as you hold to a rock in a river. Larry has been restless and angry for a while, she said. Delays in the weekend work they had planned, infuriated him. There had been another blowup at the garage, too; a mistake he made caused the boss to yell at him in front of a customer. She was full of righteous indignation. It wasn't fair. They treat him like dirt. His tension and misery are their fault and are causing him to tighten like a coil.

This morning he didn't give her the special look and sign they exchange when they separate. He takes her little woven necklace and gives it a tug and they look into each other's eyes. I had to bite the inside of my cheek and be sympathetic.

When she looked at me again, there were tears in her eyes. It was the first time he had

let her off anywhere that they didn't say their
good-bye. He only turned, gunned the engine,
and rode away. She kept hoping he would go
around the corner and come back. She looked
utterly bereft as she described his hand, impatient on the accelerator.

She had gone in and let her job take her,
putting out new stock, taking care of her teen-
aged customers, enjoying their rapid dives between trivial and profound: "Which is my true
clothing style?" and "How will I spend the
rest of my life?" She laughed at this a little,
and then shifted in the chair and looked at
me bleakly. She feels much older than they
are. She said, "Was I ever like that?" sounding
like a sixty-year-old woman looking back.

But as she talked I could see she was trying
to put off the moment when she would have
to tell me something worse. At a quarter of
three she got a call from the police. The
woman said Larry was in custody. Hope asked
if he was all right. The policewoman said yes,
but still violent. Hope took a big breath and
went on, like a swimmer, doing laps. The
phone she was using is in a place where anyone could hear. Luckily the other two clerks
were busy. She asked why Larry was in custody. The charge was assault, destruction of
private property, menacing, resisting arrest,
public nuisance, and other things. He was in
the custody section of the hospital. Hope
asked if she could see him. The officer said

it would be better if she didn't.

It hurt me to see how she has changed, our soft, dreamy girl. She knows the routines now, and she has gone into maternity clothes. The baby is moving.

She said she worked the rest of the day and then came here. She didn't want to go to Justice and Frank, who would say "hateful" things about Larry. His bike is at the garage and she was fearful of going there. The cabin was too sad without Larry and impossible without transportation.

I wanted to say, "Stay married to him and you'll have lots of nights like this," but I played my role and told her I wanted her here, that I would take her to the hospital or jail tomorrow and to work, and that I would help her get through whatever she had to. She began defending Larry again.

I asked if Larry had been drunk and she looked into my face with such empty and terrified eyes, I wished I hadn't raised the question.

She didn't know if he was drunk this time and it's terrifying her. If his arrest is because of one of his rages, alcoholism isn't his major problem. She was crying by then and I settled her into her mother's old room. When I checked two hours later she was sleeping, cradling her little belly.

Now I'll try to blank out the picture and still the voices in my own head, take the as-

pirin against the arthritis that wants me up all
night, read something soporific, and try for
the shore she swims to so easily.

*Love, M.*

# *October*

꒰ꔛ꒱

We went to the hospital's police custody unit. Larry had been drinking yesterday. They think he started when he left Hope at work, and by noon he had had enough to register a blood alcohol level that would put most people into coma. No one noticed until about one when another mechanic quit for lunch. Larry had been working alone, according to the boss, who asked him if he was finished with the replacement of a water pump. Larry stared back at him with a look of such rage and hate that he was afraid to turn away but backed off, the way you do with a cougar encountered on a trail. Then, Larry came after him, moving like a sleepwalker and knocking away what he felt, rather than saw, in his path. The boss eluded him and ran inside the building, but by that time Larry was destroying machines, smashing the plate-glass window of the office, and doing between two and three thousand dollars worth of damage. The boss called 911 and the cops had to mace Larry before they cuffed and restrained him.

Hope listened without comment to the

whole thing. The policewoman kept her recital dry and objective, and now and then I snuck a look at Hope for a response. Her face was unreadable. She might have been asleep. Psychological questions aside, Larry has done the very thing that will most readily destroy his chances for a future, house, and job in one fell swoop. They live practically rent-free, but the living depends on Larry's job. What will they do now?

I saw none of the effects of that knowledge in Hope's face. She asked a nurse if we could see Larry. He was still in restraints. The nurse looked at Hope, saw something I didn't see, and added, "This is a custody unit, but we have good staff here and we'll take good care of him." Hope's eyes immediately filled with tears; I think she was surprised at the suddenness of them.

We went for coffee. There was half an hour before her workday began. She asked if I could pick her up at five.

I said I would take her home or back to the cabin if she wanted.

She said she would stay with me until Larry was free. I tried to hide my joy. She said she needed to go to the garage to pick up Larry's cycle and talk to the Boss. Did she think she could get Larry's job back?

She said no, but they had worked so hard on the house, perhaps she could talk the Boss into coming up to see it.

I'd wait until tempers cool, I said.

Hope said she needed to reassure him (sweeping again, cleaning, patting, how the woman fixes, makes it pretty, makes it nice).

Let me tell you this: All the women I've loved in my life (my third-grade teacher; my cousin Hilary; you; Danesha Forrest, when we went south) had courage, and until the moment Hope spoke that sentence, I thought courage was the prime virtue. Sense is. I want her to leave him. I don't want her to set that jaw and learn that simple, joyless stare, as though she were setting herself to look out on a plain where nothing would ever grow. I wanted to yell at her, "Don't be brave, be <u>smart</u>. If you are smart enough, you won't need to be so brave."

I said none of this. She wouldn't have heard me. At five, I drove over to Wild Duds, picked her up, and took her to the garage. I sat in the car while she went to talk to Larry's boss. I noticed that the two missing windows of the office had been replaced with plywood, and a big, crudely lettered sign told people the garage was open for business.

They came out almost immediately, Hope and a heavy-shouldered, dark man. He was talking, all of him, hands, face, mouth, and walking so rapidly that she was forced to run to keep up with him. He was obviously taking her on a tour of where Larry's cyclone had touched down — here, here, here. Her face

279

was turned away, following his words, nodding now and then. Finally, with a wave of dismissal, he turned to go and she put up a hand and stopped him.

She wasn't pleading or arguing, but making a series of statements. He began to nod his head. Then she smiled, just a little smile. He walked behind the building and came back with the bike. It had also been wrecked, its frame bent at a thirty-degree angle.

By which I knew how far out of control Larry had been. That frame had been twisted by being thrown with great force. It was his proudest possession, the last thing he would have wanted to destroy. I got out of the car to help her with it, and we wrestled it into the trunk. One of the workers found a piece of wire and we wired the hatch down over its clumsy mouthful of metal.

When I drove I pretended that was taking all my attention. Before we started up The Hill, she said she wanted to check on the cabin.

So we turned north and went the few miles to the turnoff in silence. When I found the old road she looked at me as she had looked at the Boss, the appeal for understanding, again. I said no more.

*Love, Marz*

*Dear Gram,*                    *October 3,*
            *Not Wild Horse Dream Ranch,*
                    *but waiting to go back*

I'm writing this letter to tell you I'm staying with Grandpa for a while. Larry had a slip off his program and there was some damage at the garage. He's all right, now. I saw him yesterday. I know he was sick and everything, but they shouldn't have cut his hair. It's his Indian heritage and I almost didn't recognize him the way he was. When he was arraigned they had him in a shackle and one of those awful orange jumpsuits and his beautiful hair gone. They read out the charges and had him with a lawyer who didn't do any of the things you see them do on TV. They wouldn't let me near him then, because they said I could be passing something to him, but later I got to see him, and we talked through that plastic wall. One of the policewomen smiled at me because she was at the hospital the last time. She meant well, maybe, but that hurt as much as seeing Larry shackled.

Grandpa has been very kind to me. He took me home and let me bring three of Larry's horses back to hang up in my room, which he says used to be Mom's room.

She and Dad are being very mean. All they talk about is how I have to leave Larry and have his baby in a safe place. What do they think our house is, the desert? I told them

281

plenty of babies are born all over the world in good places and bad and we have lots better than that. Don't they realize that our house has Larry's hands and mind on almost every inch of it — that's what makes it dear and safe. Don't they understand that?

Larry understands what happened. He said he let the criticism get to him and he stopped going to his ADEPT meetings for the last few weeks (which I didn't know). I talked to the people on The Program and they told me I should go to a program regularly, too, the one for families of alcoholics. They said it's not unusual for an alcoholic to go off The Program and think he can do it on his own. They will welcome him back without moralizing or yelling at him, which is more than my own mother and father would do, but he has to start over, and so do I, on day one, two, three, the way we did back in July. They said I shouldn't keep the calendar, but Larry should, that the responsibility and the pride about his not drinking should be his. I'll do anything it takes to save Larry's life. No one understands how good Larry is and how hard he tries. No one knows how loving he is.

Grandpa invited Aunt Sol over to talk to me but it didn't work. I am Larry's woman, his mate, his wife. If we can't live here without his drinking, we'll go to Dakota and live on the Sioux reservation and make our way with Larry's mother's people.

Your example is one I admire. You are putting your body and health on the line for what you believe, to show people where you stand. I admire that in you because other people — like the kids in school — are always complaining about how bad things are, but they never want to <u>do</u> anything to fix them.

Larry won't be able to go back to the garage, I know that. He's too proud to beg for his job again, but we may be able to keep our house until we can afford to move because his boss is basically a good man. Larry says he has learned a lot at the garage and may be able to get an even better job when he gets out of jail. He's going to stay on The Program this time and never drink again. He knows how bad drinking is for him. He said he thought he could drink just one drink in the morning to steady his nerves for the day so he could face the criticism of people at work.

Don't let people try to tell you how it was — even Grandpa is against Larry, although he never says it and has been specially good to me. Someday, Larry will prove his true self. Then the whole family will know how good he is.

*Love, Hope*

Hope and I went up to the courthouse yesterday for Larry's arraignment and plea. She
had assumed I would hire a lawyer and was
angry when I didn't. I think she has been
watching TV in her mind, seeing his justifications — poverty, race, youth — played in
splendid oratory — tears in the jury's eyes —
yes, a jury. I told her Larry would resent it if
I intruded myself into his plans for a defense,
and by that ploy got out of doing it. I don't
want to be blamed if things go badly. He saw
the public defender and was advised to plead
guilty. He did look riven, pale, trembling, still
sick. The judge asked him about the possibility of making restitution. There's not a prayer.
Larry has no job and what he could earn will
barely allow survival. His boss was there, and
told the public defender that if Larry went
back on the ADEPT program, the full program, they could continue on at the cabin.
Larry looked at him as though he had never
seen the man before and Hope began to weep.
"He's a kid," the garage-owner mumbled,
"and we've all done things we're not proud
of when we're that age." Larry swore that he
and Hope would continue to maintain and
improve the place. I only pray the health department doesn't get wind of anything — literally or figuratively — and go out there to
learn the cabin has no water and no septic

system. The boss is a good man and was obviously moved by the situation. Maybe he's even a little stuck on Hope. As she stood in the court, she looked very demure and gentle and with the little swell of pregnancy just beginning.

Insurance will take care of the windows. Larry will do thirty days and be responsible for going on The Program, which can be started in jail. He got sixty days suspension from his full sentence.

In the waiting room before he was taken away, he and Hope hugged like lost children, weeping. He promised to stay on The Program this time, to stay sober, to remake himself.

After she got off work, I took Hope to check on the cabin and then back to dinner. It will probably be that way every day during Larry's thirty days, taking her to the job, picking her up, checking on the cabin, then back home to eat dinner and watch TV or read, or talk, and then go to bed. It's no life for a young girl, even a pregnant one, but she says the peace of it will be good for her. Curse me, Tig, for selfishness; I'm looking forward to having her here.

*Love, M.*

I learned about Larry's trouble when I went for Blake's custody hearing. A group of men was lined up at the end of the hall, wearing the orange jumpsuits. One of them looked familiar but I couldn't place him. A bailiff came to the door and called: "Walks Away." I saw Hope and Pa coming down the hall, but we got called for our hearing.

Blake lost custody of the boys. Why did I think a woman judge would help? Blake's wife and her new husband were there looking like Ozzie and Harriet. Blake's ex cried, begged. She had run away four years ago, she said, "in the shock and horror of finding Blake in a homosexual liaison." She had thought he might have AIDS. Her flight had ended in Atlanta where she found a job and met her present husband at church. They were happily married, in good circumstances, and ready for a true parental relationship with the sons she had missed so much.

Blake's lawyer's questions were too sarcastic. "You fled in horror and left your <u>children</u> behind? 'Oh, gosh, I forgot to bring the kids?' " She let four tears break over her lower lids. "I knew Blake wouldn't <u>hurt</u> the children. That was before he brought other gays into the house, and made it a meeting place for transvestites."

Blake had told me that his wife knew he

was gay before they married. She wasn't interested in sex, but wanted a family. He was personable, building a practice, and would provide well for her. She gave a grimace of disgust and said she had come in upon Blake and Anton one day. Blake's lawyer tried to make her admit that her disappointment had come when she found him less ambitious than she thought he would be.

They asked me about our friendship and the normality of their home life. For a few minutes I fielded questions about the lifestyle around their house, which was male. Had I seen any gay sex practices? "Certainly not." It was the high point of the hearing.

Blake's lawyer asked why Mrs. Ex had decided to press for a change in the custody arrangement. It was seeing the pictures, she said. How had the pictures come into her possession? A friend.

There were the photos — at a bad one, heronner would pull breath as though air was being sucked out of the room, and then she would pass the shot back to the lawyer.

It struck me that she looked like one of the cross-dressers.

We take our lumps in different ways. Dad goes mute; you chatter; Justice gets glassy — cold and dry. I yell. Anton left, pulled his mind away. He answered the judge's questions yes, no, with no feeling. The more she pulled, the less he gave.

Then the social workers and the ad litem testified to all the outward stuff, home visit impressions — good; the relationship with the children — good; financial capability, appropriate lifestyle. But the case was gone. The judge lifted her eyes from the pictures and began the "even though: . . . Blake was a good father, blah, blah. Anton, the friend, had positive influence. My boys and I were positive influences, blah, blah. <u>But</u> . . .

"But family <u>means</u> blah, blah . . . Society demands . . . mother where possible . . ."

She finished. Blake was white and sick around the eyes. "When?" I could barely hear him.

As soon as possible, the judge said.

"Now," the mother said, across her.

"You can't!" That was Anton. He said they hadn't prepared the kids.

Blake sounded like he had swallowed gravel. Time, please, a month, two weeks —

The husband said they had to go back with the kids. They had been here for three weeks; it was now.

Was the judge hearing this? Did it seem normal to her that Blake and Anton were the only ones giving a damn about the effect this would have on the kids?

Blake was pleading for visitations, summer vacation, single days, scraps after a hurricane for her to bless. The judge said the kids needed a conventional home. "If the father's

288

home is cleared of harmful influences," she saw no reason why holiday visits might not be allowable. The bailiff brought the boys in.

I think she had spaced out how young they were; when she saw them she gave a little startle. How do you explain custody to them, one, a four-year-old? She dove in, using that obnoxious tone adults use to kids. Erik kept moving closer to Blake. "He's my daddy," over and over.

The mother moved in. Erik was making plans, talking in a monotone, out loud but to himself. Shawn lay down on the floor and cried there, too weak to stand. I went home.

I just explained, or tried to explain, all this to Sam and Cary, who argue, as I did, as Blake and Anton did, as Erik and Shawn did, that what was happening was wrong. Erik's big into fair and unfair. Cary was afraid it would happen to him.

I was tired, angry, sad. The boys had lost their best friends and an almost-family. Would Daddy do that to us? "If he tries," I said, "I'll tear out his liver."

*Sol*

*Moms,*                                    *October 6, Niwot*

Blake's boys are gone. The bodies are gone, but the spirits move in the rooms, touching everything. Anton went to work this morning,

289

but came home in the middle of the day. Worthless, he said.

I've been over there trying for something to <u>do</u>. There is no family to pick up at the airport, no ceremony to plan, no flowers to put in water. We have no ritual called Custody Loss.

The two of them were sitting in silence, Anton on the couch, Blake on a chair. Later, we were all in the kitchen, and they passed back of one another, shrinking-in. It wasn't a couple spatting. It was pain so raw that the sufferer doesn't want a touch. Anton is shot with guilt. He doesn't know who it was who took the pictures, or how Blake's wife found the opening. Everyone in his group denies having been the one, and suspicion will probably sink their meeting.

The hate calls are back; messages on my answering machine, and theirs, tinny voices chattering four letter words, rough ones threatening to geld one or both of them. We make weak jokes about producing a series: "SAVE YOUR VOICE: With our handy tape ($8.98 plus shipping) YOU may have a full thirty-minute spew suitable for all races, gays, lesbians, and every major religion."

Some of the calls have been from gays, whose way of comforting was to vent a woman-hating rage. Part of the pain is the sense that the world outside their doors is fearsome and ugly. I leave them in a fog of misery.

Things around <u>here</u> haven't been all that

290

sweet. Sam blames me for letting it all happen. Didn't I tell them, the judge and everybody? Didn't I say how Erik and Shawn were doing what they were supposed to? "They were good in school, Ma, Erik did all his homework, and Shawn has quit picking his nose. Ma, it isn't fair!" Cary only looks at me with a stare. His friends are gone and their house is no longer an arm of ours.

Blake and Anton tell me not to keep the boys from them. Our trip to the Botanic Gardens' rain forest is still on, but I don't know how we can all pretend there's any other subject to talk about.

I don't think Blake and Anton's love can survive this. Anton can barely watch Blake writhe. God damn Mrs. Ex. She took a lot of the joy and some of the success out of my life, too, and Sam's and Cary's lives. If I knew voodoo, that lady would be screaming and scratching until she let the kids go.

On that civilized note, I close.

*Sol*


*Dear Marz,*           *October 7, Monroe, Ky.*


I know my call was coincidence, but there was an urge to talk to you that I still can't explain. After the call I got your letters about Larry's awful mess and letters from Solidarity about her loss.

291

How is Hope? Has she talked to Justice and Frank? I'm afraid that in her innocent way she's creating more of a strain between us and her parents. Justice and I had just gotten easier with each other, and now that Hope has chosen to be with you, I'm afraid Justice and Frank will feel cut out.

I'd been telling Poppy how I left you all comfortable and, I thought, contented: Hope in high school, enjoying her friends; Justice and Frank with nothing more on their minds than their annual fight about their vacation; you beginning to plan for your retirement; Solidarity getting her balance after the divorce.

Now, I wish I were back home. Poppy asks how I could help. Who wouldn't think my presence an intrusion?

In that restless mood I stood at the entrance to the Mammoth Cave complex and passed out my questionnaires, feeling sympathy for the tourists coming through, tired mothers, restless kids, footsore men. A motorcycle gang rode up on their Harleys, doffed their helmets and goggles, and were revealed to be white-haired retirees, riding the country as we were walking it. We chatted. Their children were grown and married, their grandchildren lived in distant places, some had great-grandchildren, and now, they said, "We're on our own. We're seeing the country." I asked them if they kept up with things at home. "Hell, no," one old man answered, laughing. "Good luck to 'em — I'm out of it."

I asked if it got boring going without a definite purpose.

A woman answered, not understanding the question: "When we get tired or bored, we pick up and go. We've been to practically every state in the union."

Their questionnaires were illuminating, too. They wanted good roads for their Harleys, cheap motels or campgrounds, and easier Medicare. They wintered in the South, summered in the North, and lived cheaply on retirement pensions and Social Security. In outlook they might have been fourteen years old, but without the anxiety teenagers have.

Later, they stuttered off in a blue mist of exhaust.

Part of me envied their indifference. Part of me was annoyed by it. Poppy led me away, muttering.

Because of our schedule, we didn't get to see the Caves, either.

*Love, Tig*


DIARY ENTRY        *October 7, Monroe, Ky.*


Money problems. A new advance crew has been drafted and they have made themselves beggars to keep us going. We got some help from an advertiser who photographed us as

293

background for a commercial. Some Walkers refused to participate, but they didn't refuse the gas and food money it bought.

Every decision takes forever. Thank heaven for our itinerary. Its places and dates keep us moving.

Two more couples have left. The Jeffreys were a real loss.

We have pulled long, long strands between ourselves and our families at home, but the need for contact is overwhelming. Witness the lines of us standing at open phone booths late into the night for a word from home, from son or daughter, sister, brother, lover, friends. I think I'm the only one calling a husband.

The paradox is that <u>were</u> I at home, I would be less a part of the family's lives. Our distance has brought us closer to one another. Hope told me of her pregnancy almost as soon as she knew it, confided things about Larry she never would have, face to face. Ben writes; Solidarity has surprised me, too. I doubt that Hope would have gone so readily to stay with her grandfather had I been there. Two grandparents would have been one too many, and made it a capitulation. Marz is a man alone, a man needing something, and Hope responds to that like earth to sun.

*Dear Solidarity,* October 8,
Campbellsville, Ky.

Your letter made me want to scream at the injustice of what the judge ordered. Is there any means of appealing her decision?

I fumed at first but later I realized that relatively few years ago there would have been no consideration of a gay person's custody of children. There is more equity in this country than there was then. It makes the remaining inequity show up in a harder light. When there's hope, there's struggle, and more suffering.

I hope Blake and Anton will save something out of this — visits, calls, letters, until the situation eases. I would have been desolate if you had been taken away from me because of my behavior, which was my self-hood, then. I was on trips, in jail. Had your father wanted, he could have forced you girls away from me.

Since Kevin's leaving, Poppy and my status has changed. We are older, slower, tiring sooner, and so we have been put at the bottom of the list among The Walk's necessary drawbacks, the children and the loners. The comedown is interesting, if wearing. It's been years since I was a low-status person, a charge. I had to think back to my jail days to get an adequate memory of that indifference to my opinions and needs. When Poppy and I begin to speak in Bunion Rub, people sigh. If I have a suggestion, I give it to a family person or to a respected person. Only then will it be heard on its merits.

I feel for Sam and Cary in their loss. When I was in third grade, my best friend moved away. It was the deepest friendship I had, almost the only one, my parents being as they were. I felt lost and helpless and my father trivialized the loss because he defined personal friendship as a self-indulgence. That seemed wrong to me, even then.

Love, Moms

Dear Mother,　　　　October 7, Grant Street

My son-in-law is in jail and my daughter is staying with Dad, which I've decided is for the best. When she's here, she's defensive and blames Frank and me for her situation and Larry's bad time and even for our natural anxieties about her health and safety.

I've gone up to the house and she and Dad came here for dinner Sunday evening. Hope is eighteen, and in maternity clothes. She's worried about her husband who is in jail, and who will then be on a series of "Programs." She's worried about whether the two of them can stay in an isolated hovel. She's worried about money to pay the bills for her pregnancy and delivery, for the baby, for all the expenses after. She reminds me of an immigrant, an illegal alien, a ghetto or barrio mother who has mortgaged the present for a future held in the hands of a drunken boy.

There are smudges of sleeplessness under her eyes and pulls at the sides of her mouth. This is my daughter, <u>HOPE</u>, a girl who should be working at Wild Duds for college money or to spend on clothes. She should be wondering which of a dozen promising paths she will choose.

For years I had pictured her in college, then meeting someone from a family like ours, people we could meet and get to know — a familiar, safe life for her and for the rest of us.

You know that I'm a conventional person. I'm not brilliant or talented or possessed of the inner will you used to praise so in your friends on picket lines. I'm a simple person, married to a good man of ordinary but not stellar ambition. Of our three children, Hope is the one for whom I had the clearest dreams.

I know what you'll say: Larry <u>will</u> be treated, the baby will come and be loved by all of us, maybe Larry will become stronger, maybe he'll leave and Hope will be able to start again. I don't understand her anymore and the simple dream I had — a dream about going on vacations together, making baby plans together, painting a room or talking together on the back porch on a summer afternoon — is gone.

This letter was supposed to be about my being reconciled to Hope's staying with Dad. I wanted to know, like, respect Hope's friends, to be some part of her life. I wanted to get more than her loud resentment about how The System is treating Her Man.

*Justice*


*Dear Grandma,*          *October 9, Grant Street*

I saw Hope at Grandpa's yesterday and she showed me her stomach. I don't mean she got undressed, but she pulled her top back so I could see the little bulge — it's different from a fat person because it's all in one place, and when I think there's a baby in there, it makes me feel kind of creepy. We were supposed to learn all that stuff in Family Living Class but it didn't seem real until I saw Hope.

Don't tell anyone but it was a really funny feeling. Part of it is a feeling of being interested. The baby will grow inside there and then come out, head down, all formed, somebody, a <u>person</u>. Part of it is a feeling that it's — disgusting. It's so <u>public</u>. The more Hope sticks out the more people will know there's a baby in her and what she did and what she will do, and they can imagine her <u>having</u> the baby just by looking at her. I'm glad you can't tell on a man what is happening to him.

Because I have had an <u>experience</u>. I wasn't

dreaming anything. I didn't like it. Public.

Love, Ben

Moms, October 10, Detox

I've been up to see Dad, and Hope told me the details. I listened as long as I could and then I told her to dump him. She cried. Dad was in the kitchen while this was going on — he's getting good: chicken with little rounds of kumquat and a marmalade glaze, rice with bits of kumquat rind kind of burned, and <u>homemade</u> coconut ice cream.

Hope asked me how I could be so cruel. I said, "Because I work at a Detox center and I've been treated to every one of those excuses a hundred times." She said the ADEPT programs never told her to dump the one you love. "They <u>said</u> it, you just didn't <u>hear</u> it." I told her that and we were off again. Dad called us to dinner and I saw the hopelessness of trying to talk sense to her. We went in and ate. I got a chance to savor everything like a real gourmet because no one said a word all the time we were at the table.

It was typical of me to be tactful as a rock through the bathroom window. Dad gave me a look. I hate that look.

I've never seen Lover Boy when he wasn't being a complete horse's ass. Next day I went to the city jail and said I was his aunt. They

299

brought him out looking bewildered. He recognized me after a minute or two. It took an hour to get him to relax. His health is okay — they have them cutting brush up in the mountain parks during the day, but there is a lot of idle time, and he's got three more weeks to serve.

We talked. Three years in Detox has made me extremely sensitive to con jobs, and there's a lot of the con in Larry, psycho-buzz he's picked up from dozens of case workers over the years, but I got a hint that there was something else, under the labels and the lying. I think he loves Hope as much as he can. He sees a picture of their lives that's not like hers — and which is unrealistic. He's got a case of tribalosis, too, going on about a past no Indian ever lived, but his dreams are about family, not tribe. I kept seeing Little House on the Prairie or a sixties back-to-the-land idea. I told him that Hope was doing well at Wild Duds, that she liked the work and the people. I was waiting for arguments from him, and envy, but he said they would need that money and that he was happy that Hope liked her work. Maybe he meant it. It was the only good break they had had, that and the cabin. He would work also until they had enough to buy some land.

I asked him why he threw his cycle through the plate-glass window. He said he was always fighting the drunken Indian picture everyone has. He always wanted to prove what they said was wrong. He let things on the job get to him and he got drunk. "When I'm drunk I feel free. It's always free to screw myself up."

I'm trying to give you an idea of what the feeling was like as we talked, and I can't. Night thoughts after binges are always like that, deep, self-knowing. There was more, though, than the usual self-hate. I'm not romanticizing this — he's only a puzzle now, but there is a spark of something in him that Hope may just coax into fire.

*Sol*


*Dear Marz,*        *October 13, Lancaster, Ky.*

I'm glad you stayed up yesterday and my call didn't wake you. I have no excuse for calling so late. I was tired, footsore, and blue.

New Walkers have joined us. We have a new flavor and Poppy and I are gagging on it. I can best describe it as ultra pep. It's as though the new Walkers have been recruited from a cadre of exercise coaches and gym teachers. Yesterday Poppy spoke out in Bunion Rub: "This is a Walk, not a gym class. I won't do mandatory calisthenics <u>ever</u>. When I go into town it's to do questionnaires and not to pose as a fitness poster girl." The advocates began to go on about the image we

301

should be projecting. I looked up from under my half-crumbled straw hat. "You sound like Hitler talking to Leni Riefenstahl."

As soon as the words were out, I realized they didn't know what I was talking about. Poppy was laughing beside me but she and I were probably the only ones on The Walk who were familiar with Hitler's phys-ed glorification. "We're Fresnos," Poppy began, and I heard a muttering of "Tell us again." She praised The Walk's diversity and said that no one should try to mold it into something it wasn't. Silence.

Sleep well. I'm happy and relieved that Hope is with you. God bless Ben for telling me in writing what he would never have said face to face. It meant a lot to me. Tell him when you see him that I think he's the berries. Tell him that's thirties talk, but we old birds are free to be language museums . . .

*Love, Tig*

*Dear Tig,*                    *October 13, The Hill*

I've been to see Sol's neighbor, Anton, to discuss his idea about my taking up consultation. (I think I mentioned it — renovation of historic houses.) He is an architect, and we had talked about the idea casually during our State Fair weekend.

He welcomed me in and I told him I had

heard about Blake's loss of the boys, now in Atlanta. His anguish was almost palpable. We went down to the finished basement where his studio was and I marveled at the completeness of his setup. He said he did work there and faxed it. Then, he looked at me as though he had forgotten why I came. He said he planned the room so he could be home more for the kids; then he made a sound that wasn't a laugh, and said it was odd how quickly a plan could become unsuitable. Now, he wanted to get out, to do as much work as possible at the office. Last year the partners were wondering if they needed an office. With faxing, and E-mail — He was rambling, filling the empty room with sound. Abruptly, he stopped and said, "I'm glad you came." He had done some preliminary research — and he took out a sheaf of computer printouts from a folder. I thanked him. He looked at me bleakly. It was a relief to dip into something new, that wasn't his usual work . . . and he drifted again. Then, "Here . . . let's look," and with a visible effort he turned to the pictures and began to place them one by one on his work table.

They were fascinating. They were photos of the places in old houses where rot, water, the settling of soils, and a dozen other conditions had weakened the structures. If a person studied these pictures intently and followed the included plans of the houses, which were on the facing pages, he could assess the practicality of doing remodeling, renovation, or even structural repair. There's a growing interest in the remodeling of old houses, Anton told me. He is sometimes called in to do this work — modifications that would change a house into professional offices, for example, or business and factory buildings into living quarters. The structures may or may not be sound, depending on the uses that are planned for them.

I began to look closely at the pictures and the plans. Soon we were working together with a set that Anton had made for another house with different problems. We began to shift the plans to show different possibilities. Blake came home, looked in, said hi, and went back upstairs. When we were finished, I was tired the way one is from stimulating, satisfying work. We went up and found it had grown dark. I was amazed. I had gone over after bringing Hope home. I had planned to stay an hour, and here it was almost nine o'clock.

They asked me to stay for dinner, but because of Hope, I wanted to get home. Anton said he would take me to see some old houses where what we had studied could be seen on site.

I thought the evening had been good for him, too, that for the three hours we had been working he had put his pain to one side and gratefully allowed himself to imagine and re-imagine those fine old houses with me. As I left, he shook my hand and said, "Sol is a lucky woman."

I was touched. I said, "She told me she was, because of you and Blake."

So I have an idea of a possible future career, one with fewer intrusions and more satisfactions. The field may be crowded or too heavily regulated. I'll need to study a great deal, too, building codes and the appropriate laws, old construction methods and modern ones, but I'm excited about this in a way I haven't been for years, and my retirement savings might set me up in this work until I can build a clientele.

Ben and I are going to Leadville next weekend to study the city.

*Love, Marz*


*Dear Gram,*                    *October 15, The Hill*

I went to visit Larry today and he's so much better that it lifted up my mood. He said before that he didn't want me going to the garage to talk to his boss. Now he says it's okay. Mr. Anson's a good man and that makes me wonder why Larry was so against him all last month when he kept complaining about working at the garage. I need to figure that out but I can't ask Larry, and when I start to think about it, it seems disloyal. I have the idea I'm opening a door into someone's secret

305

room, watching what I shouldn't. By the way, Aunt Sol went to visit Larry. He says she's okay. It made me feel good to hear that we are not all hypocrites and racists.

I will take Mr. Anson up to the cabin and show him everything we did — the floor, the paint, the shoring, all our work, and how we will pay for what Larry did. I miss being there, even though I know it's best if I stay with Grandpa because it helps both of us. In nineteen days, Larry will be out of jail and into the residential program and I'll be able to visit him more. This time we will both stick to the program. I know that time has changed him and he won't drink again.

He has come to our jail visits less depressed, and more serious. He says he is using the work they do up in the mountain parks to toughen himself and restore his health. I don't think he would have said that before. He wants to use his experience not to prove racism but to rise above it and be strong and wise.

I know you will be happy for us so that's why I'm telling you. My parents still think Larry is a drunken bum, a nothing. Mom came up last week and made me so mad I still burn up when I think of it. She wants me to divorce Larry or at least leave him. Wonderful. Me, pregnant and needing Larry, him in jail and needing me. But I'm changed, too. Last year I would have cried about this but not now, I'm just mad.

My boss, Steve, knows that Larry has been in some kind of trouble. He thinks it was an accident on the motorcycle. He thinks I visit Larry in the hospital. I didn't tell him that; I just let him think it. He has put my name in for training in the management program. Most of it can be done by computers, but there's a two-week paid training at the head office in Chicago. Here's our plan: Larry will be out of his program in two months, and our baby is due at the end of February. If I start the program soon, I should be able to finish the computer part by late December and that would be when I'll be really showing. Depending on when the Chicago part is run, I can go there and finish before the baby comes, because once that happens, I'll be taken up with her (yes, now I think of it as "she" and "her"), and then, when I'm ready, I'll find an assistant's job in a larger store. They have stores in malls where there is day care. You have to pay for it, but it means I'll be able to take breaks and lunches with her so I can breastfeed her.

Yes, we are practical and serious. I talked to Larry about the plan and he approves and is eager. In management, I can hold a job while Larry builds at home, and later, on our land, we'll have a place where we'll be almost self-sufficient. Larry says he never faced the idea that school isn't for him, but building is.

I have seen his work and so has Grandpa. Why not let him do that, be that, while I supply the rest of what we need? It's a perfect plan, I think, being half Indian and half White, like we are.

*Love, Hope*

DIARY ENTRY *October 16,*<br>*Old Landing, Ky.*

We split four ways. The Gym Teachers, The Spirituals, The Political Activists, and The Laid-Backers. The splits were endemic in our beginnings, I guess. There were always people doing push-ups, sit-ups every night and morning, who got up earlier than Camp Rising to do those things. There was always the company of the preachers and the teachers, always a few for whom The Walk was a pilgrimage.

The trip is changing. Our goals have inflated on the rising air; up we go in little baskets of our self-importance.

It makes for rancor at Bunion Rub. The Spiritualists demand silence after 9:30 P.M., and now, at specific times during the day. In the damp chill here, tempers are short. The Preachers exhort, the Gym Teachers exhort; few of us remain to reaffirm the original rationale of The Walk: to learn, to listen, to see, to elicit answers to our questionnaires, and to provide, with our presence, evidence of the seriousness of environmental issues. Poppy and I are more vital on The Walk than ever.

DIARY ENTRY                    *October 18, Athol, Ky.*

All around us is land that looks rich beyond the dreams of Westerners like me. Hardwood forests, big rivers, huge lakes, all amaze my Colorado eyes. The leaves of these oaks and maples are bigger than my hand, the trees branch sixty feet above me. Pines here are wide rather than tall, their needles soft and feathery with the wealth of acetic earth and plenty of water. But they stand too close together for the way trees should form a wood. Around them foliage clutters the ground. There's a kind of walled mass of growing things. Walking in the woods is a strange and unsettling experience because unless there's a trail, one can't even see the ground.

We have been heading into mining country, not like Colorado's, where tailings spill down the bare mountain fronts like the spills down the vests of careless diners. Here, whole mountains are left like broken teeth, fronted but not backed, and the slags aren't mineral sands but rubble, as though there had been a war.

The people here have been much polled, questioned, and studied. They are tired of interviews, lists of questions, government attempts to bring work to the area now that so many of the mines are closed. They are inured to the interest of casual wanderers with questionnaires. No one asks us questions about The Walk or invites us to dinner or church suppers. A Fresno murmurs, "I wish we had a flood like the one back in Morehouse." It was over a month ago and in another world.

The most egregious of our Gym Teachers has pulled a tendon while on a Pep-up Run, and she and her partner have left The Walk. Ha! Served them right.

*Dear Hope,*                    *October 19, Lost Creek*

I get letters from your grandfather telling me how happy he is that you are staying with him. I know it's not what you want, but in the meantime it's a joy to him to see you and get to know you in a closer way than he could have at a hundred family occasions.

And your mother and father are relieved. Justice is, in a way you will some day come to appreciate, a charitable and generous mother. My mother was hurt and angry when I sought support beyond her and my father. It was an immigrant thing. I was always apologizing for friendships I made outside The Movement, or the family.

Are you going for checkups? Please sign up

at a clinic or get to a doctor for regular exams. You are working hard at the store and you have tensions in your life, and worry about Larry. Marz praises you in your eating, your having given up junk food for the baby's sake. That makes me proud, but knowing a doctor or being a regular at a clinic will stand you in good stead in case anything sudden happens.

I came upon a little something in a small town we passed through three days ago. It was made by a local craftsman and it's for you and the baby. The package will be arriving soon, and it will be addressed to you at our house. DO NOT OPEN IT until I get home. Tell your grandfather to keep his fingers off it also. It is to be my surprise and I want to be the one to show it to you.

We are in gorgeous country, here, in my favorite time of year, and I am waiting for the breathing out of the season, in the colors of autumn, all against blue sky.

*Love, Gram*


*Dear Grandma,*        *October 18, Grant Street*


Jason has broken his arm and will be out of all competition, maybe even off the ski team this year, but will only be skiing for fun.* At first I laughed. In all the old movies, it's al-

---

* Footnote: What a shame!

ways the snooty lady who gets the biggest pie in the face. Later I got sympathetic because Jason's life depends on sports and competing. All his friends are that way and they use it as friendship, too, so unless he is on the teams and doing the games, there's nothing to talk about. A bunch of them came over to visit him on Saturday, and they all sat around and stared until someone started to talk about their last game and then they all replayed that in barfing detail.[†] As the season goes on there will be new games. Describing <u>those</u> activities will be like describing good food to someone who didn't eat it.

It has done nothing for his attitude. He stalks around here mad at everyone, blaming <u>me</u> because I was standing on the corner while <u>he</u> rode <u>my</u> bike to prove a point I didn't want proved in the first place. My bike is now in the hospital with a bent frame. "<u>Sorry Ben</u>"? Forget it.

Here's the good news. Grandpa and Aunt Sol's neighbor, Anton, who is an architect, are going around to some of the old houses in Denver and in the towns that Denver has eaten like Pac Man. They used to be separate towns with farms and ranches in between. That's part of what I need to know, how the city grows over the towns, so they are taking

[†] Footnote: I went by every half hour and it was another quarter of the damn game. They were running the thing in slow motion.

me with them and we will go to the museum or the town hall so I can use the maps there. Some of this I can do after school, but I also got permission to skip some seventh and eighth periods. Grandpa went to school and arranged it, and I am big-time excited.

Here's how to work things in a family: either don't have kids at all, or have seven or eight of them. Jason's arm and my bike and Grandpa taking me around on school time have temporarily pushed the worry about Hope's being pregnant and Larry's being in jail out of the way. Did I tell you I visited him last Sunday? He seems peaceful. Hope thinks that's wonderful. I don't.

*Love, Ben*

*Dear Jason,*

It was bad news, hearing that you broke your arm. Ben told me that it will keep you from the competition you love so much, and I'm especially sorry to hear that since I know how much it means for you to be part of something big, where many people work hard for the same goal.

Is there any way you could turn your idle time into something useful, perhaps developing a quieter hobby or in some way making lemonade out of the lemon you have been dealt? Maybe this sounds too preacherish now, but it might be fun to work on.

We are in Kentucky. People burn wood in their fires here that we would save for furniture. They can't imagine burning pine or spruce in a fireplace. The first time I saw an oak log thrown on a fire, I wanted to douse the blaze and save the log. Some of the people here want a return to mining, even with all its dangers.

The people on The Walk with radios — battery operated — complain that they can't get anything on them but stump preachers and country music. One of them said all the songs are "Mah hort has done been stomped on in the rain."

Heal soon and well.

*Love, Grandma*

*Dear Ben,*        *October 24, Leatherwood, Ky.*

Yesterday we spent time in Viper, Kentucky. One of the Fresnos had family there long ago, and when the itinerary was being planned, she got them to make a detour through it. Never underrate the advantage of being in at the beginning. The detour, as you can see on your map, resulted in a big jog to Harlan and the coal country again.

It was an old farm place, with a quiet, long memory. I'm amazed there are any of these places left. Molly's whole family once farmed it. Now only one couple is left, but the grave-yard remembers, stones even from the late sev-enteen-hundreds, repeating names and inter-twining marriages. The Second World War began to move people out of Viper and Vicco, Cutshin, Slemp, and Leatherwood. Include war in your studies of why people move. The men go into service and see new places, the women get work in the war plants and facto-ries. I understand their leaving; what I don't understand is why they so seldom return. The land is beautiful. If it isn't farmed, there might be some other use, small industry or manufacture that would keep people working. I wonder why they don't all retire here and bring savings and pension money back to these places.

You wrote that you had visited Larry in jail. He was peaceful, you said, and Hope was pleased, and you were not pleased. Why not? What did you see that she didn't? They say love is blind, but it isn't. Need is blind. Hope needs something so much, looks for it so in-tensely, that her distance vision blurs what's in front of her.

Can a bicycle frame be fixed, or will you be forced to buy a new one? Are we talking big money here? It's a pity that you and Jason have such different personalities and interests. Tell him I hope most of his pain is past, and that his healing goes well, and I send my love. Time must hang very heavy for him. It's difficult for people without quiet hobbies.

Love, Grandma

Dear Tig, October 21, The Hill

Anton, Ben, and I went to Leadville late in the week. I wanted to take Jason along as well, but he turned down my offer. Justice swears he is doing impressions of the heroes in Foxe's <u>Martyrs</u>. When he hits St. Steven, Justice says, she will oblige by stoning him to death. In any case, Anton, Ben, and I made a harmonious threesome.

I'm grateful to Anton; his architectural knowledge is very useful and his contacts with the owners of the old houses we visited, even more so. He wears well, and seems glad to have my company and interest these days. His house — his and Blake's — is now too big and too small, he said. Even today there was a pang at leaving Blake alone. He wasn't fishing for sympathy, only stating a reality to us. Ben sat and listened, his eyes like millwheels. Later, I asked him what he was thinking and why he was so silent.

He said that adults never talk about real things in front of kids.

I asked him how he took what Anton said.

He said he never thought grown people had so much happening beyond their control. It's like being a kid again, when your family de-

316

cides to move and you have to leave a place you may like and start over in a new school, or a new neighborhood where you might not fit in at all. His friends' parents get divorced and the youngsters are suddenly shifted, taken, reduced. He said, "We always think: 'When I'm grown up this won't happen. Then, I'll be in control.' "

I was surprised by that, though why, I don't know. My own childhood's greatest problem was boredom, not dislocation. I suppose I envied the movers a bit, going off to faraway places.

We plan more trips. The trips themselves are instructive, and studying the plans and seeing where the houses' weaknesses have shown up over the years is better than any number of structural classes. I think this will be a good field for me. I'll be getting in touch with construction people who do this kind of work.

We had snow this morning. Here comes winter.

*Love, M.*

*Dear Grandma,*        *October 28, Grant Street*

I had a great time Saturday with Grandpa and Anton. At the museum they ran off a copy of an old map, and that let me trace the streets and what has happened in the town's

317

shrinking down from a huge population during the gold rush days. Grandpa and Anton were looking at two old houses up there. Next week we may go to an old section of Denver.

You were asking about Larry being peaceful in jail. I wanted to answer you, so I asked Hope if I could go with her again when she visited him. She said yes, but she looked at me funny.

They have a big table, a long one, and you sit on one side and the prisoners come in from their door on the other side and sit down. There's a Plexiglas partition, but you can talk through the hole they have drilled in it. I guess you've seen the whole thing on TV.

It's really hard starting out: How are you? Fine. I was the one who asked him what his schedule was like, how he spent the day. As he told us, I tried to understand what he was saying besides the words. He said it was good to be in the mountains even though it was cutting brush. He laughed that the habituals, drunks, mostly, let down and idle through the day. "They lean on their rakes," he said. When he is working they tell him not to push so hard because it makes them look bad, but he needs to keep in good shape because when he gets out of there, he'll be working hard. It was what Hope wanted to hear and she had this smile lifting up her face. It sounded great, what Larry said, but what was wrong with it was in the way he sat, or maybe his hands, or maybe the look on his face. What he <u>was</u> argued with what he <u>said</u>.

I tried to copy the look in front of the bathroom mirror at home, trying to feel and see how his face and body were when he was talking to us. I didn't get it right.

Then I thought: What if Larry is really <u>happy</u>, not on the surface, but in himself, happy about being in jail. You're not supposed to be happy in jail. But jail is kind of tribal, which Larry likes, and it's kind of "Cool Outsider," which he likes, too, and they give you rules and food and times for everything, without your having to think very hard or decide anything. I WOULD HATE IT!! I would be so depressed I wouldn't have the strength to work out, to be as peaceful as Larry is. If he is happy in jail, how can he be happy outside?

Maybe I'm all wrong. There's no one I can check it out with. Hope looks into Larry's eyes and pours love over him like warm syrup over pancakes.

So here I am, bike-less, or will be until I can save up. I've been to the bike shop and they can straighten the frame, but it will cost some money that Jason is not willing to part with. He says there was something the matter with the bike or he wouldn't have fallen. I want to jump up and down on his face. Then I think about Larry getting drunk and throwing his own motorcycle through the window of that garage and some part of me really understands that.

*Love, Ben*

*Moms,*                    *October 28, 3:00 A.M., Niwot*

It's too late at night or too early in the morning. Sam just threw up again and after cleaning him up I can't get back to sleep. Kids go to school and catch whatever is going around to bring it home like the cat's present. We are all stuck in The Usual. Up there, the snowline wakes up, stretches, and starts moving toward us. I see ice, colds, dead batteries. God help me if I get sick.

Anton stays late at work. Twice he has gone out with Dad to look at old houses. Blake is alone a lot, now. I've given him dinner. He sits like rigor mortis. "Anton thinks I blame him," he tells me. Blake needs Anton, but Anton can't stand suffering — he's like those people who won't visit their friends dying of AIDS. His friends say he needs to get back to life — it's been almost a month. As though that's time enough.

God, how I miss the way it was, us running over there, Sunday brunches. Sam and Cary still talk about if and when, but even if Anton did leave, it would be months before Blake could force Mrs. Ex to let the kids visit. He calls. She won't let them talk. She says they have to adjust to the new life. Maybe after a few years, she says.

I think Anton's working up to splitting so Blake can have a hope of seeing his kids some day. I make dumb suggestions. Everyone makes dumb suggestions. It's a way of showing interest, to keep from saying, "This mess offers no hope whatever. You will suffer until suffering wears itself out."

It's 3:00 A.M. I am not the only sleepless one on this street.

*Sol*

# November

ৼ

We went up to see Hope at Dad's, yesterday. In three days Larry will be released into his Substance Abuse Program: two weeks in a closed facility and two more in an open setting. We thought it was time to make her set some limits regarding him. When she and Larry were living together we were closed off from her, not welcome at their cabin, nor visited by them. Frank told her that we had a right to something better than that.

She looked more rested. Her hair was clean and her gestures were calmer. Her little stomach was high but nowhere near as big as she pretends it is. She looks over it as though it were the full moon.

After a stilted lunch, Frank raised the topic of Larry's treatment. He said we deserved visits and assurances of Hope's health and we had a right to contribute things to help with the baby's safety. Hope froze. Then she said it wasn't right for us to try to come between her and her husband. He would soon be in treatment, facing a difficult self-examination. She would not lay trips on him

323

about what he should do.

I told her she had a child to consider, that she should be making arrangements for a hospital.

She said that Larry had been talking about having the baby the Indian way. There's an Indian midwife in Denver who practices tribal methods. They would be seeing her.

I was less horrified than Frank was. As he sat beside me I could feel his body contracting. I knew his face would be hardening and his jaw clenching as it ground on his anger. I asked if this midwife had been state certified and had access to a hospital.

Hope flared back at me. Why should the state determine tribal ways? Why did I always assume the worst?

Hope has seen her husband in shackles and twice in hospital restraints and asks me why I assume the worst. I sat there and wondered which was my prime emotion, anger or heartbreak. For one revealing moment I felt sorry for Larry, a boy, desperate to find a footing on a ledge he can't seem to see or use; second-rate Indian, third-rate white man. My son-in-law.

I'm complaining by mail to keep from hurting Frank still more. I haven't told any of this to friends because they would pity me or think I was being disloyal to my daughter and her husband, and some of them would give me Hope's own gabble. Some would blame me for her problems. I'm tired, exhausted with arguments with myself when I should be sleeping.

*Justice*


*Dear Gram,*                    *November 2, The Hill*

Larry is out of jail. He got out two days early because of going into the Substance Abuse Program and there he can wear his own clothes and not have handcuffs when he visits. I'll be able to see him at the family counseling sessions and Grandpa says he will come with me as family. Mom and Dad had to promise to come twice, at least, but I don't think they will do any more than they have to. They don't want us to succeed together. The locked part of the program is close enough to the mall where I work so I can go up there during my lunch hour and eat with him. That means he'll stand at the window and I'll be on the sidewalk outside and I'll eat my lunch there and we'll talk to each other, even if it's only by signs and smiles and waves, but that way I'll be with him and strengthen him the way I couldn't do when he was locked up. I also found a backyard place where the clients get exercise (they are clients there, not prisoners) and maybe I can sneak around and see him sometimes because visiting hours are only once a week during the first two weeks and I miss Larry so much I can hardly stand it.

I called the tribal midwife and told her I wanted a Native American birthing procedure. At first she didn't want to see me but when I told her I was married to Larry, who is half Sioux, she said okay. Grandpa took me there. Don't think she waved a bunch of rattles at me or painted my face. She is licensed and did the things regular doctors do — my weight and blood pressure and pulse, and she told me not to drink, but to have plenty of clean water and a good diet, and she asked me some questions that were different from the ones Mom's doctor asked. She uses Indian herbs, for teas I can drink, and there are special things for me to do at crescent moons and at full moons. She also told me about Larry's last name, Walks Away. The man who first had that name was a Sioux who left a treaty meeting with some White delegation. It was trying to get his band to come in to the reservation. He Walks Away was famous, she said, and Larry should be proud to be descended from him. I asked her if she was in contact with a hospital and she said yes; it was U. of Colo. Medical Center, and she would be in radio contact if we needed it. She will come anywhere, INCLUDING OUR CABIN, so that's decided. I will have our baby at our home, with Larry there. She said it was okay if we didn't have running water. She said we could get a five-gallon container and keep it on hand. No electricity? She said she would bring all the light we needed, and everything else we needed she would have on a list. Larry will be near to help me and she asked me if I had a woman friend who wanted to be there, and I thought about you. Would you come if I called you the minute I started labor? If it works out, you could fly back and be with me, but if not, maybe you could come as soon as possible after. Will you?

*Love, Hope*

*Dear Marz,*     *November 6, Ash Camp, Ky.*

I was glad you and Hope were home when I called from Harlan and Kingdom Come. I was so moved by Hope's request that I be there with her at the birth of our great-grand-child that I had to call and say yes. Here, too, are the letters, the second sheaf for you to put in the box.

Each warning to Hope has hardened her resolve to go on her own. She may be deluded but she's not stupid. She must be more conscious of her situation than we realize. Perhaps these letters will form some kind of primer for our family, not about what child-raising experts say is normal or desirable, but the way life is. There are separate, strong personalities involved here, each with a past and the baggage of that past. We don't begin anything!

I see this in the midst of rural depression and decline hidden in the glory of autumn hardwood forests and mountain land of eye-filling beauty. The questionnaires come back with a cynicism bred of answers given for a generation. This is land that has been much wept over and studied.

<u>Why</u> <u>don't</u> <u>the</u> <u>old</u> <u>come</u> <u>back</u>? Now and then on the road, we look up or down a hill or into a hollow and do see two or three well-made, neat, new houses with satellite dishes in the backyards and new pick-up trucks in the driveways. They shop somewhere. The drugstores carry four kinds of arthritis medicine and three kinds of bunion pads. I looked. Not every old person wants a seasonless sunshine.

We will be leaving Ash Camp for the scenic route into Virginia. The trip will be more leisurely up to Washington, D.C., to be there around Christmas. You said you would come. Please don't let our last meeting turn you away from this one. I promise I won't argue this time. It will be pure vacation, and on some of our old stomping grounds. I want to spend two or three nights with you in a good hotel, or if you want to rough it, camped out on The Walk. I'm interested in your post-Kevin view of us. Please, come.

Tell Hope I will make arrangements to leave The Walk and fly home to be with her whenever the midwife says she is beginning — sev-

328

eral days or a week before. We can work that out when the time is nearer. I want to be there, and I'm happy you are.

*Love, T.*

*Dear Mother,*          *November 4, Grant Street*

I have just learned that it was Dad who took Hope to visit that tribal midwife. Yes, I knew that she had wanted to go, but I hoped that the difficulty of finding one and the further difficulty of not having the means to get to her would keep Hope from the danger and foolishness of such an idea. I had made an appointment with my ob-gyn — taking her was a wish of mine. I have had few such wishes gratified — that I could buy Hope's wedding dress, meet a family, help with a wedding, enjoy Hope as she thought about starting married life — Larry took Hope away from all that.

She got pregnant and I thought there might be another chance for us to laugh and plan, to go out for lunches, to get maternity things. I wanted to help her — that went up in smoke, too, but good Lord, at least she should prepare herself correctly! Instead, she told me that her grandfather had taken her into Denver to see that tribal woman.

What is Dad thinking of? Hope is not a Native American, and Larry isn't, either; not in a tribal culture. They're playing games, both of them. Why does Dad go along with the fantasy? I was reconciled to Hope's going to stay with Dad. She and I argue, I know that. Wasn't it wonderful, I thought, that we have more family to help her, family we trusted. I suppose I should be accustomed to disappointments when counting on this family. It has all too often fallen apart on me. I spent my adolescence being called for when it was convenient for you, then neglected. When you and Dad came back together I was expected to forgive and forget. I have, or have tried to.

I will say that this Walk of yours has brought out things in me I thought I had gotten over. Now this. How could Dad have done such a thing?

*Justice*


DIARY ENTRY      *November 8, Elkhorn City*

Nothing quiets gym teachers like a week of icy rain. We move through sullen mists and a clinging chill throws back the sounds of our steps and our voices and even of our breathing, making them hollow and ghostlike. And rain. For the first time I realized that this Walk would encounter winter.

The rain. Its cold clings like an incubus. Our sleeping bags are clammy and our sweaters cling like coats-of-mail, weight without warmth. I hear hacking coughs from some of the tents.

Poppy found me weeping, thought it was because of the rain, and began to bustle, a habit of hers. Then, she realized it was grief and she pried the sad old truth from me: Justice's letter and our years-long wrangle. She had intuited as much from a stillness around the mention of Justice's name. She brewed me some illegal tea and put something in it that took me right out of my socks.

The Walk is snappish now, and we pick fights. For five days Bunion Rub has been held in the lea of the water truck. Ancient nomads must have known such periods of quiet harmony in the camps and other periods of ill humor and outright strife. I'll tell this to my "tribal" granddaughter some day.

Money, too. The running-shoe company that promised to sponsor this section of The Walk has reneged. Poppy has been writing to her college alumni newsletter for help, but relatively few of us belong to service clubs or lodges and the people in these towns are taken up with their own causes. In this weather, no one comes out to interview us so there are no news releases. We wonder aloud who has done more and who less, who hasn't contacted a rich relative, and who is too proud to tap a likely source.

*Dear Gram,*                    *November 6,*
                         *The Hill with Grandpa*

Grandpa tells me I should balance things, and that if I do, I will come out ahead. On the good side, I'm really healthy and have been drinking the herb tea Shining Lady gave me, and doing the meditation she said I should do, preparing us by taking time out in the morning and before bed to send messages to the baby's spirit. She approved of the necklace Larry made for me, but she told me to knot each tail of the braided thongs because she said that during pregnancy there shouldn't be ends loose in anything I wore. As soon as I'm ready to have the baby, I'll undo all those knots and we'll chant.

I've begun the management course. It's programmed, on the computer. I can learn at my own rate, which Steve says is very fast. The course is supposed to take a month, but I've been doing double lessons, two hours every evening. I'll be training for assistant manager, which I can do at the same store for a while, only with higher pay, waiting for work in a bigger store. Except (this is the best news), WE will be that bigger store. Our store has been growing, and is very successful. We have increased our receipts and inventory at almost the highest rate in the whole Rocky Mountain area. We have put on a new part-time girl, so there are five of us, and management from head office has come to see about locating us a bigger store here. Steve says a good part of our growth has to do with me, and I don't think that's only a compliment. I feel things and seem to know what the kids want to wear. I make sure by getting to know their ideas when they come in. If a lot of them turn down a fashion, I ask the ones I know — my regulars — why, and they tell me. What they say makes a certain kind of sense. That's what makes the work fun — you're not just selling clothes, you're thinking. Back in August, when the buyer came in to show us the new lines for the late fall and winter, Steve and I met with her for two hours and Steve made me tell her my opinions. By the time we were done, she was taking notes.

There's bad news about seeing Larry. Two days ago, I went over to the facility at lunchtime. He stood at the window and told me with gestures and saying the words that he wanted to meet me in the exercise yard at 4:30. I took my afternoon break late and ran over there to be with him. I think I told you that his exercise yard is behind the building. It's closed off by the backs of buildings and a fence, but the fence has a hole in it. I wiggled through the hole.

Larry was there. Their exercise yard is surrounded by another fence, chain-link and very high and with barbed wire on top. I was so glad to see him outside, away from that awful visitors' room at the jail, out of those orange clothes. His long, beautiful hair is growing back. He stood at the fence and we started telling each other things. Then he put his hands up and so did I, and he put his mouth to the fence and so did I, so we were kissing through the diamond holes of the links, but we couldn't get much more than lip to lip, and we were laughing and saying our feelings, full of happiness and love. All of a sudden there was somebody with him and somebody with me and they made him lie and be spread-eagled against the fence. Me, too. They searched him all over, even in his mouth. Mine, too, lying up against the fence, and they felt and patted way up between my legs and in my clothes and pockets and in my mouth and in my hair, messing my hair and Larry's, too, and they told me if I came back there again they would have me arrested. "Visiting hours only!" the man yelled. "And only in the visitors' room!"

I felt so humiliated. All the time they were searching us they were yelling at me, asking me what I was trying to pass to him, and why I was trying to screw up his program and where was I getting the drugs. I kept arguing and they kept yelling. I was afraid for the baby, pushed up against the fence, and for the baby's spirit, because of my fear and the questions they were yelling in my ears.

Finally they let me go, and said they would

close the hole in the fence and put barbed wire in the space, because they saw how I had gotten in. I had to go back to the store in that upset, with my hair all wild, and I was crying. I had to go back behind the row of stores and in by the alley way, so no one would see me. I got my purse and tried to fix myself up in the employee's washroom, but my eyes were red and Steve knew there was something wrong, which he thought was my pregnancy and I let him think it. He was sympathetic with me, for the rest of the time I was working. I looked and felt terrible. Even Grandpa noticed it when he came to pick me up. I began to tell him on the way home, and he took me to the cabin and I told him the whole thing.

I want so little. I want Larry back, and our cabin, and our baby, and I'm working hard to make it all happen, and everything is so <u>stuck</u>.

Tomorrow, we go to The Program. Mom and Dad said they would be there, and Grandpa and I will, too. That should show everyone our support for Larry. Dad seems to be less angry at Larry than Mom is, and she's more angry at me than at him. They both said they will do the whole thing, The Program, which surprised me.

So, maybe Grandpa is right, and there's more good side than bad to my life, now. I'm going to get ready for bed and drink my herb tea and communicate love to our baby's sweet spirit.

*Love, Hope*

P.S. Thanks for the mystery box. Grandpa put it in the closet in Aunt Solidarity's old room.


*Dear Justice,*      *November 10, Millard, Ky.*

Hope writes that you and Frank are going to the therapy sessions for Larry. I think it's a wonderful idea.

Larry is fragile, Hope is less so. Perhaps, her pushing you so far away is fear. She's making enemies of you because she thinks that strengthens her alliance with Larry. By supporting his therapy you aren't letting that happen. I want the very best for all of you in those sessions. Write to me if you can, about what they are like, even if you find them boring or simplistic. I'd like to follow what's happening and how you are.

I know your recent relationship with Hope has been a source of pain to you, as your letter showed. I can only say that the last word hasn't been written on Hope and Larry. Therapy may show them how unready for marriage they are. If they do split up, it will be sad for her for a while, but I think for us, not sad at all. Your <u>life</u> has been good, hasn't it, in spite of a difficult youth?

The Walk is moving up a particularly scenic route into West Virginia. There are rivers here and a lake that at home would be classified as an inland sea. The rain is over, but everyone is still coughing.

*Love, Mother*

*Moms,*                    *November 8, Niwot*

Out of the sickbed at last. Sickness, mine or others', is my nightmare.

Home is still the pits. The new kids Sam and Cary hang out with are two blocks away, and no substitutes for Erik and Shawn. We can't pass the house next door without feeling the loss. Blake and Anton wave to us and sometimes invite us in for cookies, but they're miserable, and the misery drags itself on to us and clings.

Anton stays away; leaves early, comes back late. This past Sunday he caught me. Why don't we all get together for dinner? I made my salad and your upside-down cake and took the boys, fighting it now, next door.

The house used to be so orderly. Now it's fussy — the kids looked scared to sit down. Anton worked at talking to them and after a while we eased up. After dinner the three of us started to clean up in the old way, kidding. I thought we would make the evening. When we drifted into the living room and sat down, I knew that supper and clean-up had been a truce, time out.

Who took up the verbal dagger first? Search me. A witness can't usually tell. A word about the window-shade may be an opening shot; next thing you know, the blades are out and there are guts all over the floor. They were trying to carry on the fight over my head, past me, around me; both of them, gray with rage, whitish at the lips. "One can't know, if one was not <u>here</u>." "When one has been <u>here</u>, one wasn't noticed." I tried to pull things together — The second set of weapons was net and axe. I collected the boys and left.

They couldn't stop; my wanting couldn't stop them. Now and then there was <u>helpless-ness</u> on their faces.

Sam and Cary were whiny. No one had gone in to check on them in the other room and they ended up in a hassle. Instead of going across our yards, we walked around the house to the back, like cat-burglars. We were all <u>ashamed</u>. Later, Cary asked why we didn't move to where Erik and Shawn live.

"You're <u>grown-ups</u>. <u>Grown-ups</u> can go wherever they want."

Sam said, "Grown-ups fight, and when they do, it's worse than when kids do."

They once had the fantasy that Erik and Shawn would run away, come here, and we would hide them. We all need E-mail.

I called Blake and Anton. Blake answered. I told him for God's sake to get into therapy. I said I didn't want to lose either of them.

He thanked me. I could tell he hadn't been listening.

*Sol*

*Dear Gram,*            *November 8, The Hill*

Our family session was yesterday evening. I was tired from work, and nervous, too, but I went. We were uncomfortable from the start. Larry was the only one who looked normal, not tight and nervous. Everyone had to say something. First we each had to tell Larry how his drinking affected us. Then the therapist forced Mom and Dad to admit they didn't think our marriage was a good idea, that we were too young. She asked them if they were racist, and they said they didn't think so. I said I knew they <u>were</u> racist; all white people are. I got angry and they got angry, but then the therapist said we should get back to Larry. Mom got to say how scared she was for me to be in the cabin, far from her and "medical help." Dad said that the times Larry did visit he was hostile to everyone and would take it out on me. Then he said they wanted Larry to admit that he and Mom had some rights.

I could tell it was hard on Larry to hear that. I could see him go into some other part of himself when all this was going on. It was unfair, all of us climbing on his case, and tearing off pieces of him. I said that, and the therapist said that in therapy the idea is to get Larry to know where we were coming from. "Larry is unable to see things realistically," the therapist said. "He needs to establish controls on his behavior." She began to talk about outcomes and how Larry didn't see ahead to the outcome of his actions. I said that wasn't true, because we spent lots of time talking about when the baby comes and how our lives will be.

They sat and stared at me and the therapist said <u>that</u> is a <u>distant</u> goal, and where Larry was weak was in the daily goals you set on the way to your final goal. Later the therapist said she thought I should see her privately for a few sessions, and Grandpa said he would take me. It means he's going to be chauffeuring me to The Hill every night, or to therapy and The Hill, plus part of weekends to the cabin. He said it was important, and he wanted to do it. When he said that, it made me feel dependent, so he said I could drive <u>him</u> all those places. Later, he said <u>I</u> could take the car to the cabin and to therapy. He said it would be costly but he would do it. "Costly?"

"Tranquilizers," he said. He would be popping them like breath mints. I am giving him a demo of my driving tomorrow.

I only wanted to tell you that Larry was the

best one at therapy. Everyone else was angry and dumped on him and he didn't come back at them.

*Love, Hope*

*Dear Tig,*                    *November 8, The Hill*

You asked for a report of that family session I went to at Larry's program . . . The therapist had each of us tell Larry what his drinking was doing to his relationships with us — each of us. She said to make the statement as specific as possible. I told about the sledding party, back in March, and then about having to take Hope to the garage to talk to Larry's boss, having to watch her as she began to plead with him.

The memories came out as sanctimonious and self-serving. "Your drinking has separated us from you, and from our granddaughter who has had to take sides in order to defend you." Nice try, but is it true? When does a grandfather get a choice of grandsons? Look at our own: Jason thinks I'm a harmless, if senile, old party who can't ski very fast. (He forgets it was I who taught him to ski.) A gift at birthdays, a presider at Thanksgiving. Ben values me and I love him. It's all choice and need and personality — How does Larry see me? I don't know. I want to help him, but I can't if he doesn't see me as worth listening

341

to. This is not what the therapist wanted to hear, and not anything I could say.

The next thing on the agenda was the therapist asking Larry if he had heard all of us. Larry said he had. We had lots of expectations of him, she said, but was he required to fulfill all of them? "As many as I can," he said. "I have lots of problems with my interpersonal relationships."

Something went off inside my head. I had a flash of a vision of Larry sitting in a dozen other chairs hearing and saying this. He must have had years of such sessions; therapists and school officials, medical and psychiatric evaluations, juvenile authorities, foster families. He has the jargon. Maybe these words once held wisdom, but they have been used so often that the plating has worn away. Poor Interpersonal Adjustment, Inability To Relate, Addictive Behavior, Acting Out. We heard them all as we sat there, from Larry, from the therapist. It was a shorthand talk they gave and took. Why not, I thought. He has been a client all his life. It's what he does for a living — he clients, he patients, he inmates. A century ago, he'd have been one of those eternal converts, being saved and lost to be saved again at the next revival, his weakness dressed in another vocabulary.

We were next asked to tell Larry what each of us hoped our relationship would be with him. Again I put forward a handy lie because

I didn't have the time or will to sort among half-truths. "I'd like to be welcome in your lives," I said. She nodded. I had said the right thing.

Frank followed my lead, repeating much of what I said. He even shot me a look of complicity when no one else was watching. Justice tried to tell Larry and Hope she wasn't a racist. The words came out sounding petulant and defensive. She tried to tell Larry what her dreams for Hope were, the mother and daughter things. It sounded as though she was wanting Hope dependent. Hers was the only honest voice in the crowd — even Hope tailored her talk to what was expected.

Was the therapist at fault? I don't think so. Family now has dysfunctional as its adjective. That was in the therapist's head and in Larry's, and in ours, too. The woman is too young to remember when parental modified love. Now, it modifies incest. Justice's wish to share Hope's life sounds intrusive, but Hope is eighteen and still a dreamer. She and Larry say they want to be homesteaders, but she has discovered a gift for business. Larry has good skills (you should see the work he has done on that cabin) but I don't think he has the gift for isolation frontier life requires, or the stability to pursue such a life. Could he grow into that stability? I don't think so. None of that is being investigated here, nor will it be. This is not the place. Where is the place? I don't know.

Hope has faith in The Program, The Therapy, and in the complete power of love to heal all the sickness of the soul. Whenever Larry delivered himself of one of his well-worn passwords, she glowed like the Northern Lights. Sometimes she turned that glow on me.

After the meeting, I wanted to go out some place for coffee, to get Justice and Hope together for a little, but everyone wimped out and we separated.

She didn't mention the session again. She knows, somewhere deep in herself, that I lied, and that I, too, am blind to what she sees so clearly in Larry.

What do I feel? Sitting there, I felt numb. Tossing in bed, sleepless, I formulated my real message to Larry: I wish you and Hope would separate immediately. I wish she would have her baby and give it to a fine Sioux family to raise. You took Hope in her idealism before that idealism could be wedded to any sense at all. She will be wiser for having known you, but she is meant for better things than sitting in jailhouse visiting rooms and parrying the inquiries of therapists to come.

*Love, Marz*

P.S. I have been reading a little since the session and have been faced by conflicting theories that try to explain Larry's behavior. 1. Genetic predisposition. 2. Environmental.

3. Chemical imbalance in brain. 4. Brain damage. Medicine does not have an answer for #1 and #4, but I will try to ask someone about #3. Might Prozac help?

*Dear Grandma,*      *November 10, Grant Street*

I am going ahead with my city in the basement especially since I am bikeless and it's going to be winter soon.

I was sitting, looking at it and I had an idea about how people move in crowded business areas in cities and malls. You would think that everyone would want to be in a busy area, but maybe not. It might be better for some business to be close to the busy area, but not in it. What about houses? People want to be near stores, but how near?

I can hardly remember back to when I thought demographics was about how rich and poor people moved. Now I have to add age and convenience for people to get the things they need every day. It gets really interesting and complicated, and yesterday I heard some of my teachers talking about some of the "better" areas around Boulder and I started to think that people are influenced (along with all the other things) by where other people think it's best to live, even if it's inconvenient. How will I show that?

*Love, Ben*

P.S. I am saving to get the bike fixed. Thanks for the tee shirts.

*Dear Marz,*                              *November 12,*
                                          *Sidney, Kentucky*

How are you feeling? I need to hear your voice. We will be staying an extra day at Williamson, W.Va., for repairs on the truck and on us. I'll call you. We all have had colds. The weather hasn't helped, either. It has been foggy and rainy for the last four days.

<u>But</u>. I never knew how varied mountains can be. These are not stark as ours are, but are covered with softening quilts of trees, light and dark, in the rain-hung mornings. Here I see what a job it must have been to clear this land for farming all those years ago. The roads we walk are densely grown, close on both sides with foliage. Those roads must have been fearsome when they were paths. Bears, wolves, Indians — there's the possibility of being lost half a mile from home, among these trees.

And there is water close, almost anywhere. We pass lakes, creeks, pools, ponds, we cross rivers. We hear water running, and the road leads up and away from the water and down to it again, seen sometimes, heard almost always.

The answers to our questionnaires have become ambiguous. People talk about urban sprawl, but there is none within miles. The problems they mention are a TV-generated reality. Locally, land management has helped the area greatly. People say the water is cleaner than it was in the thirties, forties, fifties, yet on the questionnaires they seem to see total failure in that category.

Is my trip worth a year out of our lives together, one added to the ten you call our unsuccessful separation? I think so. Justice still feels she was abandoned, but you remember that the girls traveled with me as much as the authorities would let them. I was protesting, or in jail, it's true, but not as often as Justice thinks. Solidarity enjoyed the changes more than she did. We stayed in the homes of supporters of the causes, sometimes a mansion, sometimes a cramped apartment. I remember spending almost a year with a couple in near splendor with the girls going to private school while we organized the Massachusetts protests. At that home we had a butler and maids.

I wish we had written letters in those days, or kept journals. We were going to change life so totally, that anything before those changes seemed irrelevant. We wrote manifestoes, but I remember a mistrust of private reality. The idea of a person sitting in an island of quiet and writing private thoughts for private purposes was subversive, smacking of elitism and betrayal of group loyalty. In the future I envisioned, I would merge into full belief instead of hovering on the edge as I had done all my life. I never shared the certainty of my radical friends. Here I am again, twenty or so years later, still truly of no one's faction.

As I think about the words I'm writing, I remember myself ten years older than Hope is now. Seen from this distance, I think I was no less confused than she. It dawns on me that she may have as little chance to put her doubts into words as I did then. To whom does she confide? As I see her in your letters, she's always certain of her future with Larry. In her letters to me, she's waiting and sometimes yearning, but never unsure, either. She presents an eager face, tells of her happiness at Wild Duds, her studying for advancement. I don't think she can talk to Justice or Frank. She sees disapproval plain on their faces, so any doubts she has about Larry's complete recovery would seem disloyal. Has she any doubts about him? If she does, where does she go to say them, and hear them in her own ears? If there is someone, a friend, a confidante, it would ease my mind greatly. Might the therapist be that person?

*Love, T.*

*Dear Marz,*          *November 13, The Road*

I just got your Nov. 8th letter, the one you wrote after sitting in on Larry's program. If he has as long a trail of state intervention as we think, they must have tried him on various tranquilizers and so on, to manage his violence. I guess it wouldn't be a bad idea to request he be checked out by a competent neurologist. Would The Program allow for that? We could pay for it, although Justice and Frank might prefer to. Why not ask them?

Of course it would be better if Hope and Larry separated, but I can't preach that to Hope; she wouldn't listen, and I would become just another enemy. You did what you had to do, and while I think you are not a great success as a liar, you're as good as most. Your problem is that you never liked lying. It confuses you and muddies the picture you want to have of yourself. Poppy is trying to teach me to lie without giving myself away by all the physical things I do — picking-and-smoothing at my clothes, stuttering, grabbing at a small hank at the back of my hair, separating it, winding it around my finger. I had no idea I did those things; it's a regular performance.

Is there more than Larry's youth, background, and alcoholism? The more I think about it, the more I think we should follow it up.

*Love, Tig*

349

*Dear Gram,    November 13, Grandpa's House*

I visited Larry again yesterday and I have a meeting with him and his therapist tomorrow. I think I'm working too hard or something, because I feel tired all the time now, tired and sad. Grandpa lets me off without doing my share of the housework because he says my studying is the most important thing. The good news is that because of the holidays, they're making the training session shorter, a concentrated week after Thanksgiving. Larry will be <u>home</u> and have the cabin winterized and the new roof put on by the time I'm back.

Things are working out and I should be jumping with joy, but instead there's a weight on my spirit. I haven't told this to anyone. Larry would think I was saying he isn't doing his share, and he is. That awful therapy happens to him every day, people digging and scratching at his spirit with all those questions. Mom and Dad would think I was complaining and they would say I was too young for real life. Grandpa would think I was criticizing him and that I wasn't grateful for everything he has done for me.

It will be better when my study program is over and my trip to Chicago is over, too, and I'm back at the store and back home at our cabin. I'll be given more responsibility at work after I have my training certificate, and I'll be paid more.

I found out my boss, Steve, had to argue plenty to get me into the training program because I'm still pretty young, and because I'm pregnant. Management doesn't like pregnant women in the program because permanent people get maternity leaves. I'm grateful to Steve for standing up for me. I told him I intended to stay with Wild Duds as a career.

Another thing. Steve knows about Larry. All about him. It's funny, because with all my being so careful to keep the hard parts of my life with Larry separate from everything else, something I didn't know and couldn't control opened my secrets up and shook them out like flags on the 4th of July. Walks Away is not an ordinary name and people remember it. Steve's brother is married to a woman whose brother works on Larry's Program. Maybe Steve mentioned me or maybe the brother mentioned Larry, but it happened at a cold-weather picnic they had last weekend up at the brother's house. This afternoon I took my break and Steve came back to the little office where I was drinking my juice and eating my bran muffin — now I eat only healthy things. The door is kept open when we are in there because it's a company rule, but the other girls were out front working so no one else came in. Steve sat down to drink a Coke and eat a candy bar. I laughed at him for his choice and said he should get a better diet, and he started picking up the crumbs that had fallen from my muffin, tasting them and making a face. Then he said, "I know about Larry — about where he is and what he's doing." It sounds cruel to write, but the way he said it was very gentle. I sat there with some muffin in my mouth that I couldn't swallow. He told me how he found out and then he said he knew my husband had some kind of sickness, and that I visited him somewhere, but he thought it was the hospital.

I said that Larry was doing very well on his Program and soon he would be on work release. I said that the <u>other</u> time, the <u>other</u> Program wasn't long enough and it didn't go deep enough. This time it's going to work.

Why did I say there had been another time? It sounded so awful. I saw he knew that, too, that this wasn't Larry's first experience with being in a Program, or even in jail. Steve's brother-in-law maybe knows more of Larry's past than I do — all the times he had been in foster homes or juvenile detention.

He stopped eating and his hand came toward me. He said he didn't tell me this to make me betray Larry. He wanted to tell me I didn't have to lie or cover anything up.

Then, he smiled a little and said that if I needed to take time off for meetings or daytime sessions, I could. I thanked him. When he left I cried.

I want to be simple and not have to make up a lot of lies about where I go anymore, but

I feel — ashamed. Will Steve look at me in a different way, or pity me, or think I'm stupid for marrying Larry? Ben said something once about being pregnant, that it's embarrassing because everyone knows what you did to get that way. This is how it feels to me that Steve knows about Larry's sickness. Later, I said, "Larry is sick. It's a sickness." He didn't answer. He doesn't believe it and he didn't want to tell me he thinks Larry is a delinquent who doesn't have any self-control.

All afternoon I was weepy. I know it's being pregnant. Shining Lady, my tribal midwife, told me that the spirit of our baby was watered by tears and laughter, and that I would find myself laughing suddenly and crying suddenly and that I should be happy in that and not be ashamed, but it's embarrassing to be at work and all of a sudden find your eyes filling up. I got through it okay, but when Grandpa picked me up, I got in the car and sat there bawling and he got scared thinking it was something wrong with me and wanted to take me to the hospital. When I told him it was nothing, just watering our baby's spirit, he sat there all confused and was afraid even to pat my shoulder.

*Love, Hope*

West Virginia. We have gone back to ending
Bunion Rub with a song instead of exhorta-
tions to calisthenics. We still dance into each
new state. This morning three new people
began to do the limbo, and for a moment, the
Fresnos pulled in their breaths, remembering
the dance as Kevin's — remembering him,
with a pang. Then Murray Siger turned,
winked, shrugged, and said, "Why not?"

So, Kevin is still with us, or with some of
us. We are sixty, now. Five of the Walkers
told us they had only the summer to give and
left early in Kentucky. We have 250 names
of Walkers who stayed with us longer than
two weeks. The braid of people moving in
and out of The Walk continues to change it.

Poppy's clinging cough seems better. I
wouldn't continue without her, and the reali-
zation is saddening. I built my life on my
independence. It was much of what drove me
away from Marz into our ten-year pseudo-
separation, and some of that old need was
behind my call to this Walk. I haven't been
free for years, but I didn't realize it until now.

The independence I aimed for all my life is
not attainable and not even desirable. At sixty-
two, I don't need much help physically, but
who knows when I will? I have seesawed between my needs for freedom and for commu-

nity. What a thing to learn from a Walk whose purpose is Environment — trees but not people, water but not communal need.

Our newest Walker is the scion of a glass-door-and-window family now interested in solar applications. He also says the family fund will stake us for the duration. Maybe. We haven't yet faced the challenge of snow, icy rains, and cold as a constant. If he stays, we'll be rich. If he leaves, we won't. Experience makes me cautious and caution lets all the air out of enthusiasm.


*Dear Gram,*                    *November 15, Grandpa's*

In two days, Larry will be finished with his in-patient program and will be on his own during the day, working or looking for work. That will be two weeks, and then we will go back <u>HOME</u>!! I will be six and one-half months pregnant — and will begin making clothes and buying things for the baby. I have to make myself begin to plan for the baby, and to find the little bed and bath things. Mom called to tell me she had leftover stuff in the attic that we can fix up, even some furniture we used when we were babies. She says some of the things have Jason's and Ben's teeth marks on them. This weekend, I am going through <u>your</u> attic, and Aunt Solidarity's attic, and Mom and Dad's attic on a baby-raid. Mom suggested that in the therapy session. I shut her up because I was still scared of <u>having</u> baby things before there <u>is</u> a baby, but then I saw Shining Lady and she told me I would have to begin, during this time, to think about the baby's body as well as its spirit so then I called and we made this plan.

Shining Lady has had four children herself and was a nurse on the reservation. She has black hair that's very smooth and it's in a big rope down her back. She's shorter than I am and fat, which she says keeps her strong.

I went to a session with the social worker at Larry's Program. I knew I wouldn't like it and I didn't. She asked me questions mostly, but I got the idea she was trying to pick at me, trying to make me confess something.

There's this bad thing and it's called Being An Enabler. I heard about it in the other Program. She was trying to make me confess to that. Enablers lie for the sick person or excuse his drinking or doing drugs or abusing. They are part of his problem. But something doesn't fit: the therapists tell the sick person that he has low self-esteem, but when we try to help that, to build the person up a little, we get accused of enabling. I did excuse Larry's behavior to his boss, Mr. Anson. "Why?" the therapist asked me. <u>Why?</u> We needed that job and our cabin. If I didn't excuse Larry to Mom and Dad they would hate him even more. Larry has a terrible tem-

356

per <u>when</u> <u>he</u> <u>drinks</u> and he knows that and so do I and so does Mr. Anson and so does my family. <u>I</u> know how good he can be, how competent and strong. Larry quit high school and everyone <u>knows</u> that. What they don't know is that he has lots of artistic qualities and he's a wonderful builder. Why shouldn't I say <u>those</u> things and not be blamed as An Enabler? Hasn't Larry heard enough bad news about himself?

She wouldn't answer any of these questions because all she kept doing was asking me, "Why do you think that way?" and "What makes you say that?" I left angry and I didn't want to be. The same therapists who talk about Enablers talk about Unconditional Love. They say that abused children are those for whom there is no Unconditional Love. What do they think Larry is, if not an abused child? He is not <u>my</u> child, and I know that, but if that Unconditional Love cures and nourishes the spirits of children, when does the gift stop giving? When does the one who loves become an Enabler and not a teacher of love?

*Love, Hope*

*Dear Tig,*                    *November 17, The Hill*

We had the second family session, this one dealing with the stages alcoholics go through in frustration, rage, and denial, and what programs are available for Larry, for Hope, and for us. Justice and Frank listened but said little.

I'm afraid my feelings about Larry as Professional Patient have colored my picture of him. As he and the therapist talked I turned my attention to Hope. Only now and again did I see in her a flash of doubt, the minutest momentary pucker of a muscle around the eye, the quick look away and then back, as though the look away had been disloyal and was repented of.

In any case, patient has progressed to job-hunter. Larry admitted that working with the public was, for the present, beyond his capacities. He will seek those jobs where there is minimal contact with demanding customers. He said he would take any job. It was then I saw another quick flash in Hope, speed of sound, and gone. How had it been before? the look said. It was replaced by her sky-tinting rainbow smile. Her love would enwrap Larry in light. For a moment I had the urge to say, "Stop the session — she's doing it again," but the look was gone and there was no chasing it with a net. I settled for second best and made a comment that maturity is a fading of the arrogance that insists on the primacy of our dreams. The meeting ended. I met with the social worker for a moment and asked her if it were possible that Larry's problem was caused by chemical imbalances in his brain, or by an injury to the brain. She said she had looked over his records, years of them, and had seen no such evidence. I asked if the program would allow consultation with a neurologist, for which the family would pay. She said certainly, if Larry agreed.

This time I demanded we all go out for coffee. We went to the mall, to Häagen-Dazs. The talk was stilted and desultory, but at least we were looking at each other, telling each other the ordinary things of the day: Jason's arm, Ben's disappearance into the basement to his model city, Frank's problems with changes in the tax laws. I watched Justice, taking tastes from Frank's coconut ice cream. She looked more lost and bereft than Hope. When I asked her about the conflict-resolution program she is introducing in grade schools, she shot me a grateful look, and gave me a short description. It's an interesting idea; you should ask her about it. Frank and Justice suffer in different ways — Justice in words, Frank in silence. Justice despairs, Frank seethes. I have it better than they do. In being host to Hope, I'm <u>doing</u>, playing a part in her life, and that lessens the anguish.

Hope's troubles with Larry and his with the law have affected Ben and Jason, too, and they are the family members we have left out of all the meetings. Jason says he doesn't want to come. Ben wants to help, but says he doesn't know how. I took Jason to a school game last Friday, and on the way over, I asked him what he thought about Hope and Larry's problems. He shrugged and said Larry was an asshole and wouldn't say anymore. When I ask Ben, he looks so forlorn that I don't take the questions further. I know he likes Larry in a way Jason doesn't. He admires Larry's skill with motors and building, a skill Ben lacks completely. Larry responds to that admiration with an openness he gives to no one else. Ben has been to visit Larry in jail. Jason seeks refuge in sports and friends, imitating himself as a happy-go-lucky jock, impatient with his broken arm and eager to get back to a life without paradox or ambivalence. Ben watches and suffers.

We got invited to Cary's first school program. Hope and I went with Solidarity and sat through the program, which seemed endless, although the kids were cute. Hope went as a motherhood trainee, and watched everything rapt as a cat. She's getting ready for her trip to Chicago and wants to be finished with all her assignments in plenty of time. She's Justice's daughter in that, and Frank's. It's moving, really, to watch the habits, the propensities as they make themselves plain down all the generations.

*Love, Marz*

*Dear Gram,*          *November 19, Grandpa's*

I did the baby raid. I understand a little of how Mom feels to see me pregnant and sort of re-live her days of having a baby. We went to our house and up to the attic. There was a rocker there that I took, that will fit fine in our cabin and where I can rock and hold the baby. There were some little blankets and other things I took, too, bedding and stuff. Then we went to Niwot, to Aunt Sol's, and we sat around and told stories and I cried. Then we went to your and Grandpa's attic, and opened the baby boxes. I found the little baby books you made for Mom and Aunt Sol and we all got soft and weepy and it was lots of fun.

When I was with Larry at school, my friends didn't like him — I think I told you about that — and when I got pregnant, my friends dropped me cold. It wasn't because I was pregnant — Annie Royce is pregnant, and so is Patty Daniels. It was because I was with Larry. Denise said she was scared of him. She's in college now, in Pennsylvania. She said she would write, but she doesn't. I see some of the girls sometimes at Wild Duds or on the mall. Yesterday it was Toni. She came into Wild Duds, not knowing I worked there, and when I came over, she stared at me and said Hi. I said Hi. Then I asked her how she was doing.

She said fine, but she kept looking to one

361

side of me or to the other, like she was waiting for someone else to show up. I tried to make it be all right, so I asked what she was doing.

School, she said, CSM, in Golden.

She didn't ask me about my pregnancy or when I was due or anything. She probably thought Larry and I had broken up and I was going to be a welfare mom. I wanted to tell her about the management program, that I wasn't just a part-time person but a full-time employee and respected and that I would get maternity leave and in a few years manage a store. I couldn't, though. The management program tells us to be completely professional when we are at work. I asked her how we could help her.

She told me she needed something to wear for field camp — geology. She started looking around. She didn't find anything at Wild Duds, but that was because she was embarrassed to see me. I didn't tell Steve that there are people I drive away.

I thought — I had the dream that my school friends would find out about me working and come in and we would get back together. I have fantasies about them giving me a baby shower. I even dreamt about it once or twice, a bunch of us, me laughing and opening baby presents.

I tell myself not to mind. I'm going to Chicago, a woman, not a girl, and I'm beginning manager training that will keep us on the track toward our goal, Larry's and mine. <u>They're</u> still <u>girls</u>. But it still hurt.

*Love, Hope*

*Dear Marz,*       *November 22, Lawton, W.Va.*

Something is poetically sweet-sad about this landscape, mountains and long vistas of deciduous forests at the tail end of autumn. The bare trees are carding long mists and slow rain. Autumn has cleared the covering foliage away. Good.

We walk, playing Civil War, imagining The Walk a march. Our heads turn, we listen for the crack of a rifle, see at the corners of our eyes a gray tatter in the mist. We advance, wondering how they advanced in country like this. We passed a dead cow on the road, smell well before sight, and a coverlet of crows working the corpse. Poppy came close to my ear and said, "Yankees been here. Look alive. I'll warn the others."

"But <u>we're</u> the Yankees, stupid."

"Oh, God, I forgot. Let's go raid us a farmhouse."

Will you come to Washington? Say yes and I'll call you with details. Can we meet the people we were, the outwardly shy secretly grandiose young people who met at the first orientation session of the Brotherhood Literacy Program?

From Hope's letters, I get her version of reality — Larry in his therapy and you and Justice and Frank and the therapist all there, and her own picture of herself. In the beginning her letters about what was happening differed widely from yours, but now they seem at least to be describing the same incident, even though she is still partisan. She is not easy or comfortable with the Program's therapist. Is there a way she could find another? I got an unfortunate answer to a question I asked you — who is her confidante? No one. She has no friends her own age. Her closest contact besides you is Steve, her boss at the store, but that can only go so far — her loyalty to Larry and picture of herself can't be compromised before him, or before the family. Do you think she could accept a therapist? You say Larry has always been a client, a patient, a recipient. He might not want Hope to become one. Have you asked Larry about the neurologist? What does he say? Thank heaven you are there to help her.

*Love, T.*


*Dear Ben,*                          *November 23,*
                          *Rainelle, West Virginia*


I'm sorry for waiting so long before I answered your interesting letter. We are in mountains now, and walking is more difficult, and slower.

We race to make up our time and find our campsites, set up, eat, have Bunion Rub, and then fall into our bedrolls until the wake-up sounds. I never knew how much of this country is mountainous. Surprise. Perhaps it's another thing for you to figure into your understanding of cities. We usually imagine our cities on flat grids, with just a few dips and rises, like Boulder, but height equals view, or does when the city is beginning. You will have to study cities like San Francisco to see what happens when they are built on one hill or many hills.

The study you have begun could supply a lifetime of fascination. Does that thought excite or depress you? Lots of us have dreams and visions that quit on us or get worn out in the middle of our lives. We are left standing, looking around at a bunch of cartons filled up with ideas and excitements we have outgrown, wondering into what new boxes we plan to put the rest of our lives.

In another 20 days or so we will have crossed America, almost sea to shining sea, and but for perhaps 200 miles total, all on foot. We walked the middle, more or less, and not in areas of high population. Cities offer separate problems. If there is another Walk in that, another grandmother will have to do it.

This trip has given me a feeling of the shape of the nation and some of its mood. This feeling is at great variance from the one I hear in talk among my friends and in print and on the radio. We've preached the worst, and over a lifetime we have come to believe it. There's plenty to do, but don't listen to too much negativism. It weakens resolve and might make you think your work lacks value. It doesn't.

*Love, Grandma*


*Dear Antigone,*                    *November 23,*
                    *Central Boulder Rehab Facility*


It has been five months since I met you in Pueblo — it was this time in June, I think. Lots has happened to me since then, and some of it was bad. I am in an abuse Program and we have learned that abuse of drugs and alcohol includes other abuses, too. One is an abuse of our family. As part of my Program, I am required to apologize to the people I have done wrong things to and one of them is you. That's because of Hope and also because of the money you sent to Hope on her birthday, which went up my nose in cocaine and down my throat in booze. I'm sorry for the pain I caused you and also the worry about Hope, due to my drinking and my abuse of her while I was drunk. I hope I can become a person worthy of your respect and a grandson-in-law you will respect as well as a father of your great grandchild.

*Working for sobriety, Larry Walks Away*

*Moms,*   *Niwot*

Anton has split. I thought he would. There was too much guilt and too many things not to talk about. Their other friends were no help. Many of them hated Anton's cross-dressing.

Blake comes home and sits in front of a TV he doesn't watch. When I go over, it's an effort for him to talk. I see his light still on when I go to sleep.

*Sol*

*Dear Larry,*   *November 28,*
*Marlinton, West Virginia*

I got your letter when we were in a place called Cranberry Glades Campground. They tell us that the Native Americans of the area used to gather those cranberries and pound them into the antelope and deer meat they had from hunting. The combination of fruit and meat is a Native American tradition, they tell me. Now that we have you in the family, that fact meant more to me.

We are rooting for you and Hope to find the way to make good lives for yourselves. I'm sorry you spent that money the way you did, but along with my forgiveness, I want to send you the message that I don't want to be shut out of your lives when I come back. Please

don't confuse the family's interest with inter-
ference and our wish to help with meddling.
We will try to be careful about your feelings,
but our interest is not something critical of
you or Hope.

I know you are courageous. I saw that
plainly in Pueblo. I pray that you call on that
courage to help you in the fight you are now
facing. We all want you to win it.

*Antigone Warriner*


*Dear Tig,*                    *November 29, The Hill*

Yes to Washington. The congressmen and
senators will all be home for the holidays.
Photo-ops will have to come later. I want to
find the places we went, the old brownstone
where we took our training, the coffee shop
and the drug store. Are People's Drug Stores
still there? I remember sending your folks an
aspirin bottle with People's label. I thought
they would chuckle. They saw it as my ridi-
culing The Movement. It made for a chilly
meeting, remember?

Thanksgiving was as good as it could be
without your being here. Thanks for the call.
We had the turkey and trimmings at Justice
and Frank's. Then, Hope got us all to go to
the center and have dessert with Larry. I
wanted to take Larry aside and ask him if he
would consent to see a neurologist, but the

timing wasn't right. Larry had the largest family participation of anyone there and it was probably the first time any of his occasions was well attended.

The third packet of letters arrived yesterday and will go with the others to be read when we are old, about eight months from now.

The day before Thanksgiving I got a letter from Larry. As part of the Program he has to ask forgiveness for wrongs he has done to people in his immediate circle. It was boilerplate. He called me Martin. I wanted to go over there and smack him. Why? It's not his fault; I guess I'm lucky it wasn't "Pops." Asking forgiveness might be a good idea, but it makes me wonder what I really feel about the things our family has suffered because of him. The letter I sent in return was a masterpiece of ambivalence. I want him sober, sane, working, and out of Hope's life. I want Hope to have the baby and put it up for adoption. A second choice would be that Hope divorce, raise the baby, and later marry a good man who will accept the child as his own and give it some brothers and sisters. Yes, that.

That's not what I wrote. The letter I did write, full of the forgiveness business, was also full of hypocrisy, prompted by the Program. Was it right to lie the way I did? I wrote what I <u>wish</u> I felt: forgiveness, acceptance. He knows better — he must. What does <u>he</u> feel?

Is he serving the Program or trying to wake some virtue in himself, or is he like the rest of us, a mass of contradictory feelings intricate as Celtic knotwork? If only I thought it would do some good.

I went up to Niwot to see Anton, Sol's neighbor. Blake told me Anton had left. Blake looked terrible, stiff with pain. When I went to his office, Anton, who looked even worse, apologized for not telling me about the sudden move. He wants to meet with me after Christmas. I thanked him for his help. He said he had enjoyed our work together and I feel he really did.

Tomorrow I will go down to the courthouse to find out about what is required in the way of certificates, permits, etc. I also have an appointment with two people presently in the work. You say you will be coming home changed. I have also been changing. I won't quit my job, until retirement, but a new career is opening ahead of me. It's one that may eat up savings until it begins to produce. How do you feel about being the principal breadwinner for a time? I haven't been so excited in years.

*Love, M.*

# *December*

꩜

*Dear Marz,*                    *December 3,*
                          *Cave, West Virginia*

So, Larry wrote to you as Martin, did he? Well, I was Dear Antigone. My letter was only half boilerplate, so I take a different view of the salutation. No one trains kids to say Mr. or Mrs. anymore. Had he been more guileful, it would have been Sir.

The <u>Program</u> <u>was</u> in it, yes; <u>abuse</u> and <u>sobriety</u>, which I can't imagine him saying. My answer was also uncomfortable, but I had an advantage you didn't: I have seen Larry under the best possible conditions and he knows it. I have witnessed his resourcefulness, courage, gallantry. He has seen gratitude and admiration in my eyes and that, as the man says, don' hoit.

Larry will read what he imagines we wrote. I don't think he is mature enough to see us realistically. Does Hope? As for us, we are blinded by Hope's sweetness, her youth, our love. There is less excuse for us than for her.

We had a Thanksgiving pause in The Walk, which has shortened its mileage as the days grow short. The celebration was marred by

371

two speeches from people who felt the feast was an insult to Native Americans. Columbus Day is gone; Halloween is going. Christmas has been subverted. At this rate, we'll end up celebrating Water (in June), Rocks (in November), and Mud (in February).

Tomorrow: West Virginia into Virginia. Poppy and I will two-step. We have practiced and we are very good.

Our constituency has changed again. The Gym Teachers' numbers and influence have shrunk. The ideologues are still with us, orthodox environmentalists who wear only natural fibers and won't use anything not immediately biodegradable. Their numbers are increasing and will, I think, continue to increase as our group becomes more urban.

The Walk feels safe. The word environmental as a definition sometimes readies people to hate us, and there have been mumblings here and there, but nothing like Pueblo. The worst is a patronizing attitude, such as one might have for a feeble-minded grandmother. Things change once the locals take part in our questionnaires.

Have you thought, dear man, that your new career might mean something new and good for me also? I've known for some time that your work has been less satisfying, burdened with rules, regs, and gridlock. You have been coming home tired in a way that isn't caused by ordinary work or daily annoyances. It's worth a lot to me to see you happy with what you do. Let's sell the house. The library will take me full time and, with savings and all the rest, I don't foresee a problem, given reasonable health for a while. As for accepting a lower standard of living, there's no better preparation than a year on the road, eating day-old bread and drinking juices of completely unidentifiable constituency, except for the sugar. I am queen of bean stews and watered soup. We might even move to a cheaper area, out of Boulder, and save a fortune.

I just had a flash of us telling Hope and Larry we are going tribal and setting up a double tent next to them.

*All my love, Tig*

*Dear Gram,*                                   *December 4,*
*Hotel Cameron, Chicago, Illinois*

In two more days Larry will be finished with the in-center part of his Program. In four, I will be back in Colorado, not on University Hill, but <u>HOME</u> with him, where we belong. Grandpa has been wonderful to me but I have counted every minute it has taken until Larry and I can be together.

I went to the cabin before I came here, and saw how much we need to winterproof the house. Larry's plan is to do that and then get any work he can — there are help wanted signs all over town for supermarket people and restaurant staff. That can be until spring, when he can get construction work and that will see us past the worst. The people at The Program say the first year is the hardest.

Here I am in Chicago, working hard on this management program with people all older than I am, and thinking about Larry and our lives together. I have been splitting my mind in two halves, but my heart — the part I write to you about — is all in the scrub-land country under the wide, wide sky, in our brush-covered covert-place, Larry and I.

Good news about school for him. There are two or three training programs he is eligible for in technical electronic or mechanical fields. He needs a skill we can take wherever we want to homestead — some place which will be near a large town or small city where we can have land not too far from where we can both get jobs. We have talked about it to the counselors and they tell us it could be a sound plan.

Four days and I will see him again. I'm a little scared. They have talked to me so much about <u>my</u> hurting him, about that <u>enabling</u>. They have made it hard for us to be natural and easy with each other. It's as though we are bringing other people into our home, people who will always be asking him what he means by this or that action, and me what I mean by this or that word. I want to scrub their influence away in the shower we will take when I come home, all the outside-ness, all the jail-dirt and the fumes of guards and prisoners and the contamination of cruelty and anger. I want them all flowing off both of us.

There has been so much shame. People thought I didn't see or hear, because I didn't let myself react to the things they said and the expressions on their faces. They said, "Mrs. <u>Walks Away</u> is here," as though it was funny. Some of them made comments about redskins. After I passed one said, "That's that Indian's wife? Well, she's got the lump, all right." The Lump. I wanted to die. That night I called Shining Lady because the words wouldn't leave my head and they were poisoning the baby. She said I should get a friend who has a sauna to let me use it, and to include sassafras bark and eucalyptus leaves in the steam, as a healing medicine. That is what Larry and I will do together when I get home. I am using the work I do here in Chicago to make me worthy, working hard so that Larry and I will deserve the goodness that will come to us when we are clear of shame and humiliation.

You can see that we need to get away from the cruelty of people in the White World. Grandpa reminds me that not all of it is cruel. I do like my friends at work. I love you and Grandpa and my baby brother, Ben. DO

375

NOT tell him I called him that because <u>he'll</u> have to have a sweat bath he'll get so mad. Even Mom and Dad try hard and I don't think they are really racist, even though they don't understand Larry or me. Some of the world is cruel, though, and wounding to the spirit. It takes huge amounts of love and courage to overcome that. It's what has to build up in Larry, and it's always being depleted.

Soon, soon he'll be with me and our love will begin to build again.

*Love, Hope*


*Dear Tig,*                    *December 6, The Hill*

Hope is off on her management class and when she comes back, it will be to the cabin. Larry is finished with the in-patient part of his Program. I picked him up at the Center and took him back out to their place. On the way I talked to him about seeing a neurologist. He slid out from under it, not deftly but the way a car skids — there's no control, all of a sudden. I didn't feel violence in him but simply a sense that he was no longer — <u>there</u>. He chuckled and then said it was white man's medicine. He had been examined; they put electrodes all over his head "like Frankenstein." Had he ever been on medication? "They do in some of the places — it's supposed to keep the inmates quiet."

He was giggling as though I were telling jokes. I wanted to ask when the evaluation had been done, but I realized I couldn't say anything more.

When we arrived at the cabin road, his equanimity seemed restored. We left the car and walked the way in. He was telling me plans to cut a turn-around spot for convenience. We saw the cabin and he began to hurry, motioning to me to follow. We walked around the cabin, noting what needed to be done to make it livable for the winter. The problem is water, primarily. They have the good stove I got them last spring. He's vented it well, and there's plenty of wood available, scrap and dead wood all around for the taking. He also burns lumberyard scraps that he gets from somewhere. My next gift to them will be a chain saw. The cabin is nothing grand but is livable. There are clever systems for showering and saving water, and a composting toilet — it's not as primitive as one would think, and as I noted this innovation and that, he came alive and I saw instants of what Hope sees in him. He wants a simplicity she is growing out of. It's sad, really. He wants what he can touch, make his own, effect on his own, because the modern world is too bewildering and complex for him. Hope is doing well in it, off to Chicago with an armload of workbooks, computer discs, and VCR training tapes. Part of Larry accepts Hope's skill because it will allow him to make the homestead, and the life he needs. The other part of him — who knows? It's proud, suspicious, and has been violent. His behavior is a mystery to me. I have now seen him in company, in jail, on The Program, and on his own. You have written about him as defender in a mob scene. All the pictures are different. Nothing coheres.

I went home to a too-large, sound-deadened house. I'm aware of how much Hope filled these spaces, how I looked forward to picking her up each evening, even when we had to swing over to check the cabin, or go to therapy sessions. I looked forward to our planning dinner, making it, watching TV, or taking in a movie at the Twin — our tastes aren't the same; she usually saw one film and I another. It seemed to <u>me</u> there was lots of laughter and enjoyment with it all.

I was often aware of her listening, as we sat at dinner, for a clink of dishes and a rattle of tableware down at The Center where Larry was. At night when we were home after therapy meetings, I felt her turning as though to catch a word he was saying to someone down there. Sound rises. She was living a mystical physics that bore Larry's footfall up to her.

So, though she was never entirely <u>here</u>, she was here enough to shine the days for me. I miss her, and missing her makes me miss you more than ever. She has taught me how to listen for the faint, distant sound of The

Walk's camp-plates being scraped, scraps of dinner, scraps of voices over the work: "What's our next stop?" "When do we get to Manassas?"

Sleep well. I will see you in Washington.

*Love, M.*

---

*Moms,*                          *December 8, Niwot*

A date, yesterday evening; another dud, an almost. We went to the Comedy Club. There was a foursome two or three tables away — you may know how close they seat people in those places; everyone up your nose. This was a rowdy bunch, lots of laughing, but there was one braying laugh so constant I found myself waiting for it. There <u>was</u> something weirdly familiar. At a break in the show, I got up and so did the laugher. I looked over at her and looked again and knew I was seeing Anton, a cross-dressed Anton — I felt the same fear I did when I first saw him. But this wasn't private and strange-looking; it was public and dangerous. He saw me and I motioned with my eyes, subtly, that I was going to the ladies' room. He hesitated, then followed, without giving any clues.

There was a little powder room in the Ladies'; women came in and out of the stalls and walked past us. Some did double takes, but no one stopped.

"I'm Lily, here," he said. "Here, it's Lily, and it's <u>she</u>."

Anton's lip was trembling with nervousness.

"Overdone," I said.

He grinned at me and said it was a cross-dresser's style.

Where was he living now? I told him I missed him.

He said he missed me, too, but couldn't stay with Blake anymore. It was like a morgue.

I tilted my head toward the club outside and asked if they knew he was Anton, and cross-dressed.

He shook his head.

Wasn't that dangerous?

He said not really. The other girl in the party was a professional escort who knows the game. The game was to get the men drunk enough so the girls could slip away. What if that didn't happen? He said he wasn't without weapons, and kept in good shape, and he did a small bump-and-grind, winking. He was thinner. I told him so. He said there was nothing like misery to trim a girl down.

I asked him why risk this.

He said there was only one way they could really tell it had all come together, that the depilatories, the girdles, the hair, the nails, the exercising, the work at the mirror, was all the way it should be.

What about the group, his cross-dressing friends?

He said they lied to each other, friend-lies. "Darling, how sweet you look," lying. The only way to know for sure was with a man, who saw you as a woman . . . He gave me a little move and said, "I gotta go."

I touched his shoulder and told him to be careful, please, to take care of himself.

He patted my back the way my women friends do, and then winked and said, "So long, Sweetie," turned, and left.

When I went back to our table, theirs was roaring away and Anton's laugh was exploding over it like shrapnel. It didn't sound like female laughter, but it wasn't masculine, either. How much could he get away with?

Whatever fun was in the evening evaporated; I pleaded tiredness and came home. What would Anton do when the date was over and the man who had poured him full of booze and listened to the wide-open laugh wanted more than a goodnight kiss ("Surely you put out, that dress, that walk —")? There was nothing soft in Lily's image. It was all hot to trot, pornographic haste and need, no delicacy, all urge. There's insult in that costume, where nothing is held back, shy or secret except the last thing, too late for the man at that table. Wouldn't Lily's date feel used, taken, made a fool of?

Anton is a talented architect. I've seen his work. His big effects are balanced. He uses simple, restrained lines; his temperament is classical. That means restraint, reserve, you'd say <u>modesty</u>. These are supposedly feminine effects, and I should know — I've battled the damn stereotype all my life. Does any part of me come on like <u>that</u>?

And there you have it, Moms, my evening out.

*Sol*


*Dear Marz,*          *December 9, Shenandoah*

The weather is forbidding. We hurry to towns for warmth. Waking up is agonizing. We grouse and bitch.

Now and then, strangers visit the camp, and last night a motherly-looking black woman. She stood at our tent, stolidly, small and wide, wearing the forty-pound coat of disguising years over what I guessed had been a skinny body. Her face was an unglazed earthenware color, crazed with wrinkles so symmetrical they might have been carved. Why was I staring? Why did she break into smiles, standing there warm-eyed, daring me to recognition? I said, "I know you," and she laughed. Her laughter broke her disguise into pieces and the buried name came out of my mouth. It was Enelia.

Poppy yelled, "<u>Enelia</u>!" and we started the hug-and-squeal of long-parted women. Enelia Seeley is now a grandmother, named McConnel. Oh, Marz, she looks like <u>her</u> grandmother!

It could have been all those years ago, summer, and us seventeen again, staying with Enelia's grandmother in that weathered house because it was off by itself and not in Taylor Grove's "Niggertown." Do you remember all that, how our being away from the settlement meant the local constabulary could turn a blind eye to our existence? I hadn't thought of Enelia's grandmother, that forceful, frightened black woman, in years.

When I told her she laughed and said it was a compliment. "Grandma passed back in 1980, but she did live to see me go to college and my two boys graduate from college, too." All their diplomas were on her bedroom wall.

I'm quoting so you will hear the words and imagine the soft drawl, and Poppy and me holding our breaths to hear her.

Mamma Sarah stayed in that house long after the settlement was gone, the shacks fallen in. The children got electricity for her in 1969, but she wouldn't have water in the house. How I remember working that pump. Enelia lives in Harrisonburg now, and works at the University.

From her tote bag she pulled a photo album. We sat down on my sleeping bag and looked at the young, frightened people we were then, white strangers in a Negro settlement in enemy territory. I had forgotten how young Enelia was — twelve or thirteen, and skinny, with those tight braids — the pickaninny of minstrel shows. Marz — there <u>you</u> were. I had forgotten how golden you were, how lanky-easy you looked standing among us. There were all the college students gone south to teach, to bring textbooks and maps and globes to youngsters who had never seen such things. Poppy was remembering names I had forgotten.

What a mellow evening! We peered at the pictures and talked and talked. Many of the images were posed, everyone trying to look dignified, but some were taken at ease, eating, standing at the doors of clapboard schools. The white kids all looked too happy — smiling too much — I know we were mostly feeling dislocated and frightened. None of that fear showed on our picture-faces, but the discomfort was evident in our gestures, our stances, how we grouped ourselves. We were trying so hard to be comfortable; we were so much <u>bigger</u> than our hosts and many of them looked frightened.

Do you remember Taylor Grove? I know you worked in another settlement, but do you remember the Seeleys? I <u>know</u> you remember their old dog, <u>Gardeen</u>. I had first thought the name was <u>Garden</u> and only after I had called him did they say <u>Guardian</u>. He was a dog of immense dignity and presence, never jumping or running but head up, walking as a military man might walk on inspection, and he sat as neatly and watchfully as a cat.

I vowed we would never forget that dog, and I haven't thought of him in years, but there he was in the pictures, watching us, managing a group of children or standing solemnly with the leaders of the community. I stared at our big, white leggy presences, in shorts and sleeveless blouses, which were not summer wear in the black rural South of those days. I asked Enelia if we were as much a curiosity as we seemed, now.

She thought, judiciously, and said we were — confusing much of the time. The locals of the settlement were familiar if not comfortable with white people. There were those they trusted but kept at a distance, and those they tried to keep away from, who were a danger. We fit in neither category.

I was amazed at what I was now seeing: ourselves there as the people of Taylor Grove must have seen us.

Enelia described us as down there giving our all, staying with the poorest of the share-croppers, marveling at what they thought was ordinary life, their gardens, their spirit in church, their capacity to endure. We came into their homes with that respect, that marveling, but we demanded a lot, too. I asked what that was.

Friendship, she said, intimacy, even love. Some of us had wanted more from our hosts than they had to give. We were leaving, after all, when summer was over.

I remembered. What she said was true. Good days, we agreed; hard days, too. Enelia added that but for the start we made — we and others — she wouldn't have her satisfying work and her children, theirs. Then we talked about all of them and all of you.

This morning as The Walk started, Poppy said that I looked thoughtful. I shrugged and said that I had been so proud of myself for going down to Taylor Grove. I didn't realize how naive I was or how little I saw of what was really going on.

She laughed and said, "They also serve who partially understand why they are there. I was no better than you. My hair was really red then, but I was never as beautiful as I thought I was."

*Love, Tig*


*Dear Marz,*                 *December 11,*
                           *Waterloo, Virginia*


The day after Enelia's visit, I was still chewing over the experience and examining the memories. I was humming the way they did in Taylor Grove. Do you remember that murmured sound so many "Negroes" carried around with them as background music? "Lord, I ain't no ways tired." "Fix me, Jesus."

"Walkin' in Jerusalem."

By noon I was thrumming with it. Poppy had picked it up and the murmur was going back and forth between us:

Me: Aren't you ready?
Poppy: Aren't you ready?
Me: Aren't you ready?
Both: To walk in Jerusalem, just like John.

We kept having to remind one another that none of our teaching or the later sit-ins or prayer groups had been here, but in the Deep South. All day we walked and hummed and people passed us, going up or coming down The Walk, and smiled. We must have been glowing, wreathed in memory and the hum.

*Love, Tig*

*Dear Grandma,*     *December 12, Grant Street*

Wow, what a present. I like getting the tee shirts but this is much better. I never thought those small places would have maps of their towns and photos taken in the 1860s, and all the way up to now. The Harrisonburg ones are almost complete. I know it was work for you, but it's the best thing there is to show me what I need to know. Towns and cities grow in different ways, but when a population declines do things go into reverse, like a movie run backwards?

My model has gone far away from what I

started with — early Boulder. It's more like Harrisonburg now. Will you do Washington, D.C., for me? They must have lots of stuff. I know you don't walk through large cities. Right now, that's fine with me, because towns are best for what I need. I'll get into big cities when I understand what happens in the smaller ones. It's something to look forward to. Anyway, thanks a lot!!

Family news: Jason is still a muscle-brained pain in the ass. He ruined my bike and never paid me back for fixing it. He's too big to beat up. I was reading about child-labor laws and they are a good thing except for lumps like Jason. When he's sixteen, he'll put his stupidity into a car and drive it around town, spreading stupidity wherever he goes.

He has signed up with the ski team, which is good news. He'll be out of my hair, at least. I saw Hope and Larry yesterday. I went up to the cabin to bring Hope a dress Mom sewed for her. We have had two or three big snows and the cabin has places that need to be insulated because the cold comes in and runs through the whole room. A week ago, I helped Larry put up shelves and next week I'll do some more. For Christmas I'm going to get them a gift certificate at a hardware store.

*Love, Ben*

*Dear Jason,*

Out of the cast at last! Congratulations. Ben tells me you have signed up for ski team and although you missed starting out with them, there's a whole season ahead. The catch-up shouldn't take too long.

I wish you would write. It would be interesting to hear about you and the team and what school is like for you, classes, friends, etc. It's a great relief to be able to sound off to someone and know that not only will she be glad to read what you say but will keep your confidences and not blab them all over town. You also have much to tell me.

For example, I know what teams do when they win; what do they do to get over the bad feelings they have when they lose? I am having something of a team experience on this Walk and it's quite a revelation.

*Love, Grandma*

*Dear Gram,*                    *December 13,*
                    *Wild Horse Dream Ranch*

I'm home! <u>We're</u> home, <u>Home</u>. We're still careful and quiet and light-footed around each other because we don't want to break into that happiness and spoil it. I know we'll get easier and more natural, soon. My trip to Chicago was good for me in a business way, and in a personal way, too, and it's not just that I get a certificate and a little more money, but it means that I can tell Larry what I learned there.

I met and talked to lots of people and I found out that many women are married to men who are Non-Traditional Earners. That means that the woman of the couple is in the business world or a profession and the man is in the arts or has seasonal work, or teaches or does nursing or keeps house. A lot of the couples have babies. The men were home with those babies.

I'm not saying that this will be our model. I'm saying that's what's happening all around and we don't have to feel odd or weird that I make the money and Larry builds and keeps our home and will be homesteading for us while I earn the money we need. I think he had to apologize to some picture in his head that he didn't fit. Men's jobs have changed even more than ours have — Larry would have been a warrior in his own culture.

Grandpa has been picking me up to go to work, and when he brought me home from the airport, he said we should think seriously about getting a <u>vehicle</u>. He was ready for Larry's anger or his being insulted, too proud to accept any help, but Larry surprised both of us by listening. A man at Grandpa's office is moving and wants to get rid of an old but very usable pickup truck. He wants $400. If we went over and saw it and ran it and wanted it, Grandpa said he would buy the pickup and then sell it to us for a small amount per week, or something that Larry and I could manage. Then Larry could drive me to work in the morning and use the truck for his own work during the day, to carry lumber or any of the things he needs. We're going to look at the truck tomorrow.

Mom and Dad wanted us to go over there for dinner when I got home, but I wanted to be alone with Larry. I expected a big blow-up over that, too, but it didn't happen. It isn't because they understood what I tried to tell them. They are tip-toeing around Larry and me because he is just out of The Program and I am pregnant and they're afraid he'll break into pieces.

Ben came up on his bike. It's fixed. He says he will visit us until the snow is too deep for him to come. Larry is trying to teach him some things about building. Anyone watching Ben would think he was stupid, even though we know he isn't. It's like his hands don't listen to what his brain is telling him. Larry told me he never knew anyone who kept on trying again and again after lousing things up as badly as Ben does.

Take the shelves. We have slowly been insulating the cabin, but there are still no inner walls for most of it. This morning, Ben came with some plywood he had left over from that stupid miniature city project of his. (I don't tell him it's stupid.) There were four long pieces. We nailed them up where we needed shelves and places for hooks to hold tools and clothes poles. Ben must have used thirty nails on one of those strips and left no place for the brackets to go. When he finally did get a shelf up he was so glad he wanted to take a picture of it. We all got to laughing so hard we could hardly stand up, and that made his clumsiness all right, but I know that even though Larry laughs at Ben, he respects Ben for other things. Ben was telling us some of his ideas about cities and how people use them and Larry said later that he thought Ben might be rich someday because of those ideas. Then, he looked serious and said, "I always thought people got rich because they inherited money or stole it or took it from other people, but you could . . . a person could get rich from an idea he had and that made sense to other people." I could see he was thinking about that.

Here's my new schedule: it's a forty-four-hour week because we stay open late Thursday and all day Saturdays. I come in late three days a week, but I close the store. Larry was sore when he heard about the extra hours. He said Wild Duds' management program was just a fake thing to get more work out of me. He gets his anger back with what he thinks. He blames The System for taking it out of ordinary people like us. I tell him I'm learning all the time, buying, design and the logic of the store, bookkeeping, recording, policy, all of it. "What for? Just so they can get work out of you."

"Yes," I say, and now I don't let him tell me things I don't agree with, because they say that would be <u>Enabling</u>.

"They just make you work more."

I saw then that Larry wants to see life the way it is in jail, where people try to get privileges without giving anything but forced or phony cooperation. I told him that it makes more money for us to help us get some land and build our own homestead without it being a secret kept from the health department.

But it is close to the holiday time when Larry gets depressed. I remember he did that last year, back in high school. I remember him saying angry things when people were being happy about the holiday. Last year, Larry said, his mother sent him a Christmas card. I would like to meet her. She doesn't even know she's going to be a grandma. She would be proud to know I'm having a tribal midwife.

*Love, Hope*

The weather is holding, mild for the season, the cold fresh, with an edge. We are on the high of our first arrival, sea to sea (we won't <u>see</u> the ocean until New Jersey). I am feeling bridal nervousness about meeting Marz. I want this visit to be glowing, full of the best of our old days. I got Kim Duda to give me a haircut and I have been oiling myself to get rid of the camp skin, face like an alligator's with windburn and work, hands that can sand wood.

I hope Washington will have kept echoes of our first meeting, Martin Warriner and Antigone Klein, young students full of principle and eagerness, hiding their uncertainty and labile emotions from everyone, including themselves. I laugh at both of them now, but the laughter has affection and forgiveness. Maybe we'll catch sight of them from a bus, or through the trees as we stand across the street from the building in which we trained.

*Moms,*                                    *2:00 A.M., Detox*

Christmas is coming. We are tying down the tables, getting ready for Detox's mob scene out-of-control ski accident we call The Holiday Season. It's a great excuse, so the regulars are beginning early. We start building our clientele from the high school and college when the schools let out. It will be interesting, you and Pops not being here for Christmas — I can't remember that happening since the mid-eighties when you were protesting up in Montana. Jussy will serve a scaled-down model for all the kids. Hope and Tonto will be going to some Native American hate festival in Denver, and I signed up for work here in the Rumpus Room, all because you won't be around.

You didn't show up at my sixth-grade graduation because you were in jail, and every time I started having friends or settling somewhere, you pulled me away or sent me back to Dad's. I see now that even with that, you and Dad are the axle of us. If there's an <u>us</u>. We're all different; I probably would never have met or known anyone like Justice, if I didn't have her as a sister.

*Sol*


DIARY ENTRY                          *December 18,*
                                    *Washington, D.C.*


Marz came to the campground again and had to be reintroduced to The Walk, all our new people. We and our D.C. sponsors set out a dinner on the campground. One asked how it felt to have come so far. I was about to answer when Patricia said that not all of us were Fresnos. This led to our being singled out again. How did we feel about the D.C. to Massachusetts leg of The Walk? I said it was like hitting a wall. Why should this part be different?

"Interest," Patricia said. "Attitude," said another. "People here are blasé." "Weather," someone said.

The sponsors laughed. One said he was proud of us for what we had done. "The blasé factor is no higher here than it is anyplace else. Don't be fooled."

Little by little our spirits and mood rose. Todd got up. He came in at Arizona, he said. "We did the desert, we did the mountains. If we can do a ten-thousand-foot mountain pass, we sure as hell can do New Jersey," and we all broke out cheering and laughing.

The Walk has found its new challenge.


DIARY ENTRY                    *December 19,*
                               *Mayflower Hotel*


We had hoped to retrace the steps we had once made down the summer streets of D.C. in the early fifties. My memory of the city was a summer one, wet heat and a memory of greenness — of big trees in the quiet neighborhood where we trained, worn brick in its old streets, the feeling of being back in a historical time.

396

Our neighborhood was gone. The trees were gone, the row-houses with their tiny gardens were now high-rises, sheer wall and window glass. The small city is now huge. Enelia's voice had faded in the rumble of traffic and the changed season. We went to a museum, a movie, to dinner, and we had a long, sweet reunion, but after months in a sleeping bag, our hotel room seemed overheated and the bed as fatally giving as quicksand. We spent the night trying to compromise on the heat.

And we talked about the years I was away; about our remarriage; about the criticism Marz endured. Half his office had expressed disapproval of his weakness and let him know they considered him pussy-whipped to take me back.

I asked about the last twenty years.

He gave me C-plus or maybe B-minus. He reminded me that I had picketed Rocky Flats when half of our neighbors worked there.

"I picketed for <u>them</u>, too, the safety of their children."

"I'm not disagreeing. You never realized any of the trade-off costs."

I was too proud of myself, wasn't I?

Now I'm back at camp. Marz stays warm at the hotel, visiting us as we ready for the winter part of our Walk northward. We have begun to nerve ourselves by reminiscing, picking among our medals: "You were there —

wasn't that weather awful? I was ready to leave The Walk, but then it got <u>worse,</u> so I <u>had</u> to stay." "Remember the ice storm going up that pass?" "Remember the mud?" "Remember the fog?" For the men, the associations were positional, geographical, with names, dates, places, locating. For the women, the associations were how we felt at this place and that. "Remember when I cried and couldn't stop, when the flood was cresting?" "Remember when you fell off that cliff?"

Marz leaves tomorrow, a better good-bye than the one at his previous visit. I'll be able to call more frequently, now. Any Walk in the future will surely be equipped with cellular phones, and the last of the letters will have been written.

*Dear Gram,*                    *December 19,*
                    *Wild Horse Dream Ranch*

I'm writing this at work, during my break. Business has been booming — gifts and Christmas things for parties. I'm so out of that scene: Steve's comments about it might as well be in another language.

We will go to a Native American event for "Christmas," and there will be speeches and some dancing. I have been to enough of these to know what will be said and who will say it, and I wish I could get up and suggest that we should do more than be angry at Indians who assimilate, but my blond hair and Anglo features stand in the way of their listening to me. I want them to be busy building good Indian ceremonies, where they do <u>celebrate</u>. They will have to create these themselves because the older people of the many tribes are so different.

Larry was depressed by it, too. Since he came home, he has been working on the cabin, but money is very scarce and we have to save up for the building supplies we need. His old boss, Mr. Anson, came by. He's still letting us stay there for the work we do fixing the cabin up, but I think he is doing it because I am pregnant. The pity makes Larry mad.

Please don't think he is drinking. He hasn't had any since he left The Program. Sometimes we go to the Native American Twelve Step Programs they have in Denver. He doesn't like the local ADEPT groups because he says they are all too white and upper class. I admire him a lot for not drinking but I wish he was happier. We got married to be happy and I am, most of the time, a lot of the time. Shining Lady tells me that pregnant women are often struck by arrows of sadness and this is true. The arrows come from negative forces trying to wound the spirit of the baby.

The truck we got from Grandpa's co-worker has an oil-seal leak. The leak is small, but it made Larry very upset. That's because it takes a major overhaul to fix it and while we can drive the truck, the problem will get worse and worse. He feels betrayed because he says if he had known there was that problem he might not have bought the truck. He said that to Mr. Anson while he was up inspecting the cabin. Mr. Anson said that for what we had paid for the truck, he was surprised it was only that. When we have the money, he said, he would agree to do the overhaul for us, and Larry could help do it and save on the labor. I thought it was a good offer, but Larry said later that it was only another cheat, but I finally told him to see it as a good thing, and especially from Mr. Anson, whose windows Larry had broken. When I feel those arrows that might hurt our baby, Shining Lady said I should make myself a special tea. Since I got back home I must have had a gallon of it.

Thanks for the little baby set you just sent. It's so cute. I put it away in a special box I have for the baby's things and I keep the box covered because I'm still superstitious.

Some of the wonderful horses Larry made for me are beginning to fade where they gallop and prance near the ceiling of the cabin. They are getting dusty, too. I will take them down this weekend and maybe paint them with enamel paint so they will stay nice. They were only made of construction paper, which has gotten dry. I want them to last forever. I wanted Larry to paint them himself but he can't take the time. We have a chemical toilet in the outhouse. We need a covered walk between the house and the outhouse so we don't have to be in mud and snow or rained on when we go outside to use it. He made me promise not to tell Mr. Anson about the plan.

I have gotten a raise but the money gets swallowed up.

*Love, Hope*

*Moms:*                                    *December 20, Niwot*

I'm okay but Jussy's really taking her lumps. Hope, who promised to show up now and then, never does. Jason thinks he's in a rooming house. Frank is pissed at Jason and heartsick about Hope, and his pain is no help. Ben watches it all, but he's not yet fourteen. Ask him about movement of people inside a city and he'll do three-quarters of an hour with slides and video, but he goes stumbling-dumb with all the emotions and silences in the house.

There were years when I envied Jussy and Frank for the family spirit they had, the laughter, fun with the kids, fun with each other. Seeing them now is like visiting Lewis and me before we separated. Lewis kept his injuries as though they were national treasures. I hate

401

to remember us. Jussy's house always looked like normalcy to me, and the way she raised her kids was more practical than mine. Now she's seen all that turned upside down by Hope — who's living a sixties parody — and Jason — the jock from outer space. They must be scared stiff of saying anything to Ben, having made such a stunning mess with the other two. They leave Ben to his passion. Jussy said it wouldn't surprise her to go down to the basement one day and find Ben shrunk into miniature size and living in his model city.

The prospect of Sam and Cary's adolescence looms. Thank God it's a few years away. I hope you and Dad are okay. How does he feel about The Walk now?

*Sol*


*Dear Grandma,*　　　*December 21, Grant Street*

Thanks a million for the Washington, D.C., maps. I just got permission to make two presentations in school based on them, one in math and one in social science. You were right about making school do what you want. Everybody is sick of me, and when I raise my hand or get up to do a presentation, the kids all start sighing and rolling their eyes like marbles. Too bad. I'm getting through school.

And I have a friend, Dennis, a new kid. He's what they call a Radioactive — a fallout from the riots, fires, and earthquakes in California. He's not interested in demographics, not much anyway, but he is interested in war, and I've started him thinking that demography has some answers for him. <u>Anybody</u> thinking about <u>anything</u> is a pleasant surprise to me and to him, too. We talk about ideas a lot. He's an Only, so no one is on him to make him compete for anything, sports or popularity. His dad works in a bank as a kind of forecaster. When I was over at Dennis's house I talked to his dad a couple of times and he's the only grown person I have met who seemed interested in the <u>theories</u> behind demographics. He says the aging of the country is going to make huge changes in the next forty years. This isn't to insult Grandpa, who listens to all my ideas and helps me, or Dad either, because he helps, too, but they are interested in <u>me</u>, not demographics, which is okay up to a point, but Dennis's dad <u>wants</u> to talk about demographics.

I saw Hope yesterday, and she is really pregnant, now. I'm trying to get over the embarrassment of her sticking out like that in public. I got some paving stones for her and Larry to use in their yard and the way to the outhouse. I told her to tell Larry to come and pick them up. If they use the stones they can get to their outhouse without swimming, ice skating, or skiing this winter. You can see they aren't like some people who are poor because they are lazy. Please don't get mad because I said they were poor. I said it to Mom the other day and she went up like Mary Poppins and then she started crying. She thought I was blaming <u>her</u>. That's why she hates Larry. She doesn't want Hope and Larry to be poor. But they have to be. Larry doesn't understand middle-class people and they have always been enemies to him.

I want to tell you I think it's a great thing, your walking across the country.

*Love, Ben*


DIARY ENTRY                                    *December 22,*
*Finksburg, Maryland*


Marz left for home yesterday. I saw him off and took a bus back to where the camp was breaking. We are in a let-down — post-Washington blues.

It had rained last night and was just above freezing. We were so cold and wet we needed the work of walking to keep us warm. The food wagon served hot tomato juice. The man ahead of me in line was new; a tall, bearded man. I got his side view, had a start, took my juice, and followed him. It was Kevin.

I was dumbstruck. I stared. He laughed. The beard made him look older. His hair was even longer, gathered at the back. And he was heavier — the weight not all muscular. He had lost some grace.

"Say hello," he said, then, "I hardly recognize anyone — lots of changes, too."

I said that a lot of those changes happened because of him.

He didn't drop his gaze. I let myself go. I said food trucks make The Walk, a provisions van, a water truck, and money. Advance people make The Walk, a core of leadership makes The Walk. All that was stolen from us by a thief and a liar. He stood still. My voice had risen but it wasn't a rise in frequency. It was the intensity that turned heads, most of them briefly, since most of the people now on The Walk didn't know who Kevin was. But Dr. D. heard me and turned and I saw the same shock on his face that must have been on mine. Kevin laughed again, high and embarrassed. He was facing me the way Kevin always did, giving his listener his total, full attention, and he didn't see Doc's expression change. Then he was felled by Doc's blow, sharp and violent, coming from the side. If not for the beard, the strength of it might have broken his jaw.

Before Kevin could speak he was on the ground and Doc was bending over him whispering in a harsh, strangled voice, that he was going to go for the police.

Kevin, trembling and shaky in the knees, got up slowly, watching Doc carefully. I'm used to movie brawls; men leap up or lie still and there is none of the fear, or the hard breathing, or the ugliness of their hate. Kevin was shakily on his feet, saying that Doc had no right — and then he sniffed up some blood that was welling from his nose — to decide what would happen on his own.

Doc said there was a steering council.

Half the council was made up of people who had come after Kevin's time. Some of them had heard snatches of talk about what had happened. Some had no clue. Doc and I explained, briefly. A council member said the problem had to wait for camp, and a meeting.

So we waited. Kevin walked with us, surrounded by wary Fresnos. As soon as we made camp, the council met with the Fresnos and Kevin.

John Sievert explained what Kevin had done.

One council member said that short of physically restraining him, how could we stop him from walking with us?

Dr. D. said we should call the police.

Patricia, council member and Fresno, said that calling the police would stop The Walk. There was a warrant out for Kevin in Missouri for the theft of money and equipment we leased in California. If The Walk was willing to stop for the time it would take to prosecute Kevin, we might get satisfaction. Maybe four or five of us should leave The Walk and set up there, but even with the police involved what would stop Kevin from bailing himself out and disappearing again . . .

Herb asked where the money was.

Kevin said most of it was safe, but it was corporate money and Kevin had signed all the checks, as a member of the council. The problem was civil, not criminal. Who could prove which group was The Walk and which was not? As it was now, less than a quarter of the group had started with it. One in five had come on since Poplar Bluff.

I was watching Kevin, remembering the leader he had been. He was standing near us, ringed with Fresnos. He showed no sign of shame or embarrassment, but looked levelly at us all in a friendly way. Still, it seemed to me that his movements were somewhat stilted and his timing was off.

Dinnertime came. People brought us our dinners and we continued talking. Bunion Rub started.

Bunion Rub has changed since Kevin's time. Doc D. got up and took the staff and began to explain what Kevin had done. No one spoke. It was winter darkness and difficult to pick out the faces in the firelight. In less than his allotted time, Doc told what had happened at Poplar Bluff. When he had finished, Kevin called out that he wanted to give his side of the events. Doc thought a moment and said he could.

Beside me Poppy drew in her breath.

Doc explained to Kevin how the rules had changed, allowing each speaker five minutes.

Kevin began to explain his leaving The Walk. His followers had urged him to live what they preached. Taking the trucks had bothered them, but had been vital. Until they could build, they slept in the trucks and used them to haul supplies. They had planned a community where the philosophy behind The Walk would be realized. They had never meant to keep vehicles or equipment. The leased trucks would be returned on time; most of the equipment taken had been spares. The money was necessary to the survival of the commune but a careful accounting had been kept and would be paid back by him. He had come back to tell us so.

At one time he might have exercised so much charm on me that I would have been convinced. No more. He was working too hard. Perhaps it was my not seeing him, having to depend on the sounds and hesitations of his voice, that made me know how forced, how strained for sincerity he was. I looked around in the cold. Everyone, even the kids, was silent, rapt.

It occurred to me that Kevin and his group had left us a mere four months ago. It had seemed like a year.

Poppy talked about having to scramble to replace the trucks, about the near collapse of

The Walk. When she sat, Kim Duda stood, gave a sentence or two and then was overwhelmed with weeping.

I was ashamed of the complex feelings I had, disillusionment with the anger.

John Sievert got up and asked Kevin what he wanted. Kevin stood. He and the group were doing well. In a year or two they would begin to repay what they had taken. If we dropped the charges, which he hadn't known were instituted against him, we would have his signed promise that money and equipment would be returned. We would need to know the location of the commune, where it could be reached. Might he stay the night? It was dark. Cold. Tomorrow he would head back to the commune. He had fifty dollars as a bond, which we could hold. Five of it would pay for the night's meal and breakfast tomorrow, and then he would be gone. Was there an extra tent?

We were camped near the reservoir three miles from Hereford. He pitched his tent in the center of camp and before bedtime appeared in front of ours. He said he wanted to tell me, me especially, how it was, why they left without notice, why they took what they did. I needed to understand . . .

I said I understood but I was tired of him. We've been through a lot recently, trying to keep The Walk from becoming just another slogan on a wall. His case was irrelevant, not to The Walk, to me.

Wasn't I curious about what happened?

"No," I said, lying.

He left and I began to write. It's past midnight and we have The Walk to do tomorrow. I wonder about the women who went with him — which of his enchanted girls is pregnant, now? Shari? Jessica? Innocence is a one-day blossom.


DIARY ENTRY                          *December 26,*
                                    *Near Conowingo*


Kevin was gone after breakfast. The day's Walk was a good one, the pulled calf muscle, healing. Night. I was in my sleeping bag, dreamless. The noises were faint to me at first, voices, running feet, then louder sounds, and then I was up and struggling to sit and Poppy was saying, "What's happening?" in a strangled voice. There was a shot, then several shots. Someone was shooting, and I thought, stupidly, "How can this be? Poppy got rid of the guns, back in Missouri, in the river."

Poppy called to me. The shooting stopped.

There was more shouting and running feet coming close, then next to our tent, someone running and gasping, then a cry and the fall of a body, almost on us.

Poppy was shouting.

I thought our tent pegs had caught someone. I grabbed the flashlight we keep near and struggled into a jacket. Suddenly there was a light, the whole camp lit up, and someone adjusting the mechanism of a bullhorn. It blooped and then went silent. Poppy and I put on shoes and crawled out into the light.

Next to our tent someone was lying, panting in its shadow. We scrambled up, our light showing us a young woman. She was in black; her face was blackened. "I was trying to get away," she kept saying. "They were holding me prisoner."

I stared at her. The voice was familiar. I chased a name, but it outraced me. "The dancer, Jessica . . ." Poppy had caught it, Rinaldi.

The girl struggled up. Behind us we heard someone say, "Step aside, ladies, and let us do our jobs." We turned. It was a panoply of buttons, leather, and badge, and a riot nightstick held in a leather fist. From all around the camp people were moving out to the central area — police, our people in night gear, and intruders with their faces blackened.

Their disguises made an easier separation between us and them. Uniformed men — there seemed to be more than one kind — searched the camp. They found two or three more of the intruders hidden under trucks or inside them, and two in the johns. Together they made a band larger than the number of people Kevin had taken away, or so it seemed to me. The women were loaded into a police van, the men handcuffed and driven away in other vehicles. Two cars stayed behind, their officers standing for a few minutes smoking and talking until the cold drove them back into their cars. Someone said they would be staying with us until morning.

Suddenly I realized I was freezing and in my nightclothes with just my jacket and no gloves or hat. Some of us were standing sock-footed in the clinging chill of the night. The officers turned their spotlights off, then the motors of their cars went still.

"Let's get back in our sleeping bags," Doc was shouting, "before we all get hypothermia."

I don't know who actually slept. I got up to make cocoa for the police, and eventually the wake-up call came. Since Poplar Bluff it's been Don playing his trumpet, not reveille but show-tunes and the occasional request number. We soon learned the call had come an hour late, and people struggled groggily from the hard-won warmth of their sleeping bags. We were all confused; even the rise-and-shiners looked caught out. The police had gone.

Immediately after breakfast we broke camp and just before setting out, Doc called us together in a close circle at the side of the water truck. It was icy cold. He said he would explain quickly and get us on the road.

They didn't yet have details, but thought Kevin's commune had been taken over by some rougher people. Kevin had promised or was forced to promise them something before they destroyed him and them. He promised them us. He came here to make sure we were still on schedule, learning that The Walk was doing well, that we had no security, that we had replaced everything, and that we had lots worth taking. Doc thought Kevin might have deluded himself about their using guns. Our one-time leader was well out of his depth.

How did the police get involved, someone asked.

Patricia had become suspicious of Kevin's rosy picture. She convinced the council we needed help. She and John left The Walk and went to the Harford County sheriff, where her description of Kevin's group as a violent cult got his attention. He called the State Patrol and the Park Rangers in support. John and Pat would be leaving The Walk to press charges and later to testify. The Walk will go on. The sheriff had said he would call ahead to the law in Pennsylvania to keep an eye on us.

We began to cheer. Patricia of all people — she of the waffling uncertainty, of the tears; John Sievert, whose interpersonal skills are rudimentary; Doc, who is not a man of imagination — those are the people who saved The Walk and maybe our lives.

413

We sang all day; we sang "Who's Afraid of the Big, Bad Wolf?" and "Stouthearted Men," and a dozen other chest pounders, savoring the joke that it had been <u>our</u> wit and perseverance that had done the job. Later, Poppy commented on my meditative mood.

"Where is <u>my</u> perception? Where is my good sense? How will I get through the rest of my life if I'm this gullible?" I had begun to tremble.

Maybe it's a good thing that a life only lasts a lifetime, since so much depends on luck.

*Dear Marz,*                    *December 27,*
*Near Unicorn, Pennsylvania*

We celebrated Christmas a day late and sang carols across the Maryland-Pennsylvania line. Our lateness was due to Kevin's showing up and trying to rob us again. Doc, John, and Patricia got to the police in time, so Kevin and Co. people were caught and no one was hurt. We are on the move again, but not yet on schedule. I will tell all when I see you.

The weather is now very cold, but our walking has toughened us in an unexpected way. I never knew how the Indians survived, how anyone survives without central heating. The answers are clothes and action. In storms, we hole up, the way they must have, but we seem to be learning how to deal with cold very well.

The danger is in getting wet, but we will be near Lancaster soon, and when we get there, we will replace these walking shoes with something more appropriate to cold and slush.

I'll call you from there. How about meeting The Walk somewhere in New York? — not the city, the state.

*Love, Tig*

*Dear Tig,*                    *December 27, The Hill*

Boulder had its first big snow two days ago and in melting the road crew discovered massive leaking in the bridge over Davis Creek. The cause was careless snow removal, so that improperly diverted run-off water undermined parts of the bridge support. There was a big newspaper article and charges of incompetence spewed over everyone involved. Yours Truly included. I've been having news conferences with media people and acting as spokesman for the department. I told the interviewers what the problem was and that it, and the bridge, will be repaired. It has been a slow month as news goes, so everyone has been treating this as though the bridge had collapsed and hundreds killed and injured. Someone wants a Pulitzer.

Otherwise I am fine. I took Solidarity out to dinner and a movie last week. She works hard and I think appreciated the break. We talked. It was good.

Are you sufficiently dry and warm? Enclosed is a check to cover the purchase of some warm clothes and more of that chalky over-sweetened, disgusting instant cocoa you and Poppy drink.

*Love, Marz*


*Dear Grandma,*      *December 26, Grant Street*

Merry Christmas. We had a big snow and I went up on Saturday with some of the guys and skied. It was lots of fun and we didn't have to race. <u>Of course</u> Jason is out for the ski team. The glassy-eyed girlfriend Kim is kaput.

Yesterday afternoon I hitched a ride up to Hope and Larry's. The snow has shown up some bad trouble underneath the cabin which is why the floor had been so warped. Larry was trying to drain the water away from the cabin because any support that's put there washes away. While we were trying to get enough stone for shoring around the supports, he dropped a rock on his foot and got really mad. I don't think it hurt his foot, except for a minute, but it made him feel stupid and Larry hates that. He started yelling at us and when Hope asked him later how long he was going to work he got even madder and told her to shut up. I realized something.

It's that I don't hear much swearing or yelling at home. People don't call each other names, except for Jason and me, and that will stop when we get older. It's because at home people think you're doing the best you can even if things don't go right. Does that make sense? The funny part of it all is that I didn't realize this until I heard Larry. Unless he learns not to do that, and I don't know if he can, their baby will grow up in his yelling and blaming. I'm going to be its uncle. Maybe I can explain to that kid how it really should be so he doesn't get the wrong idea.

When we're alone or with Larry I don't mind it that Hope <u>really</u> looks pregnant, now. When we're at home she doesn't wear her professional clothes, only big shirts over her jeans and a big, old coat she got from Dad. Her face has changed, too, and remember when I told you her hair made her look old? Now it fits her. She looks like a grown-up woman. Jason is still a kid. I am still a kid, but Hope has moved away into another place, like a neighborhood where we can't come yet. Did she have to choose to go there or did she just wake up one morning and <u>was</u> there? It separates me from her, and it scares me, too. When I think about it, it makes me want to hang on to something so I don't get swept away.

*Love, Ben*

*Dear Gram,*                                    *December 28,*
                              *Wild Horse Dream Ranch*

It's cold and snowy now. We take the batteries out of the composting toilet and put hot bricks under the truck to make it easier to start. We also have a cover I thought up to keep the engine warm. Larry had a part-time job for Christmas and he's got a possible job in the spring for construction people he wants to work for — people who are on the adult side of The Program. They told him they would take him on if he stayed on ADEPT and came to meetings. He never has been on the inside of things and now he is, in a way, people being willing to give him work, because he is one of them. I thought that made them a kind of tribe, but Larry got mad when I said it. Indians are very proud and sensitive about things white people don't see as important.

Larry wants to spend our Christmas money on a trip before the baby comes. This place is hopeless, which I see now, as winter shows us how difficult it is to keep water out of it and there will be mud in the spring. Even though we live here almost free, I am eager to start saving for something ours and permanent. I'm glad I don't have to pay a doctor and hospital. Larry asks me how we will ever get anywhere if the baby takes all our money?

We see our dream so clearly, but it's behind heavy glass, heavier than a store window. In

places I can even make out sounds from behind the glass, the baby crying, a chain saw
cutting wood for our house, sounds of nature,
even trees in the wind. In other places there
is silence and a wave in the glass makes the
things I want to see watery and indistinct. At
night I imagine myself jumping on my horses,
urging them to take us behind the glass and
to <u>be</u> in that place and working on that real
dream-ranch.

*Love, Hope*

# *January*

❧

*Dear Marz,        January 2, Outside Reading*

Now, technology comes into its own for me. Enclosed is a copy of my diary report about Kevin's midnight raid, which as you will see was primarily an auditory experience for us as we huddled in the tent. I copied it on a machine that seemed to be waiting for me in a small convenience store. I did have some idea of sparing you. (I had no idea the story would be picked up by the media.) Take the copy as my apology.

In my defense, you will see how quickly it all went and how little we actually experienced. The emotions that remain are an astonished gratitude that Doc, John, and, above all, <u>Patricia</u>, could have been so alert and resolute when Poppy and I had missed what was behind Kevin's plea for understanding. I cringe at my lack of perception. Why did he try to convince <u>me</u> of his goodness? Do I remind him of his mother or does he only see a credulous old woman?

The main inconvenience on The Walk, now, is all the clothing we have to put on every morning and take off every night. There are hats and coats to be worn even to go to the johns. We wake up warm and cozy from almost hibernating sleeps and moan as we struggle into icy garments, trembling at their clammy touch. We dance in the rhythmic shivers that are almost paroxysms, teeth going like castanets. We are walking fewer miles and spending too much time warming up in public buildings in the towns we pass.

Three Walkers have left and one is a loss to me, a girl from Missouri who felt the winter cold too much. The loss reminds me of how little we looked into the soul of things when we envisioned this Walk. How easily we praised the idea of a braid of people moving in and out, never dreaming that this series of gains and losses would affect us emotionally. There is a blow to morale every time someone leaves, even in illness or trouble at home. People are not interchangeable.

There are new Walkers, now and then. My memory for names, always feeble, has declined even further. I demand at least a month's notice from anyone expecting me to remember his name and summon it at need. Patricia reminds me that the total number of Walkers, come and gone, has been over 300. It is my excuse.

I hate it that you are catching unearned criticism about the bridge. What are the odds that Mrs. Good hasn't called you five times to ask you if the news report isn't a cover-up for a conspiracy involving <u>all</u> the bridges in Boulder County? What about the neighbors who stop you as you shovel the walk to pester you about the safety of the bridge? And what about the overpass downtown?

I am really, really sorry I didn't tell you the Kevin thing in a call.

How is everyone? What do you hear from Hope? How are Justice and Frank?

In spite of cold, rain, and snow, we are well, and The Walk is moving up the map, and into the polar bear regions north of Reading, P.A.

*Love, Tig*

*Dear Ben,*                                    *January 3,*
        *Circumnavigating Reading, Pennsylvania*

My winter letters will be short because I take my mittens off to write and must warm my fingers at the light. Illegal heaters and stoves have blossomed inside our tents. We pretend not to see and not to smell them, and even the most law-abiding Walkers sport the tell-tale soot-smears of their use. Our conversations, once about the best dinners we have eaten and the best beds we have slept in, now concentrate almost entirely on memories of warmth. Like gourmets over the perfect meal, well-traveled Walkers pull out their stories of sunshine in foreign parts. Have you ever been to Tucson in April? Acapulco? What was the best week, the ideal day? The idiot who mentioned a New England autumn as her favorite time was pelted by snowballs and forced to the back of The Walk.

It strikes me that for years, our family has gone on gradually, growing up as we grew older. As soon as I came on this Walk, everyone began great changes: you found a deep enthusiasm, Jason broke his arm, Hope married and found herself soon to be a mother, Grandpa is planning a new career, Aunt Solidarity seems to have lost two real friends, we have a Native American in the family, and he and Hope are dreaming of wild horses and homesteads. Wow.

What is your friend, Dennis, like? Does he belong to a war-games group or does he follow the interest on his own? I have a good friend on this Walk, Poppy, and now know how the behind-the-camera world of filmmaking works. You, too, will come to know a lot about Dennis's interest. It's the best way to learn anything — fun without responsibility.

When we were down south we felt echoes of the Civil War. Now it's Valley Forge.

*Love, Grandma*

*Dear Hope,*  *January 4,*
*Circumnavigating Reading*


How are you? Do you see your folks often? Yesterday I began remembering you, Jason, and Ben when you were little. Jason was a spirited little boy, but when he grew into the sports he loves I couldn't join him physically or spiritually. His impatience met my apathy and the result is that I seem irrelevant to his life and he seems withdrawn from mine. You and I have more in common from the start. Do you remember our Sunday walks?

This Walk is foundering in the dark. Cold, wind, and the brevity of daylight drag at our feet. It's a plot by a miser. We don't want to stop altogether so we do five or six miles a day, sometimes as many as ten. We sing prison songs and chain-gang songs and laugh at ourselves for being over-dramatic, but we also feel the cold and the rain and the snow. I love you. It's cold. Take care of yourself.

*Love to Larry, Gram*


*Dear Marz,*  *January 5,*
*Circumnavigating Reading*


This evening, a visitor. It was Evelyn Ware, no name for you to conjure up a face to match. She was part of the Vietnam protest years. How had she heard about us? And this location? She mentioned a name I hadn't heard since the seventies.

Evelyn is now a short, preserved-looking woman, intense, drawn, with hair as black as Poppy's is red. No greeting, but "You've gained weight." Now, there's tact. We went into the tent and lit the lamp.

For a moment I remembered Enelia, her dark face, her soft voice. Evelyn's picture collection was all blare, screaming faces, absolutes, and no doubt in us. I shouted out of this picture and yelled out of that. A line of us: Evelyn, looking no less drawn, only younger; Poppy; Billy Kirchner; someone whose name I have forgotten; and I, stood exhorting. I read our manifesto again and winced. She turned the page — there I was with the manifesto — and Claude, being dragged away. "He's yelling at the Pigs —"

We did yell a lot, didn't we? I had forgotten how arrogant we were. Evelyn was puzzled at my lack of enthusiasm.

"We got the world's attention," she said. "We made them stop the war."

I stared at her. Did she really believe that?

She stared back at me. "We were heroes," she said.

My Vietnam stand had cost me a great deal, and I did it in the conviction that I was saving the world. I had left ordinary life, taken Justice and Solidarity into situations Justice says she still remembers with anguish. Evelyn turned the pages of the albums: attractive young people with faces full of hate. I knew I was being a disappointment to Evelyn, who wanted nostalgia and praise.

I asked her what she has been doing since our protest days. Finding safe houses for fugitives, she said: Weathermen, the front, the Red Network, the Hundred, others.

There must be years of albums, I told her.

She looked at me intently and said she had to keep those pictures in her head. Her house might be searched. I remembered what I had missed in her all those years ago. It was balance, humor. People were dying, she used to say, and while one person was dying in Vietnam, how could we laugh?

"It's a wicked, corrupt establishment," Evelyn said.

I had once believed that but also that we were incorruptible, ourselves. She still did. I was attracted to the intensity of her face, the leanness, the white teeth, her smile, smiled often at the justification of her truth. Evil is all around — see it? See it?

We went over the pictures again, playing "Where are they now?" Some of us had become orthodox in other ways: feminist, religious, vegetarian. My friend Sonia had joined a religious commune in Arizona; Suzy is a banker's wife. Evelyn must have come knowing about my Rocky Flats protest and my arrest, wishing it had been brutal, for the greater glory. She was hurt and angry when she left; I had given her none of the validation she sought.

Darling Marz: What changed in me? How did the change happen? The pride I had in my protest days was with me when I started this Walk. Somewhere along the way, the past changed.

Being presented with one's own arrogance and self-regard is not pleasant. I have been prouder of myself than I should have been, all these years. I have been marching under a banner that had my own picture on it. Protest? Sure — it's in my blood, for three generations at least, but maybe I can lower the banner a little, for a look at the world.

*Love, T.*

*Dear Hope,*                    *January 7,*
*Boyerstown, Pennsylvania*

We are stalled again in a storm, one which broke from what looked like a clear sky and good traveling. We woke to a blue day, and set out in a brisk wind: superb walking weather. In another hour, a magic show of incredible effects was set in motion. The day went dark, the wind lifted an icy sheet of snow and flapped it against the ground. Snow began to come, not falling, but thrown, projected against us. We unpacked as quickly as we could, set up camp with frozen fingers, bone-chilled and wet and now, as the Aussies say, we are lying doggo until this is over.

Even now there are shadowy, bent figures going back and forth between the tents. Friends visit and drink our still illegal but now universal hospitality: hot drinks — Coke, grape juice, cocoa. Lovers visit their sweethearts and there is even more than the usual back and forward, come and go of their meeting. This Walk, as Ben would say, is demographically skewed toward young people. The overwhelming number of Walkers, as in no tribe on earth, are young and unmarried. The Walk is full of passion and tears.

We are to arrive at Woods Hole on the 29th of March, collect ourselves and prepare our report for presentation on April 1, enjoy the conference for that week, spend the next week breaking camp, taking vehicles back, then dispersing. We will have a farewell party and then we will be our old selves again but wiser, we hope, and infinitely better informed.

I have arranged to leave The Walk in the last week in February, if that is still your due time. I am delighted with the idea of being with you at home, to be there in your labor and delivery, and to share your first sight of your own child, our great-grandchild. The words are thrilling to write. Your invitation means that you will have to go for your checkups often in the last weeks of your ninth month and you will need to let your parents know all the details. I will be calling them regularly for news.

Here is a sensitive thing: I delight at being asked to be with you, but is there a way you could also let your mother play some part in things? She loves you and wants the best for you. She can't help interpreting what she thinks the best is. You write so beautifully about your wealth — the love you have for life, for your husband and unborn child. Please think of sparing some of that wealth for <u>my</u> daughter, who was born to <u>me</u>, just as your baby will be born to you. You are not required to take her advice, any more than you are required to take mine; only allow her a place in your life at this crucial time.

Think about this, please. Ask your midwife, too.

*Love, Gram*

*Moms,*                                    *January 10, Niwot*

I got a call from one of Anton's friends to tell me that Anton was in the hospital. It was a beating so bad, they thought he might lose an eye. All his facial bones were smashed and there was internal injury, too. I called ICU. Only family. Later I went down there, ready to say I was his sister. Sometimes, working in Detox gives advantages that make up for its

430

floor-level social status. Friends work the ICU and I got in as a co-professional.

He was conscious, barely. I saw his chart. Whoever it was had gone for his face with a fury the doc said he hadn't seen before. They had done nine hours of surgery on Anton, eight on his face. Brain injury? They don't know. He was found on the street, thrown out of a car, and what clothes were still on him, were women's.

I called Blake. No answer. When I went home the house was dark. I thought I'd sit up and wait for him, but I fell asleep in that soft chair by the window.

I did half the next day on automatic pilot. At noon I called Blake's office. He had heard the news. They would let him see Anton in a day or two, he said. He sounded <u>hollow</u>, the way people do when they're using a foreign language and don't know what the individual words mean.

*More later, Sol*


*Dear Tig,*                    *January 12, The Hill*

Solidarity's friend Anton was badly beaten and left for dead. I got the news from <u>The Camera</u> — that chronicle that's supposed to be about strangers' miseries.

Sol called later and asked me if I would watch the kids while she went to see him.

While I was there, a man stopped by next door and left a message. Others cruised by in cars. When Blake came home later, I went over. He said, "If Anton dies, our world, gay and bi, has all the experience necessary for a moving funeral. In the past fifteen years, I've organized thirty-three of them." Once again there was that tribal message, feelings raw against the abuse of outsiders. I made no comment.

Solidarity has had to tell Sam and Cary. It hadn't occurred to me that the boys would be part of this spreading mess, but of course, they are. They will have to be armed against tactless comments by neighbors, teachers, schoolmates, and drive-by strangers. We can't give them any real protection.

The Great Leaking Bridge Exposé has fluttered off the front page and back to C 23, and The Public's Right To Know may presently be keeping a street person warm. Its revelations showed me yet again how terrified the bureaucracy gets, and how ready to sacrifice me or anyone else below administration level at the drop of a word to the media. We have patched the bridge and re-graded the approaches. I took the county men over the area and when I showed them how they were contributing to the problem, they said they would change their snow-plowing patterns. That's all it took. We could have done that without massive inquiries and the threat of heads rolling.

On Saturday and Sunday I go to Louisville to look over a three-house-project. Hope, like the springtimers of her tribe, has left this house and disappeared from my life. She said she would call from work when I might come to the mall and take her out for cocoa. She didn't. She said they would come by — she and Larry. They didn't. I miss her. In my anger about Anton, the house project has more meaning. I can follow his plans and keep him part of what I'm doing. I went down to the library this morning and did some more study. Our idea of the proper size of a room has changed considerably in the last century. Many and small seems to have been the style back then and that helped give stability to the structure itself. You had more weight-bearing walls. Probably because of stronger, lighter building materials, our taste has gone to fewer and larger rooms in the same space. As I wrestle with this problem, I am in more or less friendly contact with the architect on the job.

I can't meet you in New York; the money is short and our D.C. trip took just twice what I had budgeted for. I do plan to take my vacation early and pick you up at the end of The Walk in Woods Hole. Hope tells me you will be coming to help the midwife, Pink Lady or whatever her name is. Drop in here, too.

*Love, Marz*

I went to see Anton earlier today. They've put his face together, and his eye back in it, but everything is bandaged shut, stitched together, and wired in place. He can write a little and he hears and can make grunts for yes (1), and for no (2). He wanted some things he still had at Blake's, among them, a little velvet bag with two alabaster balls — the ones people use to keep their fingers and hands limber. The bag was in the basement, he said, in his dressing room. There were other things, too, and some books for people to read from.

I went to the house and used the key Blake and Anton gave me before all this mess — it feels like years ago. While I was there, Blake came and we talked.

He has decided to leave Colorado, maybe even to leave law. It hit me suddenly that what he was planning was to move to Atlanta where he would find a place close to Erik and Shawn. Mrs. Ex would give him visiting rights or partial custody or he would show up at every toney party, every gala, society function, board meeting, charity affair, money-raising function, and school parents' day. Like dogshit on the doorstep? I asked. On all the doorsteps, he said, on all the doorsteps in upper-class Atlanta.

I asked him if he wouldn't wait until Anton was better. He shook his head. The house was being put up for sale and his partners were buying him out of the practice. He would be gone as soon as he could.

But the beating — Anton's suffering — They had been lovers, friends. Blake said it was the beating that had decided things for him. Anton had chosen the beating and the danger. He would go on choosing it.

Jesus, Moms, I don't know enough about cross-dressing, straight or gay, not nearly enough to argue a case against pure choice, choice that looks suicidal. Is it compulsion? How deep, how basic? Is it a simple habit a person can decide to give up, like smoking? I said it was beyond me, and Blake and I went downstairs, and into the dressing room. Good God, what a spread. There were enough costumes to fit out a thirties musical. What part of us did he want and not get? For all the silk and shimmer, the place was orderly and I found what Anton had asked for. I brought it along with a Walkman and as many tapes as I could carry.

Anton seemed happy to get everything but it was difficult to know because he's a gentle person and wouldn't have said he lacked anything.

He knows Blake is leaving. I want Blake to visit often before he goes, but who am I to want anything? The lives are theirs, everyone says so. Sure. Yes. I know.

*Sol*

435

*Dear Marz and Solidarity,*  **January 18,**
**Martin's Creek**

Your letters were held up during the storm here and I just got the packet including Solidarity's letter about Anton — I have not so far had a friend attacked. The people we love should wear stickers on their clothes, something like the list of contents carried on products. Anton's sticker might have read:

> This is a named individual and possesses a family and friends. DO NOT INJURE THIS MAN. His contents are: kindness, generosity, humor, great capacity to love. He also contains risk-taking behavior. Because of this, and his ambiguous packaging, you may disapprove of him and rage at him, but do not end his life. The grief you cause will far outweigh any fleeting sense of outrage you may feel.

I fantasized doing this for you and Justice when you were little girls, and young women. You were so trusting and eager, wanting friends and experience, wanting the world's totality because you thought the world was totally fair and good. I loved that in you and didn't want to spoil it. It horrified me that the world didn't know or care that you were ours, and loved. Cruelty was out there, selfish will, aggression, ugliness. If only I could tell people, let them know who you were . . .

How long will Anton be hospitalized — how long recovering? Is there medical opinion on that, yet?

*Love, Tig*


*Dear Grandma,*        *January 16, Grant Street*

I am going to spend time up at Hope and Larry's to work on the house and time on my city, and time teaching Dennis to ski because I'm hoping he will make a good ski-buddy. Dennis takes me to the war games. The games fill the entire end of a shopping mall and they are set up on tables. At each table a battle is fought. Two "Generals" sit at each table and people gather round them while they fight the battles the same way or another way. Dennis has been studying weeks for this. Two of his battles are ones nobody's ever heard of. He says <u>everyone</u> wants to fight Gettysburg and the Bulge, but if you sign up for the really insignificant ones, you can be a general and there's not so much pressure on your board.

Dad and Mom brought a whole lot of insulation and plywood up to Hope and Larry's. Aunt Sol got sheets of fiberglass that's translucent to make a little roof between the house and the outhouse. The ground is frozen so they won't be digging anything, but they have the supports braced temporarily with vertical pieces bolted to the 4 by 4's which are on the ground. It's like a breezeway, roofed over and with its side on the side the wind blows from.

Larry had a job wrapping packages during the Christmas rush. He said he didn't like the pressure of it. Hope worked extra at the store.

Why didn't I ever know how hard it is to make enough money? Dad goes to his job and comes home every day and never tells us. I know about tax season being busy, but I still don't see how a person can work and work and be poor anyway. Larry says I'm improving — from a fifth-rate worker to a fourth-rate one. By the end of a year, I may improve into being useless. The way he says it doesn't hurt, but the work is really hard.

*Love, Ben*


*Dear Gram,*                    *January 17,*
                    *Wild Horse Dream Ranch*


I talked to Shining Lady and she agrees that my mother should be at the birth. She said that in tribal days all the women relatives gathered at a birth and that she will keep Mom from taking over or trying to get me to go to a hospital if I don't want to. Larry is very impatient with all this business and I don't blame him, but it's hard when you are given baby things and can't show them off or when you have worries and can't tell anyone. Sometimes I talk to the girls at work, but only one has had a baby and understands. Steve came in with an old-fashioned copper washtub last week and gave it to me. I will be able to wash the baby in it. There's something else to cheer about. There's water — two faucets in the wall in back of the mall and with a short length of hose we can fill up our plastic containers and water jars fifteen gallons at a time and take them home every day. Larry comes in for his job and then when he picks me up, we go over and fill the containers. Yesterday I had a hot (warm) bath!

The cabin itself is getting okay and there's a breezeway going up, but I still worry, and it's not good if I show that to Larry. We haven't saved anything and yesterday he took off the whole day and went looking for land instead of showing up for work. He says land is too expensive around here. He's talking about moving to rural Wyoming or going to the Dakotas. Wild Duds has stores all over the country, but I don't think any of them are near vacant land in the poorest parts of the state.

I know there will be expenses when the baby comes. Larry does, too, and it makes him angry and bitter sometimes. I wish spring would come. There are people on his Program who say they will have work for him, then.

*Love, Hope*

I visited Anton again. He's out of ICU and they've cut his pain meds. The doc told him there would be lots of plastic surgery. The thought of being ugly and deformed scares Anton far more than his present pain. Are gay men more vain than straights or just more up front about it? They're feeding him through tubes and IVs. He is already much thinner and says that when he gets out of the hospital he'll look like an AIDS sufferer. Any skinny gay man is suspect, he tells me, and tries to laugh through his wired jaw. Some of his words get through the metal webs along with coughs and whistles. He says when he sneezes his skull lifts.

And there's still so much pain. And no one is working too hard on catching the ape who did it. An officer came up and took a statement, but Anton only knew the guy's first name and that he was from out of town, a conventioneer, he said. The car was a rental, but there must have been blood on it. Surely the people who took it back noticed that and the cop said not necessarily so. Anton had lost consciousness long before he was dumped out and the man used his dress to soak up most of the blood from his face.

I want justice. I want things to be made right. I want things to be the way they were when we were all friends and close. Anton has

lost all his front teeth. He told me he went to
the tooth fairy for a withdrawal but those were
all milk-teeth. He said he asked for a professional discount. Gay humor. He was hurting
so bad; I saw it in the small part of his face
not hidden in bandages. He'll be blind until
they can trust the injured eye to be firmly
reattached.

Is this more than you wanted to know?

*Sol*


*Dear Grandma,*                    *January 19*

He hits her.

*Love, Ben*


*Dear Marz,*                    *January 23,*
                    *Milford, Pennsylvania*

Have you seen Hope? Is she all right? If
Larry can strike her when Ben is there, what
has he done when they're alone? He can't be
allowed to hurt her. He must be made to
know she is not to be hurt. Ben tells me he
has stopped drinking, and Hope herself says
so, as though that was all anyone had to know.

I know; he may hate his violence as much
as we do; God knows it has given him nothing
but pain and ruin, but Hope's pain is now
and her choice of him to love didn't include

441

being at the end of his fist. Who will stop this? How? Can you get them to separate until he gets whatever therapy will stop it? Can't you all go up there, you and Justice and Frank? Do we all stand by and let this happen? I think of her all alone up there, dependent on him and so vulnerable, no neighbors, while he rages, no phone for police, or Frank or you; no protector.

They lie to each other, both of them. He told her he wanted the baby; I think he was merely proud to prove his manhood. She dreams about an isolated ranch while beginning real success at a job that demands she live near a city. He says he wants his heritage and he sits and manufactures it from New Age fantasies and shreds of Noble Savage fiction. God, I'm so angry and so frightened at what they have set in motion — please go there, all of you. Drag her away.

I'm babbling. I know you have no such power. Talk to her, at least; tell her it's for her baby's sake.

*Tig*

*Dear Gram,*          *January 21, The Cabin*

There has been a big mess and mix-up and most of it is my fault and Ben's fault. Here's what happened:

We had a big freeze this week and the floor-

442

ing in one corner buckled where we hadn't seen water coming in. Larry has worked so hard on that floor and was so proud of it that when even a little of it got warped he was really angry. We fought and he did hit me, but it wasn't hard and he did it because he was angry at himself for not seeing how the water was coming in from the hill on that side. HE WAS NOT DRUNK. He does not drink anymore.

Later, he was so apologetic and sad. He had lost his temper and that's one of the things he does when he drinks. It was a discovery for him that he can lose control of himself when he isn't drinking. I had been arguing with him, saying the wrong things. When he is in a temper, it's wrong to try to make excuses for what happens, like I was forgiving him. Why didn't I see this before? It's what they told me again and again in The Program, that it's wrong to defend an alcoholic's actions or faults. He saw the water stain and the way the floor wood had swelled up in that corner. I shouldn't have rushed in and said everything was all right and that it was only the corner, anyway.

So he lost his temper and hit me.

I don't know if you remember — I told you that I got a sort of shadow on my face. There's a cream that covers it and you blend it in with your skin tones. I use it when I go to work and I used it then to cover the bruises.

In ADEPT they tell you that the alcoholic needs to be confronted with the results of his action, but Larry wasn't drinking and it seemed too cruel to both of us for me to walk around with my bruised face for days when he had already told me he was sorry.

Ben came up to help. He has been spending his weekends up here, working while he is on his vacation. They want to get the breezeway in before we get another big snow. Now, Larry says that work on the breezeway should be put off while he tries to find a way to shore up the cabin and divert the water on that bad corner. He got a jack from Mr. Anson — one of the big ones you can jack up a truck with, and it was just to use for Sunday. Larry's idea was to jack up that corner of the cabin and put some flat rocks under there just temporarily until summer when we can dig — the ground is all frozen now.

It was hard because it was so cold and wet. We had trouble positioning the jack because we had to dig out some earth under there and the ground was wet and frozen, too. I can't help too much, feeling the strain and forgetting how big I am. I start doing things and can't follow through.

We got the jack in and Ben was positioning a rock to push it under. The cold was beginning to make me tired and a little sick. Ben and I were in position because the rock was too heavy for Ben to work alone. We were going to shove it under and when Larry yelled we couldn't see the rock so it got pushed against the jack the wrong way and rotated so it was wedged in a way it couldn't work. Larry started pulling the jack out and then the level slipped so the jack got wedged under the house. We started again. The second time the rock slipped and kicked against the jack and the jack slid out from under the house.

We were all tired and cold and Larry lost his temper and shoved me out of the way. I started to slip and that's when his hand came up accidentally because he really wasn't hitting me, he was trying to get his own balance. Right after that I saw Ben staring at me and I realized that the cover-cream had all been rubbed off my face and he could see the bruises there, where Larry had hit me before.

Gram, it was awful — he started to cry. He was standing in the churned-up slush, where we were working, just standing there, crying. Larry and I didn't move, either, and didn't know what to do. Then Larry got disgusted and said something bad and walked away.

What could I say to Ben? I tried to tell him how it was but he only cried until he got all stuffed up. I asked him if he had a Kleenex. He shook his head. I went to the outhouse and got him some toilet paper.

Then I tried to make him stay for supper. "Larry will come back and need us to help. He'll be better when he comes back because

445

he's trying hard to control his temper."

Ben shook his head and got on his bike and went sliding away up the muddy road. When Larry came back I told him Ben had to go home to do something there. I haven't heard from him since, but I want him to come back. Ben is the only friend we have who isn't old. I have people I see and like at work, but I don't invite them up because they wouldn't understand why we live this way. When they invite me to their houses I don't go because we are busy with the work here and because Larry wouldn't like them, and they wouldn't understand him.

When I get some time during a break, I'll call Ben and try to get him to come back. I can't get the picture out of my head, his crying like that.

*Love, Hope*


*Dear Ben,*                              *January 24,*
                              *Port Jervis, New York*


You have been a good brother to Hope and a good brother-in-law to Larry. Please don't leave them. I see them in my mind flailing around, needing help, but unable to see the situation they are in. You may think that help-ing Larry means you approve of what he does. That's not so. Hope has cut herself off from all her family and friends. Larry may even

446

resent your grandfather for the help he has given.

You are seeing Hope as grown now, gone away from you, but that grown-up self is just an outline. She and Larry have chosen to grow up in the most difficult way, isolated, even though Hope has a job. Please be a help.

We are in New York, now. I have begun to be impatient for The Walk to end. Too bad, too, because we have more than two months left to go. I plan to take a week away to be with Hope when her baby comes. Maybe then she will be able to accept help from the folks. Hope says that Larry is struggling against his rages and trying to overcome them. Can he do it without help? I don't know. I don't even know what help he could accept. Larry has been client, patient, inmate, recipient all his life. He has had what therapy our juvenile facilities know how to give, but he wasn't ready to accept it. Will that change? Hope says they are still on the ADEPT Program and that is helping to keep Larry sober.

We seem to be in for some good weather. Even our ecologically pure Walkers now depend on the battery-operated radio that brings us news and weather. There's a new weather person on The Walk every week, and she carries the radio close to her body to keep the batteries warm. If the forecast is correct, we praise her; if it is not, we yell at her. Weather, which is a factor in ordinary life, has become the factor in our lives. We have been forced into modesty and to praise the technology many of us cursed.

Enclosed is a ten-dollar bill. Use it to buy marshmallows and toasting skewers, then go up and toast marshmallows at Hope and Larry's with my compliments.

*Love, Grandma*

*Dear Mother,*     *January 24, Grant Street*

My gracious daughter has asked me to be with her at the birth of her baby in an unheated cabin with no water or electricity and an Indian midwife. I said I would come. My friends, whose daughters have their babies in well-equipped hospitals, say that I should "make her" have the baby in a safe environment. They have mistaken their good luck for prudent planning and skillful child-rearing.

Now and then she lets me take her out to eat at the mall. Last week I cornered an overwrought Ben and forced the information from him. He told me there were bruises being covered by makeup.

I am a civilized woman, reared by civilized people. I am on the school board and the water committee and the League of Women Voters. I have been wishing to hire a hit man to kill my son-in-law. I have been planning ways of killing him myself, going up there with

448

a gun and blowing him apart. Hope would grieve for a year, name her baby Larry, and be free of the need to deal with that abuser face-first. No moral compunction keeps me from doing these things. All that does is my fear. Where are such hit men found? Could I be blackmailed? Would I be caught?

I hate Larry for showing this part of me to myself. I am furious at Hope for putting me in this position. Poor Ben. He liked going up there to help, to learn to build things. When I forced the facts from him, he collapsed in tears, saying, "We have to do something." I asked him what we could do, and he mumbled something about kidnapping.

I haven't told Frank yet, but he suspects something. If I <u>tell</u> him, he will think he has to act. I won't give up, but I can't stand being in this position.

How did I lose my ability to protect her? Now, I'm in danger of losing Ben's trust as well; I can't raise an army and take his sister away by force.

Frank is attending another series of workshops on the new state and federal tax laws and I'm getting ready for more polarization in the school board — far left versus far right. Through all of it, worry about Hope threads itself like an ugly sinew, tightening and loosening with mood, news, and time of day.

She says she is healthy. She says she's watching her salt and I don't notice any swelling to speak of. Her color is good and her eyes clear. I haven't seen Larry since he sat in the therapy session and promised us he would be part of our family. Hope has told us not to drop in up there, but since they have no phone, visits must be elaborately planned. On two occasions, she called from town and headed us off.

*There is where it stands. Justice*


*Dear Hope,*　　　*January 26, Bear Mountain*

It's no good your saying there was a mix-up. Ben saw your bruises, your mother noticed them also, and you and Larry have kept none of his promises about being members of the family, visiting and accepting visits. Larry says one thing in his Program and lives another. You make excuses for his temper and his cruelty.

Are you both still on The Program? Are you going to meetings, at least being a part of <u>that</u> community? Is Larry telling those people the truth about his rages and his broken promises? Larry thinks the world is against him; please don't let him prove it.

I am fine. The Walk is in New York now, moving up the map. Everything is older here, longer settled. People seem to stand closer to one another, to live in tighter proximity; even the trees crowd. The closeness may have given more protection from family abuse: people heard, people saw. I remember, then, that men striking their wives and parents beating their children were, not so long ago, defined as normal. Standards have changed; expectations have changed. Stop thinking of your mother as an enemy. Your isolation in the cabin is dangerous because neither of you can control the weather, your health, or Larry's rages. It must be obvious to <u>Larry</u> that something is wrong with his behavior. You do have the power to put your foot down and demand honesty from him.

*Love, Gram*


*Dear Tig,*                    *January 27, The Hill*

The Louisville project is coming along fine. Three or four times in my professional life I have been granted foresight and come up looking like a genius. I had the right clue there and now walk on water for these folks (performances Sundays 2–3 P.M.). It was a structural weakness compounded by careless remodeling. I found it because I was looking for it, but we will be able to pump some concrete in under pressure and undo the remodeling with some new inner beams, saving all three units. The price will be steep but not prohibitive for what we will recover.

The bad news is that I want to be there for

all the work and that means taking more personal and sick-leave time from my job. I've used up my vacation time along with two or three days I was with Hope during Larry's troubles. I'm not supposed to be moonlighting while the sun is still out. Garvin knows about my outside project; I'll ask him if I might put in longer hours with fewer days this month. If I can convince the Louisville people to do the major reconstruction work on Mondays only, I'll be able to make sure the work is done as I want it done. You can tell by this how excited I am.

I was up at the cabin to see Hope and the bruises. They are real enough. I made that appointment by stopping by at Wild Duds during her lunch hour, which cost me mine. Larry was working on the house when I got there. I went to where he was trying to shovel away the recent drift of mud from the hill in back of the cabin. I said, "Listen, man, I'm a structural engineer. Let me help you with this. I won't boss it; I'm a good worker and no stranger to any of your problems here." He told me what had happened that had gotten them so upset — how the jack had slipped and gotten wedged, etc. I gave him a suggestion and recommended he borrow the jack again and said we'd do the thing together. We set a date. I told him his basic idea was sound and that he had done damn well so far, which I believe.

You are, by now, dancing up and down with frustration. Why didn't I tell him to stop hitting our granddaughter? I couldn't. He knows why he shouldn't. Hunkered down with him in the mud, it became very plain to me that I had no authority except my presence, no way to advise him, no less order him to shape up in his marriage. He's not stupid. He knew why I had come. Then, I thought that if I shored <u>him</u> up in some way, helped him — structurally, as it were — he might be calmer. If he were calmer, it might reflect in his treatment of Hope. Did you think I could threaten him? We both know how empty any threat would be. If only Hope would say, "Rescue me," armies would be massed at the roadhead.

She came out while we were working. She looks drawn, with only six or seven weeks to go in her pregnancy. The cold and the wet made her look a little gray and she was shivering inside the big jacket she was wearing. My silence wasn't cowardice but discretion. I wasn't falsely cheerful or insincerely warm. In fact, I was a lot more honest than I had been at the family therapy charade.

*Structurally yours, Marz*

*Dear Marz,* $\qquad\qquad$ *January 29,*
$\qquad\qquad\qquad$ *Mohansic, New York*

We are bogged down again by weather, freezing fogs, and ice. The morning was so bad that we didn't break camp, getting up only to eat and use the toilets and go back to our sleeping bags. The youngsters tried to make a fire in the afternoon but without success. Later we went to one of the family tents and told stories. This weather is bad for me. It gives me time to brood.

$\qquad\qquad\qquad\qquad\qquad\qquad$ *Tig*

# *February*

჻

*Dear Gram,*                    *February 1, The Cabin*

Don't flip: I quit my job. Larry needs me
here. He says he will try to find work, later,
but if we get the house in good shape and the
hill banked, we'll be okay here until spring. I
will be helping him with the rock wall and
we'll be able to save time, not having to take
me to work and pick me up every day.

Steve wanted me to stay at Wild Duds and
the truth is that I didn't want to quit. It's just
until we get on our feet and the baby is born.
It's true that I have been feeling a little draggy
at work. Steve said if I would wait three more
weeks I could have full benefits. Larry thinks
that's a hook to keep me working longer hours
— and since I'm on the management track,
they have gotten longer.

We really need the money. When spring
comes, the construction business will start
again. Colorado is in a building boom and
Larry is sure to find a high-paying job. I will
stay home with the baby and then, when he
or she is old enough for day care, I'll try again
at Wild Duds so we can save for our land. By
then, Larry will have the confidence he needs

to see that my career is secondary to <u>us</u>.

It's tough waking up at 6:00 A.M. and going out to that icy privy, getting dressed in the cold room, then waking Larry up to take me to work. This way, we'll only have to go to town once every other day, to do laundry and pick up water. If I stay home, we'll be able to do the retaining wall and also finish the breezeway and not fight the snow or wet to get to the privy, <u>and</u> we'll need a big stock of wood before the baby comes. I can help with all that. Larry is nervous about the baby. My working makes him even more nervous. I said I'd be close to a phone if I kept working and then I could call Shining Lady from work. He told me that the people at work know we are poor and are going to have our baby in a tribal way, and they laugh. Maybe they will even call some agency about us. I started to laugh, and I said, "People don't care that much about us, and I haven't told anyone about Shining Lady or having the baby here."

He said that <u>Steve</u> cared, that I didn't know it, but he wanted me. He said he looks after me when I walk away, his eyes follow me, and he made his fingers like rays coming forward from his eyes.

Larry is afraid that Steve has been listening to me. Steve is white and middle class and Larry has picked up on that. I didn't mention that Steve knows about Larry's having been in jail and about his being on the ADEPT

Program. Larry is very sensitive. He feels everything very deeply.

I hate to give up my job, but maybe it's for the best. It's not <u>real</u> <u>life</u> like being at the cabin is, and we do need to be together in harmony, Larry and I, before the baby comes. I <u>am</u> beginning to feel bulky and tired. I was two different people — one at work, wondering about styles and into predicting fads and how people look; and another person at home, worrying about winter and water and handling the garbage. It used to be a secret high for me to know I went between the two worlds and was competent in both. It pleased me but it shouldn't. I should be one person, one thing.

Please don't criticize this, Gram — when you come you will see how I am right. When I came up here to live with Larry, he cried. He said he never thought I would be so faithful and true to him. That's when I knew that people could move beyond their own little worlds into something greater and deeper. Please understand this.

*Love, Hope*

*Dear Mother,*        *February 3, Grant Street*

I went to the mall yesterday and thought I would drop in on Hope. I went into the store, resolved to smile my way through our talk. A salesgirl told me she wasn't working there anymore. I stood, stunned, not knowing what to do, and I guess I gawked at the girl until she got embarrassed and moved away from me.

I left the store and drove out to the cabin. And there she was and there <u>he</u> was. He gave me a nod and left.

They have no phone; now she won't be at the mall. When would they pick up mail? She and Larry have kept none of their promises about visits or contact. She is now completely isolated, unavailable. I told her so.

She took me to the back of the cabin, around to where the ground was banked up behind it, and she began to talk about their making a retaining wall. This was what she had stopped working to do, or to help Larry do. I stared at her. Didn't she <u>remember</u> that Larry was supposed to be going to school or working at a job?

When I saw her at Wild Duds I usually gave her money, a hundred, two hundred dollars. Frank gives her money also. We had agreed to pay for the midwife and the expenses of the pregnancy and the birth of her baby. I wanted to tell her she would get no more money from us.

I couldn't. She started talking about her love for Larry and the unborn baby. It was blackmail. Does she know it? Does she care? She made another promise about visiting us,

458

and that she would call at least once a week from town. She will not visit us. They will not visit us or call. She might, just once, and then come to believe she did it twice a week.

Will she never wake up, look around at her future with her dream-mechanic and dream-rancher and see that those dreams will never be realized, and leave him? She's nineteen, and there's still plenty of time. She was sitting on one of your old chairs — the ones we had when we were growing up. I asked what would happen now that I couldn't give her money.

She hadn't remembered. Why does that hurt so much? She looked at me in wonder as though she had once misplaced all that reality and was surprised to find it again. She shook her head and said we could meet in town — she would ask Larry to make a schedule, or they could meet me at the supermarket. "We do have to shop." She sighed, and then she said that Larry would be job-hunting soon. He'd be gone most of the day and I could come up and see her, but only if I didn't criticize Larry or try to make her be disloyal, or try to get her to go to a hospital instead of having Shining Lady come.

I told her again that Larry had broken all of his promises, every one of them. Couldn't she see?

And she turned her back on me and went into the tiny back room and came out with a baby blanket someone at the store had made for her. It had a pattern of little horses on it, appliqué — it was a lovely thing.

This was why I wasn't welcome at the cabin; I didn't see any of what was important.

The friend who made the blanket understood about the horses Larry had given her. "They're all around this room and you don't even notice." I looked up and there they were, some torn and faded, a dwindling herd around the ceiling of the cabin. She pulled that damn leather braid out from under her dress. The tribal midwife had instructed her to untie the knots in its fringes so that the birth would be easy and the cord wouldn't wrap around the baby's neck. I didn't know whether to laugh or cry. I asked what if something happened? They have no phone, no way of contacting anyone. Larry might be away —

"Babies don't come all of a sudden," she said, hugely experienced in such matters. "There's a phone at the park."

I left. The park she mentioned is four miles up the road, and there is a telephone there. It's on a stand, in the open. I drove back looking for any neighbors and saw none.

Justice

Dear Hope,                    February 5,<br>Shelton, Connecticut

Please, please reconsider your move. I'm

not speaking of love or need but of solid economics. If you stay at work, you can get maternity benefits and that will mean having enough money so Larry can try for something he likes better than food service or garage work. You can tell him that Steve, your boss, might be tender toward you, but that is a brotherly care, not a romantic one. Seen every way, your staying at Wild Duds for the required time makes sense. Remember Shining Lady's advice: your child's safety and spiritual growth are the prime considerations. That means your putting yourself in the best situation possible: cheerful and safe days at work, evenings and weekends at home with Larry. Please think again about the decision you have made. <u>Larry doesn't want to be jealous or abusive</u>. He is incapable of control, and your pregnancy has made things worse, not better, because of the tension you have put him under. You need to stand up for yourself and your baby and answer his fear with self-confidence. This marriage has too much against it. Help him. Help yourself. Please.

*Love, Gram*


*Dear Justice,*          *February 6, Bethany, Conn.*

What a picture — you as Larry's hit man. The worst thing about your rubbing him out is that when you are caught, Hope will find out, and won't even show up at the jail with cookies for <u>you</u>.

When I went south without a mandate from the Party and did teaching independent of any political directing, Papa declared me dead, co-opted. He disowned me. Mama, hating my "blindness" and desertion as much as he did, called and wrote and sent us money out of the tiny amount she was able to save guiltily for her own use. She cried over me, but she didn't disown me. Now, the shoe is on the other foot, and our children are disowning us. Maybe it doesn't matter which one of us makes the peace, who cedes power and who holds it: father, mother, daughter, or son. I wonder where Larry's mother is and if we could find her. Hope's mistake is terrible. I think we have a right to insist on seeing her, taking Larry on, forcing him to his promises.

I haven't felt myself flag physically until this month. I've been reminded by my own exhaustion that winter was the winnowing time for tribal elders. Cold is constant and I'm afraid of getting any kind of injury or sickness. At this age, every injury heals so slowly. Even so, The Walk will not have been a mistake for me. I'm learning a lot, experiencing a great deal. When this is over, I'll know more about the times I live in and the me who is living in them.

Maybe that's all that can be expected.

*Love, Mother*

I talked to Pop yesterday about Hope's retreat into the bushes. He wants to find a way to deliver Larry to a doctor. I decided to go ahead with a little idea of my own.

We have a computer here, which is tied in to the state's medical record system. I accessed that, and with a flick of the wrist was able to get Larry's file and also his info from Social Services. I know him top to toe and side to side, the good news and the bad.

He's been gone over, physically, pretty well. There were two or three neuro workups after rage-fits he got into during his earlier adolescence. All was normal. Whatever chemical changes go on in his brain, they don't respond to drug or other therapy. He's had various medication in foster placements; none of them worked. He has also had new stuff, on a test basis. Some of it might have helped but he dropped out of the study.

What seems to work is jail. Dad and Ben noticed how much better he is when he's there. Dad wondered how Larry could accept loss of freedom, choice, <u>autonomy</u> so easily. It's because Larry needs an iron system: the Marines, without a pass; a monastery, with no time off; or — prison, where every line is drawn and every step is ordered. According to more than one person who has studied him, all the control has to come from outside because there's none <u>inside</u>.

His ma, by the way, has a record of her own: alcohol, drugs, and a little prostitution. Her last known address was in Leadville, but she's not there anymore, or not at that address. There's other family, but none of them are interested in Larry. If he ever gets to Cañon City, he'll be with more relatives than he's ever known he had.

Bad shit, as Leonardo says. What's worse is that you can see him struggle. He's smart, capable, and creative. He's a blind dog in a slaughterhouse and all around him people are moving past, working, living, making decisions and living with them in ways that are beyond him, using gifts he can't see or name.

Lots to do on a slow day in Detox.

My nitwit niece needs to get out of there. Wild Horse Ranch. Can't someone drug her oats? Nope. She says she <u>loves</u> him. Pffllt!

*Sol*


P.S. Blake has gone to Atlanta. Anton is in a nursing home and will soon leave it for his apartment. He says he'll go to L.A. for his plastic surgery. We moved all his computer material to the apartment, and all his boas, wigs, and stiletto heels there, too. Give it up? No. He'll leave and take it with him to some place where he can dress up again. Will he go out again on one of those dangerous dates? He shrugs.

*Dear Tig,*        *February 10, The Hill*

The job in Louisville is proceeding but I can't get the contractor to guarantee they'll work on my free day. I do get agreement in detail from the architect and I go there on weekends to check things out. He remains pleasant and cooperative — I hope he's not jollying me along while he goes his own way and lets the principals or the construction people try to do it on the cheap. I do not walk on water. I walk on a series of carefully arranged submerged rocks.

Still, things are good and I'm looking forward to this new work. Everything will be better when you come home to see about Hope as she delivers our first great-grandchild. You will be staying here all that week, won't you? Things will be best when you come home for good in April. You did choose one helluva year.

*Love, Marz*

*Dear Grandma,*     *February 13, Grant Street*

Is there such a thing as smart coming out of stupid or success out of failure? When I think about my life, it's hard to remember there was a time when I didn't know the words I use now to show what happens in cities. It seems like I always had those words, even though I <u>know</u> I couldn't. I got interested after I decided I didn't want to be on the ski team. That was early last year.

Now, I wonder if my interest happened because I <u>was</u> really interested or because I am a doofus at sports and wouldn't have been any good in competitive skiing because I am a doofus at <u>doing</u> things.

Larry doesn't want me up at the cabin anymore. He didn't throw me out or anything, but I <u>know</u> that's how he feels. Last weekend he and Grandpa got the jack under the house to put in the shoring because it was dry and everything went fine. This weekend Larry and I were supposed to get at the retaining wall and start work on the breezeway, too. Larry kept me changing from one project to the other. First I thought that was a good idea. Moving those heavy rocks is hard work and Larry had a bunch of rebars he was pounding into the ground behind where the rocks were going in for the wall. He asked me to pound some and I did a terrible job. They splayed out and bent and everything. The thing is you have to get the force exactly right on the rod, like hammering a nail. So, Larry had to get the rebars out and some were bent and it was a big waste. Then we moved stone and I was better at that, but I'm not strong enough for the weight of the stones we had to set and I kept falling and the stones kept slipping.

When we went to work on the breezeway

it was even worse, because I can't hammer nails without bending them, and I almost broke the sheet of fiberglass Aunt Sol got for the top of the breezeway. Larry was disgusted; I know he was. Hope asked me to stay for dinner, but I said I had to do something else and I got on my bike and rode home. I don't want to go there anymore. It's not that they treat me bad. I know Larry likes me, kind of, and I like him when he isn't hitting Hope, and Hope loves me and I love her. But I don't like seeing myself doing a bunch of stupid things and screwing up.

I better stick with my little models downstairs. I can move houses and stores around and study zoning and follow what happened in the city photos and maps you are sending me. I never thanked you for the Washington, D.C., neighborhood maps and photographs you sent. Everyone knows about the Capitol and the monuments, but now I know D.C. was a great neighborhood city. Grandpa says you met there, and had your courtship. I like that word.

*Love, Ben*


*Dear Marz,*                    *February 14,*
                    *Devil's Hopyard, Conn.*


Good walking weather at last. The snow stays on the ground here, melts, and then freezes or decays like heaps of bones left out in a cold sun to go gray and spongy. My new boots are light, warm, waterproof, and worn with the right kind of socks, not sweat-producing. They have the extra virtue of being politically incorrect. The purists on this Walk don't want leather, fur, plastic, coal, or oil derivatives. If a product isn't made of soybean husks, the hell with it. No one mentions the energy required to make the soybean husks into cloth, paper, or leather. The group has just voted to ban Styrofoam cups, <u>even</u> the ones we get in the convenience stores where we go to warm up. I <u>love</u> those overheated, overlit places, and the Styrofoam cups that keep coffee hot.

Did I dream this? Going through a town we went down one of its back streets. The fronts were all white wood, old cobbles, oak trees the size of Liechtenstein, clean-lined white-spired churches. At the back were the Dumpsters and overflowing garbage pails one sees everywhere, complete with the fluttering plastic which <u>does</u> degrade into tiny, brittle shreds that look like sea-kelp drying in the sun. There, behind the Dumpsters, were small groups of people. On down the street at one Dumpster stood three elderly women — white-haired and fragile, one of them caged in her osteoporotic bones. They were huddled in jackets and scarves, shivering. Why were they there? They were smoking. All down that back street by ones, by twos, taking drags in the punishing cold.

Once more let me tell you that I'll be happy to go full time while you build a business. We'll talk more when I get back for Hope's delivery. We say Hope's delivery as though we <u>knew</u> exactly when it was to happen. I'll be ready whenever the call is sounded.

Her isolation worries me. Her giving in to Larry's needs worries me. He has no job; they have no money. It's natural for Justice to buy Hope's maternity things, to supply the occasional food order, to send her away from lunches with a hundred dollars in her purse. It's natural for Hope, in love, to be most sympathetic to Larry's calls on her for sacrifice. All that <u>natural</u> life has become forced by his needs into unnatural shapes. Who will call a halt, at last?

Maybe the baby will bring Hope to defend herself when she has something smaller and weaker than herself to defend. Hope has ambitions. Larry has defenses. The baby will <u>cry out</u>. None of the talk about Indians and white people, prestige and need, none of the defenses will be worth the breath that carries that baby's howl.

My thoughts and energy are beginning to leave The Walk and circle around that cabin.

Love, T.

I've been tearing my hair. We're so used to instant contact with our faxes, phones, and beepers that we aren't used to waiting three to five <u>days</u> for information to be received.

Hope is in the hospital. <u>This</u> form of communication that relates not to the stopwatch but to the calendar has the virtue that there's time for an account. I'll tell you the news as I received it.

They called. She's so stupidly wary of Justice and Frank that she put our number in her purse. It was almost 2:00 A.M. and I thought the ringing phone was a clanking elevator. I didn't identify it until the fifth or sixth ring. It was Boulder Community Hospital and Hope was there, in "guarded condition." I called Justice and Frank, then went to the hospital.

Where was Larry? I looked for him in the emergency room, hoping to get the story, but he was nowhere in sight. Soon there was an overwrought Justice, and Frank in the emotional lockdown he goes into at times of stress. The nurse was minimally communicative. I think the purpose of the summons was for the hospital to assure itself that someone would be responsible for the bill. We sat for hours propped like the mannequins the store no longer wants, chair sprawl, couch sprawl, giving room to the father of a motorcycle drunk, the mother of a girl with a cut hand, then to sleep-blunted tourists fetched up on the icy road.

At last a doctor came and told us the baby was still in place and would probably be all right. Hope had "sustained internal injuries." That was at eight in the morning. I looked at him through grainy eyes as he talked to Frank. Then we let Justice go and get us something to eat. Then we sat, tried to read, paced, and dozed again. Another doctor came and asked to see the person who had brought Hope in. At nine they told us she was going to be all right; the bleeding had stopped (what bleeding?). I went home and then to work; Frank and Justice stayed.

We saw her that afternoon. She said she and Larry had been working on the retaining wall and some rocks had given way. Late in the afternoon, she said, she had felt a strain and stopped work. The strain eased, but after dinner, exhaustion overtook her and she fell asleep, waking up after a while with pain and a cough in which she thought she brought up some blood. She woke Larry and he brought her to the hospital. "Where is he?" we all asked, like a Greek chorus in a play. She began to cry, not, I think, for the first time that day.

Justice asked her what had happened. Rocks had fallen. "On your <u>face</u>?"

She said she had been trying to set them up on the wall.

"Rocks fell on your <u>face</u>, Hope?"

The social workers and doctors had kept asking her that, she said. Why didn't they leave her alone? She wasn't bleeding and the baby was safe. Whatever was wrong was beginning to heal. It was only the bleeding inside that had them worried.

We talked to the doctor. He said there was no mystery. She had been punched in the face and kicked in the stomach. She was sticking to her stupid story to protect him. While she did, their hands were tied. When there's domestic abuse, it usually escalates with the wife's pregnancy. She wouldn't bring charges, and when she left the hospital she would probably go back into the situation. He gave a helpless look and a little shrug.

He sounded matter-of-fact, almost bored, and I felt anger begin to flood me and words erupted I wasn't conscious of thinking. Whom did he think he was talking about? This was a girl who had grown up with every gift of self-respect and confidence. The doctor stood with that damn patronizing look until I wound down. Frank said, "We won't let her go back into the situation."

"Good luck," the doctor said.

I know, I know — there are plenty of middle-class girls and women walking the world with scars over their eyebrows and swollen lips and cheekbones shadowed with black and blue. Why would I think cruelty and passivity have a geography or a credit rating? I wanted it to be happening to someone else, someone I could push aside.

Later we had a conference with the social worker. She came in to Hope's room carrying a file of some size — Larry's record, his and Hope's history as clients, and the news that the couple had been considered High Risk. There was a little red tab at the top of the file, which gave it a special place, I guess.

The Immediate Family (what am I, a day late?) was allowed into the room, first. Freed of official constraint, I went to the nursing station and got a friendly older nurse to talk to me. They had been afraid for the baby, she said, and there had been a slow bleed that had gone on inside of Hope for four or five hours, a seeping from the blow to the stomach. They were not planning to do surgery. There was some worry that the placenta had been partially torn away from its place against the uterine wall or that the sac might have been minutely torn, and that was why they would be keeping Hope for two days or so.

I went home and fell asleep.

I'm at breakfast, now, or supper. It's night again — I'm using the little portable typewriter which now has toast crumbs in it. I'll go to the hospital before work, and when I come back from work. I have things to tell her.

*Love, Marz*

I'll slip the letter in the mailbox on the way home; communiqués from the front. Are the soldiers of the future going to carry laptops?

It's after nine, and regular visiting hours are over. I want to get the happenings down before they float away.

She looked yellow in the bluish hospital light, and the bruises — there were more than I had expected from the doctor's description. I had heard about two blows, but there were more — marks of grabbing, throwing — some hair was gone. This time, I gave her no space.

I asked her what it would be in six months — teeth out? jaw shattered? What, in a year, ribs broken, pelvis? At this rate, she might survive for a year before he does something the surgeons can't fix and that marking crayons won't cover.

She started to cry. I told her to turn it off, and get used to pain.

"You don't understand," she said, yet again.

I told her that had been her theme from the beginning. Why did I have to understand anything? He makes the decisions, she gives the concessions, and I'm supposed to understand something. Understand this, I said: "He doesn't keep his promises. Separate from him until he begins to keep his promises — job, school, counseling, alcohol abuse program, until he stops the abuse." I said I wouldn't submit <u>myself</u> to this suffering anymore.

Aha, she had her defense. He wasn't drinking — he hadn't had anything to drink.

Didn't she see that was even worse? I was yelling at her by then. He may love <u>you</u>, but he doesn't love the baby. What happens when it cries or fusses? Grow up!

He was sorry — he had brought her here . . .

"Yes, so you wouldn't die on the floor of the cabin. Good man."

I tried again. I told her that Larry couldn't help himself or do what he wanted to do or be what he wanted to be. He didn't want to batter her. "Stop making him do it."

She was crying again. She had tried, tried so hard.

"Take your face away from his fist," I said.

She said she would think.

I let her think. I came out here to write this. I know she won't press charges and the more he beats her the less attractive she will look and the less proud of her he'll be and when he has blurred her and marred her enough, he'll smash the image for good. We don't understand, she says. It's her conversation stopper, that she understands and we don't. She's right; I don't.

Is Larry's case simpler than we believe, or more complicated?

Either way I'm tired and angry. Tomorrow I will come back and see what she has thought about it all. Justice and Frank want her with them. To her, that means capitulation into childhood again. If I invited her to stay, they might accuse me of interfering. I have to sort that out with them and the social worker. I would be very happy if she came to stay.

*Marz*


*Dear Tig,*          *February 17, The Hill*

Hope is here. The last three days have been a month long, but Hope is <u>here</u> for the necessary bed rest.

She wouldn't talk to the battered women's volunteer, but they take pictures automatically now, before the women are cleaned up and sutured together. The volunteer got seven or eight photos of Hope and held them out to her, prints and negatives, in case she planned to bring charges. Hope refused to look. Later, we had an intense half hour with her, as she wept in denial and hysteria. Justice and I made her give up the stupid lie about rocks falling on her. She told us they had been setting the rocks and she had felt strained. The work was going too slowly for Larry, who was building up a rage. She remembered asking him when he was going to begin looking for a regular job. They needed money. It was time for her to start supper and the food supply was low. He closed up, a look like shutters going down over his eyes. She tried to back away, but he grabbed her and threw her on the ground.

From there it was all figuring how best to protect the baby. We listened to this, but I don't know how. She gave no details, but I had better knowledge than she of her injuries. I had gotten the photos from the volunteer, and I held them out to her again, putting them before her on the little rolling tray, 1, 2, 3, like poker cards in a hand. I told her to look. She closed her eyes.

I said if she went back to Larry now, she'd never make it to term. Neither would the baby. Look at the bruises, here, look at this bruise on your stomach. Do you see that red mark, there? It's the mark a boot makes.

Justice has recently begun to understand my argument: saying that abuse is bad for Larry makes the most sense to Hope. We began to argue that a separation would be good for Larry, that the strain of his inability to support her and the baby was harming him. We argued for an hour, the social worker came and argued, and we had at it again, but it was those pictures in the end, the blood around her teeth, the bruises, the way a scalp looks when a clump of hair is pulled from it, that made Hope stare at them, her vanity assaulted by their ugliness. She agreed to a separation.

The social worker talked about the help available to Larry. She wanted Hope to go to a shelter; to see other abused women and hear their stories, but when there was room with family, family took precedence. Justice asked Hope if she wouldn't come home to Grant Street.

Hope shook her head and then looked at me.

The delight in me began to bounce around in the sudden space she had created for it. The social worker asked if there were a way to contact Larry.

Hope nodded.

The social worker became brisk and began to talk about Larry's therapeutic possibilities.

Hope had no sooner decided than her resolve went limp. She cried, hanging on to that leather thong around her neck, that when Larry was happy, he was tender and sweet, full of love for her and the baby.

I saw Justice's face go hard and the social worker's face go neutral. "Of course he is," she said, lying in her bridgework, "and that's why he has to be protected from acting out inappropriately." I almost laughed at her mouthful of bafflegab. Then she said Larry didn't get up in the morning and think, "Oh, boy, another day to beat my wife." He was as much a sufferer as she. We can't leave him without a way to deal with his own nightmare. Give him this chance.

Hope wavered a little and then came back, nodding again, her eyes full of tears.

So this morning she was released from the hospital and I brought her here. Justice and Frank went to the cabin to get her clothes and left a note that Hope could be contacted through the social worker. I went to work, telling her to keep the doors locked and not to see Larry face to face until he had begun some kind of therapy. One of us should always be with her. She has agreed.

We are all exhausted. She said she slept the whole day through until I got home.

*Love, Marz*


*Dear Marz,*                   *February 20,*
*N. Scituate, Rhode Island*


I read your letter and bolted for the phone. Thanks for your patience. Then, I called Justice, who was resigned to Hope's decision about staying with you. She realizes that Hope needs face-saving (excuse the pun) and couldn't go back to her teenage room with everyone slipping too easily into the pre-Larry days.

Had I been home, Hope would have seen no open place she might fill. If she can stay resolute, Larry will drift away, save himself or lose himself somewhere else, and I wish she would give the baby up, too, and start again.

That's a dream that won't happen. Hope will keep the baby and make a symbol of it as she did with Larry. One worry at a time.

I hope Justice doesn't try to alter Hope's plans while she's with you. Shining Lady is an ally; I like her advice. She has kept Hope eating well and staying calm through some very troubled times. I know Justice would like to erase the entire year. She hates Hope's life at the cabin, her pregnancy, and her growing familiarity with the psychiatric and correctional arrangements of the city. Hope sees this as valuable life experience, real learning. Justice sees it as an unmitigated waste.

Hope will never accept that verdict. She's been too many places and learned too many things. Even her work at Wild Duds was connected with Larry and wouldn't have happened without him. I think that unless Justice gives Hope full marks for all that, credits her with it, honors her for it, they won't ever make peace.

It's wrong to drop Larry out of our lives; we can't, anyway.

The Walk goes on; two state-line crossings; Poppy's and my Charleston has become "an act." People have been writing gaseous verses and comic speeches and songs. In these poems and speeches we have become more conscious of ourselves as "an act."

That's all to the good if it informs — good if we bring it to what we do. I'm worried that it may tip over into preciousness. There's talk of a book, of making us a permanent group. This Walk is heroic stuff, some of it. Hope feels the same way, I guess. Without that whiff of romance, what would we try?

What looks <u>romantic</u> to us must look <u>authentic</u> to her. Thank heaven for your being there.

Love, Tig

February 22, Niwot

Moms,

I went up to see Dad and there was Hope, beating-colored and swollen. Ain't love great? Maybe it was lucky Larry flipped — she would have hung on for years doing the dance — violence, abjectness, shame, apology, sweetness, surreal peace, and then the ratcheting of tension and it all begins again.

She still thinks she's more important in that cycle than she really is. <u>She</u> ends the peace, <u>she</u> causes the tension, <u>she</u> makes <u>his</u> violent rage by some look, gesture, mistake. "Kiddo," I said, "you're a cliché by now, one of a crowd. Women like you could fill a stadium." That was what the social worker wanted to show her by sending her to a shelter and letting her see the other faces and hear the other stories.

The good news is that they are separating, which Hope agrees to for Larry's sake. "The baby and I were a strain on him." She told me how he was struggling to support her, to work, to finish the cabin. She was working hard, too, making more money than he was and not seeing what that was doing to his pride. I don't think happy and successful men beat their wives, she said. No comment.

Dad looks relieved. It's nice to come home to someone waiting, dinner in the making, talk about the day. I miss Blake and Anton for that. I like it from Sam and Cary, the school talk, who hit whom, who called a name.

No hint from Hope that she will give the baby up for adoption. We are all going to be made to re-a-lize that this baby has an Indian heritage. She wants to buy cassettes of Indian music and drumming to play to him in utero.

*Sol*


*Dear Grandma,*       *February 23, Grant Street*

Last week there was a couple, a cabin, with half a retaining wall and half a breezeway, and problems about water and mud. This week that's all over and everyone is trying to forget it. I'm glad Hope is with Grandpa and not getting beaten up, but I can't get used to the idea of the all-of-a-sudden-ness in everyone's life.

Mom doesn't want me to mention Larry's

name. Hope wants me to talk about Larry all the time. I like Larry for some things and not for some others, so I'm mixed up in ways I don't want to be. Is their marriage over, and is he just going to fade away somewhere? No, because there's a baby, which has his genes and stuff and is going to be as big in Hope's life as Larry ever was. What if Larry gets into school and studies and goes to work and takes drugs to stop his temper and learns how to stop hitting people and comes back then? I don't see it happening that way. I think Hope will have the baby and raise it and it will be some part Indian, so Hope will try to make her idea of race-peace be in that child.

When I see Hope and she talks about Larry, I feel funny. I always thought people decided things for ordinary reasons. People build cities, and the cities' changing is something you can learn. Demographers say that cities are the sum of lots of personal decisions. I always thought that the personal decisions were logical and clear. They were clear to me.

But there is another part, and that's about what people dream, and I can't think about that without hanging on to my desk like you hang on riding the roller coaster. Even the roller coaster obeys the rules of physics so you don't fly out. Hope and Larry are all about wish and dream and pictures in their heads. It makes me dizzy.

Don't think I am crazy or need to see a

shrink. Hope looks at me funny when I say things like this, or talk about how she and Larry are different. Are they? Is everyone half falling out of the roller-coaster car? This is very hard to talk about. Jason would have a three-month laughing jag if he found out.

*Love, Ben*


*Dear Gram,*                    *February 24, The Hill*

I owe you more thanks: I found out you wrote to Grandpa about my going on with Shining Lady and not having to have this baby in a hospital just because I am separated from Larry. The baby is still half Indian and my pregnancy has been Indian. Mom got started right away about me going back to the obstetrician and not seeing Shining Lady; Grandpa told me to go where I felt easy and secure. I told Shining Lady about my separation and she told me what to do to minimize its effect on the baby's spirit. She came here and looked it over. She says this will be easier. She wants you to say prayers for the baby morning and night and to stop throwing any water out of your tent — I told her where you were. She said you should be careful to pour it slowly on the ground. When March comes you should get a rawhide strip and knot thirty knots in it and untie one every day as soon as you wake up. Will you do those things?

They are to put you into harmony with the baby's spirit and mine.

I am getting a little clumsy and heavy and sometimes I get tired and sleep most of the day. I don't know whether it's being almost in my ninth month or because I am separated from Larry.

Everyone said to me how he didn't keep his promises. They were right, but how could he have kept them? He didn't have the money to buy things for the house or to keep the truck going. It hurt him that I started a career and he couldn't. All that and a baby was overwhelming to him. That made him angry with himself. As soon as some of the weight is removed from him, he will be able to get up, to move forward, and find his way, and then we will go back together in the right spirit.

So I am at your house again with Grandpa and it feels right to be here, now. I would die at home, feeling like a little girl again. This way I can help Grandpa and he doesn't try to make me hate Larry. Shining Lady says that hunting parties and war often separated husbands and wives and many babies were born when the men were away.

Grandpa says I improve his quality of life. I think that means he has better meals. Shining Lady gave me a diet and we follow that. We both cook. Grandpa says if he hears about the Food Groups one more time he will scream. He says that in fun because he is eating better. Larry didn't want a balanced diet, either. Are all men like that, not wanting to eat right? They both say that casseroles weaken the masculine spirit. Is that right?

I guess I missed out on being with other newly married women, sharing recipes and stuff. It would have been fun to find out about getting bargains and learning how to do things the best way and laughing and comparing how it was with each of us. Did you ever have that?

This is really embarrassing: when I laugh or cough I wet my pants. Now I have started to wear a pad so I won't be caught. Is that normal? It makes me feel worse than any other part of this, backaches or how I used to be sick every day, and throw up. So, you see, Larry was right to make me stop working when he did.

I went down to the store early today, to Wild Duds, and I talked to Steve. He said I looked beautiful and I started to cry, but I didn't think he saw that. Could I come back when the baby was born and six weeks old? Yes, he said. It made me feel good. If I could get child care I could stay with you and Grandpa for a while. Then I wouldn't have to be in special housing.

That's the news from here.

*Love, Hope*

*Dear Marz,*                                      *February 26,*
                        *Barrington, Rhode Island*

We have made the earliest date possible and will spend the extra time going slowly across bridges and bays into Massachusetts, then around Cape Cod, to end at Woods Hole. Then, we will tabulate our questionnaires and write up our own notes on the places we have passed. What will emerge will not be the unified impression of each place we had expected to elicit, but 70 or 80 impressions depending on The Walkers. Even Poppy and I have different views, some of them radically different, depending on where we looked and to whom we spoke. Where I see quaint she sees shabby. The value of The Walk is that instead of one view of any given place, there will be majority and minority decisions, and a kaleidoscope of reality that should yield a depth and dimension missing in the ordinary report.

I am dreading this month. As we near the coast, the cold has been joined by a viscous and subversive dampness, a blunt, obdurate, and unyielding blanket of it. When I get back home I will never leave the high, dry Rockies where air is a gas, not a liquid.

*Icily, Tig*

*Dear Solidarity,*                    *February 27,*
        *Portsmouth-Tiverton, Rhode Island*

I'm so glad you are bringing Sam and Cary to see Dad and inviting him to Niwot. Neither of us was great as the grandparents of toddlers. This used to bother me until I began meeting other grandparents who admitted that they, too, weren't capable of the joy they wanted to have until the grandchildren were six or seven. Then, the relationship bloomed. We didn't give you much help with baby-sitting, but I think we are readier, now. I'm looking forward to the experiment.

It has become clear to me why people camp in the summer, and not in the winter.

I thought I was developing cataracts, but it was only five days of fog.

                     *Foggily, Ma*


*Dear Hope,*                    *February 28,*
        *Portsmouth-Tiverton, R.I.*

A secret about casseroles: leave out the cheese, call them stews, and men will eat them. The cheese makes it a casserole. Your grandfather has strong ideas about food. Cheese has uses; they are as follows: 1. on sandwiches; 2. as powder sprinkled on spaghetti; 3. in a cheeseburger. Period. Cereal is to be eaten in the mornings only. Once I tried to give him polenta as a side dish, and he stared at it as though Martians had brought it down in a space ship. Oranges and bananas are <u>morning</u> <u>foods,</u> and cannot be eaten at any other time. Ask him, and you'll see. Bacon belongs with eggs, not in salads. Sunflower seeds are fed to chickens. Chickens are edible. Seeds are not. There are other rules and maybe you can get him to bend them a little. Our neighbors eat sushi, so I know that there are older men eating it outside the borders of the islands of Japan.

The Walk has severed all my ties to time-appropriateness in food. We may eat stew in the morning and cereal at night. I seem to notice that it is the men on The Walk who get whiny when we have last night's reprise at breakfast. Where is the pioneer spirit?

I am happy to hear you are taking care of yourself and the baby. Get Ben to take you out and get your folks to do the same so you can have some fun in this last month when the waiting gets to be such a bore. I will remember not to throw water. It would be ice before it hit the ground.

*Love, Gram*

# *March*

*Dear Ben,*                                    *March 1,*
       *Westport, Massachusetts, Campground*

I know you have lots of feelings about Hope and Larry's separation; I wanted to write about something you said about yourself, about your incompetence at building things.

That may be true, but don't decide yet. Larry likes you, but I think he had a need just then, to drive you away, and how much easier than to make you feel clumsy and useless by giving you work beyond your experience? I don't think he did this in a conscious way. It was his need. Don't pass <u>any</u> judgments on yourself until you are at least twenty-five years old. I say this because when I was your age I decided I wasn't athletic. The decision was made on a trip I took with friends to a resort, where I tried skiing and ice-skating for the first time. I put on the skis and fell down. The others skied away. Half an hour later I was still floundering in the snow. I got the things off and walked back to the lodge exhausted and humiliated. Then, I sat through lunch while my friends glowed and crowed about the wonderful morning, and allowed themselves to wonder where I had gone. Then we went skating.

They all knew how. They were encouraging but they had forgotten the work and time it takes to learn to <u>slide</u>. The fourth time I went sprawling and couldn't get up without help. I decided as I lay on the ice, wet through, chilled beyond feeling, shins aching, shoulder bruised, that I was not athletic. I didn't put on skis again until your grandfather kidnapped me to Eldora for my fiftieth birthday. I don't regret the skiing I missed as much as the judgment I made on myself all those years ago.

The separation <u>I</u> had made between body and mind denied me half a lifetime of fun. The sign I am posting says:

**Don't fall in this hole.**
**Read the sign.**

*Love, Grandma*


*Dear Justice,*        *March 2, Fairhaven, Mass.*

I'm writing this to crow about my grandson. If I wrote it to him, it would embarrass him too much, but what a joy he is. I love him for so many things, not the least of which is his ability to see beyond my wrinkles and gray hair to someone to whom he can speak naturally. Thanks for him. He's a gift that causes me to smile inwardly whenever I think of him.

492

How is Jason getting along? Is he skiing, now, even if not with the team?

And there is Hope. In all the anguish and worry about her safety, and in our knowing how blindly romantic she is, how stubborn in that romanticism, I don't want to forget how decent she is, and how gifted with an ability to be happy.

It's a selfish time of life, her age, but God knows that selfishness could have been manifested in any one of a dozen less attractive ways, some more harmful than this. Her romanticism is about love, not despair. Could that have brought out the worst in Larry? We are suffering for Hope, all of us, but at least we are suffering for the right reasons.

I haven't said any of this before because we are usually too busy living to meditate on life.

I love you, Justice. I respect Frank and I'm proud of the life you have made together. I delight in the family you have brought us, and I wanted you to know that.

*Love, Mother*


*Dear Gram,*                    *February 28, The Hill*


Larry came today and he looked so wounded. Grandpa sat just in sight of us, working on some papers, but we knew he was listening. We were sitting at the kitchen table at each end so we could see each other, and I was picking at the place you said Mom had picked at with a knife when she was little, making a hole there under the edge. I told Larry I was going through with the separation. It was going to be a legal one, and that meant that we were separated <u>now</u> but could change back when he was really in school or really on a job and had done the work he needed to do on his temper and his rages. He said, "I know I fucked up." Grandpa's head came up with that sudden alert look you see on squirrels or chipmunks, that "What? What?" We both laughed and Grandpa scowled and went back to his papers and we laughed again. Then I said, "I have to be here; it's because of the baby. I was bleeding and you really hurt me this time."

"I'm not drinking — you know that."

"You kept kicking me and you wouldn't stop."

"I need you to be with me. I never mean to hurt you. You know that."

He said it so quietly. We were both almost whispering. This was about 2:00 P.M. You know how your kitchen gets lighter, then, with the sun heaping up light in the corner near the stove. We had been in shadow, but as we talked the light got to us as though a hand had pulled a curtain away and the light wanted us.

Larry said that Mr. Anson came out to see the work he did. I was eager to hear what he would say because we had worked so hard,

Larry and I and Ben and even Grandpa.

He walked all around, Larry said, and inside. There was the floor and he showed how Mr. Anson's eyes opened up to see how it was fixed.

I kept looking at Larry sitting in his shaft of sunlight; his face was quiet while he talked. He has none of the play acting and bragging that used to get me so sick of <u>boys</u> when I was in school.

There was the floor, shelves, stove. Outside were the shoring and the breezeway. See? Water doesn't run under the cabin anymore. Mr. Anson was impressed.

I remembered all the work we had done, even those stupid shelves Ben worked so hard to make. If you put a can on its side, it would roll to the left on the lower shelf and to the right on the upper one. Don't tell Ben. I thought I might start to cry so I asked Larry if he had a job.

He said yes, at a motel. It's pretty good. He's a general handyman.

I was so happy. It's just the right job for him. He said he had to give a reference for it, so he gave Anson's name because Anson was the only one who knows his skill.

There's one bad thing and that's he's supposed to be available for emergencies. He couldn't tell them he has no phone, so he gave them this number, and also mom and dad's number.

I didn't want to talk about the bad things he had done, but I had to, because it was the whole reason I couldn't stay with him. When I did, he looked so miserable. Then he said, "I don't know why I have my rages. I start to think things. I don't want to think. Once, I got pills for that." You should have seen him. He bent over and was trembling like a shaky old man trying to get a pill out of a bottle and then scattering them all over the place. We laughed and Grandpa looked up from his work again. Grandpa's look made me stop. Why would he want to keep us from laughing?

Larry said I was the only person who ever gave a rat's ass about him.

I know that sounds gross when you read it, but it means he knows how I love him.

He said it was harder when he isn't drinking. When he gets a mild buzz, the feeling softens up and there aren't any edges. It's the edges that trip him up; they go sharp.

His face was like it gets when he's figuring how much wood or stone we'll need for a project, and I could see his hands trying to work the words like rope he was using to tie things together.

Love isn't only making love — I always knew that. I love the look he has when his mind has traveled into his hands and into the work. He'll go inside it, so far that when he's figured it out, he'll straighten up and say, "It's getting dark . . ." in a kind of surprise because he didn't notice the time passing. Those are the best times because I'm his hand or his eye and we're one body, one wish and two energies to work on the job. He has no arrogance then, which people say he has at other times, no impatience and no anger.

He said, "I can't control my drinking. When I drink, one of the edges that goes soft is the edge that says when to stop. I have stopped drinking. I'm going to get control of my anger, too, because it isn't at you."

I asked him why he had hurt me, then. He said he didn't know but he did know that he wanted me and our baby and being together. He wanted me to dream for him and have faith in him; that he needed my faith.

I said how he had broken his promises. He nodded and said he knew that.

What about this job?

He smiled and said he liked it. His other jobs had the weekend off and that's when trouble happened. On this job he gets off at four and when the days get longer he'll have time to work on the cabin. He looked at me and there was such pain on his face — He said, "You don't trust me yet. Here it is, two o'clock, and I'm not working."

Then he said he had told them ahead of time that he would work four to six tonight to make up the time. I could see then that it wasn't a punch-in punch-out job, and they were treating Larry like a man, and not a boy, and that would give him the feeling of respect he needed. I was glad.

He got up and started to leave. We had a minute standing up, me so big and pregnant and him wondering if he should try to kiss me. We wanted to, but Grandpa was there, and got up, too, and Larry held out his hand — but Grandpa wouldn't. Larry left. Then I cried. I wish Grandpa could forgive Larry.

*Love, Hope*


*Dear Tig,*                    *March 5, The Hill*

Hope wrote about Larry's first visit, but I'm writing now about the second. I came in on them, being peaceful enough, at five this afternoon. He had brought her some more of those horses, plywood this time and cut out with a jigsaw, probably at his work. I was furious. The visits were supposed to be monitored, the conditions had been set up and agreed on. This was instead of "hello" and Hope looked wounded. Larry said he had come to deliver the horses. He and Hope had just said hello. There was no harm in that. I said it wasn't about good or harm, but about promises, things Larry agrees to do and doesn't do.

Larry said he was working and the people like his work.

I asked if they would like to know he had

been making stencil cut-outs at their shop, with their shop tools, when he should have been working.

He said he had come to tell Hope that he had made these as models and showed them to the boss. The boss said they'll put them up on the doors of the units with the room numbers on them. He'll be painting those doors in the spring and when he does, he'll have a different model for each of the doors and the number on each.

What could I do but congratulate him for that and remind him that he should have waited until I was at home before coming. He could have called her, faxed, . . . I nearly said sent smoke signals, but I caught myself. It was a promise! Hope looked bereft. Larry took off, and the four horses were put in the window instead of the plants you had there, which have died, droopy and stringy in your absence. Hope sulked through the evening, leaving me to feel like Blunderbore, the fairy-tale giant.

I told her again that I didn't want Larry here when I was out. She had promised that and so had he. I reminded her that too many of their meetings last year had been done in secret. "You are separated — remember that." Did she hear me or was she nodding and shrugging as a body filling in for a mind gone into dream?

All the while I have been leaving the house at six A.M. so as to get to Louisville to check the work going on in the houses. The concrete will be poured soon, requiring four days of good weather for optimum curing.

Frustration at work. A TV journalist followed our road crews, documenting the time spent in coffee shops and napping in the trucks. Some of the men are obviously "Impaired." Now the commissioners want to get everyone on the county payroll to justify every half-hour block of his time. We will waste hours tracking down half-hours. They should have fired the ten biggest loafers on the road crew and thanked the journalist for documenting everything. It would have brought all the rest back into line.

You will be pleased that I called Justice and told her what had happened. She thanked me, though she was annoyed at not being able to do much herself.

I am beginning to envy you that damn Walk, snow or no snow.

*Love, M.*

*Dear Grandma,*               *March 6, Grant Street*

I went to Grandpa's yesterday.

Hope saw me trying not to stare at her stomach and she asked me how it looked. I said like someone trying to hide a volleyball.

Then we were starting to argue about the size of the ball until I yelled, "Okay, beach ball!" and she threw me down on the floor and threatened to roll over me and kill me. For that little time it was the old Hope and me and it felt so good to remember we once fooled around like that.

I want her to keep her baby. Mom and Dad and Jason and Grandpa and Aunt Sol don't. Jason?

I asked Mom why Jason would have an opinion about Hope's baby. It's not that he says she'll have to support the baby. He just says, "She should get rid of the kid." Mom says Jason is lost in a fog of his own body's chemicals and can't identify his real feelings. I'm the only one who sides with Hope. Grandpa is trying to act fair and never says what she should do, but his hands, his legs and feet, do things that make me know how he feels. Hope must see this, too. Mom and Dad say, "You are going to give it up for adoption, aren't you?" Aunt Sol shakes her head. I forgot to include Sam. He just had a birthday — seven. He asked me why Hope was so fat and I told her she had a baby inside her and Sam wanted it to be born so he could race it against his friend's rabbit. When I said it would lose, he stopped caring.

So, Hope wants it and I do and Larry, I think, wants it, too, and that puts us against everybody else, I think maybe even you. It's none of my business, either, except that I will be the baby's uncle and that's not the only reason. Here it is:

When Jason smiles — <u>really</u> smiles, and it's not an expression we see much anymore, but when he does, he looks like Dad and that makes me believe in genetics and all that science stuff they try to teach us in school. When that baby is born it will have <u>us</u> in it. I don't want that us-part to be given away to people who won't want it there because it is <u>us</u> and not <u>them</u>.

*Love, Ben*


DIARY ENTRY *March 9, Marion, Massachusetts*


Buzzards Bay and we'll spend ten days, collecting our data, writing our notes and diaries, and getting our report into shape to present to the convention. We will be camped in a large park. The town is close in case of storms and a hotel there has given us use of two fairly large rooms for preparing our reports and will let us use its laundry rooms as well.

Without computers, we'll use <u>people</u>, the eighty of us, a work-force at the command of John Sievert and Patricia who have been giving a lot of thought to the collection of the data and how the reports should be done. The answers in the questionnaires will be read and gathered for each locality and then for the states and regions.

We will arrange piles of questionnaires at Answer Stations to be read, and sorted. Then we will carry them to the next station. An Internet user calls the process <u>Walk</u> Net. There is nothing scientific about this core-sample through the nation's middle. We have no cities, few suburbs. But a picture will emerge, including movement into and out of cities, along with the way people feel about how their areas are changing.

I'm looking forward to the work. We have earned these figures, and the knowledge we will be getting, subjective as it is.


*Dear Marz,   March 10, Buzzards Bay, Mass.*


I have been writing all day, culling perceptive sentences out of the questionnaires, underlining them in red and taking my turn at one of the rented typewriters, clickety-clack down and back.

The Walk has become the Office of the Census — 80 people tabulating thousands of pieces of information. We foresaw none of these needs — space to work, paper, pencils, and whatever machines people are willing to lend or rent to us. Luckily, the people here became interested in the work, and we have gotten superb cooperation.

Now and then we come across one of the questionnaires <u>we</u> took. We remember, or don't remember, where it was taken, the day, or even the person who filled it in. Poppy runs over to me with the questionnaires from the two older women we met outside Las Vegas, and we smile and remember the sun pouring warm honey over the afternoon as we sat on their patio and talked.

Kevin rises again. Here and there are questionnaires with his initials, and the names or initials of people who went away with him. I wonder now how much of this collecting work that he considered so tedious, he actually did.

Poppy and I were interviewed a month or so ago by a magazine, and yesterday for a local paper. Our age has been mentioned here and there, and the magazine has promised us a copy when the issue in which we appear comes out. The paper will concentrate on our courage and age-spots. The magazine took pictures of us, Poppy fresh from another dye-job. The outdoors — wind and sun and cold — have done their work on us as on the monumental mountains we have traversed. We are creased, eroded, wind-blown, and sun-scoured. We look like the hundred-and-twenty-year oldsters found in the Caucasus, or the raisin-faced sons of slaves someone photographed down south. Poppy's red hair makes her look like a dishmop with an attitude. I have let my hair grow — it got in my eyes, but now it's long enough to gather in back, Pilgrim-father style. I look like a witch down on her luck and scraping the bottom of the cauldron. When I get back home, I'll have to use neat's-foot oil.

*Love, Tig*


*Dear Ben,     March 12, Buzzards Bay, Mass.*

I will be issued a copy of the report we make of this Walk, the questionnaire material, etc., and will save it for you to read. As we count and measure and evaluate, it occurs to me that there might be something there for you — a how and why people move toward and away from your cities in the first place. Your populations are not stable. People move into and out as well as within the cities, and the places from which they come may play a role in the city's character.

Your argument for Hope's keeping her baby was moving to me and tells me you are thinking more of the family than I had been. My thoughts are for Hope alone and of what would be easier for her — maybe not even better, only easier. As it is, we will have very little to say in the matter. Hope has decided.

There's a special beauty on this coast. We are seeing it in what I thought was a season of iron-gray seas, gray skies, boiling clouds that overflowed their vessels in heaves of snow, almost gray itself, and mute. Then, yesterday we came out of the hotel where we have been working and everything had gone suddenly, gloriously blue. The sea was blue — not blue-green but dark blue as a newborn's eyes, the sky shattering its blueness against the white snow in a blinding glare of light, the air whipped blue up out of the sea in waves; even the gulls had changed their color from muddy gray to pearly white.

The people here say it is seldom the same for two days at a time but the same scene remakes itself, weather and season changing it every day. Maybe we will come back here some day, you and I.

*Love, Grandma*


*Dear Hope,*     *March 13, Buzzards Bay, Mass.*

I'm furious. Newspaper and magazine articles have come out about The Walk, both of them featuring us as its oldest participants. The magazine interviewer seemed awed. I said that 62 and 64 were scarcely considered old anymore, but yes, it was a special challenge for people of our years to do a Walk of this length, winter, etc. Poppy gave a wonderful statement about how in one's sixties one finally realizes she won't be around in 30 or 40 years and begins to consider the heritage she is bequeathing. "One looks beyond Family," she said. I said those whose children are grown sometimes feel a loss of purpose. Projects such as this replace that element. The interviewer was amazed that my husband was not on The Walk. "How could he let you go off for a whole year?" she asked.

"Perhaps he understood that the happiness of one partner conduces to the happiness of both."

Poppy smirked at her and said, "What if this were a <u>job</u> and it was the <u>husband</u> who had to go abroad for a year and the <u>wife</u> who stayed home, making visits two or three times? Would that be considered so exceptional?"

I thought we came off rather well.

That was until I read the article: "SPIR-ITED OLDSTERS ON THE MOVE." We were portrayed as two characters out of an "I Love Lucy" plot, bouncing around the land-scape. "My husband is as happy as I am," the woman quoted me as saying; "<u>Husbands</u> leave their wives all the time." The article strongly suggested that we were trying to recapture our youths. It mentioned Poppy's giggle and for-est-fire hair color and ended by calling us "madcap."

We recovered from that just in time to read the newspaper article which intimated that we had forced The Walk to accept us, and that our walking was part of our struggle for the rights of the elderly. <u>Elderly</u>? Poppy was speechless; so was I.

When looking at people of our ages — women in particular — there's an urge among many young people to distance themselves. This can intensify until they go deaf and blind to everything but parodies of us.

How are you doing? How are things going between you and Marz? Are the days restful, if not happy, while you wait for Cadwallader or Aspidistra? (We used to call our unborn babies that.) Rest and relaxation are what I want for you, a time-out before the effort of giving birth and the years'-long effort of caring for a baby, then for a child.

I did that one wrong — I gave the time away. I said, "I'll take my trips in spite of being pregnant." It made me feel heroic, necessary to a higher cause. Your mom, for instance, was almost born during the McCarthy hearings, and we did marches, then. I was at Little Rock when she was a baby and I did the Vietnam protests in spite of Solidarity. Looking back now, and especially with Justice, I ache at having given away an entire nine months. I could have used that time as a time apart, a sacred time. I notice this is something you are trying for. Why wasn't I thinking, reading, resting, walking, watching the change of the seasons, seeing the shapes of snowflakes? Women have closed the door on most of that, but there should be some of it, don't you think, the ninth month at least?

Please exile worry. Your separation apparently includes Larry's visits. Take your grandfather's wishes to heart on that. He needs to be with you when you visit, for your sake. You make promises and so does Larry, and both of you forget.

*Love, Gram*

*Dear Marz,*         *March 15, Buzzards Bay*

We have been tabulating the results of a year's Walk, upwards of 50,000 question-naires and our own daily observations. We take up two meeting rooms of a large hotel.

Earlier this afternoon, I saw Heather Sievert walking across the floor with an armful of questionnaires. She asked me to get the door. The load had been read and entered, and was going into the van for recycling.

I thought that was a messy way of handling piles of paper. When I saw her go out with another pile, I got some cord, put on my heavy jacket, and went out to the van to bundle the two loads. The back of the van was empty. Puzzled, I was about to go and look for Heather when I saw her coming out with another load. She turned on the walkway to the back of the hotel. I followed.

She was stoking a refuse-burner, patiently, 30 or 40 sheets at a time, in the stinging cold, warming her bare hands at the fire she was feeding. I yelled and she turned, surprised, opening her bent arm so that some of the questionnaires went windborne into the claws of bushes.

I got two, seeing Kansas stamped on one, Missouri on another. They hadn't been finished. She looked cornered, and then said the Council had decided.

I won't bore you with the details of how I got the Council to tell me what it had decided and had begun to pull off, but its purpose was The Greater Good.

What's The Greater Good in destroying the questionnaires? Success is bad. John Sievert, hand on my shoulder in that patronizing gesture that made me want to leave him with a bloody stump, told me that any reports of small-scale success would blind legislators and the public to the need for total systems of renewable energy and tighter controls on air, water, and chemical pollution. He will be applying for grants, he told me, and the statistics will have to justify a real need. People won't see the need unless we show them, make them see . . . He is turning our inquiry into propaganda. When I said so, he looked at me with the same patronizing look and said, "When was it anything else?"

I felt like a fool. Did The Walk know?

I went to the middle of the floor, shouting to everyone over the din of 80 people typing, writing, and moving the collections of papers around the room. It took a while to get them all stopped and silent, people looking annoyed at the interruption of work. I told them what I had seen. When I finished, they stood or sat where they were, in complete silence.

People on the Council came forward and began to explain. The report on which we were working had no <u>scientific</u> value. It was purely subjective. Five miles up or down from where we had taken our questionnaires, a different set of situations might be occurring. Even if we went to the same places again, the responses would differ. All this I granted, but said that if we made propaganda of it, it would lose <u>whatever</u> value it had as a document worth reading.

I looked around. People were standing, listening, waiting. Herb Kvarner began to talk. Do you remember him? You said he looked like a pecan, brown, in hair and face, all his features shading into one another. He began to talk about grant money for worthwhile projects — re-forestation, open space, protected areas for wildlife. Other people had projects, using The Walk to sponsor awareness. That awareness would need validation, with clear, unambiguous figures. All the Council was doing in destroying some of the positive responses was making the contrast sharper.

Others spoke, for and against. Herb spoke again. The "delineation" had already begun; most of the "questionable" papers had already been destroyed. They would wish to keep ten percent of the favorables to round out the picture. "Why bother?" I asked. "Since this is propaganda, why not make it a clean sweep?"

Someone said that the Council included Fresnos who had done the whole Walk believing in its original mandate. I spoke out as a Fresno, reminding people how it was in Missouri when we lost Kevin, because we were not a political party or an ideological movement.

In the end, we voted. Thirty for censure, for stopping the "delineation" and adding a mention of the destroyed questionnaires. Forty-six voted to "adjust" or "delineate." Ten abstained.

So the trip has changed as it changed during the Vietnam protests, as it changed for me during the later Peace movement. We voted down the moderates then, and polarized an impossible Left and an impossible Right.

Poppy and I and fifteen or so assorted Walkers have stopped working on questionnaires. We'll help cook for The Walk, or go to work on its bookkeeping, a job that needs to be done. I'll do anything for The Walk except be part of its newly discovered Political Soul.

I'm feeling my age. I'm feeling duped and stupid, but this time I didn't let the tide carry me.

Our lack of cooperation on the questionnaires is drawing stares from people. They work awfully hard. At Bunion Rub, I asked why there was a need to mold and sculpt to provide statistics that could be spun up like candy. Why not simply fake them all? People glared back at me. I have apprenticed myself to Murray Siger, who is getting the food and water trucks ready for the trip back to Arkansas.

*Moodily, Tig*

*Dear Gram,*    *March 10, The Hill*

I need to write this. I hate to do it. Larry has been visiting almost every day. He says he is still working, that he takes off in the afternoon to see me and then goes back to the job and works later, but I'm not sure that's true. Maybe he tells the boss he has to shop for paint or wood or something and gets off that way. He says he is still doing repairs on our cabin, that the retaining wall is getting completed and the breezeway is almost done. He does that in the early morning and after his job for an hour or so because the days are still short.

I tell him I will stay here and have our baby. I tell him we will be separated for a year and then I will see if he is working steady and not drinking and if he has been doing therapy to control his violence.

Yes, he knows, yes, he understands, but maybe he isn't listening. He goes away when I talk about that and he's not behind his eyes. "Where's <u>Grandpa</u>?"

I tell him he's not supposed to visit without Grandpa here, that he promised.

He says he would have promised to turn purple to see me. I'm his wife; I should be with him. He points to my braided necklace.

I told him that was about hoping he would keep his promise.

I told him I would come with him if he worked this year and didn't drink and went to therapy or ADEPT or one of the other programs. He breathed out hard, the way you do when you are disgusted. I told him he had promised all those things and he got a little angry and left.

I'm worried about him leaving work to come and see me and I'm worried about wanting him back and knowing he shouldn't be back until he is more steady and settled in himself.

Grandpa needs to know that Larry comes during the day. It will be tough to tell him, but I guess it's important because Grandpa gave me a long talk when I first came, about keeping promises. The problem is that when you make the promise, you see a picture of what the future looks like with you doing what you promised in it, and it looks clear and possible to do and even easy — there you are, taking classes or being a single mom working at Wild Duds and waiting for Larry to be ready, and there <u>he</u> is, working on a job and doing therapy in a group and the picture is so clear and feels so right, you say, "Oh, yes, <u>that</u>," as if you were pointing at it in a store window to choose it for yourself.

But that's not how it happens, is it? What happens is that when you get up the next morning you aren't that person you saw in the picture and when Larry comes, he isn't, either. The promise was made by the people in your head, not the people who are here, now. Then you get confused between what the dream was and what's here.

I know you will want me to tell Grandpa. He will think I have been lying to him. I hate that because he has been good to me.

Love, Hope

Dear Tig,                March 11, The Hill

Last night I came home and we had our usual comic argument about what we would eat for dinner. I always demand something like chicken-fried steak, mashed potatoes and gravy, "and for <u>dessert</u> . . ." Hope tells me what the menu actually is and I pretend to protest and rage and we end by going into the kitchen to fix it. Last night, as we worked together, I sensed she was nervous about something. Of course, I thought it was the baby, that Hope had been bleeding, or was in pain.

Her hands naturally fall across her stomach, now, and in her nervousness, she was rubbing it the way little kids rub parts of their bodies when they are distressed, unconscious of doing it. No, it wasn't the baby.

I touched her sweatered arm.

She told me Larry had been coming around, wanting her to go back with him. I forced my voice down and told her that her lip was nearly healed. "Maybe the mark of his kick has faded, so you're almost ready for more. If he breaks your jaw next time you'll have six weeks away." She dropped her head and started to cry.

God, I hated that. I lost my temper; telling her not to snivel, but to talk, to tell me why she let him in. It was all the old guff. Larry can't be shut out, he has been shut out all his life, he needs to know we care, blah, blah, blah. I told her I cared so much, I wanted to be part of the family he has said he needs. He has a family, now; let its rules stand for once. Tell him. Make him know.

She said she would.

Tomorrow I will call in sick and Hope and I will go out to Louisville, where they have finished the basics of stabilizing the structure. If Larry comes, Hope won't be here. She says she will not see him unless I am here. I called Justice and told her and she says she can come and stay with Hope in the afternoons until Larry gets the message. Hope doesn't like it, but there it is. She feels Justice's eyes on her.

A sweet, short snow has just fallen. Ben and I will go skiing this weekend, I hope, and Justice and Frank will chaperone Hope, or we will take her with us to sit in the lodge and read or sew. She says she doesn't mind doing that.

Tons of fun. Wish you were here. Really.

*Marz*

*Dear Mother,*         *March 13, Grant Street*

I went over to Dad's to talk about Hope's plans and when she met me at the door, I had a shock, seeing her so heavy in her pregnancy. Her hair is longer now, and she wears it in a braid. It seemed dull. You know how a woman's front sticks out so much that food tends to fall onto it — she had stains down the front of the nice blouse I had gotten for her. I started to cry. She stood at the door, weight on one foot and then the other, waiting with elaborate patience for me to stop. Dad came and took my arm and led me inside.

I tried to explain by saying I remembered my own pregnancy. Dad put out some of their cake and we sat down at the table. He told me he had brought the baby's things from the cabin; they had made a nursery in Sol's old room. Hope sleeps in mine. She is planning to have the baby there and not in the hospital and Dad nodded and said it was okay with him. Shining Lady. I haven't met her yet, and when Hope went to the bathroom (I had forgotten that, too, all that pressure over the bladder), Dad told me the midwife was all right. There's lots of New Age hokum, he says, but there's also a degree in nursing and one in midwifery — State of Colorado. He saw them on her wall. She lays on the nutrition and exercise in a way Hope can tolerate, which she wouldn't accept from us. Shining has also told Hope that being apart from Larry won't scar the baby. Hope came back and I told her I knew that Larry was coming when she was alone, a thing he promised not to do.

She argued. Her face got that set look.

I said she was setting up the same situation she had before.

Her face contorted and I thought she would cry, but she got hold of herself and we were all still for a while because we could see she was trying for control. There was time to look around.

They do all right; the house is clean, but I saw that the kitchen was where they lived. There the order was Dad's, not yours. Books were piled on the counters because Dad likes to read at the table. Hope's sewing was on top of the TV because she likes to sew to TV, which they have moved into the crowded kitchen. Everything's for convenience, nothing for graciousness. The dining and living rooms have an unused look. They have retreated into the heart of the house.

Hope was talking. Larry needed roots, she said, a reason to keep working. She said she was scared to send him away, to shut him out, just because Dad wasn't here.

I was suddenly alert: Scared of what?

"I'm scared of what he might do," Hope said, in the small voice of her childhood.

I told her I would stay with her during the day. She pleaded with me not to. I suggested she come with me and spend the time where I am. I promised not to pick at Larry.

She tried to sound playful. Go to the water board meeting? Go to the school board? When we didn't laugh, she said she would graduate from high school and get a college degree, too. "I have done what adults do, only in the wrong order," and then we did laugh, not at what she had said, but at the way she looked while she was saying it, little-girl-pregnant-woman, and with a fussy-little-old-lady inflection at the end.

*So. Justice*


*Dear Tig,*                    *March 14, The Hill*

Yesterday, he came again and I headed him off, trying for the pleasant, laid-back approach.

He stayed for half an hour to show me I couldn't drive him away and when he left, I went to the computer and sent in some things needed at work. I had started with a good mood, having carried out my duty as guardian of the gate, but as the afternoon went on, the day seemed to darken for me, why I don't know. I was angry at Larry, angry at the situation, annoyed at Hope, irritated at the county, my boss, cholesterol, and the ozone layer.

The Louisville project is now taking up my late afternoons and sometimes my evenings. I've been taking Hope with me and Ben has joined us once or twice. Hope isn't interested in the project and it's cold in the car, but I can park her in a nearby coffee shop with her magazines or some baby-sewing.

The only two subjects in her purview are Larry and the baby. Any other discussion films her eyes over and draws her mouth down into a tired, forlorn droop that annoys me. Ben isn't interested in the house project, but he has a map of the town and has drawn in the buildings and developed a theory as to why they were kept during what he calls The First Great Change — the 1920s. We talk about his ideas as we drive down — the three of us, and it's a pleasure to have him along even though it always requires a big, Italian dinner afterward.

It's good to get the news of your closing phase, even if the news is bad. In your letter you said The Walk's psychological destination had changed. I believe you. I can't believe it started out political and aimed to cook the questionnaires. Something about the energy expended makes people want to get more out of an idea, or project, than what there is in it. Funny, though; most faking is done to put a positive face on things. I'm eager for you to get it all over with and come home.

I think Hope realizes now that Larry can't be depended on. He comes when he wills and his motivation lasts just long enough for him to describe it. I suspect he isn't working at the motel any longer, although he says they give him the afternoon off whenever he wants it, because he works so hard the rest of the day. He says the cabin is now winterized and that the breezeway is finished. These are the incentives he offers to urge her to come back.

Our own cabin has suffered some damage. A seventy-miler blew the Garsons' maple over and one of the big limbs hit our roof. We will have to make repairs and a window needs to be replaced, but there isn't any real structural damage. Windows were broken all over Boulder and Gallagher's Roofing has put me on a waiting list.

*Peace be on your tents, Marz*

*Dear Gram,*                    *March 16, The Hill*

I feel like I'm walking in a mist. I see Shining Lady every week and she tells me that I'm fine and that the baby seems to be getting into position to be born, and yet I feel sad for it and for me. We had the dream that this baby would mix the blood of his people and mine and that would be a sign, foretelling the end of racism in America.

Now, with Larry and me separated, it's going to be just a baby, who won't have all its heritage.

Larry has not been at his job. When he started coming around here Grandpa said it was strange how Larry could take so much time off to come and see me. Yesterday, I called the motel to tell Larry not to come here during working hours and they told me he had been fired two weeks ago for not showing up to work and for walking off the job. He hadn't been working for any more than a week before he started coming in late and leaving in the middle of the day, the man said.

Grandpa was right. Larry was missing work to see me. Maybe if I hadn't been here, he would have stayed at his job, because there was no place else for him to go. And Grandpa was right when he said we should be separated. When Larry comes this time I will not let him in. I am going to write a note and tell him we need to be apart until he gets himself something steady to do.

I called some of my friends from school and their voices were all far away. "Oh. Hope. Hello," as though the words were in a tunnel and had to travel slowly because there might be something dangerous ahead. They all had excuses for not wanting to go out for the day with me. Denise used to be my best friend. She said, "What if you started to have your baby while we were downtown?"

Then, in the next breath, practically, she told me that she and the other girls from our class had a big baby shower for Stacy Ippolito, and how much fun it was.

Why do people hurt one another like that? Even if it was racism, because it was Larry's baby, I don't understand why they do it. I started to cry but I kept my voice very steady until I could hang up.

So I will call Ma to pick me up and take me to some meeting. Larry will read my note and realize I mean it and will not be there for him.

*Love, Hope*

*Dear Grandma,*          *March 17, Grant Street*

Yesterday Grandpa and I went skiing. Even though he got tired, it was still a challenge to keep up with him.

We talked about my studying cities. He said he grew up in Kansas City, which he liked, but he never thought about why the rich people were on one side of town and the poor on the other. "Few people question their own living conditions as theoretical constructs."

I like saying that: theoretical constructs. I said it over in my head as Grandpa was talking about the neighborhood he grew up in. He said there were so few cars then, the kids played in the streets. A car might pass once in ten or fifteen minutes.

You lived in New York, Grandpa said, and during the Second World War you had a blackout. What was that? You will have to take me skiing when you come back or to some place where we can talk about <u>your</u> neighborhood, and theoretical constructs.

*Love, Ben*


DIARY ENTRY          *March 18, Buzzards Bay*

I was lying on my back, staring up into the grease-fittings of the water truck, when it occurred to me that the questionnaires had been numbered. All we had to do was to note the numbers missing from the sequence. I quit my lubrication job and rounded up ten of the dissenters. Many had found other work or quit The Walk. We have begun to tabulate the missing numbers from the finished batches. The others won't stop us, partly because they don't want a fight and partly because they will have achieved their aim. The report will have been cooked and the grant applications, etc., will not be using the raw data. We estimate a loss of 15 to 20 percent of the responses. The statisticians will keep ten percent of the positive responses to give verisimilitude to the report.

That means that 25 to 30 percent of the respondents felt that things are better, environmentally, than they were 10 to 20 years ago, or 20 to 40 years ago. The people who answered that things had stayed the same are being retained to swell the sample.

Rumors of our death have been exaggerated.

And, I have found I like using the grease-gun on the chassis. Murray said he would teach me the whole tune-up procedure.


*Dear Gram,*                    *March 19, The Hill*

Larry keeps coming. I have not let him in. The first day I went out and left a letter in front of the door for him. I explained that I knew he had lost his job and had not kept that promise, either, and so I wasn't going to see him until he got straightened out. It was gone when I came back, so I knew he had been there. The next day I was here and it almost killed me to hear him knocking, then ringing the bell, and then trying the door. I didn't let him see me.

Yesterday he was here again and he was pounding on the door for half an hour. When he went away, I saw that <u>he</u> had left a note for <u>me</u>, and I read it. He said I was unfair, that he gave up booze for me and took shit jobs, and even stayed in Boulder because of me, and made the cabin livable for me and it was unfair for me to leave him after all that.

He's right, really. When we met, he was planning to hitchhike to the Navajo or the Sioux reservation to start reclaiming his heritage. He changed his plan when we started going together.

Still, it hurt when he said shit jobs. Mr. Anson has been very good to us. Why doesn't Larry see that? The job at the garage was a very good one — the work was hard, but Larry could have made it training to be a mechanic. The motel job was even better. <u>He</u> said so. The motel manager told me they liked him at first because of his talent in fixing things. The manager was an AA person and Larry had told him about being on a program, too. The manager said he didn't think Larry had been drinking.

Yesterday I told Grandpa that Larry had been here and he said we would get a restraining order so Larry would have to stop coming around. Grandpa said it wouldn't hurt Larry except if he tried to see me before I was ready.

I don't want to do anything against Larry. I only want him to get a good job and start building up his life. I don't want to be sad about Larry anymore. He can't succeed if he only thinks about me. Grandpa says that Larry uses me as an excuse. If Larry is stopped from coming here, maybe he will find a job he can stick with.

*Love, Hope*

*Dear Marz and Hope,*          *March 19,*
                              *Buzzards Bay*

I was relieved when I called and heard you were both all right. Do you need me to come home? I can stay with Hope while you are at work, Marz. Let me know.

The weather has relented and in a few days we plan to finish the tabulation of our questionnaires and turn them into recycled scrap paper at the local schools. After the conference, we will have one more job, getting the equipment returned to its donors. We are now signing up who will take the borrowed things back, who will ship the tents and equipment, who will help in the dozen last things that need attention.

I'll be calling every day or so, checking in with you. Marz — I've sent the fourth packet of letters back, certified. Watch for them. Will we all be surprised to read them, ten years from now?

*Love, Tig; Gram*

Sam's birthday — Bunker Hill? Desert Storm? Every kid should have <u>one</u> of these. Maybe by the time Cary's comes, I will have forgotten this one: eight kids on a treasure hunt — house and yard. It took me most of two hours to write and plant fifteen clues, and it took them all of twenty minutes to find them. Then there was cake and punch and the eight were demanding and cheeky about the food.

The little creeps made me feel poor. Cake and punch for eight kids, plus Sam and Cary, and the brother of one of the kids his mother left here would have been a belt in the budget, so I got a mix, made the cake myself, and iced it. It got lukewarm reviews from the critics, who had been expecting a fancy bakery cake with Ninja turtles or superheroes sculpted in frosting, on matching party plates and cups — we did the job on our regular dishes and the jelly glasses I save for juice. "Where are the party napkins?" one gourmet demanded. "And where's the ice cream?" I told him ice cream liquifies too quickly at a party with the heat from the candles on the cake.

I guess I remember my friends sniping at the clothes other girls wore, but I thought boys didn't do that. This bunch of finicky consumers-in-training made me want to dump them in the creek. They spent an hour up in the boys' room looking at their toys with leveling eyes — "I have a space commander." "I have Ninjas." I locked the door of my room in case they should want to go in there with jewelers' loupes and check out my rings and bracelet.

Sam took it well. I asked him later if it bothered him not to have all the toys the others talked about, and he said that stuff was only good when it was very new. "Things like the painting set and the Etch-a-Sketch you got me — they last a long time," he said.

"That's so." I wanted to kiss him. Cary yearns for it all.

*Sol*

*Dear Gram,*                    *March 21, The Hill*

We went down to the courthouse and applied for a restraining order and they wouldn't give one to us because of what the District Attorney called <u>condonation</u>. The times since we decided to separate, when Larry came over and we let him in, constituted condonation, the D.A. said. There had been only two times I had shut the door against him, the D.A. said. He hadn't done anything new to warrant this action. I said yes, he had. He had lied about being still on his job. The D.A. said that people lose their jobs all the time.

Grandpa said that Larry had been <u>violent</u>. That I had been in the hospital.

The D.A. looked at me, and told me to file for divorce. There couldn't be a restraining order without that. Because I had let him in meant I obviously felt I was safe.

I wanted to say it wasn't like that, that I didn't feel safe when I let Larry in, and I realized I had lost some kind of power by sympathizing with Larry. I said I couldn't let him stand out there. He thinks no one respects him enough as it is.

The D.A. shrugged again and Grandpa and I got up and left.

We're supposed to tell Larry that we don't want him coming around at all anymore and that I am filing for a legal separation which will include no contact. There were no police reports made when I was in the hospital because I didn't want him arrested and in trouble again, and that now stood against us when we wanted Larry to stay away.

Grandpa is disgusted and angry and while he says he isn't angry at me, I know I'm part of his bad feeling. He told me not to let Larry in. I said I wouldn't. We walk around each other and are unhappy.

Now I want the baby to come. I'm heavy and clumsy and I feel like a house sometimes, and I struggle getting up from chairs. Grandpa says I'm really graceful in comparison with some pregnant women he has seen.

The days are warm and soft. I know the spring snows will come, but by then I'll have my baby and I'll be happy to stay inside. Because of Larry, I haven't gone out by myself for a walk or to lie in the sun and laze around reading the clouds the way I used to do back last year.

Yesterday, Shining Lady came to the house again and we got everything ready that I would need, and packed the things in a plastic bag. I have one more week to unbind the knots of my fringe and then everything will BE READY!!

Love, Hope

Dear Hope,                    March 24, Eastham

I got your letter and am answering it right away. I will begin to travel home when you untie your last knot, that is, unless you call me sooner. By the time you get this letter, I will have called you with a phone number that will get me here. It will be a delight to call you, even if the answer is, "Yes, I'm fine; no, not yet; good-bye."

Don't let Larry in. Go with your mother or stay in the house. If Larry comes, call the police. I will be there soon and will stay with you.

Love, Gram

I'm not ready to write, but you deserve it. Hope is dead. The baby is dead.

You remember my calling and Hope telling me to come. Years ago, or a week, we hurried to Hyannis, jubilant, pieces flying. Hyannis to Boston, to Denver.

In Boston I called the house again; no one answered. On the plane I slept most of the way.

Shining Lady would be in the house. Hope might have been in hard labor just then. If the labor was long, hard, or complicated, people wouldn't answer.

We don't ever meet at the airport — I take a bus. I called again, and got the answering machine. The bus ride was endless. When I got to Boulder, I called again. No one picked up. I took a cab home.

There was a van parked in front of the house: a cleaning service. I wondered why they should need <u>that</u>. I went to the door, but without my key, I had to ring, and a tall young man in a uniform opened and stood staring at me. He asked if I were Tig.

I stood gaping at him. He looked down at his uniform and then said, "Investigative unit." I couldn't make sense of it.

I thought: complications. She's in the hospital.

A car had pulled up ahead of the van. It

was Marz. He got out and came quickly up the walk, calling my name.

It was something that sent his voice ahead of him, almost an octave higher than his normal tone, and it was meant to keep me from turning again and going inside. He began to run toward me. My mouth went dry so my voice was cracking when I asked what had happened.

He stopped in front of me, almost skidding, although the walk had been cleared of the recent snow. He took me in his arms. I dropped my backpack where I stood. I told him Hope was dead at the same time he told me.

I saw her in my mind, in an overtaking, sudden hemorrhage, maybe the placenta having torn off suddenly and rupturing blood vessels, too sudden to call the midwife or 911. Perhaps she had fallen. I asked about the men. Marz said they were investigating.

I said, "The baby is dead also, isn't it." He said yes, both of them.

I wanted to cry, but couldn't.

Marz said we would be staying with Justice and Frank until the work was finished here. He turned me away from my house and pushed me toward the car, saying I should sit in it and wait.

I wasn't able to move. It seemed too far. I thought, "I've just crossed America and this walk is more than I can do." Then I stared around me.

Shock dulled me. My gaze moved here and there, over the houses, the trees, the ground. Only as I caught sight of the two large black plastic garbage bags at the end of the walk did I see color. A fluttering, yellow, plastic ribbon was sticking out of one of them. I stared at it, thinking, "There must be a breeze; that piece of ribbon is moving." Then the fluttering stopped. The ribbon lay against the black background of the full bag. I found myself moving down the walk to where the bag was, to tuck the ribbon in. I pulled the bag open and it was full of the yellow plastic ribbon. Printed. "Police — Do Not Cross — Police." I stood and wondered what the words meant.

Why would someone collect ribbon with those words on it? Marz was there. He said, "Jesus." I fell into his arms.

So now I know. Larry had come, waited for Marz to leave, and then tried to make Hope let him in. He called to her, he wept, raged, begged, demanded. The neighbors had said they were about to call the police, when she let him in. He went into the kitchen. He probably demanded she go away with him. He pulled her to him by that woven leather necklace he had made and kept pulling it tighter and tighter until she was dead. On the floor. Then he went to the refrigerator and made himself a sandwich. When Marz came home Larry was asleep in a chair in the kitchen and

Hope was dead on the floor. Marz called 911 and went outside in the evening cold to wait for them. When they came, he pointed to the open door. After some time Larry was brought out and the van came with the investigators and the yellow plastic crime-scene tape. Marz went to Grant Street to tell Justice and Frank what had happened.

*Tig*

# April

### ᴖ

I'm glad you called. I know it took forever to get me. It's shattering. I would have left The Walk and come like a shot, but I knew I would have been as welcome as a case of the clap. Damn the girl. Damn the boy. Why don't they know how valuable they are before they throw themselves away? Useless, that question. I want to be with you, at your side, in your hair, complicating everything in my feeble attempts at comfort. I'm lonely, so I cry a lot and then I'm mad, so I curse and sulk in our tent. You sure blew the end of this Walk.

We gave our report at the convention yesterday, the one sculpted by our fearless council. Then, the Buzzards Bay Twenty, as we are now known (you present in absentia), got up and gave its addenda. (Nine more people on The Walk have joined our protest, not because of the truth of our cause, but because they thought we had gotten a raw deal. Go figure.)

We had written a two-page paper about the meaning of the missing figures, about the mis-

537

take of propagandizing environmental studies, and about the danger of polarizing the movement. As John Duda read, people in the hall began to stand up and yell. All over the hall, they were getting up, applauding, requesting time at the microphone. He was barely finished, when a roar went up and dozens of hands were raised as people demanded the floor.

For a full five minutes there was pandemonium while the first speaker stood there. When quiet was restored, she began to give examples of the arrogance and lack of deftness on the part of environmentalists in government and quasi-governmental agencies. One spoke of an eventual backlash from these abuses that will harm the cause. Other speakers began to voice the doubts and misgivings they had suppressed to preserve the movement's unity of purpose.

The afternoon meetings were entirely changed. Instead of preaching, people were talking about trade-offs and relative values in the environmental movement.

Stay away. The positive effects of your absence, as demonstrated by what's happening here, are almost incalculable.

*Love, Poppy*

They blame us, Justice and Frank; they blame Marz and me. Yesterday the police released Hope's body and we buried her. The funeral people asked how we wanted her dressed and we stood and stared at them, Justice and I. The men had gone somewhere. What would fit her, now? The question made us stare stupidly. The coffin will be closed.

Solidarity was here, also, and just to see her was a comfort.

We wanted a religious funeral. Jewish, although no one belongs to any congregation. That might change. A house with eaves is needed in the rain. And they blame us. Justice and Solidarity. Frank has retreated into cold rationalism. He and Marz work off a list: the cabin emptied of her things, Mr. Anson told, the newspapers informed, friends, the school, etc. Marz has pulled away into that busy-ness and Justice blames me, Marz and me.

<u>Me</u>? I wasn't there. That's why. <u>Marz</u>? He <u>was</u> there, and he didn't protect Hope. Accusations are in the turn of her head, in her gestures, and in outbursts of pain. Why didn't Marz call her to protect Hope? Why didn't we send Hope home, where they could have guarded her?

I said again, Hope didn't want to go. She wouldn't have gone.

Justice turned on me. Hope had written to

me. Hope had told <u>me</u>.

How did I weigh those letters? I sat in the aura of the question and tried to think, to remember. The last few letters are with my things in Plymouth, but the rest were sent to Marz a week or so before I left. They might be studied for what Hope said or didn't say. Maybe Justice is correct and I didn't give Hope the hearing her fear deserved. Maybe there were hints, messages I didn't see under the messages I did see. Later, I will go back and read her letters.

Jason is barely there. He spends what time he is commanded at home, silent. Sympathy slides off and he wipes his looks and words clean of it. There's a stunned look in his eyes.

Ben stands in the middle of rooms, forgetting why he had come into them. He cries and hates himself for crying, he tries on reasons and discards them one after another, or else is mute with suffering. Justice, in her pain, Frank in his, barely look at him. Yesterday I talked him into taking me down to the basement to see his model city. It's not beautiful. He hasn't built it for a sense of design or serenity. His stores and houses are cubes and rectangles of plastic. There are no trees. I got into a bit of a tiff with him, saying that the presence of big, old trees is a hallmark of a fine neighborhood. We were arguing spiritedly as I presented my proofs. For twenty minutes or so, we argued. Would there be a way to prove this?

Ask a real estate agent, I said.

His face lit with eagerness.

And then something reminded him that he was Hope's brother and his eyes filled up. He looked at me reproachfully. What had I done to make him forget that his sister was dead and that he might have prevented it?

I asked him if he thought he could have prevented what happened. He said he should have kept on going to the cabin; when Hope came to Marz, he should have stayed with her, strengthened her. "She sent me away and I was mad," he said.

I told him that was fantasy, taking on more than his rightful load.

He looked at me out of a terrible pain and said, "I'd feel better thinking I failed her than thinking she didn't care enough about me to call me."

*So we lumber on, Tig*


*Dear Poppy,*                    *April 9, The Hill*

Hope has been buried for a week. I walk around doing things, what things I don't remember after doing them. Justice's and Frank's faces fall when they open the door and see me, because I'm not Hope, standing there, and because they feel the need to behave for my benefit. Ben is back in school. I have cleaned the house and yesterday I told Marz I wanted to go and help disband The Walk. I had promised to drive with you, returning the chuck-wagon and water truck to your friend in Arkansas. When I reminded him, he looked bereft. He has scarcely been home since the funeral. He's putting the files in order at the county office. He sees this as his legacy, a summation of all the work he has done since he started in 1966. It is the beginning of his good-bye to the agency, and marks his years of service. After work he goes to Louisville to look in on the reconstruction project. He's not required to be there, he admits. He also admits that the work takes up his mind and moves Hope from her absolute center in his thoughts to a place where he can look at her, a sidelong glance.

So Marz has projects. Ben is back in the cellar. Justice flinches at my presence, and I want to forget, too. Marz says he needs me when he comes home, but that's late at night. If we talked, it would be different, but we watch the evening news and go to bed. I told him I wanted to finish The Walk properly, one more week breaking camp.

He wants me to stay but he isn't ready to stay with me, to sit in the kitchen where Hope came for protection and where she wasn't protected. I need to end The Walk to hear about the convention and the protest paper, to pack, and take a truck to Arkansas.

No one knows this: I visited Larry today. I

was on my way past the building, aiming for the mall and the fabric shop, and it suddenly seemed that my trip had been for no other purpose than to see him.

He's small — I had forgotten that — 5'6" or so. He was half my size. He was Hope's height, and boy-like. His face is smooth — he has the skin of the Indian part of his family. The mad monster I had made, the bully, the terror-maker collapsed in my mind. He didn't remember me from our two meetings, and at first, took me for a social worker or some official of the hundred agencies that have ordered his life. I got the dull stare he uses for them. When I said my name, he got up to leave. We were in that partitioned room Marz described to me, stuck to the Plexiglas. I urged him to stay. He turned, and there it was, like Jekyll and Hyde, theatrical as that, the sneer and the half-swagger. He said he had his rights and didn't have to stay.

I said I was better than the boredom back in the jail.

He grinned, a bear's grin, no mirth at all. "What would you know about it?"

I said we were mourning for Hope and he was part of that. I told him where she was buried. He listened casually. There was no intensity there, no nerve pulling; everything seemed flaccid and loose. I asked him what had happened.

He shrugged, then said, "She was stuck on

her family, not on me. I wanted her back with me and she wouldn't come. I stayed in this crummy town for her. I worked, I put up with all kinds of shit for her, and then she wouldn't come."

I asked if he saw any more to it than that.

He shrugged again. I asked what Hope had been like for him. She had always told me how much in love they were.

"She was always talking about love," he said. "When she wasn't doing that, she was okay."

I couldn't ask him if he was sorry. He would have laughed at me. I know there's more to it than his shrug and his swagger, but I don't know how to get at it. I left, and went down the hall to where the detective was, the one who had brought me in. He's a nice man. He told me he didn't think Larry knew any more than what he had told me. Larry has been estranged from his own motives for years.

Why did I visit? What did I want to hear?

*Tig*

*Dear Tig,*                    *April 11, The Hill*

I hope this gets to you in Arkansas. You explained why you had to leave again, but I am still unable to understand. I know about finishing things, getting the work completed. I had always thought of that as one of my virtues, not one of yours. The Walk has cost us so much more than we had thought it would, financially, and psychologically. <u>Now</u> you are most needed <u>here</u>. Just because the need is that you stand and wait doesn't make it any less vital.

Back when you were protesting: the war, the bomb, toxic waste, etc., etc., I was often angry and frustrated, but I was stopped from real disapproval by the belief that what you were doing was important. I have no such feeling about your ferrying a food truck. We need you; <u>I</u> need you. I'll admit I made a poor showing of it when you were back here. What you said when you left was true; I have been staying away. Come home, now. I won't hide from the pain any longer in numbers or rebar or salvaged brick. I'll be finished with the project, and I'll need you here.

We're both in pain. I understand the hard words we had the evening before you left.

*Love, Marz*


*Mother,*                    *April 11, Grant Street*

I never imagined you would leave Boulder to go back to that monstrous ego-gratification you call The Walk, after the funeral of your granddaughter. Then, I thought, why not? She was in jail when I graduated from junior high, and on a Ban the Bomb demonstration when I graduated from high school. She had <u>plans</u> to help me shop for my first prom gown, and whatever happened to the Sweet Sixteen party I wanted? She was giving her energy

<u>there</u>. Where was it, Chicago?

I know Hope loved you. She talked about your letters and hers to you. It was a correspondence she prized, and one in which she confided so much more than she would to me. You knew about Larry's violence long before we were told, about his instability and his job-switching, and you didn't warn us or counsel Hope to leave him when she might have done so and saved her life.

You will say you are working for mankind and that the future of mankind takes precedence over individual wants and needs. That's what you used to tell us from the jail cells you were so proud of gracing. That was where you were when I broke up with Bucky Gerard and wanted to die. I needed a mother to talk to, to cry to. My mother was all over the country fixing up the world.

So I made my own family and what a joy it was to have a girl, one to be my friend, one whose ballet costume I sewed, one whose plays I went to, one whose tears I understood and whose triumphs I delighted in. That went on until she met Larry and it all changed.

We'll go on — Jason has divorced us for his friends. He tells us nothing. Ben is a victim full of self-blame. What could he have done? You might have stayed with him, but you went back to your ecological cause. Global. So much bigger than we are.

*Justice*

I've been trying to do what you told me when we were down in the basement looking at my city. I wake up in the morning, and sometimes I am so happy, I want to jump up out of bed, and then I remember where I am and that Hope is dead. There won't be any new baby and their ranch won't happen ever, and I won't be invited the way we all planned, a whole life won't be, that I was hoping would be.

Jason hates Larry and wants him on Death Row and executed. I remember that Larry tried to be someone he wanted to be, and how much work he did on that cabin and how proud he was when Grandpa helped him raise the back of it and said Larry had done more with it than was possible. I'm the only one who knows those things now. It makes me understand more, even why he killed her, even though I can't tell anyone because I don't have the words for it.

Mom and Dad won't talk about Larry or mention his name. I want to visit him but they don't let you in without a grown-up. Will you take me when you get back?

Hope was five years older than I am, and a girl. I loved her, but we weren't close, either, until she married Larry and I started going up there to see them. Now, she has made a big ache in me. I know you told me not to feel responsible or guilty about any of it, but

I do. Mom wants me to feel bad because I didn't tell her how dangerous Larry was. I think they loved each other. It scares me.

*Ben*

*Dear Justice,*  *April 20,*
*Mountain Home, Arkansas*

If I could have stopped Hope from idealizing Larry, wouldn't I have done it? If I could have stopped her from marrying him, wouldn't I have stopped her? If I could have prevailed on her not to become pregnant, would I not have done that? All those things were in my letters to her. Too much advice and she would have burned the letters, bombed the mailbox, and I would have become the enemy. My pleas were as careful as a cat testing quicksand, stories of me and my parents, examples from my girlhood, all pleas. If I could have stopped her from giving up her job at Wild Duds, I would have, and if I could have opened her eyes to Larry's instability at any time along the way — because six months ago, she might have left him and stayed alive — I would have done that.

Could I have come home and torn her out of that damn cabin, I would have done that. This country teaches independence, and it praises love. They were Hope's legacy from every one of us every day of her life. Grief is supposed to bring people together, closer; why doesn't it?

You are upset at my rejoining The Walk. You remember my causes and protests and marches. I felt I was fixing something, saving something, doing something that would guard the people I loved. I couldn't make us happy, but I could try to save us from being in a war. I couldn't put out a hand and tell Solidarity that Lewis was weak, but I could try to keep radiation from hurting her.

I was a woman of Causes, I admit it. You are bitter and angry at a woman who no longer exists, who has not existed for years. Your memory includes much and excludes even more. I took you with me whenever I could.

This Walk was not a great cause. It was an inquiry, peaceful and inclusive. I helped it be that. I helped provide The Walk's needed stability, and in the end, I helped save its integrity.

All this is a defense, one more, another. The Nation is still here, Causes and all, and so are we, making do.

*Love, Mother*

*Dear Tig,*

Months ago, back in another life, you sent Hope a package and told her not to open it until the baby was born. She brought it here and we put it away in the attic, so as not to be tempted. I forgot about it, but was up checking with Gallagher, who finally came to fix the roof, and there it was. I took it downstairs, opened it, and saw the little wooden toys, the nested boxes and wooden chain, the little wheeled cart.

I thought about your getting those things for a little baby you'd be welcoming as best you could, and whom you would probably come to love.

Why? Because you are generous. You give to friends and Causes, to an idealistic granddaughter and a demoralized engineer. Maybe, you say, protesting might help change a bad government policy. Maybe, with support, a bad relationship could be shored up, a weak child strengthened. Sometimes it works.

Justice showed me your letter to her when I asked if you had written. I read your defense of your choices and saw in it how hard you have tried, how hard you were trying here and on The Walk, how much you care about us and the world. You tell me we'll sell the house; you're busy making plans to support my new career, and there is joyful energy in that as though we weren't in our sixties, when most people begin to expect a passive peace as a reward.

Some of your fellow war and arms protesters then, and some of your fellow Walkers now, get their energy from rage. Not you; yours is from love. I want to enjoy that love, and to be part of it. Hope is gone. We'll grieve, but not in rage, and that's a gift. You're full of gifts. Sometimes I have wanted to close the flow. I've been suffering too much in private because Hope died on our floor and Larry ate the leftovers out of our refrigerator, here, where I took her in to be safe and loved.

Did you know that Hope's violent death may make the house less salable and bring down the price? Come home, my darling woman, and help me learn to live with such paradoxes.

*Love, Marz*

ANSWERING MACHINE MESSAGE:

We're in Mountain Home. The trucks are back. Poppy has rented a pickup, and we will dump our tents and equipment into it and start heading west. She will deliver me to our door like generic, recycled paper, suitable for normal use. We are planning no blue highway adventures; we want to cover the ground.

*Dear Grandma,*          *April 15, Grant Street*

I was dreaming last night after I cried about Hope. I start to go to sleep by deciding to visit a city. I have a collection, now, and maps and pictures of lots of places. I like to imagine I am a big bird who can fly at a perfect height — low enough to see people clearly and high enough to take in the form the city has.

I was flying around and I saw a kind of square and this was in a city I don't know. It was beautiful, full of white buildings, and LOTS OF TREES. I flew down and in the middle of a square there was a statue of Hope and Larry. He was holding her by that necklace he made for her and they were laughing, the way they used to be in the cabin in the beginning.

The statues were made of marble. It was a happy place. There were kids playing there and even climbing on it because the figures were people size, and not on pedestals. Hope's statue looked at me and said, "Don't forget me," and I started to cry in the dream and said, "How can I ever do that?" Then she said, "You heard me wrong. I didn't say 'Don't forget me'; I said, 'Don't forget me.'"

And I knew the dream was talking about how I should plan cities. I should plan them for lots of different kinds of people. Maybe I'll design prisons, too, to help the prisoners be more normal. I'll want a lot of beauty in my city because that's what Hope meant. The dream is important in a way I can't figure out yet, but I woke up feeling okay. I want to talk about it all when you get home.

*Love, Ben*